PRAISE FOR THE DESCENDANTS

"Freeland's command of aspects of military culture and history of American warfighting is impressive." -Kirkus Reviews

"The Decedent's careens from harrowing combat missions in Vietnam through compassionate family reunions to heartbreaking loss of loved ones in the War on Terror." -Shawn Ireland

"Larry Freeland has the unique ability to bring History alive and make it personal and real for the reader." -John Smith

"Filled with history and human emotion, I was moved to tears as this story touches the deepest sense of admiration and gratitude for the heroes and their families who live among us." -Paulette Brown

"This book is magnificent... It is so important that we know and try to understand these conflicts in our recent history." —Regina Loveridge

"...a remarkable novel! It reads like three books, each part being an incredible and standalone story." —M. Niland

"[The Descendants] is well researched and is as educational as it is engaging."-Jameson Gregg, Georgia Author of the Year

PRAISE FOR OTHER BOOKS BY LARRY A. FREELAND

Chariots in the Sky

"Impeccably faithful to historical events...a worthwhile peek into the horrors of war." – **KIRKUS REVIEWS**

"There are more than enough harrowing flying scenes and firefights on the ground that will keep readers of this genre interested." — **The VHPA Aviator, May/June 2021**

"A nicely written, exciting book. [The author] replays the feeling of time and place extremely well. Well worth reading." — **HELICOPTER LIFE, Spring 2021**

LEGACY OF HONOR TRILOGY

The Patriarch - Book 1

"A gritty, action-packed..war tale." – **Kirkus Reviews**

"... reminiscent of the carnage in Civil War battle scenes in *The Red Badge of Courage*."–**Jameson Gregg**, GA Author of the Year

"Freeland does a good job painting the picture as we move from scene to scene. ...excellent transitions." –**Bill McCloud, Vietnam Veterans of America-Books in Review II**

The Air Warrior - Book 2

"A novel of wartime bombing missions that makes for gripping reading." – **Kirkus Reviews**

"Freeland's descriptions of air combat are thrilling." –**Bill McCloud Vietnam Veterans of America in Review II.**

LEGACY OF HONOR
THE DESCENDANTS

LEGACY OF HONOR
BOOK THREE

LARRY A. FREELAND

Copyright © 2025 by Larry A. Freeland

All rights reserved. This book is a work of fiction. Names, characters, places, and incidents are products of the author's imagination or are used fictitiously unless otherwise historically correct.

Legacy of honor: The Descendants
Larry A. Freeland
LarryFreeland.com

No part of this book may be reproduced in any form or by any electronic or mechanical means, including information storage and retrieval systems, without written permission from the author, except for the use of brief quotations in a book review.For permission requests, solicit the publisher via the address below.

Cover Design Lead: Raeghan Rebstock
Editor: Janie Mills

ISBN 978-1-954000-90-2 (Paperback)
ISBN 978-1-954000-91-9 (eBook)

Published 2024 by Publish Authority,
300 Colonial Center Parkway, Suite 100
Roswell, GA USA
PublishAuthority.com

Printed in the United States of America

This novel is dedicated to my younger brothers, Thomas Lee Freeland, and Robert Scott Freeland, both of whom have predeceased me, and the men and women who served this country faithfully during the Vietnam War, The First Gulf War, The Global War on Terror, and all other excursions the United States has participated in through the years following Vietnam.

PART ONE
THE OLDEST DESCENDANT
ALAN MCCORMICK

1

THE MOUNTAIN OF THE CROUCHING BEAST

HILL 937

The night is a lonely place out here in the bush.

If it's your turn to stand watch at night, you hear all the sounds of the night. The distant firing of artillery, maybe some small arms fire, bugs making all kinds of ungodly sounds, frogs croaking, and men lying around you snoring while they toss and turn in their attempts to gain a few hours of sleep. As they lie there in their fighting positions, the night sky lights up occasionally as flares slowly descend to earth and cast eerie shadows for the men who are awake to gaze upon them.

Second Lieutenant (referred to as Lieutenant) Alan McCormick of A Company, 3rd Battalion, 187th Infantry of the famed 101st Airborne Division is manning his forward position. It's his turn at a two-hour watch. Lying there with his M-16 rifle on full-automatic, scanning the terrain up the hill to his front, he wonders if he'll survive. They have been fighting to capture Hill 937 for seven days, and tomorrow, they're going to attack up the hill again to secure the top.

The Vietnamese refer to the hill as Dong Ap Bia: *The mountain of the crouching beast.*

Approaches to and up the hill are narrow trails that create bottlenecks, forcing the infantrymen to attack in smaller formations. Troops are funneled into killing zones covered by interlocking enemy machine guns. They've devastated A Company's ranks during repeated assaults to take the hill. Lieutenant McCormick started the battle as a platoon leader, and he's now the acting company commander, their ranks having been cut significantly.

For seven days, men have moved upward, fought the enemy, seen their friends and buddies killed or wounded, and then withdrawn. They fall back to safer ground, take care of their wounded, and reorganize; then, minutes later, they go back up the hill to battle the enemy again.

Soldiers describe the fighting as feeling like they're in a human meat grinder. As they battled their way up the hill for the past seven days, they were cut to pieces by extremely accurate machine-gun fire. The ferocity of fighting and the bravery of the soldiers who push through to fight the enemy is reminiscent of Marines storming Iwo Jima and infantrymen storming Omaha Beach on D-Day. There is a nauseating smell of death in the air. Men are dying as their bodies are shredded by rocket-propelled grenades and landmines that spray metal fragments. Snipers tied to trees and hidden in firing holes pop up at will, taking deadly aim at them.

Though the hill has no tactical significance, taking it is part of Operation Apache Snow, a United States military sweep of the A Shau Valley. The purpose of the operation is to cut off North Vietnamese infiltration from Laos and enemy threats to the cities of Hue and Da Nang, located in the northern part of South Vietnam, which is designated as the I Corps. Assigned to Apache Snow are three airborne infantry battalions of the 3rd Brigade of the 101st Airborne Division (Airmobile.) They are facing soldiers of the North Vietnamese 29th Regiment, who are battle-hardened veterans of the Tet Offensive and considered the best unit in the People's Army of Vietnam (PAVN).

It's time for Lieutenant McCormick to be relieved as he crawls over to the small foxhole near him where two men are sleeping. He wakes up Sergeant Smith by shaking his foot and then his leg. As the sergeant slowly awakens, he rolls over and, looking at Alan, whispers, "Is it my turn already? Are you sure? I just went to sleep." Alan responds, "It's your turn, Sergeant. It's been quiet. You have the watch."

He responds, "Yes, sir."

Alan crawls back to his fighting position and settles in for a brief respite from the stress of standing watch. As he does, he can hear other men changing shifts to start their turn at guard. He thinks to himself, *it's a comforting feeling to know that the men take their responsibilities seriously out here, and he feels a degree of safety that their perimeter is being protected.* He's close to these men, having served with them since arriving in Vietnam in September 1968. He was commissioned after graduating from the University of Florida in May 1968, reported to Fort Benning for Airborne training, and, upon completion of training, shipped out with newly trained airborne troops for his first deployment to Vietnam. He's often asked why he chose Airborne. His reply is simply, "You have to volunteer for Airborne training, and I wanted to serve with the best."

But rest comes in fleeting moments as he thinks back to

the men he's lost since the battle began on May 10, 1969. There was John and then Charlie, both of whom were shot dead by snipers as they struggled to climb the hill. The men were close friends and died within seconds of each other. Then there was Jimmy, who was taken out by a booby trap and shredded to pieces. When a rocket-propelled grenade (RPG) hit a tree next to him, Bill flipped over and was blown backward, hitting another tree, which broke his back. He'll be a paraplegic for the rest of his life. Andy got hit in the neck and bled out before a medic could get to him. Pat was shot in the stomach, and as he rolled back down the hill, he hit a booby trap, killing him and sending shrapnel flying in all directions, wounding other men.

Replacements are flown in, but many are wounded or killed before anyone has a chance to get to know something about them. New men, often referred to as FNGs (frigging new guys) have an adjustment period before they gain some experience and become savvy to the ways of war. Commanders generally try to give their new men some time before sending them into battle, but this is not one of them. Every man is needed in this struggle. The odds of becoming a casualty in this battle are the same for men with one day in the field or eleven months. Death is random on this hill.

The odds of surviving are becoming dimmer by the day. Within a few hours, the unit will be awakened to go at them again and charge up this damn hill. How many more will the Grim Reaper take before the sun sets? Is this damn hill worth the lives of all these men? Lying there, pondering their losses, Alan feels the fear once again building within him. It never goes away out here, but thinking about it makes it worse. He wonders what it's like to be wounded and dreads the possibility of becoming a casualty. Fear makes it harder to hold onto hope. Hope is a terrible feeling to give up on and lose.

The first light of day seeps through the jungle canopy above, and the shuffle of men going about their duties in preparing for today's assault is heard around the perimeter. Lieutenant McCormick is already moving about his company, checking on the men, instructing them to check their weapons, get some food, and prepare for the assault. They will attack up the hill after another artillery barrage rains down death and more destruction on the hilltop above. To many of the men, it seems fruitless.

As the artillery barrage commences and horrendous explosions are heard in the heights above them, Alan moves among his men offering encouragement. This is no easy task, as he's tired of hearing the screams of dying men and seeing and smelling death all around him. He's also tired of waiting for it to find him here in this hellhole called the A Shau Valley. Nine months in Vietnam and most of that time has been spent chasing Charlie or the NVA (North Vietnamese Army) out in the bush, and it has taken a toll. Mindless days of boredom punctuated with moments of stark terror and sometimes prolonged days of combat, such as now, take a toll on men. Alan is no exception. He longs for the suspense to end. Kill him now and send him home in a body bag. If not, wound him now and send him home to recover, or send him back to the world alive, in one piece, and back to his family.

The artillery barrage lifts and the command to move out is given. Each company in the 3rd Battalion is assigned an area to move up the hill in a coordinated attack. It's hoped that this will prevent the PAVN from concentrating all their firepower on one attacking company. Company A starts up the hill in platoon order, spread out across a line of attack. Lieutenant McCormick is leading the first platoon as they move up the hill yard by yard, seeking shelter behind tree trunks or shell holes as AK-47 rifles and machine guns deal out death on the advancing Americans. A new man in front of Alan is hit in the face, spirals around, and rolls backward down the hill. He's gone, just like that—suddenly and with no warning. His day didn't start any differently than the other men, yet it ended in a second with half his face blown off.

His men continue forward as the North Vietnamese defenders begin rolling hand grenades down the hill, exploding around the advancing troops. RPGs are coming in from several locations above the advancing men, adding to the carnage. The second and third platoons advance and fill in the gaps formed as men are hit, fall, and die or writhe in pain from their wounds as they fight their way forward.

The men of the 3rd Battalion, 187th Infantry, are engaging a large force of entrenched defenders in close combat with their M-16s, M-79 grenade launchers, M-60 machine guns, and bayonets. They slowly fight their way upward on this eighth day of battle. The battalion is closing in on their objective: the hilltop. But as fate intervenes in the form of an intense thunderstorm that seemingly comes out of nowhere, visibility goes to zero. The torrential rains cause massive flows of water and mud to stream down the hill, stopping the men's progress. They lose their footing, can't grab onto anything to place, and slide back down uncontrollably. They curse and yell out profanities at their tormentors above as they struggle to retain the ground they covered to this point, but it's futile. Their attack falters, and unable to advance any further, the fighting ends, and the men fall back down the hill.

Once again, back where they started earlier that day, Lieutenant McCormick, exhausted, covered in mud, soaked to the bone from the rain, and mad as hell, asks himself, *Why are we continually attacking this hill with infantrymen? Why not use heavy firepower and continuous air attacks until the hilltop and its surrounding terrain are blown to hell and back? We are wasting good men and making many mothers "Gold Star Mothers" back home.*

He walks among his men, checking on their condition and seeing to their needs. One man is placed on a chopper and is on his way home. He hit a booby trap near the summit, is without a kneecap, and may lose his leg. We don't know. He hit it, it blew up, we loaded him onto a helicopter, and he's gone. Just like that, he's headed back to the world. Hopefully, he'll live to see home.

One of Alan's acting platoon leaders just made it down the hill with three other men carrying a body. Each man is holding one of the dead man's arms and legs as they gently set him down. His face is covered with a towel that had been around his neck. He had been using it to wipe the mud from his face before he was killed. There is a small hole in his forehead and the back of his head has been blown away. The men sit down near him, share a canteen of water, and help each other light up cigarettes. They are shaking from the experience, and their bloodshot, tired eyes reflect fear and hatred at the same time.

Alan walks over to them, sits down, and attempts to console them. Looking at the platoon leader, he says, "John, who is he?" John takes a long draw on his cigarette and replies, "Private Tremble, sir. He joined us the day before we started this madness."

"What happened?"

"He made it up as far as we got, then a sniper popped out of his hole right in front of us and shot him dead."

Alan looks around at the other fellows and then stands up. "John, see that his body goes out on a chopper after our wounded are lifted out. You fellows, get some rest. I'll let you know what's going on when I find out."

John replies, "Yes, sir."

More men stream into the base area at the foot of Hill 937, carrying their dead and wounded. Lieutenant McCormick moves among them, seeing that the wounded are lifted out as soon as possible, followed by their deceased comrades. Supplies and ammunition are being flown in, and the word starts circulating among the men that the press is calling this battle the "Battle For Hamburger Hill."

That evening, after the wounded and dead have been airlifted and what's left of the battalion resupplied, they settle into their night defensive positions. They dread tomorrow and what it will bring. Lieutenant McCormick joins surviving officers and NCOs for a short briefing of the day's events as the sky fades from gray to dark, with the torrential rains having ceased earlier. He learns Company D nearly carried the hill but experienced severe casualties, including all its officers. All the companies in the battalion suffered losses during the fighting, with Company D experiencing the highest.

Officers and NCOs present at the briefing are cautioned to be leery of answering reporters' questions. Several reporters caught wind of the battle and are hitching helicopter rides into the area. A sergeant speaking to one reporter said, "Have you ever been inside a hamburger machine? We just got cut to pieces by extremely accurate machine-gun fire." Another soldier who fought in nine of the ten assaults up the hill was quoted as saying, "We've lost a lot of buddies up there. Few guys can take it much longer."

After the briefing, Lieutenant McCormick returns to his company, checks on the men, then settles into his fighting position for another fretful night. Their fate is yet to be decided; they'll have to wait until tomorrow.

Lieutenant McCormick thinks back to his history classes on the Korean War and recalls a grim battle that occurred near the cessation of hostilities referred to as the "Battle of Pork Chop Hill." Another war and another battle suggesting the men were chopped up like meat as they fought to take and hold the hill.

Will we ever learn?

2

HAMBURGER HILL - HILL 937
LET'S TAKE THE DAMN THING - MAY 19, 1969

The morning of May 19 dawns early as two fresh battalions, the American 2/501st Infantry and Army of the Republic of Vietnam (ARVN) 2/3rd Infantry, are airlifted into the base of Hill 937. They are reinforcements for the soldiers who have been fighting and becoming increasingly disgruntled.

The look on these men's faces as they disembark their helicopters and gaze upon the scene before them is one of horror. They've just stepped into hell. Nothing but sheer devastation greets them. Large swaths of vegetation have been blown away, while wasted supply boxes and spent ammunition cover the ground everywhere. The stench of death hangs in the air and causes some men to choke as they first breathe it in. Glancing up the hill, the new men see big gaps in the jungle canopies where trees and undergrowth no longer exist. The continuous fighting, shelling, and dropping of napalm has turned the higher elevation and top of Hill 937 into a wasteland.

Body bags are placed in the helicopters as the fresh

troops disembark—fresh meat for the crouching beast lurking on the mountain. Stepping off the helicopters and staring into the eyes of men who have been in the fight and are now trying to relax before it begins again is unnerving. They can see sheer terror, fear, anger, and total exhaustion in the faces of these men as they move among them.

The new men arriving must be wondering to themselves as they look around at the men before them: *How have these men survived so far? What is sustaining them? What will be our fate out here?*

Losses for Alan's battalion, the 3/187th, have been severe. Two of the four company commanders and ten of the sixteen platoon leaders are casualties. A typical infantry battalion normally consists of four companies, each averaging 125 soldiers. They, in turn, are allocated between four platoons, each averaging thirty soldiers. Platoons are broken down further into squads, which is an infantryman's most intimate group, consisting of six to ten soldiers. Three to five battalions can form a brigade or regiment.

Lieutenant McCormick and the remaining officers and senior NCOs of the battalion are called into a briefing by their battalion commander. He shares with them that, because of heavy casualties already sustained, and under pressure from the press, the commanding general of the 101st Airborne Division seriously considered discontinuing the attack but decided otherwise. He's being supported by higher command. The 101st Division will take the hill.

The men are told by the battalion commander that even though higher command wanted to pull his battalion off the line, he insisted they were still combat-effective. They'll join the attack tomorrow morning. The remaining men in his command will be combined to form two companies and they'll be reinforced by Company A of the 1st Battalion, 506th Infantry. This gives the battalion three companies to make the attack once again up Hill 937.

He continues his briefing. The 3rd Brigade will launch a four-battalion attack at 1000 hours tomorrow, May 20th. The attack will be preceded by two hours of close air support and ninety minutes of artillery fire. From the facial expressions of the men present, it's clear they were not expecting to go back up the hill. They keep their reactions to themselves and refrain from any vocal outbursts. The colonel ends his briefing by telling them to return to their men, ensure they are fed, resupplied, briefed on the following day's planned action, and that they get some rest.

As they disperse, the colonel pulls Alan aside. "Lieutenant McCormick, when A Company arrives, I'll brief their CO and send him over to you. Give him an overview of what we've been up against out here and help them settle into their positions for the night."

Alan responds, "Yes, sir."

Alan returns to his company area on the defensive perimeter and walks among the men. He offers words of encouragement where he can, briefly explains the following day's attack plan, replies to any questions directed at him and eventually settles into his foxhole for a brief respite. While he has some private time, he decides to reread his last letter from Ana, his mother. The day before they were airlifted into this hellhole, he received the letter and carried it with him into the battle. Leaning back against one corner of the hole he calls home, he pulls from his rucksack the letter, slowly removes it from its plastic bag, and reads it once more.

Dearest Alan,

I hope this letter finds you doing well, staying healthy and out of harm's way. From the news we hear on the television every evening and read in the newspapers, this war continues to drag on with no end in sight. Unrest is building in this country because of that and the losses of so many of our young men. President Nixon was elected partially on his promise to end the war. Let's hope he does so soon. Enough for now about that. Here's a brief update about your family and what we're doing.

Your grandmother, Marie, is doing well and continues to be active in the Louisville community. Your grandfather, Sam, struggles with his respiratory and digestive health issues but doesn't let them get him down. He is one tough man and still enjoys smoking his pipe, drinking Irish whiskey, and playing poker with his buddies, although his group is losing members. My father is doing well. Like Sam, he's enjoying his retirement. He stays busy playing cards, ballroom dancing occasionally at Myers Lake, and working in his woodshop.

Your brothers Lee and Scott are both as active as ever and doing well. Lee is finishing up his junior year at the University of West Florida where he's continuing to excel in his studies and the Navy ROTC program. He still plans on applying for Navy flight training when he graduates and receives his commission. I think he's taking after your father.

Scott's junior year in high school has gone well.

He's certainly discovered girls. It seems like we're always being introduced to new young ladies he dates. His athletic abilities in track and field, cross-country running, and swimming meets haven't gone unnoticed by college recruiters. However, he's a handful with his independent streak and is always the maverick, looking for excitement and taking undue risks. It will be interesting to see what becomes of him when he grows into manhood.

I have some sad news about Melanie Miller. As you're aware, she has suffered from depression ever since the loss of her son, Captain Henry Miller, Jr. She has been in and out of treatment centers for the last few years and, more recently, began drinking heavily. This isn't easy for me to say, but she took her own life. She left a note, which, in summary, said she loved her husband, Henry Sr., and son, Henry Jr., more than anything in the world. With the loss of Henry Jr., she could not handle it any longer and chose to end her life and join her husband and son. We buried her next to Henry Sr. in Canton, Ohio. Both your grandparents took it very hard. Henry Sr. was your grandfather's best friend, and your grandparents were the godparents of Henry Jr. Melanie was considered a member of the family.

It's a tragic loss for all of us. Melanie married one brave man and birthed another, both of whom served their country and fellow man with honor, dignity, and courage. May she and her family all rest in peace.

Your father is doing very well and has enjoyed his return to Homestead Air Force Base since being reassigned here last year. He was just advised that we'll be relocating this summer to Offutt Air Force Base, Omaha, Nebraska, the host base headquarters for Strategic Air Command (SAC). He'll be promoted to major general and become heavily involved with SAC strategy and operations. He's excited about his new assignment. He doesn't talk to me about it, but I sense he would like to return to flying again and lead a bomber group. As a wife and mother of three sons, I think he and this family have contributed much to our country already, and I don't want to see him return to fly in another war. You are in Vietnam now, and I fear both your brothers could end up over there. How much must one family contribute? I hope this war ends soon.

Back to Scott, he's not very happy about us relocating. He'll be leaving his friends in high school here in Florida and starting his senior year in Nebraska. You were in this situation when we relocated to Puerto Rico in your senior year and know the difficulties. Maybe when you have a chance you can write him a letter with some encouraging thoughts and suggestions to help him. Just your mother talking.

That brings you current on the news from here. I'm doing fine, staying busy, and looking forward to another move. After several years in warm climates, Florida and Puerto Rico, it should prove quite an adjustment going back to colder winter weather. It has been some time since your father and I lived in a colder climate. We'll adjust, try some winter sports, make new friends, and move forward.

We miss you very much, love you dearly, and pray for your health, safety, and well-being. Return home to us soon.

We love you!
Your loving mother.

Drifting in and out of thoughts about home, Alan is tapped on the shoulder by a captain. Looking up at the captain standing over him, he slowly stands up without saluting. You don't salute out here; that could be the kiss of death. It would alert a hidden sniper to the fact that one or both men are officers, which are much sought-after targets. The captain is tall and lean, and probably played basketball in high school and college. His height alone can make him a bigger target for snipers, but out here, everyone is a target.

Alan doesn't recognize him as he speaks. "Yes, sir. What is it?"

He responds in a low-key, calm, and authoritative manner. "I'm Captain Carl Price, A Company commander. Your colonel sent me over here to get a better idea of our situation and the terrain above."

"Yes, sir."

The captain responds, "Alan, we can dispense with the rank. Just call me Carl. So, what are we dealing with?"

Alan, in a soft, discerning, matter-of-fact voice, responds. "Well, in a nutshell, we landed in the middle of a hard-core, battle-tested regiment of PAVN's. It has become one hell of a shitstorm."

He takes a moment and continues. "We've been up that hill several times already and have been pushed back down or had to pull back due to heavy rains and casualties. They're well dug in up there and seem to pop out of nowhere at any time and cut us down. We kill them, but more just keep coming."

Carl has been listening intently and makes a comment. "Alan, as you know, we're next to Laos, and they just flow in from over there. Since we can't cross the border after them, it makes our job tougher. The Air Force is bombing the hell out of Laos, but without good intel on the ground, it's very difficult to identify high-value targets to bomb." Alan nods agreement.

Carl continues, "I'm no general, but this doesn't seem to me to be any way to fight a war. If you can't go after them where they live, resupply, rest, organize, and stage from, how can you ever defeat them?" After a long pause, Carl concludes with, "Just a thought."

Alan leads Carl on a tour around his company and then a tour of A Company's assigned area. Alan finishes their tour as evening sets in. After a few minutes of light conversation, each man returns to their company area and wishes the other good luck. Alan checks on his men again and settles into his fighting position on the perimeter for another night of little to no sleep. If he survives, he'll sleep for a week if they let him.

The men of the 3rd Battalion know the looming battle tomorrow is going to be costly. They'll face the challenge with grim determination as they once again attack Hamburger Hill and, this time, take the summit.

MAY 20, 1969

Tuesday morning, May 20, finds the men of the 101st poised for their attack. Artillery shelling and multiple bombing runs of the higher elevation of Hill 937 have been ongoing for several hours. The noise is deafening. Smoke from the bombardment drifts down on the men, and the smell of gunpowder, burning trees, napalm, and vegetation hangs in the air. At times, they can hear the screams of NVA soldiers higher up the hill who have been wounded by the bombardment.

Alan moves around his perimeter, checking on the men as he encourages them. "Fellows, hang in there." "We'll be up on top of this damn hill shortly." "Soon, we'll be back in base camp drinking beer and getting some much-needed sack time." The few men who respond to him do so with no small talk. "I hope so." "Can we hold you to that?" "I just want to get the hell out of here."

One man's comment catches him off guard. "I just hope the bastards that put us here are held to account for this slaughter." Alan stops and looks at the soldier whose eyes glare with hate, and he wants to respond but doesn't. He just gives him a look of agreement. He feels the same way. If going up and down this damn hill to show them how tough they are and to rack up a high body count is the goal here, then someone should be subject to court-martial. Surely on the first or second day of this operation, with heavy contact and casualties, they could have pulled back and let the Air Force blow the top half of this hill away.

After checking his perimeter, he moves over to Captain Price's location to check in with him. "Carl, good morning. Wonderful day to charge up a hill. Don't you think?"

"I'll let you know when we make it to the top. Are your men ready?"

"They are, but if we don't take the top today, they'll be in no shape to try it again. These men need downtime."

"I saw that yesterday when we got here and wondered

why they weren't pulled out then. We best go about this day's business and hope we take the top. Good luck, Alan."

Alan responds as he turns to head back to his company. "Thanks, Carl, you too. See you on top."

Returning to his position, the sound of shelling and bombing begins to taper off. In moments, they'll get the order to advance up the hill. Alan yells out to his men, "Get ready, fix bayonets, and stay alert. We're going to take this damn hill."

It's midmorning, and the order to advance comes. The Americans launch a four-battalion simultaneous attack up Hill 937 from four sides. About two thousand Americans and South Vietnamese soldiers begin their assault on the hill's summit. Alan leads his men up as they advance slowly, methodically, and seeking cover with each movement forward. The NVA are once again proving tenacious as they roll hand grenades down on them. Mortar rounds land among the advancing troops, along with accurate machine-gun fire, AK-47s, and RPGs once again raining death upon the charging men. Some fall screaming in pain, others continue onward, crawling up the steep slope through paths and draws, shell holes and bunkers.

To Alan's right front, Mike, a squad leader, is leading his men forward as he yells out. "Keep advancing. Kill the bastards!" He rises from his cover and forces himself forward at a crouch, rifle firing as he moves when an RPG hits a tree next to him. His body is torn to shreds and blown backward down the hill by the force of the explosion. He's gone; no need to check on him. Another man in his squad takes his place and continues the advance.

Closing in on the hill's summit, Alan crouches behind a tree stump and gauges the strength of his attacking force for the final push up and over. Looking behind him, he sees several men dead and wounded. NVA gunners continue shooting at them. They seem to relish shooting the dead. Their bodies, in many cases, are so ripped up that they may not be recognizable when the battle ends. Hatred builds within him as he looks back up the hill and inches forward, yelling at his men to follow him.

Machine-gun fire tapers off as they close in on the crest of the hill. Alan continues to press the attack with his remaining men. Another hidden machine gun opens fire on them. Red and green tracer rounds fill the air and come straight at them, slicing two soldiers near Alan almost in half. As the weapon zeros in on their position, Dwayne, a medic, uses his body as a shield to protect a fellow soldier he just provided life-saving medical treatment. He's hit in the back, and the enemy gunner just keeps pumping rounds into him. Several pass through his body and penetrate the man he just saved and was trying to protect. Both men are dead. Dwayne had already served with the 82nd Airborne Division several years earlier and had been honorably discharged from the service. He re-enlisted as the Vietnam conflict heated up because, he said, "My medic skills are needed." Now he is gone.

The men, furious from the unrelenting punishment they've been taking from the enemy, rise, charge forward with their bayonets, and fire their weapons at anything moving to their front as they close in on the top of Hill 937. No mercy is given as they engage in hand-to-hand combat with the remaining enemy soldiers who fight desperately to hold their bunkers. Elements of the attackers, including Alan's remaining men, reach the crest of the hill and begin cleaning out the few enemy bunkers still resisting. The hilltop is overrun, but it will take well into the afternoon to clean out any remaining enemy soldiers. The fortifications constructed by the enemy on Hill 937 are like an anthill consisting of a maze of multiple trenches, bunkers, and tunnels.

Reaching the top, Alan gazes out over the carnage around him and wonders, *Was this worth it?*

Carl approaches him with some of his men as they spread out to continue their sweep of the area, searching for more enemy soldiers. Approaching each other, Alan yells over to him. "I see you made it."

He responds, "Yeah, it was too damn close several times. These little bastards are hellish fighters. They don't go down easy."

Alan starts to respond when a short burst from an AK-47 fired by a sniper hidden in a firing position off to his left is heard. He's hit in the left arm and thigh as he's spun around and thrown to the ground. He lies there, withering in pain. The pain is excruciating; he felt the bullets penetrate his body with a hard impact. The wounds burn, blood flows from them freely, and he yells out. "I'm hit. Medic, Medic."

Alan stands just over six feet tall and is well built with a muscular structure honed over many years of athletic competition on baseball fields and in swimming pools. He relishes surfing, which requires considerable body strength to repeatedly swim out far enough to catch rolling waves headed back toward the beach. He waits for help, wants to scream out in pain, but suffers in silence.

Carl runs over to Alan, kneels, and checks on his wounds. Some other men near Alan run over to where the sniper fired. They kick back the hatch he's hiding under and fire their weapons on full-automatic as the sniper's body is shredded.

In the attack, several medics have been killed or wounded, and Alan has to wait for one to find and help him. Medics are another prized target on the battlefield in Vietnam. While waiting, Carl places sulfur on the wounds and ties gauze bandages over them to slow the bleeding. Fortunately, no arteries were hit, and the gauze slows the loss of blood down significantly. Carl says, "Alan, it looks like your wounds are pass-throughs." Finally, a medic rushes up, checks Alan, and gives him some morphine. Alan welcomes the jab as the morphine takes effect and the pain slowly subsides.

Medevac helicopters are called in and start landing wherever they can on the hill. A Light Observation Helicopter (OH-6 Cayuse) lands close to Alan, and he is lifted into it by some of his men, and another wounded soldier is placed next to him. Both men are feeling no pain from the morphine given to them but need to get to a MASH (Mobile Army Surgical Hospital) unit quickly. Alan looks over at the pilot, Captain Bill Pennington, in the left seat and gives him a thumbs-up as the little bird lifts into the sky. Alan waves down to Carl and the men who helped place him in the helicopter. They wave back as he disappears down the hill toward the valley below, as the chopper heads for Phu Bai airfield and a MASH unit located there. Bill, the pilot, yells back to Alan. "Hang with me, Lieutenant. I'll get you back." Alan manages a weak smile and another thumbs-up as he rests his head and right shoulder against the back of the helicopter.

Thank goodness for these helicopter pilots and crews. They are brave men who infantrymen count on every day out here in the bush. Flying helicopters in Vietnam is a dangerous job. Considered the most dangerous chopper to fly in Vietnam are these little birds—called Loaches. They are expected to fly low over the jungles and grasslands in any locations American units are patrolling or engaged in battle. The aircrew's main mission is to locate enemy forces hiding in the foliage. They then call in air support to rain death down on the enemy, guide friendly units on the ground to their location, and/or engage them with their own limited weapons.

With Alan evacuated and on his way to a MASH unit, the remaining men in his company are placed under the command of Captain Price. They continue a sweep of the hilltop and clear out the remaining enemy soldiers. Finally, late into the afternoon of May 20, the North Vietnamese stronghold is declared captured and secured. Under the onslaught of the four-battalion attack, the remaining elements of the North Vietnamese retreat across the border to sanctuary areas in Laos.

The next day, the surviving men of the 3rd Battalion 187th Infantry are flown out of Hamburger Hill to Eagle Beach for some much-needed rest and recuperation, referred to as R&R. The 101st Airborne Division uses Eagle Beach, six miles east of Hue on the South China Sea coast as an R&R center.

A sign is posted on a tree trunk on the summit of the hill. It reads: "Hamburger Hill." Below it, someone inscribed, "Was it worth it?"

3
MEDEVACKED TO DA NANG

Alan is slipping in and out of consciousness as the Loach speeds toward Phu Bai. He feels the wind on his face as it whistles through the open sides of the helicopter. It's comforting and keeps him from passing out. The morphine is doing its job, but he still feels some pain. Reaching the valley floor, Bill flies at a low altitude as he races toward Phu Bai. Calling ahead that he's inbound with two wounded packs, the MASH unit responds they are a busy place. Wounded and dead men are streaming in from the battle.

As the Loach clears the valley and flies over rolling piedmont below, which rapidly changes to flat coastal plains, Phu Bai comes into sight. Bill radios the MASH unit that he's five minutes out. He then radios the Phu Bai tower and receives clearance to land at the MASH unit. Alan sees Phu Bai in the distance. His spirit improves with the thought he'll soon be in the capable hands of MASH doctors.

Bill lands, hovers his helicopter over to the MASH unit and settles onto the tarmac. Men in scrubs rush to his

Loach, lift the other wounded soldier and then Alan from the helicopter, and put them on separate gurneys. Alan and Bill exchange hand salutes. With all the activity swirling around, Alan becomes more aware of his surroundings and witnesses scenes that will haunt him for a lifetime.

Off to his right, he observes several soldiers helping to remove stacks of body bags from a CH-47 Chinook helicopter. These are the second largest helicopters in the Army's inventory, with jet engines mounted on each side and tandem rotors, front and back. They can carry internal loads to include thirty or more troops and external sling loads. They're the Army's heavy-lift workhorses.

The helicopter's whirling blades are causing considerable wind, and the men going in and out of the Chinook have difficulty maintaining their balance. The ramp they traverse is wet and slick from all the blood seeping out of the body bags. The men lose their footing and slither and stumble down the ramp, dropping body bags as they fall. Alan turns his head so as not to gaze upon this ghastly scene as he's whisked into the triage area.

It's no better inside. Men are moaning and crying, some screaming in pain or from the terror they experienced that put them here. Nurses are moving among the wounded, trying to provide comfort as they perform triage. This is where they separate men who need immediate attention and are moved into surgery from those who can wait. Those who they determine will not survive their wounds are moved to a separate area where nurses will watch over them and do what they can to comfort them while they die.

Alan looks around the large room at all the carnage. Some men are missing arms and legs. Fatigues are removed and cut from the bodies of men to determine the extent of their wounds. As clothing is removed, shredded flesh from wounds on arms and legs is exposed. Alan sees one man near him being rolled over on his side so the staff can check for exit wounds to his back. As they do, part of the flesh on his back stays on the litter he was resting on. They ease him back down as he passes out from the pain. They rush him into surgery.

Alan wants them to knock him out with something to escape these horrific scenes. Combat is gruesome and horrific, and men die before your eyes. Lying here and watching all this human carnage and suffering unfold before him is more traumatic than he could have grasped before today.

Off to one corner, he notices a nurse moving in his direction. Even in her bloody and soiled nursing fatigues, she appears angelic, moving with a purpose, very focused, and very attractive. She comes over to him, looks down, and in a soft, compassionate voice, says, "What's your first name, Lieutenant?"

Looking at her face, Alan is immediately drawn to her caring eyes and notices a slight smile beginning to emerge. In a weak, melancholy voice, he responds, "Alan. And yours?"

"Judy. Now let's see what we're dealing with here, Alan." He manages a slight grin, nods his approval, and watches her every movement.

She slowly removes his combat fatigue clothing while systemically checking the severity of wounds to his left arm and thigh. Alan wonders as she proceeds how she tolerates the filth and odor emanating from his clothes and body. He's been accustomed to living with it for the last ten days. She doesn't wince or show any visible sign that she is repulsed by his appearance and digesting smell. He wonders, *How do they do this?*

Looking into his eyes, she smiles slightly and says, "Alan, your wounds are not life-threatening. We'll get you into surgery as soon as possible. In the meantime, I'm going to give you a sedative to help you relax. It won't be long."

Alan already has an IV in his arm administering formulated liquids to prevent dehydration. Judy adds a sedative to his IV. As she does, Alan responds, "Thank you, Judy..." His world goes dark, the pain ceases, he hears nothing, and it's silent as he fades into unconsciousness.

Later the next evening, as Alan opens his eyes and looks around, he does not recognize his surroundings. It's all foreign to him. He's in a hospital bed inside a wooden hut with several beds down both sides, all of which are occupied by wounded soldiers. He's lying on clean sheets, the air is cool and comfortable with fans blowing, and it's relatively quiet. Although they are located near one end of the Phu Bai flight line, the noise from helicopters and other aircraft landing and taking off from the airfield seems remote. He feels restrained, lifts his head up, and notices his left thigh is wrapped in bandages, slightly elevated, and his left arm is in a small cast. A feeling of relief momentarily overtakes him as he realizes all his limbs are intact, and he can feel them.

His mind is still foggy, his senses dulled from all the drugs, and he craves liquids and something to eat. Seeing that he is awake, a doctor and Judy, the nurse he first encountered upon arrival, walk over to him. The doctor grabs his chart hanging from a hook at the foot of his bed and reviews it while looking down on him. He then says, "Welcome back, Lieutenant. I'm Captain Willard. You came through surgery fine and have been sleeping for almost thirty-six hours."

Before the doctor can continue, Alan tries to say something. His throat is dry and sore, and his voice is hoarse almost to the point of being inaudible. The doctor continues, "Relax, Lieutenant; you're fine. The soreness will dissipate shortly. You've had tubes down your throat, and it takes time for it to feel normal again. You're still in the MASH unit here at Phu Bai. We'll be sending you down to the 95th Evacuation Hospital in Da Nang within a few days. You'll remain there while a final determination is made whether to medevac you home for full recovery or keep you in-country. For now, just relax, enjoy, and do what the nurses tell you."

He continues with his rounds as Judy steps forward and bends down by his bed. In a soft, caring voice, she says, "Lieutenant, I'll be helping to care for you in this ward until you're moved to Da Nang. In the next few days we'll work on improving your appetite, regularly changing your thigh wound dressing, providing you reading materials and your mail. Your personal items will be sent to you in Da Nang."

Alan looks into her eyes—those caring eyes—and tries to say thank you. She clasps his right hand, smiles, and just nods. Standing up, she says, "I must finish my rounds. I'll send another nurse over who will give you some liquids, chicken broth, and Jell-O for dessert."

For the next three days, Alan makes slow but steady progress. He and Judy spend time talking and sharing a little about themselves. She is from Dallas, Texas, and will return there after her service commitment is fulfilled. She looks forward to returning to civilian life and working as an emergency room nurse at one of the major hospitals in

Dallas. Judy, like all nurses serving in Vietnam, is an angel in fatigues. All of them go about their jobs working twelve-hour shifts, six days a week, while maintaining an enduring persona. Always calm and forever patient with the wounded soldiers under their care, they are truly unsung heroes.

The day arrives, and Alan, along with several other soldiers, are loaded onto a C-130 for their flight to Da Nang. He and Judy part company, promising to write letters and maybe hook up someday back in the States. The flight to Da Nang is short and uneventful. After landing, Alan is transported by ambulance to the 95th Evacuation Hospital, which is next to the beach. His new quarters are a steel Quonset hut with air conditioning and 24-hour nursing care and attention. His living conditions are the best he's experienced since arriving in Vietnam, but it was a tough way to come about them.

Within a few days of his arrival and after settling into what will be a long recovery and recuperation routine, he is given tragic news. The day after they left Phu Bai for Da Nang, the Phu Bai airfield came under rocket attack. One of the rockets landed near the MASH unit's wooden structure housing the nurses. Some were wounded, and one was killed. Judy.

He learns a cold, hard fact, as did his father and grandfather before him. The realities of war are brutal and horrific and often result in good people losing their lives. The experiences of military personnel in war and during brutal conflicts will follow them throughout their lives. They'll try to forget but never do. How can they?

4
GOING HOME

Alan has been at the 95th Evacuation Hospital for two weeks, making steady progress as his wounds slowly mend. He's no longer required to keep his left thigh wound elevated, and the small cast, which was used to help stabilize his left arm, has been removed. A fragment from the bullet that hit his arm caused a small fracture, which necessitated the cast. With these impediments removed, he's enjoying being taken outside daily in a wheelchair for fresh air and sunshine. He's always assisted by one of the nurses on duty, and in some cases, they spend time making small talk.

Shortly after arriving here, his personal items caught up with him, including a backlog of letters from his parents, grandparents, and two from his brother Lee. He's read each of them several times. His reactions are always the same: homesick for America, he wants to fly home on the freedom bird and leave this place behind him.

His parents, Sean and Ana, are doing fine and are preparing to relocate to Offutt Air Force Base, Omaha,

Nebraska, in mid-July. Scott is having a tough time dealing with the pending move and doesn't want to leave his friends. Lee will help with the relocation to Omaha and stay with the family through the summer. He'll return to Pensacola, Florida, to complete his senior year of college and the Navy ROTC program. Upon graduating in June 1970, he'll be commissioned as an ensign in the Navy and plans to enter the aviation program.

His grandfather, Sam, and grandmother, Marie, are well and still active as ever. After the bloody Battle For Hamburger Hill, Alan has a better appreciation for what his grandfather endured in World War I in the trenches. Although Sam never talked about his trench warfare experiences, Alan has carried with him some knowledge of them. When Alan was in the fifth grade, his father, Sean, was overseas on an unaccompanied tour. Sean moved his family next door to his parents in Louisville, Ohio. It was during this time that Alan would accompany his grandfather on his monthly all-night Saturday poker games held on the top floor of the town's courthouse.

There were nine men in this close group of Sam's friends, all of whom were veterans of World War I. On many occasions, late into the morning hours and after a few drinks, they would sometimes talk about their experiences in the trenches. They assumed Alan had fallen asleep on the sofa in a corner of the room. That was not always the case, as he would overhear some of their conversations. Since being wounded, Alan has often reflected on the nightmarish fighting he endured for ten days trying to take that damn hill. He now understands more clearly how they felt and what they endured fighting in the trenches.

The most current letter from his parents, in his backlog

of letters, was dated May 24th. It indicated that they received official notification from the military that he had been wounded and was recovering at the 95th Evacuation Hospital in Da Nang. Sean wanted more information and reached out to his contacts at the Pentagon requesting more details. They responded quickly and indicated Alan was well and would make a full recovery. However, there was no mention of whether he would be sent home or remain in the country to finish his one-year tour of duty.

It has been nineteen days since Alan was wounded on top of Hamburger Hill. As his physical condition improves daily, he's noticing his mental attitude is also improving. The hyperstress, despondency, and fear factors he's lived with for most of his time in-country are slowly receding. Alan is within three months of his DEROS (Date Expected Return From Overseas) and wrestles with his inner demons and conscience. He's torn between staying with his unit and completing his tour of duty if he's able or going back home to complete his recovery. The first is a matter of honor, and the latter is simply self-preservation.

The atmosphere within the 95th Evacuation Hospital is laid-back and easygoing within his ward. The doctors, nurses, and administrative staff have created and worked to maintain a relaxing environment. Many of the wounded soldiers joke and banter around among each other and staff personnel. The nursing staff is particularly engaging and understanding and works hard to keep the men's spirits up and their healing progressing. They treat every soldier as if they were their brothers and show nothing but kindness and patience, no matter how difficult a soldier may become or how severe his wounds. Each day they make their rounds, change bandages as needed, visit, and make small talk, as they listen to wounded soldiers talk. Alan marvels at how courageous, caring, and giving these women are and wonders how they deal with all the suffering they witness day after day.

It's late afternoon on June 9 when Alan is wheeled back to his ward by a nurse after spending time outside enjoying a warm, breezy, clear sky as he gazed upon Da Nang Bay. Settling onto his bed with the help of the nurse, he thanks her as she moves on to another patient. He pulls out his writing materials from the nightstand next to his bed and prepares to write some letters. As he does, the doctor who has been monitoring his progress walks over to him, pulls up a chair next to his bed, and sits down.

Looking at Alan with no emotion, in just a matter-of-fact tone, he says, "Lieutenant McCormick, you're going to be medevacked back to the States to complete your recovery, then you'll be assigned to a new duty post."

Without waiting for an explanation, Alan reacts. "That's good news, but I thought I was making progress and would return to my unit soon. Is going back home to complete my recovery necessary?"

"Lieutenant, you're progressing nicely but still have a way to go. Your wounds are serious, and they need more time to heal. Physical therapy is also necessary for you to regain full mobility in your arm and leg. Don't worry, though; you'll be 100 percent soon enough and can move to your next assignment." He stops and looks for a reaction from Alan. "Any questions, Lieutenant?"

Alan responds, "No, not really. Although I'm surprised by this. I thought I would end up back in my unit for light duty until my year ended. I'm not complaining. The truth is, I'm glad. When do I leave for the States?"

"We're working on that now. I would guess within the next few days. You'll be sent home to Walter Reed Hospital, where you'll remain until you make a full recovery. You'll be given new orders for reassignment when they release you."

He stands up, shakes Alan's hand, and moves to his next patient. Alan thanks him as he tries to absorb and digest the full ramifications of what he just heard. There are two conflicting emotions bubbling within. One is that of sheer relief, joy, and the urge to jump up and down at the news he's going home. The other is a feeling of guilt that he'll be leaving his unit and the men with whom he's served behind in this hellhole.

Later that evening, after dinner, Alan writes a letter to his parents and informs them that he's coming home. He then writes a letter to his brother Lee, one which he's put off writing for some time.

Dear Lee,

I trust this letter finds you in good health. As you know by now, I was wounded while helping to secure a hilltop in the A Shau Valley. Not a pretty picture, nor was it something I want to do again. The good news is that I'm still above the grass and taking nourishment daily. So, all is well! As I told our parents, I was informed earlier today that I'm being medevacked home soon to complete my recovery. I can't say I'm sorry about it. I've seen enough death for now.

In one of your earlier letters, you asked if I would

give you an idea of what it is like over here for a typical infantryman in the field, or as we call it, "the bush" or "boonies." Well, here it goes.

Weight is everything when we go out into the bush. You live with what you carry. Much of it is carried on a rucksack you sling over your back. First and most important is what we carry so we can fight. This includes our weapons, ammunition, grenades, claymore mines, hand flares, trip flares, weapon-cleaning equipment, and usually an extra belt of machine-gun ammunition. Then you add food and water (I'll come back to that), poncho and liner, extra socks, footpowder, a steel helmet, and personal stuff placed inside a waterproof small ammunition can.

We carry everything that matters to us in the ammo can, which is secured to the bottom of our rucksack. Wallet, money, pictures, letters from home, notepaper, magazines, paperback books, and/or diaries, to name a few items. Lest I forget, toilet paper.

Most of us drape a green towel across our shoulders and around our necks. It absorbs some of the sweat which streams down from our heads and necks. We also use it to wipe salty sweat from stinging eyes, and it can be used to help cushion the straps on our rucksack.

Now, back to the water. Water is essential, and over here, it can be a precious commodity, especially during the dry season. When in the field, we are usually resupplied, which includes water, about every three to four days. Because of this, we'll normally carry six canteens of water to get us through to the next resupply. During monsoon season, there is normally plenty of water accumulated in bomb craters, which are just about everywhere, and flowing streams. Our ponchos help collect rainwater during storms, so with Mother Nature supplying our water needs, we can usually get by with two canteens.

When we fill our canteens from bomb craters or streams, we must treat it with iodine tablets to kill all the parasites and other junk. The water is always murky and has an odor that is not very appealing. After the iodine tablets are dropped in the canteen, we must wait thirty minutes or more before it is considered safe to drink. Several of us use either Tang, lemonade, or Kool-Aid packets to disguise the taste.

Personal hygiene in the field is hard to come by. We don't carry shaving cream, razors, toothpaste, soap, deodorant, hairbrushes, and any toothbrushes we have are used to clean our weapons. Remember, weight is everything over here when you're going out into the bush. When we return from being out in the field, everyone back at our base camp or firebase cuts us a wide path until we've had a chance to clean up and get new fatigues. We're a mess and smell raunchy.

I guess that covers it.

It's incomprehensible to the average American back home that infantrymen in the field live this way over here, but for the soldiers in Vietnam, this is our way of life. My advice to you—stay with the Navy.

Take care, and I'll see you soon.

Your loving brother,

Alan

C̶ompleting Lee's letter, Alan places his finished letters into envelopes, seals and addresses them, places his writing materials back in the nightstand, turns off the reading light, and settles himself comfortably in bed. For the first time in almost ten months, he falls into a deep, restful sleep with no nightmares or haunting visions.

5
FORT BENNING

Alan is medevacked to Walter Reed Hospital, where he spends two months undergoing rehabilitation for his wounds. He's then given a thirty-day leave to visit family and continue his full recovery. Reporting to Fort Benning the first week of September 1969, he is assigned to the 54th Company of the 5th Student Battalion, The Infantry Officer Candidate School, more commonly called Infantry OCS. He is a Senior Tactical Officer and second in command of the company. During his recovery, Alan was promoted to first lieutenant and awarded several medals, including a Silver Star and Bronze Star with a "V" for valor, two Purple Hearts, the Combat Infantry Badge, and some other awards.

It's early morning, September 30, and today started as any other for Alan since being assigned to Fort Benning. The sun is beginning to rise in the east as the clear sky slowly turns from black to grey to a pre-dawn light blue. The air lacks humidity, normal for this time of year, and is comfortable for the men performing their routine morning exercises. Alan is at the head of six platoons of 200 OCS candidates in trail formation as he leads them on a five-mile run around the airborne track. They move at a deliberate, medium pace as they pound their feet on the asphalt, making a loud thumping noise. When this is done in unison by a large formation, it has its own soothing, rhythmic beat, helping the men to stay in perfect step as they run. It's referred to as the airborne shuffle. The student cadence caller yells out, "Who wants to be an Airborne Ranger?"

The candidates respond in unison, "I want to be an Airborne Ranger. I want to live a life of danger."

Completing their run, Alan marches them back to the mess hall, which is attached to their barracks. The barracks is a three-story concrete block structure that can house up to 250 men, and has a recreation room, an armory with weapons in the basement, and a large self-contained mess hall exclusively for the company. This is a separate area for the soldiers to eat and comes from the old meaning of mess: "food for one meal."

At the entrance of the mess hall, OCS candidates must negotiate monkey bars to gain entrance. They form into two long lines, with each line behind one of the two sets of monkey bars placed at the entrance. They stand at attention until their turn comes to negotiate the monkey bars. The two lines move quickly as each man jumps up on the bars when it's their turn and swings from one bar to the next until reaching the last bar. They drop to the ground, step forward, and ask the tactical officer, an infantry lieutenant at the entrance, for permission to enter. When granted, they proceed inside. This is a daily ritual for all meals Monday through Saturday. While dining, they must sit in a rigid position at their tables with no conversations permitted and must look straight ahead. This ritual continues until they reach Senior Status, called turning blue, at which time they can eat in a relaxed manner and converse.

The OCS program lasts six months. Those candidates who make it through the fifth month will become seniors. They'll place blue epaulets on the shoulder straps of their uniforms to distinguish them as senior candidates. They're within a month of being commissioned infantry second lieutenants.

Alan is the first man to negotiate the monkey bars and stands at the top of the steps as he watches the first few candidates follow his lead. Each platoon has a newly commissioned second lieutenant, who graduated earlier from OCS, as their tactical officer. After six months in this assignment, these second lieutenants will be sent to Vietnam and assigned to infantry units. Satisfied that they are moving quickly, Alan turns it over to his tactical officers and goes inside for breakfast. He secures a tray, goes through the chow line as food is placed on it, and then joins his company commander, Captain Harry Martin, at the officers' table.

Captain Martin is a career officer who has completed two combat tours in Vietnam and is highly decorated. Alan respects him and enjoys working with him. He has a stocky build, is of medium height, and played fullback for the Ohio State Buckeyes football team. He's Airborne and Ranger qualified. In essence, he's a soldier's soldier. The men working for him and the OCS candidates feel the same way Alan does about the captain.

Walking over to the table and pulling out a chair as he

sets his tray down, Alan says, "Good morning, Captain Martin."

Responding in a cheerful voice, he replies, "Good morning, Alan. The men are looking good. I was watching you run them around the track from my office window as daylight was breaking. They are shaping up nicely."

"Yes, sir, they are. I think we've weeded out the candidates that were not cut out for this program."

Captain Martin has a mutual respect for Alan, enjoys his friendship, and would gladly serve alongside him anywhere, anytime. Alan's combat experience on Hamburger Hill preceded him in this new assignment. Alan is considered by many in higher command to be senior officer material should he choose to make the Army a career.

Captain Martin responds, "Like you, I believe we have weeded out the candidates who didn't measure up. But the real test will come when these men are stationed in Vietnam. I hope they rise to the occasion and make it possible for every unit commander to say: send me more graduates like the ones I have now!"

Alan nods his agreement and informs Captain Martin of the company's scheduled daily activities. They include live-fire exercises with 81MM and 4.2 duce mortars on one of Ft. Benning's artillery ranges. This will be followed by outdoor classes on tactics and how to deploy these weapons of war effectively on the battlefield. Their conversations also include mundane items associated with their daily responsibilities. Finishing breakfast and their conversions, Captain Martin looks at Alan and speaks to him in a low-key, casual manner.

"Alan, if you're not doing anything this Saturday evening, Mary and I would love to have you come over.

Mary's best friend is visiting, and you'll find her an attractive woman—intelligent, accomplished, and very enjoyable company. What do you say?"

Alan, caught off guard, recovers and responds quickly. "Are you sure it's alright with Mary? You two don't get much time together with all your responsibilities of commanding this training company."

Harry cracks a smile and laughs as he responds, "Not at all. It was her idea."

"I would like that, thank you. What time should I show up?"

"Say about 1800 hours."

Alan is delighted with the invitation and opportunity to meet a woman. In his capacity as the Senior Tactical Officer, he spends all his time at Fort Benning. His world requires most of his waking hours to be spent at the 54th Company. What entertainment he finds on post normally involves stopping by the Officers' Club's Infantry Bar located in the basement.

This bar is for infantry officers only, and you had better remove your cap before entering. If you don't, a bell hanging at one corner of the bar, always manned by someone sitting at the bar and waiting, will ring out loudly. If you're caught, it's infantry officer etiquette to buy everyone at the bar a round of whatever they're drinking. Alan learned this the hard way on his first visit.

As an infantry officer, Alan must stay in top physical shape and has established a workout routine at the post gymnasium. This takes up some of his time during the week. Alan's personal and alone time is spent in his room at the BOQ, Bachelor Officers' Quarters on Fort Benning.

With virtually no social life since arriving at Fort Benning, Alan would enjoy some female companionship.

Both men stand up and carry their food trays to the kitchen. As they do, Alan responds, "I'll be there."

"Mary and I look forward to it. Stay safe out there today." They head their separate ways to begin their day's activities.

6

SHARON
FIRST DATE

Alan arrives precisely at 6:00 p.m., holding a bottle of red wine, knocks on the front door of Captain Martin's quarters on base, and steps back. Harry walks up, opens the front door, and greets Alan. "Good evening. Come in, Alan. You're looking good."

"Thanks, Captain"

"Alan, please call me Harry. The ladies are outside on the back patio."

Alan follows his lead as he hands him the bottle of wine. "Thanks for inviting me, Harry."

"It's our pleasure. Just FYI. Mary has been talking you up to Sharon."

"Thanks. I'll try not to screw it up."

Sharon Sheehan is a striking young lady with flowing strawberry-blonde hair which rests on her shoulders, a beautiful, milky complexion, and an outgoing personality that radiates confidence. She works for the Coca-Cola Company in Atlanta as one of their Business Development and Marketing officers in training. As they step outside,

Harry just smiles and looks over to Sharon. The look on Alan's face telegraphs his first impression of Sharon. She is stunning, and his expression conveys that clearly. Sharon is equally impressed with Alan and is drawn to him immediately, but only treats him to a coy smile of invitation.

Mary comes over to Alan, shakes his hand warmly, welcomes him to their home, then turns to face Sharon. "Sharon, this is Lieutenant Alan McCormick."

Sharon steps forward, extending her hand as Alan grasps it. She has a firm but gentle hold of his hand as they smile and exchange greetings. Alan is smitten, knows it, wonders how he'll impress her, and hopes she'll be drawn to him.

Sharon looks into Alan's eyes and sees a warm, caring, confident man looking back at her. Both Harry and Mary, observing Sharon's and Alan's first reactions to each other, sense the chemistry between them.

Alan is slow to release her hand as it feels so natural and inviting to hold. Relinquishing it, he says in a soft, sincere tone, "Sharon, it's very nice to meet you."

"Alan, it's my pleasure. Mary has told me a little about you, and it seems we have some common background."

Harry guides everyone over to the patio table and chairs, where they take a seat. Harry pours some wine for Alan, refills the ladies' glasses, and then his own. Light conversations occur between them as Alan shares a little more about his family with the group. As they listen intently, Alan looks for any sign that Sharon is impressed. If she is, she hasn't shown it so far.

Sharing some of her background, Sharon relates that she was born and raised in Tampa, Florida, a graduate of Florida State, and just received her MBA from the University of

Florida in June 1969. Although Alan completed his senior year at the University of Florida in 1968 while Sharon completed her first year of graduate work that year, their paths never crossed. She is an only child. Her parents are both professors at the University of South Florida in Tampa. Like Alan, she enjoys the beach and has, on occasion, gone surfing. She likes sleek sports cars and LeMans racing and is a huge fan of James Garner, Paul Newman, and Steve McQueen.

Conversation among the group continues well into the evening while dining outside under a cloudless sky.

The evening comes to an end as the time for Alan to depart arrives. Standing to leave, Alan says good night to Mary while giving her a casual hug and thanks her for introducing him to Sharon. He then steps over to Harry, vigorously shaking his hand while thanking him. Harry walks Sharon and Alan out onto the front porch, says goodnight to Alan, and goes back inside.

Alan and Sharon are alone on the porch and are drawn to each other. Although Alan has only known Sharon for one evening, he believes that she is the woman he'll marry someday. Not wanting to offend her or push himself on her, he draws her close to him and gives her a hug. She is hesitant and slow to respond to his hug but does so in a manner that he finds inviting. She then pulls back slowly, not letting go of him completely, and creates a little space between them.

"Alan, we should stop and maybe continue this later in a more private setting."

Looking into her eyes as he suppresses his urge to continue, he responds with sincerity and longing in his voice. "Sharon, you're a beautiful woman, terrific to be with, and I very much want to see you again."

She looks into his eyes and, with that mischievous smile he first noticed when they met, replies, "Is tomorrow afternoon soon enough?"

BUDDING ROMANCE

Alan and Sharon meet the next day before she returns to Atlanta. They begin a relationship which only grows as time passes. Whenever Alan can take time off for an evening or weekend, he travels to Atlanta and spends time with Sharon. She lives in a small Midtown apartment near Piedmont Park. They enjoy life in Atlanta, like restaurants, parks, museums, historical locations, concerts, and performances at the Fox Theater. They are falling in love and thinking of marriage.

Alan is concerned about the fact that he's an Army infantryman and will be sent back to Vietnam at some point. His military commitment has a few more years to go before he can be honorably discharged from the service and begin a civilian career. He's uncertain about his long-term plans and is hesitant to commit to a military career. His rotation date to return to Vietnam looms closer.

As 1969 comes to an end, Alan and Sharon take a week off, and she joins him on a trip to Louisville, Ohio, to meet his parents, brothers, and grandparents. It's a mini-reunion for the McCormick family at the home of the patriarch. While there, Alan seeks guidance from his father, Sean, and his grandfather, Sam, about what he's planning to do—ask Sharon to marry him.

7
A NATION IN CONFLICT

The year 1969 proves to be a very bitter, exasperating, and distressing time in America. There have been and are many events that deeply trouble and pull at the very social fabric of the country. People increasingly distrust each other as culture wars pit pro-Vietnam war advocates against anti-Vietnam war activists, men against women, old against young, the establishment against the counterculture, Blacks against Whites, and conservatives against liberals. The year is a time of profound social and political disorder. America's values are being attacked—tested as never before, redefined, with no clear sense of where the country is headed.

Antiwar protests continue to grow as millions of Americans come to believe the Vietnam War is a lost cause and a costly stalemate, rapidly destroying the country's spirit. On November 15, 1969, the Vietnam Moratorium Committee stages the largest antiwar protest in United States history at that time. A half million people attend the demonstration in Washington DC on the Mall.

Americans serving in the military during this time experience a significant downward spiral in the general public's support of the war and the men fighting in Vietnam. For the first time in our history, the public is turning against the men and women going to and returning home from the war. They are directing their disdain for the war more toward veterans and active-duty personnel.

8

INFANTRY CHAPEL WEDDING
THREE BROTHERS

It's midmorning, March 30, 1970. The day dawns early for Alan. Outside, the sky is clear and bright; temperatures are mild and pleasant, with a hint of spring in the air. Standing and gazing out the window of his second-floor room in the Bachelor Officer's Quarters at Fort Benning, he struggles to adjust his bow tie. It feels tight around his neck, and he's been fiddling with it while waiting to leave for the Infantry Chapel. Lee and Scott are with him and do their best to convince him he looks great in his uniform and encourage him to relax. He tries, but it's not every day you marry the woman you've been in love with from the moment you met.

Alan stares outside as he momentarily retreats within and reflects on what brought him to this moment. When he took Sharon to his grandparents' home to meet his family over Christmas, every member of the family was impressed with her and could see they adored each other. His father and grandfather told him he'd be a fool if he didn't ask her to marry him. Alan felt that way from the moment they met, but hearing the two men in his life whom he holds most dear and immensely respects, made it unanimous. On Christmas Eve, while they were alone, he asked Sharon to marry him, and she accepted.

The second weekend in January 1970, he and Sharon made a trip to Tampa to visit her parents to seek their support and approval. Her parents were initially hesitant and made their views known about war, the military, and Vietnam. They expressed their concerns about Sharon marrying a man whose world involves all three. It became apparent to Alan they were not pleased that Sharon had fallen in love with him. Sharon has a strong will and her own beliefs, is very decisive, and is an independent thinker. Knowing their daughter, they become confident she has thought this through and is very much in love with Alan. Although reluctant, they're drawn to Alan, believe him to be a fine young man, and give their consent and pledge of support for them both.

Alan is brought back to the present when Lee clutches his shoulder and says, "Brother, it's time to go. We must get you to the chapel on time."

As Alan turns to face his two brothers, Scott says, "Let's look at you, big brother ... Not bad. I still don't see what she sees in you." He adjusts Alan's bow tie, then his blue shoulder lanyard, both of which are crooked.

Stepping back to admire his work, he looks over at Lee in his Navy uniform, then back to Alan. "I still think the Navy's' dress whites look sharper."

Lee smiles, and Alan sneers as the light banter between the brothers relaxes him.

"Thanks, guys. I believe I'm ready...let's go."

THE INFANTRY CHAPEL

The Infantry Chapel is a special place that has been in high demand by many soldiers over the course of the Vietnam War. It is similar to a production line as post chaplains schedule and coordinate marriages of all faiths when requested and approved.

The time has arrived. Alan stands at the front of the small chapel next to the chaplain, looking out at the pews full of invited guests. Present is Sharon's mother, immediate family members and several of her college sorority sisters, and some associates from the Coca-Cola Company. On Alan's side of the chapel are his parents, family members, several junior officers he serves with at the 5th Student Battalion, some fraternity brothers from college, and surprisingly, a few senior United States Air Force officers, men who have served or are currently serving with Alan's father, General McCormick. They made the trip to show support for the general and his family.

Alan is joined at the front with his brother Lee as his best man. Next to Lee stands Scott, who is dressed in a tuxedo. Standing next to him is Captain Harry Martin, dressed in his Army dress blues. Both Harry and Scott are Alan's groomsmen.

In the first row is his father, General Sean McCormick, in his Air Force dress blue uniform, Ana, and his grandparents.

The organist begins the processional as Sharon's two bridesmaids, followed by the matron of honor, Mary, slowly make their way down the center aisle. All eyes look to the back of the chapel as Sharon emerges, escorted by her father. She is stunning. Alan beams with joy while struggling to contain his emotions.

Sharon's father walks up to Alan, places his daughter's hand in Alan's, then takes a seat next to his wife. The chaplain conducts a brief service, pronounces them man and wife, and tells Alan he may kiss his wife. After the kiss, they turn, face the congregation, and walk slowly down the aisle. Because of the tight schedule of weddings for the day, they only spend a few minutes taking pictures. Everyone then heads the short distance over to the Officers' Club for their reception.

RECEPTION AT THE OFFICERS' CLUB CORREGIDOR ROOM

The Corregidor Room of the Officers' Club is crowded with their wedding guests enjoying each other's company, the open bar, and food. The newlyweds move effortlessly around the room, making sure to engage their many guests. Their facial expressions radiate the love they feel for each other and for their guests.

The time arrives for toasting the newlyweds. Captain Martin steps forward to the microphone and raises his champagne glass as he proposes a toast to Alan and Sharon. Looking out at the men and women before him and then gazing over at Alan and Sharon, he speaks in a strong, calm, and compassionate voice.

"To Sharon and Alan. May their love for each other grow with every passing year and their lives be enriched as they venture forward."

Everyone raises their glasses toward Sharon and Alan as "Hear! Hear!" and the clinking of glasses is heard throughout the Corregidor Room.

This is followed by many more toasts to the newlyweds.

The room is full of people talking, enjoying themselves, while the noise level rises, when Sam McCormick steps forward to speak. His gait is slow but steady, and his breathing is somewhat labored, but Sam carries himself well. Stepping up to the microphone and gazing out over the crowd, his voice is emotional but controlled as he looks at his grandson and Sharon.

"Ladies and gentlemen. I look at my grandson standing before me, and it seems like it was only yesterday that I first held him in my arms. Now, he's a man, a soldier, and a husband. I have nothing but pride in my heart and love for him and Sharon. I know they will face life's challenges with grace and courage and make us all proud. Please raise your glasses to Lieutenant and Mrs. Alan McCormick."

Sam walks over to Alan, places his glass on the nearest table, and embraces him as tears swell up in his eyes and he whispers in Alan's ear, "I'm proud of you."

Alan becomes emotional, almost to tears, by his grandfather's gesture and love for him. They've created many memories over the years, and Alan respects and holds his grandfather in the highest regard.

While still embraced, Sam pulls Sharon next to him and whispers to her, "Welcome to the family. You are very much loved." The three of them stand there embracing, oblivious to the cheers and well-wishes expressed by the people gathered in the room. Relaxing his grip, Sam steps back enough to look upon their youthful faces. and with conviction. speaks.

"Remember, when you love each other, it doesn't matter if you're only married for six weeks, six months, or sixty years. Not even a war can steal your love."

General Sean McCormick moves from the back of the

INFANTRY CHAPEL WEDDING

room up to the front. He walks over to his father, son, and daughter-in-law and embraces them. It's a moment of pure love. Tears flow freely from several guests as they gaze upon the scene in front of them, and the room slowly goes silent.

Breaking from their embrace, Sean steps over to the microphone. He scans the room, looking for Ana. When their eyes meet, he asks her to come join him. With his wife next to him, he speaks to the crowd.

His voice is controlled and authoritative but laced with emotion as he speaks. "Ladies and gentlemen, close friends, and my fellow comrades, thank you for being here today and sharing this lovely occasion with my family."

Sean pauses, looks directly at Alan, and continues. "Alan, your mother and I love you very much and wish you and Sharon nothing but happiness and fulfillment in your lives." He then looks directly at Sharon. "Sharon, you're a beautiful young lady with incredible talent, personality, and intellect. Our son is fortunate to have you by his side. We love you very much and welcome you and your family with open arms."

He stops, motions for a waiter to bring him and Ana a fresh glass of champagne, and waits for everyone to have their glasses refilled. He then continues. "Ladies and gentlemen, please join me in a toast to Lieutenant and Mrs. McCormick. May their love for each other and happiness continue to flourish in all the many years to follow." He stops, raises his glass, and takes a drink as the room full of guests follow his lead. Cheers, applause, and conversation erupts throughout the room as many wipe tears from their eyes, including Alan and Sharon.

The reception continues with conversation, hugging, kissing, and shaking hands until it's time for the final act.

The guests move outside the Officers' Club, forming two long lines leading to Alan's car. Alan and Sharon walk under a sword arch and then through a gauntlet of guests showering them with rice as they make their way. Lee and Scott decorated his car, which he's very protective of. They have carefully decorated it with toilet paper, a string of cans tied to the back, and a newlywed sign placed in the back window.

Alan and Sharon give their parents and new in-laws last hugs as Alan helps Sharon into the car. He then slides into the driver's seat, starts the car, and slowly pulls out of the parking lot. Their families close ranks together as they and the other guests wave goodbye to them until they disappear.

HONEYMOON IN PANAMA CITY BEACH, FLORIDA

Arriving in Panama City Beach early in the evening, they find their motel. It's a quaint place set off the highway and near the white sand beaches of the Gulf of Mexico. They check in and meet the owners, who give them the keys to the honeymoon suite on the second floor.

Entering their room, they find a cozy suite with a bottle of wine and a flower arrangement on a small table. They're both drawn to the veranda and step outside to admire the view. The sun is slowly setting, and small waves roll endlessly up on the beach across the white sands. While enjoying the view, they start caressing each other, which draws them closer together as they begin kissing passionately. As their passion builds, they step back inside, leaving the door partially open. They hear the surf rolling in on the beach. Alan removes his shirt, kicks off his shoes and begins to undress Sharon. They both work feverishly to remove her garments. As they do, Sharon stands bare, silhouetted in front of the door with the night sky's fading light revealing her full beauty. Alan is captivated by her angelic features and removes his remaining clothes with record speed.

This is the moment they've waited for. They're now man and wife. They fully embrace and caress each other slowly as their desires reach a crescendo. Their marriage is consummated several times into the late evening and early morning.

Over the next two days, they enjoy the white sandy beach and beautiful weather. Their evenings are spent dining, drinking, and dancing to the music of the Swinging Medallions band at a favorite hangout near the pier. Their late evenings are devoted to making love. .They cannot wait to share their lives together.

Their short honeymoon comes to an end, and they return to Fort Benning. Events soon overtake them when Alan assumes command of the 54th Company. Captain Martin is promoted to major and sent back to Vietnam at the end of April for his third tour. Alan is promoted to captain in May and alerted that he'll be deployed back to Vietnam in June. Captain Alan McCormick is going back to war. A war with seemingly no end.

9
FIRE SUPPORT BASE RIPCORD
ARRIVAL AND ASSIGNMENT

Captain McCormick arrives at Tan Son Nhut Air Base near Saigon in South Vietnam on June 20, 1970. He is assigned to the 101st Airborne Division, which is responsible for I Corps in the northern part of South Vietnam, familiar territory for him, having served there on his last tour and participating in the Battle For Hamburger Hill in May 1969. After spending the night in Saigon, he flies to Phu Bai airfield onboard an Air Force C-130 and reports to the division's headquarters at Camp Eagle, next to Phu Bai and south of the Imperial City of Hue. It's late evening when he completes his processing into the division and spends the night at Camp Eagle. He's assigned to S-2 Operations of the 3rd Brigade, stationed at Camp Evans, located northwest of Hue.

Early the next morning, Alan is flown to Camp Evans on board a Huey chopper. Sitting in the waiting room of S-2 operations, responsible for acquiring and disseminating intelligence for the 3rd Brigade, he nurses a cup of coffee. The day starts out with a slight breeze, but as the morning progresses, the hot, smelly air, heavy with humidity that drains your energy, takes over. While waiting, he feels as if he never left Vietnam. Since arriving in the country, he hasn't had a chance to fully adjust to the time difference, the heat and humidity, or catch up on his sleep. He's exhausted and could use some sack time. The coffee helps him stay awake and gives the appearance of an alert person.

The door opens to the S-2 office, and out steps a familiar face, Major Harry Martin, the senior S-2 officer for the 3rd Brigade. It's only been a few months since they last saw each other while serving together at Fort Benning. Both men are surprised and close the distance between them, greeting each other with hugs, then vigorously shake hands. Alan's initial impression of Harry is he looks tired, distraught, and serious. He's only been here two months, and he looks like he's been here forever. *My God, is it that bad?*

Stepping back from each other, Major Martin speaks first. "Damn, it's good to see you. I wish it were under different circumstances."

Alan looks at his good friend and responds, "Major, I do too. Since arriving at Phu Bai yesterday morning, I've been hearing rumblings about a Firebase Ripcord. It doesn't sound good."

"Alan, come on in my office and I'll bring you current on what's going on and your assignment."

His office is sparsely furnished. The 101st Division flag and American flag adorn the walls and some pictures of his wife, Mary, are on his desk. His window is open, and a ceiling fan hums as it struggles to keep the room from becoming too unbearable. Alan left his coffee in the waiting room, and as he takes a seat, Harry grabs two Coca-Colas from his mini refrigerator and hands one to Alan. Both men raise their drinks in a toasting gesture, and Harry begins his briefing.

"Alan, we've been in a lengthy struggle to control the A Shau Valley and are trying to kick the NVA out of that area. It's not looking good." Alan responds with some remorse and anger in his voice. "Hell, we were fighting them back in the early part of 1969—trying to run them out. Will this ever end?"

Harry, ignoring the question, takes a few gulps of his Coke and continues in a slow, methodical manner to bring the situation into focus for Alan.

"President Nixon has been withdrawing troops from Vietnam, leaving only the 101st Airborne Division fully operational. We're tasked with taking the initiative to gain control over the A Shau Valley, code-named 'Operation Texas Star.' Colonel Benjamin Harrison, the 3rd Brigade commander, sent units from Lieutenant Colonel Lucas's 2nd Battalion of the 506th to secure and rebuild Firebase Ripcord which was abandoned after the Tet Offensive in 1968. This firebase is crucial to providing fire support for our operations in the valley area. Two air assaults were turned back with heavy casualties on our first attempt to get in there. The site was finally secured on April 11th."

Alan's facial expression is one of concern and anticipation for what's coming next. Harry takes a moment, allowing Alan to digest what he's said, then continues.

"Just a bare hilltop when it was first established, Ripcord is now a heavily bunkered stronghold providing artillery coverage for other firebases and units operating in the objective area. While rebuilding the base and preparing to attack enemy supply lines, the NVA launched sporadic attacks on our units throughout the area. Their attacks began with our initial insertion into Ripcord and continue as we speak. From the intelligence we've been able to gather, it's estimated there could be as many as 25,000 NVA troops in the A Shau Valley area."

Alan interjects. "Not surprising, we're playing in their front yard, and they don't like it!" Pausing to finish his Coke, he continues. "The problem we've always had is the communists simply don't care how many people they lose while achieving their goals. We may have been willing to sustain larger losses earlier in this war, but now, we just want to keep the enemy at bay until the ARVN can stand on its own and fight."

Harry leans forward, a slight grin emerging from the corner of his mouth, and with a low-key tone, responds, "Alan, I totally agree. Unfortunately, we don't make policy. We're just ordered to carry it out. That is why you're here."

Alan peers into Harry's eyes. What he sees is a seriousness he hadn't seen when they worked together back at Fort Benning. Harry continues. "I requested an experienced infantry officer to be assigned to this office who will report to me and temporarily be attached to the 2nd Battalion working with Lieutenant Colonel Lucas. We need the best intelligence possible out there and fast. I fear they're planning a major action very soon. Are you up for it?"

"I could say something trite like, 'Do I have an option?' But a simple yes will do."

"Good. I have several meetings scheduled throughout the day, so my senior NCO will take care of you this afternoon. He'll drive you around Camp Evans, see that you draw your gear and weapon, get you settled into your quarters here, and then you can rest for a while. We'll meet for dinner this evening and stop by the Officers' Club later for a beer. Alan, I would like to give you another day or two, but we don't have the time. Tomorrow, you'll be flown to Ripcord."

FLIGHT TO RIPCORD

It's midmorning the next day, June 22, and Major Martin drives Alan to the helipad. It's another typical day in this part of Vietnam: hot, humid, and uncomfortable. Pulling up to the helipad and stopping, they shake hands, exchange hand salutes, and part company as Harry wishes Alan good luck. Walking up to the waiting Huey with its blades running, Alan slowly approaches from the right side carrying all his gear and M-16 rifle. The downdraft created by the blades feels refreshing on his sweat-soaked body as the wind penetrates his combat fatigues. Peering through the open window of the cockpit door, he recognizes Captain Carl Price from Hamburger Hill sitting at the controls and gives him a thumbs-up. Carl, in turn, smiles and gives him a thumbs-up. Jumping into the Huey, the crew chief hands Alan a headset so he can communicate with the crew over the intercom.

Carl looks over his left shoulder into the compartment where Alan is. He pushes the button on his control stick, the cyclic, and speaks over the intercom. "Well, I'll be damned. When did you get here, Alan?"

"Carl, great to see you again. I just got in the country two days ago."

"And you're going up to Ripcord? Good luck, old buddy. It's shaping up to be another shitstorm like Hamburger Hill."

"That's what I've heard."

With Alan situated, Carl introduces him to the aircraft commander. "Alan, this is Jim. He's got eighteen days and a wake-up. Then he's heading back to the world. Jim, this is Alan. We served together at Hamburger Hill last year." Both men exchange greetings.

As they take off, Alan continues, "Carl, when did you become a helicopter pilot?"

"When I got back home from that last tour, I thought it would be better to fly over the bush out here than humping through it all the time. The food is a little better, I sleep in a cot most of the time, and even get to take cold showers regularly."

"Sounds like paradise. So, you're living the good life!"

"I've been here a month, and except for the few perks I mentioned, it's as dangerous as humping the bush, if not more so at times. So, why are you going to Ripcord?"

As the Huey gains altitude and flies toward the A Shau Valley, Alan gazes out over the landscape below. Alan recalls in 1969, when he first flew around this area, how beautiful it looked from a high altitude. But the area they're flying into belongs to the NVA. They control it, and they have no intention of giving it up. They're playing for keeps.

Alan responds to Carl. "I've been assigned to the 3rd Brigade's S-2 and attached to Lieutenant Colonel Lucas."

"He's a good man, a good leader. Unfortunately, I believe he's been placed in an impossible situation. That whole area is crawling with NVA, and Ripcord is in the middle of them."

"That's not encouraging."

"No, it's not. Alan, we're approaching Ripcord. We'll fly 1,000 feet above it to give you an idea of the surrounding area. Then we'll make our approach and get you in there. One thing. Hang on. If we take fire, it will get dicey."

"Got it."

Flying high above the firebase, Alan observes that it's on top of a steep, balding rock covered in whitish-brown dirt surrounded by jungle-covered mountains. It's over 3,000 feet above sea level and about 700 feet above the jungle floor below. It looks to be no bigger than two football fields. After circling the area a few times and the men pointing out to Alan other prominent features in the area, they begin a rapid descent into the firebase.

Descending, the Huey is jostled around by mountain updrafts as they approach the landing pad. Jim is on the controls and keeps them on a steady descent into the firebase as if it's just another day at the office. Coming in on short-final to the pad, the left side of the Huey is hit by several rounds of .51-caliber machine-gun fire. The Huey shakes from the impact of the rounds penetrating the airframe. Jim is hit and slumps over his controls. The left door gunner is also hit and falls to the floor with much of his head missing. A ghastly sight. Alan's been in this situation many times on his last tour, and it comes rushing back to him. The fear, the rage, the adrenaline rush, the slowness of the action around him, and the panic in everyone's voices as they deal with the crisis.

Gun crews on Ripcord cut loose with their .50-caliber machine guns. Carl takes over the controls, steadies the Huey, and lands hard as it bounces a few times before settling on the pad. Looking back at Alan, he yells, "Alan, I've got to get these men back to the MASH unit fast. Good luck. Hope to see you soon."

Alan responds, "Good luck to you, Carl." He removes his

headset and pats Carl's shoulder as he grabs his gear and jumps out of the helicopter. Carl executes a full-throttle power takeoff, gains altitude, and speeds back toward Camp Evans and a MASH unit. Alan runs to a bunker near the pad where a few soldiers are waving him over. A moment ago, all hell broke loose on the helicopter, and as the gun crews on Ripcord ceased firing, all went quiet. Moments of stark terror, which can come at any time, are followed by the sounds of sweet silence.

Alan approaches the small group of men as a first lieutenant steps forward, greets him, and guides him to Lieutenant Colonel Lucas's command bunker. As he's taken through the firebase to the command bunker, he notices considerable damage in many areas within the base. It has the look of a firebase that's been under siege for a prolonged period. There is a distinct odor of tear gas in the air, with some of it emanating from bunkers they pass. The stinging gas and smoke finds their way into the bunkers. The lieutenant guiding Alan mentions that in that last salvo of mortar rounds fired by the NVA, they threw in a few rounds of tear gas. He says this is something they like to do to torment their adversary.

COMMANDING OFFICER 2ND BATTALION OF THE 506TH

Entering the command bunker, Alan places his gear in one corner and is taken to the battalion commander. After introductions, they move to a secluded spot and sit at a small worktable. The commander inquires if Alan's okay and not hurt, given his welcome to Ripcord. His response, "Shaken, but okay. The pilot and left door gunner were hit.

The gunner took a round to his head. I'm afraid he's dead."

With anger, tinged with remorse, Lieutenant Colonel Lucas answers with an emotional voice. "Unfortunately, that's a regular occurrence around here. We're totally dependent upon chopper aircrews for supplies, replacements, and medical evacuations. They're a fearless bunch of men."

Gesturing to Alan, Lucas offers him some coffee, which he gladly accepts. For the next hour, they engage in a conversation about what has transpired to date and the current situation.

Alan is told that after establishing Ripcord in early April, there were several fierce actions as more fire support bases were opened in the Operation Texas Star area. When the monsoon season came to an end in mid-May, the sky was full of Army helicopters and Air Force support. That is when the NVA seemed to vanish. There continues to be enemy activity all around the area, but not in any force. Ripcord is routinely harassed by incoming mortar fire, and helicopters are fired upon. Overall, the action has not significantly increased.

Ripcord has two artillery batteries of 105s and 155-mm howitzers. They provide fire support for two battalions of 101st infantrymen patrolling the jungles in the operations area, hunting for and trying to engage the NVA. Ripcord is less than a fifteen-minute flight from Camp Evans, the rear area of the 2nd Battalion. The firebase is deep in the mountains, closer to Laos than its own support bases, which gives the NVA a distinct advantage over the Americans in this operation.

The 101st Division cannot afford another Hamburger Hill

should the NVA seize and retain the initiative. Colonel Harrison, the brigade commander, was informed by division headquarters that they were reluctant to be drawn into the kind of bloody battle that occurred on Hamburger Hill. Should they become engaged in major action with the NVA around Ripcord, no additional units will be sent in. Under the old rules, fresh units would have been airlifted in to engage the enemy without hesitation. There are new rules now.

BATTLE FOR RIPCORD COMMENCES

Since arriving at Ripcord three weeks earlier, Alan, through his interaction with other officers in the 2nd Battalion, formed a grim opinion. They are facing an NVA force far superior in numbers than the Americans have in the area. What's more, the communists are willing to commit all of them to take Ripcord. The question is, what are the Americans willing to do to defend the firebase and ultimately secure the A Shau Valley area? He conveys this to his superiors.

After weeks of observing the Americans and reconning the area, the NVA begins dropping mortar rounds on and around Firebase Ripcord on the morning of July 1. The battle for the hilltop is on, and the 101st is surrounded. NVA mortar crews begin regularly shelling Ripcord, and small teams of enemy infantry engage American units airlifted in to destroy the mortar positions. Resupply helicopters come under heavy antiaircraft fire on every approach into the firebase. In a devastating end to the first day, a sapper force breaches the perimeter of a company that set up a night defensive position on another mountaintop a short distance from Ripcord. The sappers demolish the unit.

On July 2, another company's night defensive position is attacked with rocket-propelled grenades, small arms fire, and satchel charges. Several Americans are killed. On July 10, B Company of the battalion is hit with 60mm and 82mm mortar fire, killing two more Americans. During this time, repeated attacks by elements of the 101st to secure a hill with dominant terrain features west of Ripcord which would have provided security, failed. On July 12, another fortified hill that provides the enemy a direct line of fire into Ripcord is secured by a company from the 101st. They suffer heavy casualties, repelling several NVA night attacks. The company is subsequently airlifted out and not replaced with fresh troops. As the battered company moves toward its designated LZ to be extracted, the NVA reclaims the hill.

Why are we fighting and sacrificing our men like this, only to have their efforts wasted?

HELICOPTER TRIP - A SHORT ODYSSEY

The morning of July 13 begins early for Alan. He's scheduled to fly to Firebase O'Reilly, which is further north of Ripcord, to meet with his S-2 counterparts in the Army of the Republic of South Vietnam (ARVN) 1st Battalion, 1st Regiment of their 1st Division. The American 101st and the ARVN 1st Divisions make up the combined force for Operation Texas Star.

Alan secures his web belt on his waist. This belt holds his Colt M1911 .45 caliber pistol, ammunition, and a canteen full of water. He slips on his combat vest and helmet, grabs his M-16 rifle, and heads for the bunker exit. Emerging from the bunker, he steps out into a very windy and dusty day. To some degree, both wind and dust are always present on top of Ripcord. He then makes his rounds of the firebase, checking in with the officers to obtain their status before reporting to the battalion commander.

After briefing the commander, he makes his way to the helipad to wait for his ride to Firebase O'Reilly. There is a lull in the NVA's shelling of the base. However, this will change with the sight and sound of a Huey approaching the firebase, on short-final. The NVA can see and hear approaching helicopters.

Alan takes cover behind a sandbagged gun emplacement next to the helipad as the other soldiers in the area also seek cover. They know what's about to happen as the helicopter approaches. The Huey settles to the ground, and the pilot frantically motions for Alan to get in. The NVA fires their .51-caliber machine guns from two different locations at the Huey. Their tracers are seen by Ripcord gun crews who return fire. It becomes a duel of machine guns as incoming green tracers and outgoing red tracers cross paths. Amid this firestorm, Alan rushes to the waiting Huey and throws himself onto the floor of the chopper just as they lift off and speed away from the area.

The Huey escapes the hail of lead directed at it, is still able to fly, and heads for Firebase O'Reilly. The crew chief, Wayne, hands Alan a headset and then a chicken plate (aircrew protective armor vest). He encourages Alan to put it on over his other vest for the flight to O'Reilly. Fighting is also intense in that area. Alan doesn't need any encouragement, given what he just went through to get on the chopper. The flight to O'Reilly is short and uneventful.

The Huey approaches the firebase's LZ, and the aircrew,

along with Alan, can see they are also under fire from several locations. The pilot gains altitude and requests the ARVN soldiers suppress the incoming fire so he can come in. He'll then shoot his approach and get in and get out quickly. For several minutes, there is a furious exchange between the opposing Vietnamese forces of machine-gun fire and exploding mortar rounds. The ARVN soldiers on the firebase and the NVA in the surrounding area are locked in a fierce battle. Over the radio, the aircrew and Alan hear an American captain using a radio to call in artillery. He's doing an excellent job, as artillery barrages seem to wipe out the locations from where the firing originates. There is a lull in the action, so the pilot descends rapidly into the LZ.

As the Huey closes to about 100 feet of the LZ, the windshield explodes when machine-gun fire rakes the left side of the chopper. Wayne yells he's hit and falls to the floor, lifeless. Alan takes a round in the chicken plate the crew chief gave him when they left Ripcord and is knocked to the floor. The plate saves his life. The Huey's tail rotor gets hit and they start to spin slowly as the pilot decides to abort the landing. Without a tail rotor, landing a chopper on an LZ is damn near impossible.

The pilot manages to stop spinning, but as they pass over the LZ, the hydraulics go out. He struggles to gain control of his chopper but can't. The engine quits on him. He's about twenty feet off the ground as they pass over the LZ. To save the men on board, he pushes his cyclic hard right and pulls up the collective which causes his Huey to flare up and turn facing the LZ. He does his best to settle the chopper on the LZ, but they hit the ground hard, bounce several times, and roll to one side. The rotor blades beat themselves on the ground, sending blade fragments flying in all directions. These fragments become deadly projectiles, with many embedding themselves in sandbagged bunkers near the helipad. The blades eventually stop, and the chopper slowly settles itself in the dirt.

The pilots are still strapped in and frantically release their seat harnesses to exit the aircraft. Alan and the surviving door gunner crawl out through the back and make a beeline for the nearest bunker. The two pilots join them. Their first thoughts are to exit the chopper and get as far away as possible in case of fire. Incoming fire from the NVA has ceased. They brought down another American helicopter so they're celebrating a little victory.

With a temporary lull in the battle and no fire in their Huey, the pilots run back to their chopper to retrieve Wayne's body. Alan joins them after he realizes he left his M-16 on the Huey. He grabs his rifle and helps remove and carry the crew chief's body back to the bunker. They lay him gently on the ground next to the bunker and cover him with a blanket.

The men slowly regain their composure as their adrenaline rushes, and heavy heart pounding and breathing start to abate. Alan, realizing he still has on the chicken plate, removes it and finds a bullet partially sticking through the back side. He's one lucky soul as he looks to the heavens and whispers, "Thank you."

Alan and the aircrew are sitting on the ground, leaning against the bunker wall when an American captain and an ARVN major rush over to check on them. Looking down on the men, the captain says, "You fellows all right? Do you need a medic?"

Alan is the senior officer in their group and stands as he

replies. "I think we're okay. Unfortunately, the crew chief was killed."

The captain looks down at the body covered by a blanket and then at the aircrew. "I'm sorry to hear that. It's a wonder that you're not all lying there next to him." Looking at the pilots, he continues, "That was a damn fine exhibition of flying. Well done!"

The pilots just look up at him and nod their heads as an expression of thanks. He continues. "I have requested another bird in here to take you men out. It should be here shortly. If you need anything while you wait, just see the ARVN sergeant in the bunker. He'll take care of you."

Again, the pilots nod their heads and say, "Thank you, Captain." He responds, "You're welcome; good luck out there."

The captain looks to Alan and introduces the ARVN major and then himself as an adviser to the ARVN. He knows the purpose of Alan's visit and leads him to their command bunker with the ARVN major following.

COLLEGE ALL-AMERICAN OFFENSIVE LINEMAN

After spending the night on O'Reilly, Alan returns to Ripcord and continues his interaction with the officers in the 2nd Battalion. On July 17, Alan checks in on the new acting commander of Battery A's 155 howitzers. First Lieutenant Bob Kalsu assumed command of the battery after the captain in charge was severely wounded in the neck and had to be medevacked.

Bob Kalsu is not just any first lieutenant. He was an All-American tackle at the University of Oklahoma and the eighth-round selection for the American Football League

Buffalo Bills in their 1968 season. He was a starting guard for them that year, played the entire season, and became the Bills's rookie of the year. He is admired and respected by the men who serve with him, doesn't dwell on his football past, and is considered a fine officer. Particularly noteworthy is that he was eligible to stay in the States with an Army reserve unit and could have done so. This would have kept him home and not landed him here on Ripcord. He chose to place his professional football career on hold, fulfill his ROTC Army commitment, and deploy with his unit.

Bob conveys to Alan that his battery's fire missions are increasing in frequency. The 155 howitzers have a range of thirteen miles and can place heavy artillery barrages on key NVA positions in areas covered by Operation Texas Star. He believes, and Alan concurs, that this is creating havoc for the NVA. It's forcing them to intensify their attacks on Ripcord to silence his guns. Shelling from the North Vietnamese is becoming more persistent and grows worse as helicopters try landing to resupply Ripcord.

Their conversations drift back from the war to home and then their wives. Bob shares with Alan that he'll be a father soon, as his wife is expecting to give birth any day. Alan, looking forward to being a father someday, congratulates him. They part company, as Alan must continue his rounds, and Bob needs to rejoin his men at the battery.

THE TOP OF THE HILL IS BLOWN OFF

Troops on Ripcord have been living an underground existence because of the incoming fire since July 1. On the seventeenth day, the enemy moves up powerful 120mm mortars and begins shelling the firebase. On July 18, a CH-47

Chinook from A Company of the 159th Aviation Battalion, the Pachyderms, takes a burst of machine-gun fire in its fuel tank while hovering over Ripcord with a sling load of artillery shells. The Chinook crashes straight down into the ammunition storage area, causing massive and violent explosions, followed by a firestorm. That portion of the hilltop located on the southern section of the firebase is literally blown off. The 105-howitzer battery located near the storage area is completely destroyed along with the Chinook. Extensive damage is done to several bunkers in that section, and there are many casualties.

Alan concludes that the situation is deteriorating rapidly, and drastic action is needed. Either evacuate the firebase or commit significant troops to attacking and securing the surrounding hilltops around Ripcord.

ACTION ON RIPCORD INTENSIFIES

On July 19, Ripcord encounters continuous mortar fire, with the NVA concentrating on the LZ as Hueys fly in and out, dropping off supplies and evacuating wounded soldiers. One Huey is hit on short-final, catches fire, and crash lands just off the LZ pad. Everyone survives, except the copilot who forgets to duck as he exits the Huey and heads for safety. He is hit in the head by the chopper's rotor blade, which is still rotating and is decapitated.

The situation worsens the following day. An infantry company is inserted on a ridgeline east of Ripcord to find and destroy NVA gun emplacements that have been harassing the firebase. They come under heavy fire as soon as they land and find themselves in the middle of a hidden bunker complex. Another company patrolling a little over a mile south of Ripcord uncovers a communications wire running along a trail. Their company interpreter, after tapping into the wire, eavesdrops on conversations between an NVA division headquarters and one of their units in the area.

Based on the best intelligence gathered by July 21, as many as twelve battalions of NVA, over 5,000 soldiers, could be surrounding Ripcord. Found on the body of one NVA soldier is a map that alluded to a forthcoming attack on Ripcord. To make matters worse, losses on Ripcord have been so high that officers are asking for soldiers in other units to volunteer to go to Ripcord as reinforcements.

By this time, the NVA is lobbing several hundred rounds a day onto the firebase, including tear gas. They send their deadliest salvos when helicopters come in with supplies and ammo, and soldiers run out to unload the choppers.

Alan is standing next to the command bunker watching the action as helicopters attempt their resupply missions. As another Huey approaches, he hears some mortar rounds falling around the base and others he doesn't. Suddenly, from across the firebase, he hears the splitting crack of a mortar round exploding on impact and turns toward it. A round just landed near a bunker in the 155 battery of First Lieutenant Bob Kalsu. Alan feels the heat of the blast going past him and the concussion knocks him to the ground. His combat helmet flies off, and he hits the back of his head on the ground.

Alan's ears are ringing, and his head is dizzy from the fall as he slowly regains his footing. Finding his helmet and placing it back on his head, he runs over to the point of impact. There he finds several men peering down the steps into a bunker as some men inside work frantically to save two men. They're emotional and some are crying. Alan is told that Bob and another soldier were standing at the entrance to the bunker when a mortar round crashed five feet from the bunker entrance. The explosion was so powerful it blew both men back into the bunker. Bob's back was turned to the exploding shell which shielded the other soldier's body from the full impact of the blast. He saved the soldier's life, but First Lieutenant Bob Kalsu is killed by the blast.

John 15:13: "Greater love has no one than this, that someone lay down his life for his friends." His loss is felt by the entire garrison of soldiers on Ripcord as the news spreads.

On July 22, the twenty-second day of the battle, the 101st Airborne Division command realizes that Ripcord is not defensible, and the decision is made to withdraw. They have sustained more casualties up to this point in the fighting than at the Battle for Hamburger Hill. Immediate and swift lifeline helicopter evacuations commence

DESPERATE WITHDRAWAL FROM RIPCORD

Early on the morning of July 23, 1970, the twenty-third day of the battle, the NVA attacks Ripcord in strength. The 2nd Battalion returns fire, and an armada of gunships and fighter-bombers attempt to destroy enemy mortar and antiaircraft positions. Chinooks fly in and out, lifting the remaining howitzers off Ripcord. The Chinooks must hover over the howitzers long enough for the ground troops to secure the slings to the hook underneath the Chinook. Alan watches in amazement as these men work at a feverish pitch, one that would make a NASCAR pit crew jealous. The

Chinook crews and ground troops involved in this effort exhibit a level of courage similar to those men who charged through no-man's-land or landed in the first waves at Omaha Beach on D-Day or fought on the black volcanic sands of Iwo Jima. Similar courage is displayed as wave after wave of Hueys dart in between mortar salvos to evacuate soldiers five at a time.

The withdrawal happens so fast that Alan is one of the last survivors on Ripcord to jump on a Huey flying out. Looking out at the firebase as they lift off, he sees Lieutenant Colonel Andre Lucas standing in the open as he coordinates the final phase of the withdrawal. Around him are the few remaining soldiers of A Company, fighting a desperate holding action. It looks like a scene from Custer's Last Stand at Little Big Horn. The men are encircled as the NVA close in around them. When the Huey speeds away, Alan witnesses a 120mm mortar round explode at the feet of Lieutenant Colonel Lucas, ending his life. The final act is the extraction under heavy fire of the few remaining troopers of decimated A Company.

After the helicopters withdraw the remaining survivors, United States Air Force B-52 bombers are called in for carpet bombing. The battle ends. Although many NVA soldiers are killed and wounded, it's a victory for the NVA.

Given the political situation and resulting command decision not to commit more men to the battle, Alan believes that evacuation was the only option. However, to leave possession of the battlefield to the NVA is infuriating. What a terrible loss of America's youth. Alan wonders what it was all about and why.

10
BE CAREFUL AND COME HOME

Alan survives his close call with death on Ripcord and is back at Camp Evans recovering from his ordeal. The 101st Division redeployed their troops closer to Camp Eagle, Camp Evans, and the airfield at Phu Bai Combat Base. Firebases in the foothills are reinforced and some that had been deactivated are reactivated. Senior commanders are creating a buffer between the NVA controlling the A Shau Valley while operating out of Laos and Cambodia and the American and ARVN forces protecting Quang Tri and Thua Thien Hue provinces.

While serving on Ripcord for his first month back in Vietnam, Alan lost several pounds. He's accumulated many small and very uncomfortable skin irritations and infections which are being treated with antibiotics. Exhausted from his ordeal, he still has difficulty sleeping. He jumps at the sound of loud noises and is particularly annoyed at the occasional and totally random explosions of 122mm rockets lobbed in at night. His first few days back at Camp Evans are spent resting, showering multiple times each day, and eating to gain back a few pounds, though careful not to gorge himself while catching up on his mail.

Two cassette tapes from Sharon and several letters from his mother were waiting for him. He's played the tapes and read the letters many times. Since returning, he's been on light duty, shuffling paper and writing up after-action reports from his perspective of the Ripcord battle. The next morning, he'll report back to Major Martin for his new assignment.

This evening, July 30, 1970, belongs to Alan. Trying to relax and stay comfortable, he lies in bed on top of his sheets clothed only in his Army-issued green boxer shorts and T-shirt. The night air is hot and humid, causing little beads of sweat to accumulate on his face and chest. Looking up at the ceiling fan, which is doing very little to make it more comfortable, he curses at it in silence. His room is small and dingy, with only the basics provided. A rickety metal single bed, nightstand, small makeshift table for writing, a little mirror hanging on one wall where he's placed several pictures of his family and Sharon. The other wall has a rack stretched across the length of it, for hanging his clothes. A footlocker serves as his dresser and storage space for personal items. If, for any reason, someone wished to become depressed, all they would need to do is spend one day in this makeshift home away from home.

Looking over at the full-body picture of Sharon on his nightstand, he hits the play button on the cassette tape player and once again listens to her second tape.

Alan,

I hope this tape finds you healthy, safe, and doing well. I miss you very much and can't wait for you to hold me in your arms once again. It's only been a month, but who's counting? Some days I find myself struggling to get through the day without crying over you and our separation. I can't imagine what you go through every day over there not knowing what to expect or what might happen next. I live in constant fear of a letter from the Army. At my workplace there are some wives who have husbands serving there, and they deal with the same fear. Please don't take any chances. I want you to come home to me. Sharon's voice became solemn and emotional with those last few comments.

Let's change the subject.

My days are filled with work meetings, customer visits, charts and graphs, and office politics. They can be very challenging and rewarding in their own way but also frustrating and sometimes infuriating—particularly office politics. What I really don't appreciate is when some senior managers use military terms to try and motivate us. We're not at war; we're competing for consumer business. I find it amusing and at the same time, demeaning to the men and women who are serving our country and fighting in Vietnam. Over there, it can be a matter of life and death. Over here, it's making money, getting ahead, and staying employed. There, you can die. Here you can lose money or your job. But at least here you're alive and free to find another opportunity. Although I don't, I want to confront these armchair warriors and challenge them to produce their war experiences.

Sorry for ranting about this, but it does get old.

Some updates for you. Your parents are doing great. They routinely check on me and are planning to fly me out to Offutt Air Force Base, Omaha, to spend Thanksgiving with them. I'm looking forward to being there. They are great people, and your father is so reassuring when it comes to you and your line of work. If you haven't heard yet, he's been placed on the promotion list for major general and may be assigned to the Pentagon sometime in the next year.

Your mother is a little more conservative in her opinions about your profession. However, she's been incredibly supportive and has helped me work through my separation anxieties. Your grandfather and grandmother are continuing to age well, although your grandfather seems to be having more respiratory and digestive issues. They both maintain almost daily contact with me. I love your grandfather, Sam. He's a calming, rock-solid man who expresses his thoughts and convictions clearly and reassuringly. You have your father and grandfather in you, but I would probably give the edge to Sam.

Your brother Lee graduated from the University of West Florida, with his master's degree in mathematics and statistics in June. He then reported to Whiting Field Naval Air Station in Pensacola. I believe he's going through survival training now. When he's completed that, he'll start the Primary Flight Training program there, at Whiting.

Lee invited me to his graduation. I traveled down there with Rachel McClure, a close friend and sorority sister from college, and you may remember, she was a bridesmaid at our wedding. She works in Atlanta with Trust Company Bank. Rachel and I spent the night in Pensacola and went out on the town celebrating with Lee and some of his Navy buddies. They were all pilots in training and well-behaved. It just so happens that Lee and Rachel hit it off.

Your brother Scott is doing well. He graduated from high school and has been accepted to the University of West Florida. This will place him near Lee, at least for his freshman year, which is something your parents wanted. Scott is certainly a free spirit who sometimes challenges your parents. He's a good kid, though and will do well. But you already know that.

My parents are doing well, call me several times a week, and are planning a trip to Atlanta to spend a weekend with me. From my conversations with them, they seem to be softening their opinions about the men and women who are serving in the military, especially those who are in Vietnam.

As you know our country is tearing itself apart over this war. But to chastise the men and women serving in Vietnam is simply wrong.

I think I've rambled enough. Now, for some great news, and certainly a surprise for you. You're going to be a father. Our baby is due in January. Congratulations, Daddy. Don't die, be careful, and come back home to us.

All my love, Sharon

ALAN REACHES OVER and hits the stop button. Since first listening to the entire tape, he hasn't gone past that point again. He turns his lamp off, rolls to one side, and sobs into his pillow.

11

3RD BATTALION, 506TH INFANTRY, THE CURRAHEES
NEW ASSIGNMENT

After a restless night, Alan reports to Major Harry Martin's office. "Take a seat, Alan. Can I offer you a Coke?"

"Thanks, Harry. That would be good. I'll take anything that will cool me down some."

As usual, the ceiling fan is working hard to circulate the air, but it's not helping. The room is uncomfortable. To Alan it feels like the hot, humid, stale air is just being moved around a little. He takes solace in the fact that at least he's not hunkered down in an underground bunker on top of Ripcord.

Looking at Alan, Harry says, "Ripcord was a nasty piece of business. I'm glad you made it. The general feeling around here is that we may have slowed the NVA's movement through the A Shau Valley and somewhat upset their plans. Unfortunately, it's like the Dutch boy putting his finger in the dike to stop the leaks. Water just spouts out somewhere else, and he doesn't have enough fingers to plug all the holes."

Harry takes a few swallows of his Coke, as he turns to look out his open window at the view of mountains in the distance. Turning back to Alan, he continues. "The Division is going to increase our troop strength and firepower to provide more security in the areas we're responsible for protecting."

Alan responds, "That sounds good to me. Since we're not fighting to win this thing, we need to minimize our losses and turn the fighting over to the ARVN as soon as possible."

He takes a few sips of his Coke and continues. "I have my doubts about the long-term viability of the South Vietnamese military to stand and fight. They have their share of good, dedicated soldiers and officers…but they need to prove to themselves they're capable of standing on their own, en masse, and fight to win against the NVA."

Harry agrees with Alan as they talk around the subject for a few minutes. Harry then moves on to the point of their meeting and briefs Alan on his next assignment.

"During August, the 3rd Battalion, 506th Infantry (the Currahees), will be relocating from where they were operating, further south, to Phu Bai Combat Base. They will join the 2nd Brigade and set up on the southeast section of the base. They will join the 2nd Brigade and set up on the southeast section of the base. This section was once a stand-down area for battalions coming in from the field but has not been used for some time."

He pauses, then continues. "Alan, you're being temporarily assigned to the 2nd Brigade to work with the Currahees. Your job will initially involve training and familiarizing officers of the new battalion with how the 101st operates in this area. You'll join them in the field as they reopen and establish new firebases throughout their area of operations and act as their S-2 officer."

Looking at Alan and trying to read his reaction to the assignment, Harry asks, "Do you have any questions?"

With no questions, Harry concludes with, "Alan, you're now officially assigned to the Currahees as their S-2 officer. We'll be meeting with some of their key officers for an early lunch today at 11:00 hours and then you're on the clock."

ASSIGNMENT ENDS

During Alan's time with the Currahees, he serves on Firebase Brick, Firebase Pistol, and Fire Support Base Birmingham. He participates in combat patrols, helps gather, analyze, and disseminate intelligence, and interacts with the battalion CO and his officers. On many occasions, he is involved in ambushes and firefights while on patrol but remains physically unscathed. However, he's tired, frustrated, and losing patience with the slow pace of President Nixon's Vietnamization of the war that he instituted over a year ago.

Alan is released from duty with the Currahees in December and reports back to Major Harry Martin at Brigade S-2 Operations. He's glad to be back and sets about readjusting to daily life at Camp Evans. His room is not the Ritz-Carlton, and Camp Evans's environment is not similar to "Anytown USA," but compared to living out in the bush for several months, it's heaven.

During his time in the bush, Alan often thought about Sharon's words. "You're going to be a father. Our baby is due in January. Congratulations, Daddy. Don't die, be careful, and come back home to us." He's now in his seventh month in Vietnam and wonders if he'll live to return home to his expectant wife.

12
CHRISTMAS WITH BOB HOPE

It's December 23, 1970, and Captain McCormick and Major Martin are part of a massive convoy of troops driving from Camp Evans to attend one of Bob Hope's Christmas shows at Camp Eagle. After all the jokes, singing, dancing, and other performances, the show concludes with the singing of "Silent Night." Some will say it's the humidity, but most of the men become teary-eyed and emotional as the words and melody of that song temporarily carry them home to their families. Battle-tested troopers succumb to its spell, including Alan and Harry. Being over 12,000 miles from home and hearing that song made the war go away for a moment.

Returning to his room after the Christmas show, Alan finds a message from the Red Cross waiting for him. "Sharon McCormick gave birth on December 21 to a six-pound baby girl. Mother and baby doing well. Her name is Allie Marie McCormick."

Allie Marie is the name that Sharon and Alan agreed upon if they had a baby girl. Alan is overjoyed but feels helpless at not being home with them or able to do anything for Sharon and Allie. His grandfather and father before him have both been in this position. He now lives with the same loneliness and helplessness of his separation from family that they experienced. That night, Alan lies in bed and cries himself to sleep.

13
LAM SON 719-DEWEY CANNON II
FLIGHT INTO FIREBASE LOLO

Captain Alan McCormick is flying in the troop compartment of a 101st Airborne Division Huey as an observer. It's loaded with ARVN soldiers on the first wave being inserted into Firebase Lolo deep inside Laos. It's March 3, 1971, and they are part of the ARVN's 1st Battalion, 1st Infantry Division, responsible for making a combat assault to establish the firebase. Alan's chopper is last in a flight of sixteen Hueys flying in trail formation. Once the LZ is secured, two more Huey assault companies of comparable size will fly in the remaining ARVN battalion troops. The soldiers in the initial insertion must secure the area for the next two lifts. Alan's Brigade S-2 directed him to observe firsthand what was going on inside Laos. Operation Lam Son 719 is not going as planned and appears to be spiraling out of control. The senior officers of the 101st Airborne Division are desperately trying to control the situation. They need firsthand, reliable accounts of the situation inside Laos.

Captain Carl Price is piloting the Huey as he and Alan

communicate over the intercom. "Alan, what the hell brings you out here? It's nuts over here in Laos. A guy can get killed!"

"My Brigade S-2 is trying to get a better understanding of what we're up against over here. The situation is chaotic at best and a disaster in the making in all probability."

Carl responds with a little tongue-in-cheek humor. "My money is on a disaster in the making. When we cross the border into Laos, we regularly come under fire. The odds of us making it back are 50-50 if we're lucky."

Alan responds, "Our losses are mounting across the board. Even our fire support bases inside South Vietnam are coming under increasing attacks from mortars, rockets, artillery, and sappers. I've been spending some time with company commanders at The Rockpile, Firebase Vandergrift, and the hills around Khe Sanh. They all say the same thing: this is one big disaster."

They both laugh as Carl says, "That's real encouraging."

Their voices are stressed as they yell, scream, and shout profanities in rapid succession. Their fear and anger come through clearly as he listens to the Huey assault company aircrews get shot to pieces as they try to insert their ARVN troops into the LZ. One crew has to make a forced landing and another stays on the LZ because their Huey is on fire. Already, four Hueys and two Charlie Model Huey Gunships are down on LZ Lolo. It's becoming a death trap.

Over the intercom, Carl tells his crew they are going in and follows up with, "Damn, this isn't a good way to start a mission!"

As Carl brings his Huey to a hover, it gets much worse when firing erupts and rounds smash into the Huey. The ARVN troops panic, and some have to be shoved off the

Huey as others jump out and run for cover. After helping the ARVN out of the chopper, the door gunners return to firing their weapons. The NVA return fire as their tracer rounds head for the Huey and find their mark. Carl increases his throttle, lifts his collective, and tilts his cyclic forward. His chopper slowly responds as it struggles to gain airspeed and altitude to clear the area. Several more rounds hit the Huey.

The crew chief firing his M-60 machine gun on the left side of the Huey is hit in his thigh. He is severely wounded. A bullet hit a main artery, and blood sprays all over the inside of the aircraft. The pilots and Alan are covered with blood. Alan moves over to help the crew chief, lays him on the floor, and grabs the medical bag. He places gauze rolls on the wound, presses down, and secures the two tie-down ends of the gauze in a knot. To stop the loss of blood, Alan must apply a tourniquet above the wound. He rips the long radio cord from the crew chief's helmet and uses it as a tourniquet. The blood flow slows to a trickle.

As the Huey gains altitude and clears the immediate LZ area, the right-door gunner yells over the intercom, "We're on fire! We're on fire!"

Alan's been busy trying to save the life of the crew chief when he hears the frantic yell and looks around the compartment and engine area. Carl calls out over the intercom, asking if they're on fire. Alan responds, "You do have a fire and smoke trailing from the engine compartment back here."

"Roger," comes his reply.

There is no friendly base within miles, so Carl banks his Huey to the right and heads back to Lolo. On final approach, they receive more incoming fire. NVA troops are all over the place. Carl has no choice, lands his chopper, shuts off the engine, and he and the other pilot quickly unstrap and get out of their seats. The right-door gunner secures his M-60 and runs for a trench near the Huey. He sets his weapon up and provides covering fire for his crewmates. Carl and the other pilot help Alan pull the crew chief out of the chopper and carry him over to the trench.

The trench is not very wide or deep and appears to be a long-running gulley, but everyone makes it and takes cover. Lolo is unbelievably hot, and the men don't have any water. There is also plenty of activity in the LZ as AK-47 and .51-caliber machine-gun fire is whizzing over their heads constantly. Mortar rounds are landing indiscreetly around Lolo. No one wants to be on the LZ. People are dying here.

Alan peers over the top of the gulley, looking around at the LZ to gauge their situation. Across the open space near a tree line, he sees an American captain using a radio to call in artillery. He knows what he is doing because artillery is landing on locations from which NVA soldiers are firing. He must be part of a crew from another ship that was shot down since American advisers are not authorized to accompany ARVN units inside Laos. It's strictly their show. The captain and an ARVN officer appear to be arguing about something or having a tough time communicating with each other. One of many problems with this operation is that, with very few exceptions, neither the Americans nor the ARVN troops speak each other's language.

While still looking out over the LZ area, Carl moves over to Alan and says, "The crew chief is hurt bad. If we don't get him out of here and to a MASH unit soon, we're going to lose him."

Alan agrees, and as a brief lull in the action settles over the LZ, another helicopter is coming in on short final. Alan and Carl crawl out of the gulley and, with the help of some ARVN soldiers, carry the crew chief toward the helicopter as it lands. It's already been loaded down with several wounded ARVN soldiers when they reach it, but they make room for the crew chief. Alan and Carl run back to their trench as the Huey takes off.

Reaching the trench, they jump back in as several mortar rounds impact around them, and machine-gun fire rakes the area again. The Huey clears the LZ but is hit by an RPG in the engine area and explodes, falling to earth in a massive fireball. The chopper goes down too far from the LZ for a rescue attempt. From the magnitude of the explosion and resulting fireball, neither Alan nor Carl believes anyone could have survived.

Carl has a small survival radio and calls the C&C (Command and Control) aircraft to halt the assault until they deal with the NVA in the trees to the south. He tells them that choppers trying to come in now have a high probability of getting shot down. The NVA has the upper hand on any helicopters trying to fly in here and land. The assault is delayed while some Cobras work over the tree line to the south. With another lull in the action, more choppers are able to come in, drop off their ARVN troops, and pick up some of the downed American Huey crews on the LZ including Alan, Carl, his copilot, and door gunner.

Flying back across the border, unmolested, Alan and Carl part company after landing at one of Khe Sanh's helicopter staging areas. They promise to hook up later in the week and share a couple of beers. Alan walks over to a nearby bunker, where he waits for a jeep to give him a ride to the Brigade S-2 operations bunker located on the main part of Khe Sanh. Carl joins a large gathering of aircraft commanders (ACs) from the Huey assault companies involved in the initial assaults on Lolo. There are plenty of pale and ghastly faces in the crowd. After what these pilots and their crews just experienced, it's incredible that these men are still alive.

Alan walks over to the group and listens to their conversations. Some of the ACs are insisting they go back to put more ARVN soldiers in and get their aircrews out of there. Carl is one of them. They compare notes, trying to determine how many South Vietnamese and Americans there are on Lolo. They still have some ARVN soldiers at Khe Sanh, who need to be airlifted into the LZ. Some ACs insist they are going back into Laos and ask how many will join them and help. Everyone is scared to death. They know they can't leave those men out there for the NVA and also know they must do something quick to get them out.

What Alan witnesses next is nothing short of pure bravery. Every man raises his hand. They break out and head for their choppers. Alan steps up to Carl, salutes him, shakes his hand, and says, "Good luck out there, and Godspeed to all of you."

Carl just nods and heads to the Huey he was given to fly. His destroyed Huey remains on Firebase Lolo. Alan watches as they refuel and rearm, load up the remaining ARVN soldiers, gather some Cobras to join them, lift off then fly back across the border to the hell that awaits them.

KHE SANH COMBAT BASE

Late into the afternoon of March 3, Alan reports to Major Harry Martin at Brigade S-2 Operations located near the main airstrip at Khe Sanh. Alan could use a shower. His clothes are covered in mud and blood, and he's tired. Shaken by what he's just seen and endured, Alan would like very much to find a quiet place to rest and recover. Harry greets his friend and is surprised and concerned by what he sees in Alan's face. He looks dejected, disgusted, frustrated, angry, and defiant, all rolled into one expression. They shake hands, and Harry guides him over to a corner table and pulls out a chair for him. Harry has one of his men bring Alan some water and a cup of coffee.

Looking at Alan, Harry says, "Is there anything I can get you right now before we start? I need your feedback as soon as possible. We're having another division meeting later today. This operation is fucked up."

Alan responds in a low-key, tired, and melancholy voice. "I'm okay. Let's get started. Just keep the coffee coming."

Harry asks, "So what happened on Lolo?"

"They were waiting for us. It was an ambush. I don't know how many helicopters we lost out there today, but it must be several."

Alan stops, takes a few swallows of coffee, and continues. "I've seen many acts of bravery since serving here in Vietnam, both my last tour and now this one. But what I saw out there today with those helicopter crews defies explanation. They were incredible, fearless, and totally dedicated to completing their mission and saving their men who were shot down. I'm afraid there are many casualties from that combat assault into Lolo today…and for what?"

Harry interjects. "Initial reports coming in indicate we may have lost eleven Huey's, and over forty were damaged. Many crew members were wounded, and some killed…not a good day for Army Aviation."

"It may well be one of their bravest days, and it comes

near the end of this damn war for us," Alan responds with an emotional tone.

Harry changes the subject and asks Alan, "Give me your best analysis of this operation so far. You've been interacting with many company commanders at our fire support bases in and around Khe Sanh and now across the border."

Alan finishes his coffee, motions for a refill, and responds. "In a nutshell, it's "FUBAR," as they would say in WWII. To me it's another clusterfuck!"

"Explain," comes the response from Harry.

"Well, for starters, I think the whole operation has been compromised from the beginning. The NVA seems to know our every move. They're either waiting on us when we airlift in the ARVN soldiers or they move into the area very quickly after the first wave lands. They've deployed additional weapons not normally seen in South Vietnam. Our chopper pilots are being shot at by 20mm, 40mm, all types of machine guns, RPGs, and they've even deployed tanks at some of the firebases in Laos." Alan stops, looking for a response from Harry.

"Go on," Harry interjects.

"The ARVN soldiers are not well led in many cases. Their ground execution and combat maneuvering are weak. Many of the South Vietnamese are slow to engage, and some do not engage at all. They just curl up and try to hide from the intense fighting. There is no doubt they are significantly outnumbered on the ground. I witnessed some ARVN soldiers trying to jump on Hueys as they were leaving Lolo earlier today. Not good. I have no idea how many NVA are now engaged, but I wouldn't be surprised if they have two, maybe three times the number of troops committed to wiping out the ARVN."

"While on Lolo, I noticed an American captain, probably one of the pilots shot down, directing artillery and gunship support. I mention this because he was very effective at it. Simply stated, Americans were talking to Americans, and they knew what they were doing. We have a severe language problem. With few exceptions, the ARVN on the ground and the Americans in the air supporting them don't speak each other's language. That has proven to be a real problem."

Harry then asks, "What about the morale of our troops on this side of the border manning the various firebases and keeping the NVA at bay?"

Alan looks directly at Harry and responds in a serious tone. "In my opinion, it's weak at best. I don't believe the men want to die over here since we're clearly winding down and pulling out of Vietnam soon. I also don't believe they have much faith in the abilities of the ARVN to stand and fight once we do leave. So, therein lies a problem. Are we placing our lives on the line with some men dying and others being wounded for a lost cause?"

"If you don't have any other comments, what would you suggest we do if it were your call to make?" Harry asks.

"The South Vietnamese haven't reached their objective yet of capturing Tchepone. The NVA's tenacity is rapidly becoming too much for the ARVN. To save as many South Vietnamese as possible and hopefully limit our casualties, they need to end this operation soon and pull back. If they want a political victory and to save face, maybe they should send in one massive air mobile combat assault into Tchepone. Secure it for a few days, sweep the area for weapons and supplies, be airlifted back, then claim victory. I'll stop by saying I'm just a captain, but this thing has got to end quickly."

Harry looks at his friend and simply responds. "Alan, thanks for your candor. I'll take it under advisement. Right now, I want you to go clean yourself up, check in with a doctor at the MASH unit, and have him look you over, then get some rest for the next twenty-four hours. If I need you, I know where to find you."

Returning to his hooch, Alan takes a quick cold shower, changes fatigues, sees a doctor as directed, and then takes a long nap. Alan seeks out Carl later that evening to share a beer. He learns from one of Carl's crew that he was severely wounded while going back into Lolo to help rescue their remaining crew members on the ground. Carl has been transported to Da Nang and will eventually be sent home due to the severity of his wounds. From what Alan is able to learn, it is believed he will survive. Unfortunately, he may well lose his left leg and partial use of his left arm. As he flew into Lolo, his Huey took on several rounds of machine-gun fire. Alan goes to bed that night and ,although exhausted, has only a few hours of restless, fitful sleep.

ON TO TCHEPONE

On March 6, 276 Huey helicopters protected by Cobra gunships and fighter aircraft lifted the 2nd and 3rd Battalions of the 2nd Regiment of ARVN soldiers from Khe Sanh to Tchepone—the largest helicopter assault up to this point in the Vietnam War. Their assault meets with little resistance as they spread out and began searching the area around the heavily bombed town of Tchepone. The regiment finds several hundred bodies of NVA soldiers, numerous destroyed weapons, and over 1,000 tons of rice. Extensive B-52 strikes over several days preceding the ARVN air assault wreaked havoc on the town. While in the Tchepone area, South Vietnamese forces encounter only light resistance, and although they find weapons and supplies, it is not considered significant.

On March 16, ten days after Tchepone is taken, President Thieu issues the order to pull out of Laos altogether and return to Khe Sanh. The redeployment, as it is called, of ARVN forces results in pessimistic press reports claiming a massive rout of South Vietnamese units is occurring in Laos. American media carries pictures of ARVN soldiers panicking and clinging to the skids of American helicopters rescuing those they could.

Although no one would admit it, President Nixon's goal of Vietnamizing the war looked to be in shambles.

SAPPERS STRIKE

Following Alan's March 3 experience at Lolo, he remains at Khe Sanh, working with Harry as they monitor and gather intelligence from around the operational area. Alan continues driving or flying to American firebases around Khe Sanh, meeting with their commanding officers to hear firsthand what is going on in their sectors. It's not good. The tempo of fighting is increasing as the ARVN continue their retreat back into South Vietnam. The NVA is pursuing them aggressively and inflicting terrible carnage. Khe Sanh itself has come under increasing artillery bombardment and 122mm rocket attacks.

It's late evening on March 23, and Alan is resting on his cot, listening to the latest tape from Sharon.

Alan, my love.

I miss you dearly and have been counting the days until you return home. I know all of you over there have a calendar where you count down the days. Well, I have one too. According to mine, as of this date of March 15th, you have just ninety-six days and a wake-up until your DEROS date of June 20th. But who is counting?

The TV news reports and print media are not being kind to you men. It seems the Laos incursion is a fiasco, and for whatever reason, they tend to lay some of it at the feet of our troops. The pictures and newsreels we see are very disturbing. I feel sorry for our men on the helicopter crews, as they seem to be taking a terrible beating. I can't begin to understand or comprehend what they endure or how they manage to find the courage to fly back into Laos day after day.

From your tapes and letters, it appears you have stayed busy but relatively safe. I hope that continues, as your daughter, Allie, and I want you home. She needs her father, and I need my husband.

Just a few comments about our family. Your grandparents remain very active and are most gracious in their support of Allie and me. Your grandfather Sam's health is slowly declining. He's been accepted to a Regional VA Hospital as an outpatient, and they have been providing him with ongoing care and medicine for his issues. Both your grandparents are tough and independent, and they dearly love each other. They go through life not complaining and approach each day as a new beginning. They are truly role models.

Your parents are fine and regularly check on me and their granddaughter. Your brothers are doing well, staying active and busy with their lives. Lee is enjoying his flight training and, by all accounts, is doing great. Like your father, he loves to fly. Scott is in his freshman year and although seemingly doing well, has confided to me that he's not sure he's fully ready for college. He struggles with some of his subjects. Time will tell; he's a bright kid. Maybe he's spending more time enjoying college life right now than academic life. My parents are well and check on Allie and me regularly. Since they're fairly close to me, they visit occasionally.

Now for some discerning news. I'm not sure how to convey this and have struggled with telling you, but I must. Allie has been experiencing digestive issues and has trouble gaining and retaining weight. She also has breathing difficulties at times. Initially, the doctors thought it might be allergies causing her breathing issues. But they've ruled that out. I have been working with the Egleston Children's Hospital, hoping they can determine what is causing Allie's issues. They've made very little progress to date. She is a beautiful little baby girl, and it pains me to see her struggle at times with her issues. I hate to lay this on you now, but I must. I'm coping well, have much support, and hope they find a cause and treatment for Allie soon.

Because of Allie's issues and the time I've taken away from work, the Coca-Cola Company has placed me on an extended leave of absence. I'll deal with my career later. Right now, I'm totally focusing all my attention on our daughter. I want so much for her to live a normal life. I know this is a lot to try and digest right now with everything you're dealing with, but as her father, I needed to bring you current. The doctors are working hard to identify what she is dealing with and are hopeful they will soon know. In the meantime, I've been assured she is not facing a life-threatening situation but one that is manageable.

I'm going to close and get this short tape in the mail to you. Know I love you very much, miss you greatly, and count the days until we're together again.

Oh, Allie wants to say hello to her father.

(Baby cooing is heard as Allie voices her feelings for her father.)

Alan feels so many emotions at one time it's hard for him to absorb all he's heard. The news concerning his daughter is distressing. But what can he do? He's stuck here in Vietnam in the middle of an unfolding disaster that could claim his life at any moment. He rolls over on his side and weeps for his daughter as he slowly dozes off.

How much can a man take?

He's shaken awake by loud explosions going off all around the Khe Sanh combat base. It's late at night and NVA sappers are attacking the base.

Alan jumps up from his cot, puts on his flak vest and helmet, grabs his M-16 rifle, and exits the bunker. He steps out into the night punctuated by explosions going off in many locations, men running in all directions—total confusion and pandemonium everywhere he looks. The smell of powder and burning fuel permeates the night air. They're hitting the flight line and ammunition dumps. Alan, with his M-16 on full-automatic, heads toward the S-2 operations bunker to help fend off sappers.

Approaching the bunker, Alan sees Harry standing outside with his rifle, firing at some NVA sappers off to his right. He runs toward his friend yelling at him to jump back into the bunker for protection. Harry doesn't see the two sappers off to his left about fifty feet. One is holding an RPG and aiming it directly at Harry.

With all the noise, Harry doesn't hear Alan yelling at him but does turn to see him running in his direction. At that instant, the sapper fires his RPG, creating a flash as the grenade leaves the weapon. The rocket hits Harry, and his body disintegrates. The blast blows Alan backward and throws him to the ground. There's considerable ringing in his ears; he feels relaxed, but has no pain. Alan's sure he must be dead when another soldier grabs his arm and drags him inside the bunker. Some of the soldiers inside attend to him as he slowly regains his senses and hearing. Outside, the fighting slowly abates, and only the sounds of ammunition igniting are heard.

Alan steps outside the bunker entrance, hoping to see Harry alive and being attended to by some medics. That is not the case. Some soldiers are gathering what remains of Harry and placing him in a body bag. Harry, the man who introduced Alan to his wife and who has been a close friend and confidant is now gone. Mary, Harry's wife and Sharon's closest friend is now a widow. The following morning, after performing an assessment of the sapper attack, it's determined that a large force hit the base at several key points. They inflicted heavy damage to multiple aircraft, destroyed two ammunition dumps, killed three Americans, and wounded many others. Forty-five days after the beginning of the operation, South Vietnamese forces that survived inside Laos make it back across the border into

South Vietnam. The NVA pursues them into the Khe Sanh area and increases the pressure with heavy artillery and rocket attacks. American and South Vietnamese forces are ordered to abandon Khe Sanh and pull back into Quang Tri by April 6, at which time Operation Lam Son 719 will be declared over.

14
LAM SON 719-DEWEY CANNON II
RESULTS OF THE OPERATION

With the ARVN out of Laos and Khe Sanh closed, the surviving American and South Vietnamese troops pull back into the Quang Tri area with minimal casualties. Alan returns to Camp Evans to complete his last few months in the country.

The Screaming Eagles played a key role in the South Vietnamese incursion into Laos, which transpired from February through March 1971. The Laotian incursion was an ARVN show. American advisers were not permitted to accompany their counterparts across the border into Laos. Elements of the 101st Airborne secured forward support bases inside South Vietnam to facilitate their push, and the division's aviation assets provided the bulk of helicopter support for the incursion.

The American portion of the operation was called Dewey Canyon II, named for an operation conducted by United States Marines in northwestern South Vietnam in 1969. Operational planners hoped reference to the previous operation, Dewey Canyon I, would confuse Hanoi as to the actual target, Laos. The ARVN's portion was given the title Lam Son 719.

The South Vietnamese conducted their largest, most complex, and important operation of the war with decisions made at the highest levels. Unfortunately, the lack of time for adequate planning and preparation and the absence of any real questioning about military realities and current capabilities of the ARVN proved fatal to the incursion. President Nixon, eager to hasten the pace of Vietnamization, gave his final approval for the operation on January 29, 1971.

By April 6, 1971, Lam Son 719 was declared over, and the immediate results compiled. Although Tchepone had been captured and held briefly, the enemy supply caches discovered were much less than intelligence assessments estimated. The NVA had relocated most of their supplies west of Tchepone and well beyond the operational reach of South Vietnamese sweeps.

For the South Vietnamese forces, the reality of their withdrawal from Laos, which was reported by the media as a retreat, and by many a rout, cast doubt on the operational successes highlighted by the Nixon administration and Nguyen Van Thieu, president of the Republic of Vietnam. The Laotian incursion showed that South Vietnam's military forces were fully dependent upon American advisers for the execution of large-scale offensive operations. The feasibility of "Vietnamization" as a strategy to extract American forces from Vietnam at this point in the war is highly questionable.

Alan is discouraged, despondent, and disillusioned by what he's seen, experienced, and been privy to during his current tour in Vietnam, and especially this operation. He just wants to return home, rejoin his family, complete the remaining few years of his military commitment, and be discharged from the Army. He's ready to pursue a civilian career and move on with his life. He's served with many fine and courageous men spanning the spectrum of military ranks. However, the level of incompetence and seemingly total disregard for men on the front lines by some senior military leaders and those at prominent levels in the government that strategize and manage the war has proved too much for Alan.

When Alan considers the mood of his fellow countrymen and women and the manner in which American servicemen and women are being viewed, treated, and abused by some back home, he concludes it's time for him to make a change. How he'll live and cope with the Vietnam experience is unknown.

15
BANKING CALLS
RETURNING HOME

Alan returns home from Vietnam on June 20, 1971, and is assigned to the Commanding General's Staff at Fort Benning, Georgia, where he'll work on the new Modern Volunteer Army (MVA) project. His trip home began at Da Nang, Vietnam, took him through Tokyo, Japan, for a brief layover, then on to McCord Air Force Base in Washington State. After spending an evening there and receiving new orders, he's transported with a small contingent of other Army veterans to the Seattle-Tacoma International Airport.

Particularly troublesome to Alan and the men with him as they navigate the airport and wait for their flights home are the disparaging looks they receive from so many people. It's obvious they are returning soldiers from Vietnam, yet there are no smiles or friendly comments directed their way. Instead, what comments are made come as daggers to the heart. Comments include "baby killers," "warmongers," "losers," and "Nixon's war boys." Although only in Tokyo for a few hours, they were treated with respect and appreciation by many Japanese with whom they interacted. Returning home to their own country and being treated in this manner is very disheartening, disappointing, and shameful. Where is the "silent majority" in the country that President Nixon always talks about?

After bidding farewell to the other soldiers with whom he's been traveling, Alan boards a Boeing 747 for his flight home to Atlanta. Alan hurries across the tarmac to the terminal waiting area, straining to find Sharon and Allie, the daughter he has never seen. Alan is wearing his dress green uniform with all of his medals and patches attached. He cuts a handsome figure and immediately catches the eye of Sharon, as he walks inside the terminal.

Walking briskly up to them, he pulls Sharon and Allie toward him. For a year, they have waited for this moment, and now it's upon them. They are oblivious to the people around them who, with few exceptions, walk right on by and pay no attention to another serviceman reuniting with his family. Tears of joy flow as Sharon pulls back and, looking into Alan's eyes, says, "I've missed you, and now that you're home, I'll never let you leave again."

Alan replies, "You don't have to worry, sweetheart. I'm leaving the military as soon as I've completed my commitment."

They kiss and gingerly embrace. Alan pulls back from Sharon, realizing he hasn't held his daughter or kissed her yet. As they separate, Sharon gently hands Allie to him. She looks so tiny, like a little doll, and is so beautiful. She has her mother's eyes, strawberry-blonde hair and long dark eyelashes. He's unsure how to take her from Sharon or hold her. Sharon helps him as father and daughter are united for the first time.

He looks into his daughter's eyes and sees the innocence, love, and wonder of God's creation staring back at him. What a glorious moment. Sharon, in a calm, soft, loving tone, says, "Honey, let's get your bags and go home. We have some catching up to do."

Seeing the glimmer in Sharon's eyes and feeling the same longing, he responds. "Let's go." When his thirty-day leave ends, he and his family arrive at Fort Benning, where he is assigned base housing. After settling Sharon and Allie into their quarters, he reports to the infantry school building for his new assignment.

MVA

Alan is assigned to the general's command staff to work on the Modern Volunteer Army (MVA) project while stationed at Fort Benning. In this capacity, he interacts with officers across the spectrum who are involved in various experiments associated with the MVA concept. His superiors are impressed with his performance and consider him a consummate professional who could become a senior officer if he decides to remain in the Army.

Results over the MVA project's life cycle are encouraging, as both recruitment and retention of soldiers increase measurably. With the end of America's ground participation in Vietnam by December 1972, the draft is discontinued going into 1973. Findings of the MVA project are put into action and used to recruit and retain an all-volunteer Army force going forward.

Simultaneously, with the Vietnam War winding down, the military initiates a substantial reduction in force (RIF) across all branches, with the Army being hit the hardest.

Discharged veterans are having difficulties finding employment and trying to assimilate back into their own country's society. The economy is contracting, inflation is climbing to levels not seen in decades, with interest rates hitting twenty percent, everything is more expensive, and companies are cutting back on their hiring of employees. It's a tough market to be looking for a job. This environment is further complicated for veterans, given the mood in the country concerning the Vietnam War.

Nevertheless, Alan decides to leave the service and begin a civilian career. As the end of his Army commitment approaches, he submits his request for discharge from the service in October 1973. His superiors reluctantly accept his decision to leave the service. The commanding general and Alan's immediate superior, Colonel Williams, work behind the scenes to assist in his job search and set up some interviews with key banks in Georgia.

JOB INTERVIEWS

Alan entertains thoughts about a possible career with the FBI and applies. About a month before he is scheduled to be discharged, he is called into the Atlanta regional office for testing and interviews. Later that evening, after a long day with the FBI, he shares with Sharon one of his interview experiences.

"Sharon, you're not going to believe this, but I was asked multiple questions dealing with a hypothetical FBI warrant arrest situation. One of the questions floored me."

"What was the question?"

"Well, it went something like this...'You're out in the field serving a warrant with fellow agents, and the subject resists, draws a weapon, and starts shooting. What do you do?'"

"What did you say?"

"I told him I would seek cover and return fire. After a moment, he says, could you kill him if you had to? How do you feel about taking someone's life?"

"I simply responded, yes, I could kill him. If someone is trying to kill me or the men with me, I would not hesitate to take their life if that were necessary to end the situation."

"How did he react to your response?"

"He just looked at me and said your response was immediate and expressed with such certainty...are you sure?"

"I thought he was being somewhat condescending as I stared back at him and said, 'Have you looked at my resume? I did two tours in Vietnam as an infantryman. I had to take lives to save lives. I do not take that lightly, but I think my experiences over there would suggest that my answer is appropriate.'"

Alan and Sharon just look at each other, grinning, and she says, "That seems like a rather foolish question to ask you, of all people."

"When I asked him if that was a standard question, he replied, 'not really,' he was just curious."

Over the next few weeks, Alan is interviewed by three regional banks and one local bank in Columbus, Georgia. All four are arranged by Alan's commanding officers, whose job responsibilities include interaction with business leaders in the community.

Three of the four interviews result in Alan receiving job offers to join their bank's management training programs. In the case of one bank, he found the conduct of the interviewer to be outrageous, offensive, and totally unprofessional. Unfortunately, it was fairly typical of what other Vietnam veterans experience when seeking employment in the civilian world. In this case, Alan was interviewed by the bank's human resource manager, a vice president, with many years at the bank. He was nothing more than an insufferable, pretentious snob.

His attitude was condescending from the beginning, and he showed no interest in Alan. He began by saying he is only doing the interview because he was told to do so by the bank's president. Shortly into the interview, he asks Alan to tell him what he could do other than shoot weapons, throw grenades, and hunt down people to kill. Needless to say, this did not sit well with Alan.

Alan stood up, leaned over the desk, and said, "This interview is over. I would not work here if you paid me twice the starting salary."

Alan leaves the man stunned as an expression of fear spreads across his face. Alan seeks out the bank's president and tells him what happened. Alan thanks him for the opportunity to come in but says he could not work for a bank with an HR director who displays that kind of attitude. Later that evening, the HR director called him and profusely apologized. Alan responds, "Go to hell," then hangs up on him.

Welcome home, Vietnam veteran.

BANK MANAGEMENT PROGRAM

Alan is honorably discharged from the Army in early December 1973 and begins his career with Trust Company

Bank in Atlanta. Sharon, Allie, and Alan relocate to Atlanta and rent a small home.

The next eighteen months prove frustrating, disappointing, and a painfully slow process of transitioning into the banking world. While in the Army, Alan led men in combat, was responsible for many lives, made major decisions, and worked with high-level officers on many important tasks. Now he is learning how to count cash, run a proof machine, work a teller window, and collect past-due payments from loan customers. These are just some of the many basic tasks he is being trained to perform. Alan recognizes the importance of learning all these tasks but longs for the day he completes this training. He's anxious to be promoted to a first-level bank officer where he can begin building a banking career.

On many occasions, he talks about his frustrations and concerns with his dad, who is patient and understanding. As a young man, Sean faced an uncertain future after his discharge from the service at the end of World War II. His grandfather, Sam, faced similar issues when he was discharged from the Army at the end of World War I. But Sean, as does Sam, clearly discern some differences between their generation's transitions to civilian life and the one Alan is undergoing. The Vietnam War has been and continues to be controversial, which has resulted in too much hostility and indifference being directed at Vietnam veterans.

16

THE VIETNAM WAR ENDS
SAIGON FALLS

On March 10, 1975, the North Vietnamese Army launches offensive operations in the Central Highlands. South Vietnamese counterattacks fail to stop them as large numbers of troops desert. On March 13, South Vietnam's president, Nguyen Van Thieu, orders his forces to withdraw southward, where supply lines could be shorter. What began as a retreat turns quickly into a complete rout. Deserters, refugees, and troops clog roads, spread panic, and commandeer vehicles and helicopters to escape further south.

American news organizations cover this spectacle with live broadcasts and TV footage as Quang Tri province in northern South Vietnam collapses, then Hue on March 25, followed by Da Nang on March 28. Iconic footage and pictures of panicked South Vietnamese civilians and soldiers clinging to the wheels and back ramps of planes taking off are shown across the country on nightly news. Americans sit fixated to their TVs as this unfolding tragedy occurs in real time. Alan and Sharon are no exception. They become more frustrated, dejected, and demoralized by what they're witnessing night after night.

On April 9, 1975, NVA forces reach the last line of defense for Saigon, Xuan Loc, a city only twenty-six miles away. South Vietnamese forces defend the city for eleven days and fight, with great courage but finally have to withdraw on April 20. The next day, President Thieu announces his resignation on television, denounces the United States for betraying South Vietnam in its hour of need, then flees the country. By April 27, Saigon is encircled by over 100,000 North Vietnamese troops.

American citizens are already being evacuated as the NVA surrounds the city. South Vietnamese in vast numbers have been and are converging on the US Embassy, frantic for a seat on helicopters. Desperate people try to get aboard already overcrowded boats on the Saigon River. The North Vietnamese do not hinder these mass evacuations by planes, helicopters, or boats.

Operation Frequent Wind is the final phase in the evacuation of American civilians and "at-risk" Vietnamese from Saigon before it falls. Under this plan, helicopters are used to evacuate Americans and designated South Vietnamese to ships of the Seventh Fleet stationed off the coast in the South China Sea. As reports come in that North Vietnamese forces are closing in, the order is given to commence Operation Frequent Wind on the morning of April 29. The American radio station in Saigon begins playing Irving Berlin's "White Christmas," which is the signal for American personnel to move immediately to their evacuation points.

So desperate are the South Vietnamese that those who are helicopter pilots with access to helicopters fly them with their families and friends offshore to the American fleet. After landing on any ship they can and unloading their passengers, many of the helicopters are dumped into the ocean, making room on the decks for more aircraft.

While in the last throng of the evacuation, North Vietnamese troops occupy strategic points in the city and prepare for the final assault. The South Vietnamese government cannot resist any longer and offers to surrender, but they are ignored. The North Vietnamese communists, after decades of struggle, only want a military victory. At noon on April 30, 1975, a T-54 tank bursts through the gates of the Presidential Palace. This final act is seen on television across the world.

The North Vietnamese political commissar (responsible for political education and organization), Lieutenant Colonel Bui Van Tung, arrives at the palace ten minutes after the first tanks. South Vietnamese General Duong Van Minh, realizing he is the highest-ranking officer around, says to Lieutenant Colonel Bui Van Tung, "We are waiting to hand over the Cabinet." Tung replies, "You have nothing to hand over but your unconditional surrender to us." Tung writes a speech announcing the surrender and dissolution of the South Vietnamese government. He then escorts General Minh to Radio Saigon and instructs him to read it in order to avoid further bloodshed.

At 2:30 p.m. on April 30, General Minh announces the formal surrender of South Vietnam. This announcement marks the end of the Vietnam War.

FOR WHAT?

On the evening of April 30, 1975, Alan and Sharon are sitting on their sofa in front of the TV. Allie is asleep in her room. Sharon looks at Alan, who has watched the stunning collapse of South Vietnamese forces, their government, and country over the last month. Tears stream from his eyes. She pulls him close to her and holds him tightly.

"Alan, what are you thinking?"

He avoids looking into her eyes as he says softly, "What am I thinking? I'm sad, frustrated, angry, and feel genuine pity for the South Vietnamese people. They've endured decades of hardships, with many among them trying to defend their country and build a decent life for themselves. Now, who knows what their futures hold?"

He leans back and looks up at the ceiling as he continues. "And it all came crumbling down and played out on TV for the world to see. Our country will be dealing with the aftermath of this war for decades. I can't begin to imagine when we'll fully recover, if ever."

Sharon stands up, walks over to the TV, turns it off, and returns to the sofa. Alan looks into her eyes, seeking an answer to his question, what now? All he can think about are the losses of over 58,000 Americans and the suffering their families have endured during this war. Their grief will continue unabated for decades, if not generations, going forward. And for what?

17
WHAT IS CYSTIC FIBROSIS?
HEALTH ISSUES

Alan completed his bank management training program and is promoted to assistant vice president. He's well-liked by his peers. Senior management believes him to be a mature, professional individual who will be promoted many times over the years to follow. Alan works as the assistant branch manager with John Flemming, manager of the bank's third-largest branch office in Atlanta, Georgia. They work well together as John shares his experiences and knowledge freely with Alan. Alan is finally on a career path within the banking industry.

The collapse of South Vietnam affects Alan, even though he tries to put it all behind him. He experiences more nightmares, and eelings of depression, and has mild anxiety attacks. He often wakes up at night in cold sweats, shaking, and believes he's back in Vietnam in the middle of a firefight. Many times, he'll get up, dress, go outside, and walk around the neighborhood to calm down, relax, then go back to bed. On occasions, he'll crawl under the bed thinking he's under rocket and mortar attack. He's also experiencing high blood pressure, more fatigue than usual, occasional shortness of breath, and sometimes numbness and tingling feelings in his hands. He needs help.

The Veterans Administration has been no help. It's proven very difficult to schedule visits and be seen by qualified medical personnel. The level of care and assistance provided is minimal. Unfortunately, this is the experience of many Vietnam veterans. Men and women are sent off to war, and when they return, the VA bureaucracy slow-walks everything and makes life needlessly more difficult for veterans dealing with real-life issues. Sharon is deeply concerned and reaches out to their family physician.

Following the initial visit with his doctor, Alan is given some prescriptions to help him sleep at night and control anxiety attacks. He's also told to regularly exercise, practice stress relief techniques, and talk over his emotions with his father and grandfather. They know what he's going through and may help him to deal more effectively with what he's experiencing.

Over the next year, Sharon's understanding, patience, and love make it easier for Alan to deal with his demons. He makes some progress albeit slow, but he does improve. When time permits, they visit his parents and grandparents. He seeks out the guidance and counsel of the two men in his life whom he respects the most. Sam and Sean prove helpful in dealing with his nightmares, war memories, and stress-related issues. However, Alan's physical problems, although intermittent and mild, have them both concerned and perplexed as to their causes. Alan's family physician believes they could all be related to the stress and anxiety he's experiencing. Sam, at one point, mentions that he and his fellow Doughboys experienced some of the same health problems from being gassed while in the trenches.

With Sharon by his side and supporting him all the way, Alan faces his issues while working long hours at the bank to build a reputation and advance his career. During this time, Allie is having health problems of her own. They have become so severe that Sharon has once again taken an extended leave of absence from Coca-Cola to stay home with her. Allie has been a sick child since she was born. Her life up to this point has centered around doctor visits and intermittent stays in hospitals. She has repeated lung infections, persistent coughs, chronic constipation, and poor weight gain. She is a beautiful little girl, but her many health issues foretell a difficult life fraught with uncertainty.

DEATH SENTENCE

Allie awakens Alan and Sharon, complaining of severe stomach pains in the early morning hours of March 15, 1976. She cries out. They both try to comfort her but to no avail. This is the worst episode they've experienced with Allie. Both are scared. They dress immediately, place Allie in the car, and take her to Egleston Children's Hospital. They need answers.

Arriving at the emergency room of the hospital, Allie, who has been crying in pain since she awoke that morning, is taken immediately to an examination room. Alan and Sharon explain the latest episode to the attending ER doctor, who has been joined by several ER nurses. One of them ushers Sharon and Alan out of the ER to a separate waiting room. Several hours transpire as the night slowly turns gray with sunrise beginning to appear through the waiting room's large windows. The ER doctor approaches Sharon and Alan. They stand up as he reaches them.

"Mr. and Mrs. McCormick, I'm Dr. Dunford. We've stabilized Allie; she is resting comfortably now. We need to talk first, then we'll take you back to see your daughter."

He asks them to sit down, as he pulls up a chair and joins them. He continues in a low, calming, and sincere tone. He can tell they fear what comes next.

"Your daughter is very sick. We need to keep her here for a few days and run some tests. In checking our records, I see where she has been here before under similar circumstances, this being more severe than in the past."

Alan responds, "Yes, Allie has been dealing with digestive and respiratory issues for a long time. She never seems to fully recover from her episodes, and as time progresses, they become more severe. We want answers."

He looks at both of them intently and with compassion as he continues. "I'm going to speak frankly to both of you. Based on her records and what I saw this morning, she is showing the classic symptoms of cystic fibrosis (CF). I've ordered a 'sweat test,' and we're waiting on the results."

Sharon asks, "What is cystic fibrosis? I've never heard of it before. Is it serious? Can she be cured?"

Doctor Dunford looks away, then slowly back to Sharon and Alan. He continues with as much compassion as he can summon. "If the test confirms that it is CF, Allie's diagnosis is not good. The disease is terminal. At best, she will finish elementary school. There is no cure at this time. Research is in its infancy, and a cure is a long way off. We do have some therapies which that should help and to the extent they are effective, provide her some relief."

Before he finishes, Sharon and Alan embrace tightly and

console each other as they weep for their daughter. Regaining some of their composure, Alan looks to the doctor and asks, "You mentioned a sweat test. What is that?"

He responds. "Cystic fibrosis patients give off excessive salt. Discovery of the sweat defect in 1953 resulted in the development of a standardized sweat test in 1959 which helped to identify cases of cystic fibrosis."

Alan continues, "If the test comes back positive, what next?"

"We'll conduct other tests to determine the extent of her CF progression. We'll then prescribe therapies to help Allie live as normal a life as possible. I don't mean to be cruel, but this disease usually takes children's lives at a very early age, and it does so painfully."

Once again, he stops and gives them time to digest what he said. "Mr. and Mrs. McCormick, should Allie's test confirm that she has CF, we'll cover everything in great detail that you'll need to know. I want to share with you that providing medical care and treatment for CF is very expensive. For you and your family, it will be stressful and consume your time and energy as Allie's health deteriorates. You should check your medical insurance and prepare yourselves and your family members for what will transpire going forward."

Sharon pulls Alan close to her, buries her head in his chest, and cries uncontrollably. Alan does his best to comfort her as he looks at the doctor and says, "I appreciate your candor." Alan is one who wants the facts and wants to know where he stands, then he'll face the issue or issues at hand. He's not immune to the devasting news and grieves internally for Allie and Sharon. Now, he tries to remain strong for his family.

WHAT IS CYSTIC FIBROSIS?

They have some answers. Now, it's time to move forward and cope with the hand they've been dealt.

Allowing both parents to regain some composure, Dr. Dunford ends the conversation by explaining the next steps and offers his sincere sympathy and prayers for them. He promises they will do everything within their power to help Allie. One of his ER nurses joins them and offers to take them back to see Allie. Dr. Dunford excuses himself and returns to the ER.

The nurse takes them back to Allie's room. They enter and find her resting comfortably with IVs stuck in her arms and breathing through nose prongs attached to a tube connected to an oxygen compressor. They walk over to her bed, peer down at her small, frail body, and watch as her chest rises and falls with each breath of air. They both struggle to contain their emotions with little success as they weep openly over their sleeping daughter. Allie is only six years old and may already have lived most of her life.

The nurse assures them she is comfortable and will be sleeping for several more hours. She recommends they go home, and for one of them to return prepared to stay with her until she is discharged. Alan and Sharon return home. Sharon packs a bag, and later that morning, Alan takes her back to the hospital. He gazes upon Allie who is still asleep, leans over and kisses her forehead, then departs the room after giving Sharon a long embrace. Alan drives to work, tears streaming from his eyes as he desperately tries to regain his composure before arriving at his office.

Five days later, on March 20, Allie is released to go home. It was confirmed that she has CF. Dr. Dunford takes his time explaining to Alan and Sharon that CF is an inherited disorder that causes severe damage to the lungs, digestive system, and other organs in the body. It affects the cells that produce mucus, sweat, and digestive juices, which are normally thin and slippery. With CF, a defective gene causes the secretions to become sticky and thick, which plug tubes, ducts, and passageways, especially in the lungs and pancreas.

Sharon and Alan are instructed on the available therapy techniques for Allie. They include mist tents (a way to deliver humidified air to patients to help clear mucus from their airways), "postural drainage," where children are held upside down while being pounded on the back (helps loosen and drain mucus from their airways), and antibiotics for children when dealing with ear, nose, and lung infections.

They are provided information about the Cystic Fibrosis Foundation which was established in 1955 by a group of concerned parents of CF children. Since the disease is very rare, it hasn't garnered the attention or money of other major diseases affecting large numbers of people. Sharon contacts the CF Foundation and is provided information about the organization and what they offer. She tells them that once Allie is settled into a routine, she and Alan will become active members of the CF community. They want to help their daughter and other CF patients in their fight against this terrible disease.

Alan notifies his parents, grandparents, and Sharon's parents of Allie's diagnosis. He also talks with his two brothers who do their best to reassure him and let him know they will be there for his family. Lee is on active duty and preparing to ship out again. He cannot join them at this time but commits to calling Alan regularly for updates and offers encouragement. Scott is attending college full-time at the University of Florida in Gainesville. He'll call regularly, visit whenever he can, and commits to being by his brother's side should he need him for any reason. Although neither Lee nor Scott say it out loud, both brothers wonder just how much one man has to endure and why it must be their older brother, Alan. Hasn't he been through enough already?

Time moves on as Alan and Sharon, feeling no self-pity only a deep love for family and their daughter, try to adjust to their new reality and make a comfortable life for Allie.

18

CAN THERE BE A GREATER LOSS?
DESCENT INTO DARKNESS

Over the following year, Alan and Sharon settle into a routine and strive to make Allie's life comfortable. Before they lose her, every effort is made to provide her with as many enjoyable life experiences as possible, like visits to the Atlanta Zoo, trips to Stone Mountain to ride the train, short road adventures through the North Georgia mountains, and occasional trips to local movie theaters to see the latest Disney movie. One of Allie's favorite foods is cheese pizza. She loves going out to eat at "Everybody's" a popular pizza restaurant located across from Emory University and near Egleston Children's Hospital.

Day in and day out Allie's therapy includes mist treatments, back pounding to loosen the mucus in her airways and help to cough it up, and pills, oh goodness, the pills! Included are enzymes to aid in the digestion of any food Allie endeavors to eat. To help Allie take her enzymes before eating each time, they mix them with applesauce. Getting Allie to eat is a constant battle, always pleading with her to eat just one more bite of food. Some days she'll eat more than others, but her digestive issues cause her to be constipated frequently, causing stomach pain. She struggles along with Sharon and Alan, who constantly encourage her to eat.

Alan will often resort to bribes to get her to eat some food. Taking her shopping to buy another Barbie doll, trips to McDonalds for french fries, which she loves, and shopping sprees at the local toy store where she is given an allowance to buy whatever fits within her budget. During these trips, Alan walks with her throughout the store as she picks out toys that catch her eye and gives them to Alan to hold. They call this process her "thinker lists." When she has picked several items, she then sits down, lays them out on the floor or a table, and thinks about which toys will make the final cut. Whatever she picks must fall within her total dollar limit for the day, which always seems to expand to fit what Allie chooses. It's always fun to see what Allie selects.

All the energy, time, and effort Alan and Sharon devote to encouraging Allie to eat only results in ounces gained, not pounds. If she does gain any weight, it's a battle to keep her from losing what she gains. She can lose weight faster than she can gain. Cystic fibrosis works relentlessly at destroying her body over time.

Allie's daily therapy of pounding on her back to loosen mucus in her airway involves turning her upside down and sideways as Sharon or Alan pounds on her back. She always accepts this therapy and occasionally complains, wanting to delay her daily treatment. Recently, she has become vocal and complains that the treatments are hurting her. Every effort is made to respond to Allie, but these treatments are deemed necessary for helping her cope with CF and prolong her life.

As her disease progresses, she begins coughing up blood. The first time this occurs, she panics and comes running to her parents crying. They are not prepared for this either, and panic begins to set in. They do what they can to calm her and rush her to Egleston Children's Hospital. Coughing up blood is another CF symptom which will continue and only get worse. It is only a small amount at first but increases as Allie's health continues to deteriorate. Both Sharon and Alan live in constant fear of her next episode. At night, they often cry out, "Why my baby girl? Why, God? Make it stop. Please make it stop."

It isn't long after her fourth bleeding incident that Alan gets a call from Sharon. Allie's right lung has collapsed. Sharon rushes her to Egleston. She is now in emergency surgery to relieve the pressure on her chest. Lungs collapse in CF patients is common, and many patients can suffer more than one collapsed lung in their brief lifespan. Alan notifies his superiors and rushes off to the hospital to be with his family.

Arriving at the hospital and finding Sharon in the waiting room, he walks up to her and, from her face can tell the situation is bad. Sharon has been weeping and tries to control it as Alan embraces her tightly. The doctor who performed the procedure walks over to them and introduces himself.

"Mr. and Mrs. McCormick, I'm Doctor Wooten. Allie is stabilized and has been moved to the intensive care unit. She will be here for a while. Her right lung collapsed, and she was in considerable pain." He pauses to gauge their reaction and, from experience, knows they are distraught and wondering—what next?

Looking at both parents, he continues. "I'm going to take you back to see your daughter now, then we'll go to my office where we can talk." Alan nods his understanding and, with his arm around Sharon, guides her as they follow the doctor.

Entering the room where Allie is, they once again see her little frail, helpless body, devoid of excess body weight sleeping in her bed. She has IVs in her arms, a prong in each nostril with a small tube attached to an oxygen compressor making noise as it helps her breathe, and a tube running out of her chest. This is new. The doctor explains to them that they made an insertion between her ribcage and chest cavity to insert the tube. This chest tube acts as an escape valve allowing air trapped in her chest cavity to exit her body. The tube will stay in her body for several days to help heal her lung. The doctor has them sit with their daughter, giving them time to absorb what is happening. He returns to his office and asks one of the nurses to escort the parents to him shortly.

The worst is yet to come.

THE MCCORMICK FAMILY'S LOSS

Allie has been under intensive care for six days as her condition deteriorates to the stage where she is given only hours to live. For the last two days, she's drifted in and out of consciousness. When conscious, she always finds her parents sitting next to her bed. Sharon and Alan stay by her side, only taking short breaks before returning to her room. Alan steps out regularly to notify his father, Sean, who keeps family members apprised of the situation. Alan's bank is very supportive and provides him with all the time he needs. After a long, fitful night where Allie struggles desperately to breathe while never waking, she sighs her last breath and goes limp as the morning sun begins to shine through the hospital window.It's Friday, March 25, 1977, when Allie succumbs to the deadly disease of cystic fibrosis, which she's lived with since birth. Alan and Sharon, each holding one of her hands in theirs, feel her life force fade away. Both parents lay their heads on her frail, lifeless body and weep profusely. The room is emptied except for Alan, Sharon, and the little body of their daughter, Allie.

Alan looks up at the ceiling, with tears steaming, and whispers. "Thank you, God. She is now at peace. The pain she's lived with during her short life here on Earth is over. Take care of her."

LAID TO REST

Allie is laid to rest on March 30, 1977, at the Decatur Cemetery, a historic graveyard within the City of Decatur, Georgia. The day dawns cold, but with a clear blue, glorious sky. Present for her funeral are family members, coworkers from Trust Company and Coca-Cola, Allie's two CF doctors, and many friends of both Sharon and Alan. There are no small children at her funeral because during Allie's brief life only adults have interacted with her. Allie's pallbearers are Sean, Sharon's father, Lee, Scott, and two of Alan's former military buddies who drove up from Fort Benning. Alan's grandfather, Sam, and grandmother, Marie, cannot make the trip. Sam's health has been deteriorating rapidly, and he can no longer travel.

After the church service, the funeral procession drives through Decatur en route to the cemetery, tying up traffic for blocks. Until then, Alan hadn't comprehended how many people had attended Allie's funeral. It was very comforting and brought more tears to his eyes.

At the grave site, after a short service, the minister closes with, "Suffer little children to come unto me, and forbid them not; for of such is the kingdom of heaven. Luke 18:16 KJV"

Alan and Sharon remain standing with their family members behind them for support as attendees file by to pay their respects before leaving. The crowd begins to dissipate, and Alan walks up to the grave and looks down on Allie's casket. His brothers Lee and Scott move forward and join him, one standing on each side of Alan. They each place one of their arms over Alan's shoulders in a show of support for their brother in his time of grief. Tears flow freely from the eyes of all three brothers.

Alan speaks softly to his daughter. "Six red roses for you, my precious Allie. One for each year of your life." He drops them one at a time on top of her casket and takes a moment. He then says, "I thought I had it rough in Vietnam. Allie, my sweet little girl, you're the bravest person I've ever known. We'll miss you terribly, think of you daily, and love you forever, my lovely little princess. Rest in eternal peace."

19
THE PATRIARCH IS CALLED HOME
CLEVELAND VA HOSPITAL

On the morning of November 11, 1979, as the hour approached 11:00 a.m., Sam McCormick passed away peacefully in his sleep. Sam had been suffering from severe digestive and respiratory issues for several months. He was placed on morphine drips to ease the pain as he slipped in and out of consciousness. He was moved from his home in Louisville, Ohio, where he had been receiving medical attention to the Cleveland VA Hospital. Marie stayed by his side until his last breath.

Sean and Ana were notified a few days before his death with the ominous message that he was fading fast and, at best, only had a few days remaining. Sean, now a lieutenant general stationed at the Pentagon in Washington DC, flew to Cleveland with Ana to join his parents. They are with Marie when Sam dies. Marie has watched her husband deteriorate for some time and suffer greatly as he approached the end of his life. Although difficult and beyond comprehension, she welcomes his passing as the suffering ends, and he's finally at peace.

THE PATRIARCH IS CALLED HOME

With the death of the patriarch, events move rapidly. Sean designates one of his colonels at the Pentagon to coordinate arrangements for his father to be interred at Arlington National Cemetery. Sean has his father's body transported back to Canton to the same funeral home that handled the burial arrangements for his father's close friend, Henry Miller, and his son, Captain Henry Miller, Jr.

Alan and Sharon arrive in Louisville the day after Sam's death. Lee, his wife Rachel, and their baby son, Josh, along with Scott, join their brother, arriving at Louisville the following day. Lee is a lieutenant commander stationed at Naval Air Station Norfolk, Chambers Field in Virginia, where he flies Sikorsky SH-3 Sea King helicopters. He was on station in the Indian Ocean as an officer in charge of a helicopter detachment assigned to the USS Nimitz when news of his grandfather's death reached him. He was given emergency leave to return home for the funeral. Scott works for the CIA and is pulled from a field assignment to join his family for the funeral.

Sean, Ana, and Marie arrive in Louisville later in the evening of the same day that Lee, his family, and Scott arrive. The patriarch's family is together, collectively supporting each other. Sam's body rests at the funeral home in Canton for the next three days as family and friends steadily pass through, paying their respects. During viewing hours, every member of the McCormick family is present.

TRINITY REFORM CHURCH IN CANTON

On November 16 at 11:00 a.m., funeral services for Sam McCormick are held at Trinity Reform Church in Canton, where Sean and Ana were married.

Sean is standing behind the pulpit, looking out over the congregation present to honor his father. He's in his Air Force dress blues with the rank of lieutenant general, three stars, on his shoulder lapels and a full display of medals above his left coat pocket.

The sanctuary is filled to capacity with an overflow into the foyer area. In the first pew sits Ana, then Marie, and next to her is Charles Glazebrook, Sam's lifelong close friend from WWI and the steel mill. He flew in from New York to be with the family. Next to Charles is Brigadier General Ken Jones, in his Air Force dress blues, and his wife. Ken is a close friend of Sean. Both men have served together throughout their military careers. In the pew behind them sit Sean's sons, Alan and Lee, with their wives, and Scott.

Within the sanctuary are lifelong friends of Sam and Marie McCormick. Sam and Marie have touched the lives of many people over the years from his career with the steel mill and veteran's activities, and their involvement in community organizations. Sean and Ana's friends from Canton and Louisville are there. Men who served or are serving with General Sean McCormick have made the trip to show support for the general and his family.

SEAN'S EULOGY FOR HIS FATHER

Sean looks down at the flag-draped casket in front of him. His father lies inside wearing a Class A Army dress green uniform. The rank of first sergeant is affixed to his dress coat sleeves, and a full display of his awards is pinned above the left coat pocket. Sean gazes out at the people present in the sanctuary and, in a calm, clear voice begins his eulogy. "My family and I thank you for joining us today to pay honor and respect to my father, Sam McCormick. He is the patriarch of the McCormick family."

Alan listens to his father speaking as if his grandfather were still here, sitting in the pew next to him. Alan struggles to control his emotions while reflecting over the years he cherished sharing time with his grandfather, for Alan admired, respected and strived to be like him. A man of character, integrity, and courage, both moral and physical. He lived life with a code of honor and wanted his son and grandsons to do the same. Alan knows his father has and takes solace in the belief that he and his brothers are also following their grandfather's example.

THE PATRIARCH JOINS THE FALLEN

Samuel McCormick is laid to rest with full military honors at Arlington National Cemetery at 11:00 a.m. on November 18, 1979. At the conclusion of a short graveside service, an Army chaplain closes with, "We commend to you, God, this man's soul for eternity. May he rest in solemn peace with his brothers and sisters who have preceded him in death on the battlefield. Welcome him, care for him, and provide peace of mind to his family and friends, knowing that he is in your presence and care now. Thank you, dear Lord. Amen."

The patriarch joins and now rests with his closest friends and comrades in arms, Sergeant Henry Miller, his son Captain Henry Miller Jr., and Sergeant Art Wilson. All were men who lived their lives with character, courage, and honor.

20

AGENT ORANGE
YEARS OF FRUSTRATION

It's early evening on Saturday, October 16, 1993. Sharon and Alan are enjoying a beautiful sunset over Lake Lanier from their back porch overlooking the lake. When Alan was promoted to executive vice president at SunTrust Banks, Inc. in 1990, he and Sharon bought a new vacation home on the lake. Sharon's career at Coca-Cola Company has progressed to the stage where she is a senior marketing officer. They both have high-stress careers, so they find the peace and tranquility of the North Georgia mountains and Lake Lanier very therapeutic. They maintain a condominium in the Buckhead area of Atlanta for commuting purposes.

This evening, they're enjoying some red wine as they talk about Alan's health issues. It's been sixteen years since the death of their daughter, Allie. It's just the two of them, as they chose not to take a chance on bringing another child into the world with cystic fibrosis. They have each other and their busy careers.

Alan has been increasingly involved in Vietnam veteran-related activities. He, along with other veterans of the war, is trying to encourage and to the extent possible, force the Veterans Administration to respond to their issues. The list of health crises linked to Agent Orange within the Vietnam veteran community is ever-growing.

Alan's own health issues have become more acute as medical bills continue to escalate. The combined health insurance plans of Sharon and Alan have covered most of his expenses over the years, but they're rapidly becoming a heavier burden for them.

Sharon takes another sip of her wine and says to Alan, "Do you want me to go with you Monday morning for the meeting with the lawyers taking your case against the VA?"

"If you could, that would be great. Your perspective concerning what I've been living with for the past several years may help."

Looking at her husband lovingly and in a soft tone, she replies. "I've already cleared my calendar and will be by your side. They need to be convinced of your sincerity and the issues you and your fellow veterans are facing. The VA has been unhelpful up to this point."

Alan agrees as he looks over at the stack of documents he's providing the law firm at their meeting. Included are copies of his request for assistance from the VA and their repeated rejections for various reasons they made up to justify their actions.

Alan concludes with, "This firm is supposed to be very good at litigating veteran's issues. I guess we will find out."

DOES ANYBODY REALLY CARE?

During the Vietnam War, the United States government ignored warnings from researchers and scientists and told their military members serving in Vietnam that the herbicides being sprayed all around them were harmless. Unfortunately, that was not true. Vietnam veterans in large numbers have been and are experiencing tragic, disabling effects of the toxins used throughout the Vietnam War.

Starting in 1977, Vietnam veterans began filing claims with the Department of Veterans Affairs, claiming that exposure to chemicals used in Vietnam caused their health issues. The VA slow-walked their claims, requested proof from the veterans that their problems began during military service or within a year of discharge, and then denied their claims. The Veterans Administration clearly acted as a bureaucratic arm of the government, totally devoid of any empathy, urgency, or real interest in determining what America's Vietnam veterans were dealing with.

In 1991, after scientific evidence showing that symptoms of Agent Orange toxicity may take decades to appear, Congress enacted the Agent Orange Act. Under the Act, the VA declared a specified list of health conditions as "presumptive" to Agent Orange exposure. This VA term refers to certain disabilities or diseases that the VA automatically "assumes" to be caused by military service. But the list of conditions is small. Although health conditions on the list are considered presumptive, the Vietnam veteran must submit a claim with supporting proof. If approved, treatment and compensation will be provided. By 1993, over 39,400 claims had been submitted to the VA. Of the claims submitted, the VA only approved and compensated 486 soldiers who served in Vietnam and had been exposed to Agent Orange.

Agent Orange is taking a huge toll on Vietnam veterans, with many dying from their exposure to toxins used in the war. No one officially dies of Agent Orange; they die from the exposure, which causes many health issues such as ischemic heart disease and failure, lung cancer, kidney failure, and COPD-related disorders.

Welcome home, soldier. We're here to help!

21

EVERYONE'S A VIETNAM VETERAN
THE REPRESSED

Following the collapse of the South Vietnamese Government in 1975 and well into the 1980s, Vietnam veterans were essentially shunned. Most veterans refused to discuss Vietnam with anyone but other veterans. No one else seemed to understand, care, or have any interest in asking questions like, "'What happened to you in Vietnam?" "What was it like not knowing who your enemy was?" "Did you feel like you gave up a year of your life for nothing?" "What did you accomplish?" "Would you do it again?"

When Vietnam veterans first returned home, many tended not to think about their experiences and tried to move on with their lives. Within the general population, no one showed any interest in Vietnam veterans who walked among them. Many veterans began to wonder why no one cared or showed any interest. A feeling prevailed that maybe it was something they should not openly discuss. Bury it, get on with your life, and forget all about it.

With the construction and acceptance of the Vietnam

Memorial, a resurgence of appreciation for the military and those who served arose. Vietnam veterans emerged from the shadows. There was a spurt of national pride following the stunning success of the First Gulf War, which began on January 17, 1991, and ended on February 28, 1991. The National Victory Celebration was held in Washington, DC, on June 8, 1991, to celebrate the conclusion of the Gulf War. It was the largest American military parade since the end of World War II and included a small group of Vietnam veterans. During the 1990s, the American population, in general, began to accept Vietnam veterans and express appreciation for their service and sacrifices.

It was becoming fashionable to be a Vietnam veteran.

STOLEN VALOR ACT

During the Vietnam War period from 1964 to 1975, nine million military personnel served on active duty. They are referred to as "Vietnam Era veterans." Only 2.8 million Americans actually served in the Vietnam Theater of Operations, i.e., Vietnam, Laos, Cambodia, Gulf of Token, and aircrews of the United States military, flying combat missions from bases outside of the war zone. They are referred to as "Vietnam War veterans."

As the visibility, recognition, and praise for Vietnam veterans became more prevalent across the country, many cases emerged where politicians, judges, celebrities, group officials, antiwar activists, prominent persons, and average citizens lied about their military records. Some boasted about their fictional exploits, while others went further and donned military uniforms and awards. Forging government documents to use as proof of their stories also occurred.

While the phenomenon was mostly associated with the Vietnam era, cases have occurred in recent years associated with the First Gulf War and the wars in Afghanistan and Iraq.

The Stolen Valor Act was signed into law by President George W. Bush on December 20, 2006. The Act was passed to address the issue of people claiming military awards to which they were not entitled and exploiting their deception for personal gain. For example, as of June 2, 2006, there were only 120 living Medal of Honor recipients, but there were far more known impostors. There were also large numbers of people fraudulently claiming to be Navy SEALs and Army Special Forces who served in Iraq and Afghanistan.

Particularly egregious to Vietnam War veterans is the number of men claiming to have served in the Vietnam War. During the War, many young men did not want to go into the military or be sent to fight in Vietnam. This attitude began early in the War and only grew as the conflict became more deadly and unpopular with Americans. Now, there are men of that generation claiming to be something they are not: veterans of the Vietnam War. Where were they when the opportunity for them to serve was present?

PART TWO
THE MIDDLE DESCENDANT
LEE MCCORMICK

1
FLIGHT SCHOOL
WATER LANDING

It's midmorning, August 30, 1970, and Ensign Lee McCormick is on a routine solo training flight over the Gulf of Mexico, flying at 5,000 feet in clear skies. The coastline of Pensacola, Florida is barely visible on the horizon as Lee peers out of the cockpit plexiglass window to his left. He's flying a T-28B Trojan, a fixed-wing aircraft manufactured by North American Aviation which the Navy uses as its basic trainer.

While cruising at his assigned altitude, Lee drifts off momentarily, thinking about how he arrived at this point in his training. After graduating with a Bachelor of Science in Mathematics and Statistics and completing the Navy's Aviation Reserve Officer Candidate (AVROC) program, he was commissioned an ensign in the United States Navy. He was then stationed in Pensacola for flight school training.

Lee's closing in on completing his Primary Flight Training, having accumulated thirty-one of his required thirty-five hours of flight time, and has the necessary grades to advance to the Intermediate level. For his next phase of training, Lee is considering transitioning to helicopters. He's developed a fascination for what they can do and believes there are similarities between flying them and the biplanes from earlier times. Biplanes have open cockpits, a high degree of maneuverability, are easier to control, and are considered by many pilots a joy to fly.

Lee is abruptly brought back to reality as his cockpit seat shakes, and a loud noise emanates from the engine of his Trojan. The engine is in distress, making "a terrible racket" sounding like "a gearbox is failing or there's no oil." His T-28's engine sputters, begins losing power, then, with a loud boom, goes silent.

Lee transmits to Whiting Field Naval Air Station's control tower in Pensacola. "Whiting Tower, this is student pilot Ensign McCormick. I'm declaring an emergency. Over."

The tower responds. "What's the nature of your emergency? Over."

In a calm, professional voice, Lee responds. "I'm over the Gulf at 4,500 feet and losing altitude. My engine just quit. Over."

"Have you tried a restart? Over."

"Roger, it's a no-go. I've turned north. I'm heading back toward the coastline. Over."

The tower responds. "Roger, understand, Squawk 7700, and state your intentions. Over."

Lee scans his instruments, noting that his engine oil pressure is dropping like a rock, the engine is emitting black smoke, there is no fire, he's losing altitude at an accelerating rate, and he fears he'll have to splash down in the Gulf. He responds to the tower with no sense of panic.

"Tower, it's not looking good. I'm going to have to set her down in the Gulf. I'm going to fly as close as possible to the coastline. Have you picked up my squawking yet? Over."

"We have you. Navy Air-Sea Rescue has been notified. I'll give you their ETA as soon as I have it. Over."

Lee is losing altitude fast as he watches his altimeter dropping like a rock. He's passing 3,500 feet as he struggles to maintain an airspeed above eighty knots. His Trojan's wings begin rocking a little, which is an indication he may stall his aircraft. Realizing this, he pushes his control stick forward to gain some more airspeed, placing him in a steeper dive, thus trading altitude for airspeed. As the aircraft falls below 3,000 feet, his airspeed has increases to 100 knots.

Whiting Field control tower transmits. "Ensign McCormick, an Air-Sea Rescue helicopter has been launched and is headed your way. Given your present course and airspeed, they should be in your vicinity within five minutes. Over."

"Roger. I don't have much time left up here. I'm falling fast. Now passing through 2,000 feet. I can see the coastline clearly. I'll let you know when I see the helicopter and when I set up for a water landing. Over."

Lee is still several miles from the coastline as he sees the Sea King flying toward him. The pilot transmits. "Ensign McCormick, this is King 5. Understand you're having a little engine trouble today and have to set her down in the Gulf. Over."

Lee manages a grin as he transmits. "King 5, thanks for coming. I do have a little trouble. Now that you're here, I'm going to make a smooth water landing and wait for you to pick me up. Over."

The Sea King pilot responds. "That will work. We'll

maintain a safe distance at your nine o'clock and stand by for a water pick up. Good luck. Over."

Lee responds, checks his instruments again, and is now flying at eighty knots about 500 feet above the water. The Gulf is calm as he nurses his aircraft closer to the water. His gear remains up, his canopy pulled back for a fast exit. He lowers his flaps and pulls back slightly on the stick, raising the nose of his aircraft, then gingerly sets it on the water. He skims lightly over the water's surface, bouncing up and down, and slowly comes to a stop as his nose dips into the Gulf.

He says to himself, "Congratulations, not a bad landing," but the Navy is short one more T-28B trainer. He wonders if this will impact his flying career with the Navy. Will they kick him out? Pursue disciplinary action? Commend him for the way he handled an unforeseen situation? Was there something he could have done to prevent the incident? Or was it just fate? Time will tell.

Without hesitating, he unbuckles himself, stands up in the cockpit, sheds his parachute, inflates his life vest, and steps out of the cockpit onto the left wing. His airplane is starting to fill with water and sink below the surface as he jumps into the water and awaits his rescuers. The Sea King hovers over him as one of the rescue swimmers jumps into the water to join him. Lee looks up in amazement as the helicopter just stays over him with minimal movement, and the men go about their respective duties like it's just another day at the office.

The rescue swimmer reaches Lee with the suspended cable and harness. He introduces himself, secures Lee into the harness, and signals for his crewmate to winch him up. Lee reaches the door, and the other swimmer helps him crawl into the passenger compartment. He unfastens the harness and lowers it back to the water surface for the swimmer to hook up. Once the rescue swimmer is on board and everyone is secured inside, the pilot heads back to Whiting Field Naval Air Station.

The helicopter is noisy, so they provide Lee with a headset to communicate. The pilot transmits over the intercom to Lee. "Ensign, that was a textbook water landing. Well done. Not sure it was on your training program for today, but you did good."

"Thanks! I would prefer to be flying back to base in my own plane, then spending the rest of my day at the club."

Some laughter follows as Lee thanks the helicopter aircrew for pulling him out of the Gulf. Men in the Air-Sea Rescue units have a dangerous job that requires them to fly in all types of weather conditions, day or night, to rescue Navy personnel at sea and on land. Their job is not for the fainthearted.

INQUIRY

Lee spends the afternoon being checked out by a naval flight surgeon who clears him for continued flight duty. He then proceeds to his flight school operations building for an initial debriefing. Both are standard procedures for incidents such as this. Lee's given twenty-four hours to rest. During this time, he informs his parents of the incident, going to great lengths to assure them, particularly his mother, that he is fine. After a twenty-four-hour stand-down, he is subjected over the next two days to an official inquiry.

The inquiry results in Lee being cleared of any responsibility for the incident, and he's immediately returned to full flight status. The T-28B aircraft he was flying that day, although marked as ready to fly, had been in service for several years and had a long history of engine-related issues. Lee is commended for his actions that day, and for the manner in which he conducted himself. Case closed. Lee goes on to complete the remaining four hours of solo flight time and his coursework.

HELICOPTERS

Lee moves on to the Intermediate Flight Training phase of his program. He requests and is assigned to helicopters. Learning to fly helicopters safely is no small feat. Learning to operationally fly them in poor weather conditions, day and night, is a fundamental skill required of all naval aviators.

As Lee progresses through flight training, more demand is placed on his abilities to navigate, communicate effectively, remain situationally aware at all times, fly the helicopter, and make sound decisions. He's a natural pilot and successfully completes this phase of his flight training, earning a Standard Instrument Rating in early June, 1971.

Upon completing his intermediate training in August 1971, he moves on to Advanced Flight Training. He chooses and is assigned to transition into the Navy's Sikorsky SH-3 Sea King, their current workhorse.

2
NAVY GOLD WINGS

After completing his flight training and transition to the Sea King, Lee is awarded his Navy Gold Wings today, August 15, 1972. His entire family has joined him in Pensacola to see his father, General McCormick, pin the Navy Gold Wings on his uniform. Both his father and brother Alan are dressed in their military uniforms. Sam, his grandfather, is dressed in his best suit and carries himself with a military presence. His younger brother, Scott, is unable to attend as he's still in Korea, serving with the United States Army. His mother, Ana, grandmother, Marie, and Alan's wife, Sharon, and daughter, Allie, are all present for the occasion.

When time permitted during his training, Lee traveled to Atlanta to spend time with Rachel McClure, whom he met at Alan and Sharon's wedding. On some occasions, Rachel drove to Pensacola to stay with Lee as they enjoyed the beach and casual nightlife together. They've grown very close and, more recently, talked seriously about their future together. Rachel joined Lee the day before his family arrived for this occasion and now sits with his family.

As deference to his military position and rank, General McCormick is seated on the stage with other dignitaries present. He will pin a Navy Gold Aviator wing on his son's chest when Ensign McCormick is called to the stage. The entire family sits in the audience on the front row of the auditorium.

The Wings of Gold ceremony at NAS Whiting Field signals a naval aviator's official completion of helicopter training and their entrance into "unrestricted naval aviator" territory. In other words, they're naval aviators and are going out into the world to meet the challenges of their chosen profession. The ceremony, one of naval aviation's most time-honed traditions with all its pomp and circumstance, is short and ends promptly. Ensign McCormick is now officially a naval aviator.

After the ceremony and congratulatory socializing, the McCormick family travels over to the NAS Pensacola Officers' Club on the beach for a private dinner party. Until now, Lee's parents and grandparents have only heard about Rachel through letters and telephone conversations from Lee. During the course of the evening, Rachel interacts with family members, who quickly become enamored with her personality, composure, maturity, and beauty. She's a confident young lady who makes a very favorable impression on the McCormicks.

Lee was hoping to use this opportunity for Rachel to meet his family and gauge their reaction. He is in love with her and is giving serious thought to asking for her hand in marriage. As did his brother Alan, Lee seeks the opinion of his father and grandfather after they've had some time to spend with Rachel. They both come to the same conclusion. If you don't ask her to marry you, it would be a mistake. Lee's mother and grandmother share the same sentiments.

As the evening comes to an end, Lee has not only been awarded his Navy Gold Wings but could become a married man soon. Of course, that depends on Rachel.

3
ANTISUBMARINE WARFARE (ASW)
THE SH-3 SEA KING

The Navy's SH-3 Sea King is a twin-engine, medium-sized, antisubmarine warfare (ASW) helicopter designed and built by Sikorsky Aircraft. The Sea King is capable of operating under all weather conditions and is the first American helicopter that can simultaneously hunt and destroy submarines. It can also perform various other roles and missions like search and rescue, transport, and medevac operations.

In normal operations, the Sea King typically has a four-man crew on board—a pilot and copilot and two aircrew stationed within the main cabin area. When conducting antisubmarine missions, the rear aircrew operates the aircraft's sensors and interprets the generated data. Their equipment includes dipping sonar, which is lowered into the water while the Sea King hovers over a location, specialized computers for processing sonar data, and a data link enabling the rapid dissemination of sonar information to other friendly elements.

After receiving his Navy Gold Wings, Lee is assigned to

ANTISUBMARINE WARFARE (ASW)

Naval Station Norfolk in Virginia. Since reporting for duty, he has been flying SH-3 Sea Kings with Helicopter Antisubmarine Squadron Five (HS-5), nicknamed the "Nightdippers." They acquired this name several years earlier due to their trailblazing efforts in using submersible sonar equipment at night and in all-weather ASW operations. Lee is promoted to Lieutenant, Junior Grade (LTJG) on November 1, 1972. His call sign is Nightdipper 24.

NIGHT TRAINING MISSION

Tonight, December 3, 1972, Lee is flying as copilot with Lieutenant George Jones, the officer in charge and detachment leader for tonight's training mission. Three Sea Kings in the group departed from Naval Station Norfolk, Virginia at 1900 hours. They are en route to the Helicopter Offshore Training Area to conduct a scheduled night antisubmarine sonar training flight.

The sky is clear with a half-moon, a light, cool breeze, and minimal winds. Lee thinks to himself, *it's a good night for practicing a difficult operation*. They have been training for several weeks in preparation for their next deployment to the Mediterranean Sea, often referred to as "The Med." They'll be part of a Naval Task Group with the aircraft carrier USS Independence.

Routine radio transmissions occur between the three helicopters as they fly in darkness over the Atlantic Ocean at 1,000 feet above the calm seas below. Reaching their training area, Lieutenant Jones reports their position to his group of Sea Kings.

"Gentlemen, we are on-site. We'll independently perform four approaches to a sonar hover and then practice our hover trim techniques. Be advised keep a safe distance. Over."

They respond, "Roger, Wilco." The Sea Kings are on a straight line, three abreast, with over 200 yards separating them from each other as they commence this phase of training.

Looking at Lee, George transmits over their intercom. "I'll do two practice runs back-to-back, and then you'll do two."

Lee responds. "Sounds good. I'll keep us clear to our front."

Satisfied everyone is on the same page, George descends to a hundred feet above the water and goes into a hover. He holds his hovering position for a few minutes, then ascends back to 1,000 feet above the ocean. He repeats the practice approach a second time, takes it back up, and turns the helicopter over to Lee. He takes the controls and performs his two practice sonar hover approaches flawlessly. With all three helicopters having completed this phase, they're ready to proceed to the next one.

The Sea King pilots now conduct four more approaches to sonar hovers while practicing dipping their sonar domes into the ocean and lowering them down below the surface. Due to the danger associated with dipping sonar, the pilots alternate their approaches one at a time.

The United States Navy uses the AN/AQS-13 series dipping sonar system. Its components are divided into two groups: the wet end and the dry end. The dry end is the processing unit used to obtain data. It is housed in the main compartment of the helicopter and operated by trained sonar operators. The wet end components are those necessary to deploy a submersible unit, called a dome, into the ocean and retrieve it. The dome is lowered or dipped into the water from the helicopter on a cable using a hydraulic reeling machine. The operator selects the depth at which he will lower the dome into the water to achieve maximum detection probability. Dipping for submarines is somewhat like going deep sea fishing and trolling for the big catch.

Lieutenant Jones is required to report every half hour and transmits that his group is now on their third of four practice dipping approaches. Lee just finished his third practice and regained their assigned altitude of 1,000 feet. The second Sea King, piloted by Lieutenant Terry Berger, one of the more experienced pilots, begins a hover over the ocean.

His sonar operator lowers their dome over 100 feet below the water's surface. At that depth and with unfavorable water conditions below the surface, hovering the helicopter becomes more difficult and unstable for Lieutenant Berger. The sonar operator sinks the sonar dome deeper into the ocean, hoping the stability will improve. For a moment, it works. But the sonar dome begins to pull their helicopter downward into the ocean.

The pilot screams in panic as he transmits over his radio. "We're going in! We're going in! Our sonar dome is pulling us under. I'm losing control."

Lieutenant Jones instructs the other Sea King pilot to remain at altitude and calls for a rescue helicopter. While maintaining a safe distance, he descends closer to his stricken aircrew as their helicopter is pulled backward and down into the ocean. The Sea King impacts the water, its rotor blades hitting the ocean violently, abruptly stopping as the Sea King immediately begins to sink below the water's surface. The pilot is transmitting as they go under, "God helps us. Tell my wife and daughter I love...." Then silence.

Lee and George witness the devasting crash as they descend closer. Lee turns on their landing lights to illuminate the area. George flies a low and slow circular fight path over the crash site as the Sea King slowly disappears below the ocean surface. He and his crew gaze out of their helicopter, looking for survivors. Lee spots two crew members floating on the surface and then sees a third. Over the intercom, Lee transmits to his sonar team.

"Fellows, secure our life raft and get ready to drop it to the men in the water."

After securing the raft, one of the sonar operators opens the helicopter door. George hovers over the three crewmen in the water who have closed in tightly together. The downed Sea King has been swallowed up by the ocean. All that remains floating on the ocean surface are the three crewmen and some small debris from the crash. The fourth crewman is nowhere to be seen.

Lee tells the sonar team to drop the life raft to the men. George radios the other Sea King pilot to join him at a safe distance and use his landing lights to help find the fourth man. They begin a wider search of the area after dropping the raft. Off in the distance, they see lights from the rescue helicopter closing in.

Over their intercom, George tells Lee to contact the rescue helicopter and coordinate with them. He'll fly and continue their search for the fourth man.

Lee transmits, "Sea Rescue, this is Nightdipper 24. We are over the crash site and have three survivors in a raft on the water. Their condition is unknown. One is still missing.

ANTISUBMARINE WARFARE (ASW)

We are two Sea Kings and will continue a wider search pattern for the fourth man. Over."

The rescue pilot in command transmits. "Nightdipper 24, this is Rescue One. Roger, we understand. We'll take it from here and secure your men in the water. We'll transport them to the naval hospital at Norfolk. Be advised another Air and Sea rescue helicopter is en route to continue the search for your fourth man. Over."

Lee responds in a low-key, somber tone as the realization sets in. The fourth crewman is likely lost, and they don't yet know his identity. Lee is friends with all four men. The two pilots and he were at the Officers' Club last night for a beer and some steaks. He fears that the missing man may be one of the pilots.

"Roger that. Thanks. We'll stick around here and aid in the search until we run low on fuel and have to break off. Over."

Rescue One acknowledges his transmission and then goes into a low hover over the raft as the rescue swimmer jumps into the ocean. He swims over to the men in the raft, checks on their condition, then organizes their order of rescue. Each man is placed in a harness and pulled up into the hovering rescue helicopter when it's their turn. Once all the men are secured inside the main compartment, the helicopter heads toward Norfolk.

Rescue One radios Lee as they speed back toward Norfolk. "Nightdipper 24, Rescue One here. Your three crewmen are secured, enjoying some hot coffee, and they're in good shape. No discernible injuries to speak of. Over."

He then transmits their names to Lee. The missing man is Lieutenant Terry Berger, the pilot in command. He is married with one baby daughter. His wife is visiting her parents in Savannah, Georgia. That's why he joined LTJG Kirkland and Lee last night for dinner at the club.

The two Sea Kings have to break off their search and return to base when their fuel levels become critically low. They are replaced by two Air-Sea rescue helicopters, which arrive on scene, take over the search, and continue searching until dawn.

Upon returning to Norfolk Naval Station, the two Sea King crews are greeted by several members of the squadron who have gathered in the hangar. The men of the squadron remain together at the hangar, awaiting word on the fate of Lieutenant Berger. There is little conversation, as each man is lost in his own thoughts. Training is a critical part of what they do, but it is also a very costly endeavor. Many aircrew members have lost their lives and others suffered severe bodily harm while training for the deadly business they have chosen as a career.

The sun slowly rises from the east to reveal a beautiful day in the making, as the air is crisp, cool, and refreshing. The morning sunrise, with all its beauty, is soon overshadowed when word reaches the men that they found the floating body of Lieutenant Berger. He was retrieved from the ocean's calm waters and the Air-Sea rescue helicopter aircrew is flying his body back to Norfolk Naval Station's mortuary facilities. Lieutenant Terry Berger lost his life while training to defend his country and fulfill his responsibilities as a naval aviator. He is gone, his wife has become a widow, and his daughter is now without a father.

TRAINING CONTINUES FOR DEPLOYMENT

After a twenty-four-hour stand-down and a memorial service for Lieutenant Berger, the squadron resumes training for their deployment to the Mediterranean Sea scheduled for mid-January 1973.

The Nightdippers' training concludes with no further incidents. Lee and his fellow aviators are given leave over Christmas. Lee books himself on a Navy flight from Norfolk to Dobbins Air Force Base near Atlanta, Georgia, where there is a Navy Operational Support Center. He is going to spend a week with Rachel in Atlanta and visit Alan and his family before deploying to sea.

4
RACHEL
BUDDING ROMANCE

Midmorning, Saturday, December 22, 1972, Lee lands at Dobbins Air Force Base in Marietta, Georgia. The pilot taxis his aircraft close to the control tower area and shuts down the engines. Once the ramp is set up, Lee exits the aircraft and hurries inside base operations to call Rachel. The phone rings at her apartment nearby.

Rachel picks up the phone, and in an excited, anxious, and longing voice, she says, "Is that you, Lee?"

He responds in a similar tone, for its been a long time since they've seen each other. "Rachel, it's me. I just landed. I'm in the base operations building here at Dobbins."

Rachel answers, "I'll be right over. Where do you want me to meet you? I don't have clearance to get on the base."

"Not a problem. Just go to the main gate. I'll catch a ride over there and wait for you. Hurry, but be careful. I've missed you."

She responds, "I will. I've missed you too. I'll be there shortly."

RACHEL

Lee is driven to the main gate by an airman going off base to visit some friends. Once there, he thanks the airman, walks inside the main gate building carrying his travel bag, and settles onto a seat while waiting for Rachel. Lee pulls out a pipe and tobacco pouch from a side pocket in his travel bag. He packs some tobacco in the pipe chamber, lights it, and slowly takes a draw from his favorite pipe. He's taken to smoking a pipe and finds it relaxes him. He credits his grandfather Sam with introducing him to the finer qualities of smoking pipes.

He doesn't have to wait long as Rachel pulls up to the parking area in her Mercury XR-7 Cougar convertible. She spots Lee, steps out of the car, and heads straight for him. She is dressed in casual slacks with a turtleneck sweater and a brown leather jacket with brown low-cut boots. She looks stunning and moves with grace and style, which is clearly noticed by servicemen entering and exiting the main gate.

Seeing her, Lee clears the tobacco from his pipe chamber, slips the pipe into his travel bag, and hurries out to meet her. Closing the distance between them, Lee drops his bag, grasps Rachel, and pulls her to him. Standing in the middle of the road, oblivious to car traffic, they kiss passionately. Their embrace is momentarily broken when an impatient driver lays on his horn and doesn't let up. Lee guides Rachel off the road and over to the sidewalk, where they embrace and kiss again. An Air Force major walks by and says, without cracking a smile, "Why don't you two get a room?"

Lee steps back from Rachel, salutes the major, and says, "I think that's a great idea." He picks up his travel bag; they hurry over to Rachel's car, settle in, and speed off toward her apartment. After an afternoon of exploring their passion for each other, they get dressed for some nightclub entertainment and drive to Underground Atlanta in the heart of downtown.

Returning to Rachel's apartment later that evening, they retire to her bedroom and make love well into the early hours of the next morning. After a late breakfast and still nursing a slight hangover, they drive to Alan's rented home outside of Fort Benning, Georgia, to spend Sunday with Alan, Sharon, and Allie.

Lee called ahead, and as they pull into Alan's driveway, he's standing outside waiting on them.

Alan opens the door for Rachel and takes her hand as she steps up and out of the car. They hug each other and exchange greetings. Lee comes over and gives his brother a firm handshake and a hug as they greet each other. Alan then guides them inside, where Sharon and Allie are waiting for them.

Sharon and Rachel greet each other warmly. Stepping back, Rachel looks down at Allie, kneels next to her, pulls her in close, and hugs her. Allie is a very pretty little girl with long, flowing black hair, big brown eyes, and long eyelashes. But with her health issues, she has breathing difficulties at times and always seems to be dealing with stomach aches. Rachel wants to just hug her and make it all go away. Tears form in the corner of Rachel's eyes as she thinks of the suffering Allie and her parents must go through.

Lee takes his winter jacket off and helps Rachel after she stands up. He then kneels down, picks up Allie, and whirls her around while hugging her. She loves this and giggles as her parents look on during this moment of joy for her.

Lee looks at Allie and asks her, "How old are you, young lady?"

She holds up three fingers and says, "Tree!"

Looking at his brother and Sharon, then back at Allie, Lee says to Allie, "What a cutie you are!"

Lee walks over to Sharon and hugs her while still holding Allie. Stepping back from Sharon, he places Allie's feet back on the floor. He then takes a gift-wrapped package from Rachel that they have been hiding from Allie and gives it to her. It only takes a moment to open as Allie gazes upon a new Barbie doll for her growing collection.

She runs back to her room to play as Alan invites everyone to take a seat in their living room. He goes to the kitchen and returns with an open bottle of wine and some glasses. Setting them on an end table, he goes back into the kitchen and returns with a sippy cup full of Kool-Aid and takes it to Allie.

Returning, he pours everyone a glass of wine and offers a toast to good health and happy times. Light conversation follows as they trade stories and share wine together.

Later into the afternoon while Allie is napping, Sharon and Rachel move to one corner of the living room. Sharon talks to Rachel about living in Columbus outside of Fort Benning and some of the challenges of being a military wife. She misses her former job at Coca-Cola and looks forward to returning someday soon. Rachel listens intently to her stories about being married to a military officer and some of what that entails in the way of challenges and rewards. Rachel tries to assure Sharon that she will someday return to her job at Coca-Cola. She goes on to share some of her more amusing experiences of working at Trust Company in their commercial credit division as a credit analyst. Both women laugh at each other's stories of being hit on at work by men.

Alan and Lee are sitting on the closed-in back porch and have switched from wine to drinking beer as they trade stories about their latest endeavors. Lee has an urge to smoke his pipe, but in deference to Allie's health, he doesn't ask for permission. He'll wait until they drive back to Rachel's apartment.

"Lee, I've been meaning to ask how you Navy pilots hover over water and manage to stay in the same spot?"

Lee says, "It's not too hard. We have an autopilot system that helps us maintain a steady position while hovering. It can be challenging, particularly at night or in strong winds. We train hard to get good at it since much of what we do while at sea demands that we do it well."

"Brother, my hat's off to you and the men you fly with in the Navy. While in Nam, I was always amazed at how those chopper pilots could get in and out of tight spots and hold their hover over just about any spot they chose."

"Thanks for the compliment. But I wouldn't compare myself to what those fellows who fly in Vietnam did. So what's it like being back from Nam, and how do you like what you're doing at Fort Benning?"

Alan responds. "As for being back from Vietnam, it's really too early for me to form much of an opinion. But, having said that, I've found the general attitude of many civilians in the community toward our military, and particularly the Vietnam veterans, to be one of indifference. I fear this attitude will be around a long time. The Vietnam War really set back the military, especially the Army. We have a long way to go to restore confidence in our leadership and the military in general."

Alan pauses, looks at his brother, and, in a serious tone, says, "What do you think? How do you feel about it?"

"Well, for starters, I took your advice and stayed in the Navy." This brings a little chuckle from both brothers.

Lee continues, "I understand we've pulled almost all our military personnel out of Vietnam and have turned the fighting over to the Vietnamese. There is no real truce or peace agreement between the North Vietnamese Communists and the South Vietnamese people. Kissinger just put together a withdrawal plan to get us out of there. He and Nixon think it's a "peace with honor" exit strategy, but in my opinion, it's all a clever ruse. They just wanted to get the hell out of there as soon as possible. Shame on them and us."

A long silence follows as the two brothers, two men, two warriors, are lost in their own thoughts. Alan comments in a soft, calm, and melancholy voice. "I agree with you. I think it won't be long before the South Vietnamese collapse and the country is reunited under the North Vietnamese Communists."

Alan takes a moment, gathering his thoughts as he drinks some beer and continues. "As for my job at Fort Benning, I like working for the commanding general as one of his aides. I do not miss being out in the field, nor do I ever want to see combat again. I'll be submitting my resignation later next year as I approach the end of my commitment to the Army. I want to pursue a civilian career and live in peace. There are nights when I have terrible nightmares. When I'm awake, I live in fear of being sent back to Nam again."

Looking at his brother and seeing the anguish in his eyes, Lee simply responds, "I can't imagine or relate to what you've experienced. I hope you find peace and settle down into a good life, doing what you want. You know you have a supportive family behind you."

"I know. Dad and Grandad have been very supportive. They know what I'm dealing with, having been there themselves." Alan pauses and then closes with, "I hope you never have to deal with this."

Their conversation trails off as they rejoin the women. Alan seeks out Rachel and engages her in conversation. He's considering the banking industry and is interested in hearing about her experiences with Trust Company Bank. After dinner and visiting more with Allie, it's late and time for Lee and Rachel to head back to her apartment. Both Alan and Sharon have to go to work the next day.

Both brothers, Sharon, Allie, and Rachel, spend more time together over the ensuing week before Lee must return to duty. This includes Christmas Day, which they celebrate with a traditional holiday meal. Later into the evening, General Sean McCormick calls Alan's house to wish them all a Merry Christmas. He's using a speakerphone so Ana, the brothers, and the grandparents, Sam and Marie, can all join in on the call.

LAST NIGHT ON LEAVE

Lee and Rachel have grown very close to each other since first meeting at Alan and Sharon's wedding at Fort Benning in March 1970. They have fallen deeply in love. On their last night together, Lee and Rachel step outside on her apartment balcony to admire the sky with a three-quarter moon shining brightly. Although winter, this is Atlanta, and the weather can be mild at times. Tonight is no exception, as the night air has a slight chill, but it's bearable.

Lee pulls Rachel to him. In a low voice, almost whispering, he asks Rachel to marry him. She knew it was coming and, although surprised by his timing, Rachel is emotional. Tears form in her eyes as she stares into Lee's, searching for his reaction. His facial expression is one of anticipation as he anxiously awaits her response. Not trying to be coy, she pauses, and a little smile slowly spreads across her face as she responds in a soft, calm, loving voice, "Yes, I'll marry you."

Lee pulls her tightly to him and kisses her passionately. Rachel responds, then steps back as she pulls him into her apartment, guiding him to the bedroom. The next morning dawns early for both of them as Lee packs his travel bag while Rachel prepares breakfast. Over the radio, they hear the lyrics to the song, "Late December back in '63. Oh, What a Night."

During breakfast, they talk about the constraints they're under when it comes to setting a date for their wedding. They'll have to wait until Lee returns from his deployment and is given his next assignment. Then, they can make definitive plans for a date, time, and location for their wedding. Lee's time in Atlanta comes to an end and he returns to Norfolk on a jet out of Atlanta's Hartsfield International Airport.

5
INCIDENT RETURNING FROM MEDITERRANEAN SEA DUTY
BEARTRAP

To provide for the safe operation of helicopters from destroyer-size ships deployed at sea, they use what is termed the beartrap device. Known formally as the Helicopter Hauldown and Rapid Securing Device (HHRSD). It allows helicopters to land safely on the decks of smaller warships, even in heavy seas.

Landing a helicopter using a beartrap device involves the helicopter hovering over the deck while lowering a wire line with an attached probe. The deck crew fastens the probe to a hauldown cable which is attached to a winch. The hauldown cable is then hoisted back up to the helicopter and secured, and with the deck clear of personnel, the hauldown cable pulls the helicopter down to the deck. Once the helicopter is secured in the beartrap, the aircraft can be moved in and out of the hangar.

. . .

INCIDENT RETURNING FROM MEDITERRANEAN SEA DUTY

SEA KING OVERBOARD

It's mid-afternoon on October 15, 1973, and the Naval Task Group is headed home from their six-month deployment to the Mediterranean Sea. LTJG Lee McCormick is flying as pilot-in-charge of his SH-3 Sea King. He is part of Lieutenant George Jones's detachment of three helicopters. They have been flying routine ASW patrols and are now running low on fuel, with the weather deteriorating rapidly. Lieutenant Jones has instructed Lee and the other helicopter pilot to go into a holding pattern over their respective destroyers while he shoots an approach to his destroyer to check out landing conditions.

From his left-side seat, Lee watches George trying to hover over the flight deck of his destroyer. He's having a difficult time and pulls up and away from the back of the destroyer. George's call sign is Nightdipper 20. Lee transmits. "Nightdipper 20, this is Nightdipper 24. It looks pretty rough. What's your take? Over."

George responds, "It is. We have a rough sea out here. The ship is rolling up and down and pitching left and right with all this wave action. We also have high winds, which aren't helping. I'm trying to catch our beartrap as the destroyer briefly settles between waves. I'm going to try again. Over."

Lee transmits, "Roger, good luck."

George double clicks his radio transmitter switch, signifying he acknowledges Lee's transmission.

Lee and the other helicopter pilot watch intently at how George handles the situation. He approaches the back of his destroyer at a high hover, waits for a trough in the heavy sea, and hovers closer as he lowers his wire line to the deck crew. They try desperately to grab it so they can secure the probe to the hauldown cable. Repeated attempts are made as George struggles to maintain his hover in severe wind gusts.

The deck crew finally catches the wire-line and secures the probe to the hauldown cable. George then hoists the cable up to his helicopter and secures it. With the hauldown cable secure, his helicopter is slowly being reeled in toward the deck. The destroyer is rolling and pitching as the waves' height increases along with the wind velocity. George is clearly struggling to hover and maintain control of his helicopter.

The destroyer pitches up violently while Lee watches in horror as George's helicopter drifts forward and his rotor blades strike the hangar structure. He crashes violently onto the flight deck of the destroyer.

George transmits, "We're going in, we're going in...these conditions are..."

His transmission goes silent as the helicopter blades beat themselves against the ship's deck, sending metal fragments flying in all directions as the helicopter destroys itself. The deck crew has taken shelter to avoid the flying debris, but George and his crew are not spared. Their helicopter falls off the side of the destroyer and quickly disappears into the ocean.

Lee radios the other helicopter pilot. "Follow me. We need to get over there and look for the crew in the water."

They are both low on fuel and have very little flight time left to stay airborne. Flying to the scene, Lee takes the starboard side of the ship and directs the other helicopter pilot to take the port side. The destroyer slows down and has initiated their men-overboard procedures, hoping to

INCIDENT RETURNING FROM MEDITERRANEAN SEA DUTY

find the crew alive. Lee and his crew search the area along with the other helicopter crew without success.

Lee radios the Air Boss on the Task Group Aircraft Carrier and requests that they be given clearance to land on their deck and wait out the severe weather. He also requests they launch an Air-Sea Rescue helicopter to take over the search as quickly as possible. Permission is granted to land on the aircraft carrier. Lee radios the commander of George's destroyer and informs him they are critically low on fuel and will break off their search and head for the carrier. A search and rescue helicopter from the carrier will take over and look for the downed crew.

Lee's crew, along with the other helicopter crew, land on the carrier and are taken to the flight operations room for a debriefing. They are directed to remain on the carrier for the night and will rejoin their ships in the morning when the weather is forecasted to improve. Later that evening, Lee is informed that the search was discontinued, and no bodies were found. Lee is made acting officer in charge of the detachment for their remaining days at sea as they return to Norfolk.

That night in his bunk, Lee reflects on the day's incident while grieving for his friend and his family. George and he had become good friends since flying together. George is married, has two young sons in grade school, and his wife, Joyce, is expecting their third child in two months.

Before leaving the Mediterranean Sea to return to Norfolk, Lieutenant George Jones was notified that he was being promoted to lieutenant commander. Lee and several pilots in the squadron celebrated with George before departing the Mediterranean. George was a good man, a good pilot, and a fine leader. His promotion will occur posthumously and benefit his wife and family as they adjust to their new reality.

So many men lose their lives in training incidents while preparing for their mission to fight and win a real shooting war, or limited engagements as they're commonly referred to these days. Wives become widows; children will grow up without their fathers, parents will grieve over the loss of a son, brothers and sisters will mourn the loss of a sibling, and grandparents will grieve over the loss of a grandson and their own children's loss of a son.

What a price we pay to provide some peace and stability for our country and many others.

6

HELICOPTER TRAINING SQUADRON EIGHTEEN (HT-18)

The Navy's Helicopter Training Squadron Eighteen (HT-18) is based at NAS Whiting Field near Pensacola, Florida. The squadron's mission is helicopter pilot training for the US Navy, US Marine Corps, and US Coast Guard. Shortly after returning from sea duty in the Mediterranean, Lee is assigned to HT-18 as an instructor pilot (IP) and reports to Whiting Field in January 1974. Lee settles into his new assignment with optimism and a sense of purpose. Shortly after arriving, the Navy offers him an opportunity to attend the University of West Florida to pursue an MA Degree in Mathematics and Statistics. This advanced degree will complement his undergraduate degree in the same field. Lee accepts the offer and begins his graduate studies in the spring of 1974.

He maintains a full schedule, which entails attending classes at night and on weekends while fulfilling his aviation duties with HT-18 during the week. Lee and Rachel pick up where they left off before he shipped out to the

Mediterranean. Their relationship continues to blossom as they set a date for their wedding.

NAVY WEDDING

It's a gorgeous day in the early afternoon of June 15, 1974. There's a light, cool sea breeze blowing under a blue sky with small, puffy, low-hanging cumulus clouds. Lee stands at the altar of the Naval Aviation Memorial Chapel on NAS Pensacola, Florida. His beautiful bride, Rachel, is standing next to him as they hold hands. He's waited a long time for this moment, and the look of anticipation, pure joy, and happiness radiates from his face. Rachel is calm as she looks deeply into Lee's eyes and recites her vows. He has recited his and has to hold back some emotion as Rachel ends with, "I'm forever yours and will love you for eternity."

Seated together on the first row on the right side of the chapel, looking up at the pulpit, are General McCormick in his uniform with Ana, Sam, and Marie, who made the trip down from Louisville, and Scott, who drove over from Gainesville while attending the University of Florida, where he's working on a dual degree in Accounting and Pre-Law. Ana and Marie are tasked with taking care of Allie, who sits between them and holds her favorite Barbie doll while remaining quiet.

Lee's parents and grandparents gaze upon the scene at the altar with pride and happiness for Rachel and Lee. They are a striking couple, with Lee standing tall in his Dress White Navy uniform. Affixed to his coat over the left chest are his Navy Gold Wings and military ribbons. Rachel looks radiant in her full-length wedding gown, and her face glows with a beautiful, contagious smile. Members of their accompanying wedding party flank the bride and groom. Alan, dressed in a double-breasted dark blue pinstriped suit, is Lee's best man. Sharon, wearing a full-length dark blue dress, is Rachel's matron of honor.

Rachel's father and mother sit on the other side of the chapel in the first row, with several friends joining them. Rachel is an only child, and her parents flew in from Miami Beach, where they live.

The chaplain concludes the service by looking at Lee and asking him, "Do you take this woman, Rachel, to be your wife, to love and cherish until death do you part?" Lee responds in a strong, calm voice, "I do."

The chaplain looks at Rachel and says, "Rachel, do you take Lee to be your husband, to love and cherish, until death do you part?" Rachel responds, "I do."

He then says, "I now pronounce you man and wife. Lee, you may kiss your wife." Whereupon Lee gently pulls Rachel to him and kisses her. Lee's naval aviator comrades erupt in cheers, and the wedding guests break out in applause.

The chaplain has Lee and Rachel turn and face the congregation and instructs them to proceed down the aisle. The organist plays the Navy hymn as they slowly walk to the back of the chapel and wait for their wedding party to exit. Once everyone is outside, they exit the chapel's main doors and walk under a saber arch of ten naval officers with drawn swords.

Their wedding is followed by a late afternoon reception at the NAS Pensacola Officers' Club on the beach. The McCormicks once again enjoy themselves as they socialize, dance to a live band, and enjoy an open bar. Naval aviators are a rare breed who pride themselves, among other things, on being death-defying men who know how to party. After sending Rachel and Lee off for their honeymoon, the wedding guests continue to party into the evening.

After seeing his son and new daughter-in-law depart, General McCormick asks Alan and his father, Sam, to join him outside on the terrace. Sean takes this moment to inform them he's being promoted to lieutenant general shortly and will be reassigned to the Pentagon in Washington, DC. He'll be reporting directly to the chief of staff of the United States Air Force and should start his new assignment in November 1974. Sam, overflowing with pride, hugs his son and congratulates him. Alan salutes his father, shakes his hand, then hugs him.

BACK TO BUSINESS

After returning from their honeymoon, Lee settles into his routine, which involves flying training missions with student aviators and overseeing the training of several pilots at a time, all while filling one of the roles as a chief instructor and standardization pilot. Two nights a week, he attends the university, working on his master's degree.

Rachel involves herself in many diverse base activities associated with being a naval officer's wife. She develops a reputation for being dependable, very capable, outgoing, self-assured, and professional. She is the quintessential military wife.

Over the next three years, Lee develops a reputation among the men he flies with, serves with, and trains as a patriot, a man of honor, and a loyal friend. When he makes a commitment, he'll move heaven and earth to see it through.

TRAINING INCIDENTS

"To learn, one must do. To train is to learn. To do, one must train."

Training is a serious business and is prone to accidents resulting in the loss of aircraft and lives. Defending a nation requires men and women to volunteer to serve. Then, they must train to the peak of their abilities so they can perform their duties when called upon to do so. Training is essential and is an ongoing ritual of military life and service.

A series of training incidents while at Whiting Field takes its toll on Lee while serving with HT-18. He experiences, witnesses, and, in many cases is involved in investigating training incidents during his tenure. They range from minor accidents to major incidents, which often have tragic consequences.

The worst training loss during Lee's tenure involved two pilots who were married, and each man had two small children. While returning to Whiting Field in very dark flying conditions, the two pilots made a routine position report ten minutes after completing their last night-landing practice. About eight minutes later, the flight crew panickily transmitted their helicopter was going down. There were no further radio transmissions from the pilots.

A post-accident examination of the helicopter revealed no evidence of mechanical malfunctions or failures that would have prevented normal operation. Weather conditions in the vicinity of the accident site that night indicated clouds were present. Given the helicopter's flight path shortly before the accident, it was likely the pilots were maneuvering to avoid clouds and became disoriented in the dark conditions. This would have resulted in a loss of helicopter control. Pilot vertigo is the probable cause of the incident.

Vertigo is a false sense of movement, causing confusion, disorientation, and eventually, incapacitation. According to the FAA, vertigo contributes to many aircraft accidents, typically at night or in instrument meteorological conditions. Many are fatal, and experienced pilots are not immune.

TIME TO MOVE ON

During August 1978, Lee completes his college course requirements and is awarded his MS in Mathematics and Statistics from the University of West Florida. Within a week of graduating, Rachel informs Lee they are expecting their first child in March 1979. This news is followed by Lee's promotion to lieutenant commander, along with new orders assigning him to Naval Air Station, Norfolk, Virginia.

7
IRAN HOSTAGE CRISIS
OVERVIEW

After the United States ended its long military involvement in Vietnam, the country faced a growing crisis in the Middle East that reached hostile proportions. On November 4, 1979, as many as 3,000 Iranian militant students stormed and captured the American embassy in Tehran, Iran. They took sixty-three Americans hostage, and three additional US diplomatic staff members were seized at the Iranian Foreign Ministry.

The incident took place two weeks after President Jimmy Carter allowed the deposed Iranian ruler, Mohammad Reza Shah Pahlavi, into America for cancer treatment. Iran's new leader, Ayatollah Khomeini, called for the United States to return the Shah and bring an end to Western influence in Iran. By the middle of November, thirteen hostages, consisting of women and African Americans, were set free. By April 1980, the remaining fifty-three hostages had waited five months as negotiations failed to bring the situation to an end.

During this time, American military commanders

refined a plan for a possible rescue mission. Training exercises were conducted to evaluate the troops and equipment that would be necessary should a rescue be attempted. With the diplomatic process stalled, President Jimmy Carter approved a military rescue operation on April 16, 1980.

OPERATION EAGLE CLAW

The ambitious plan is designed to utilize elements of all four branches of the United States armed services: Army, Navy, Marines, and Air Force. The two-day operation calls for Sikorsky RH-53 Sea Stallion Marine helicopters and Air Force C-130 aircraft to rendezvous on a salt flat code-named Desert One, about 200 miles southeast of Tehran. The helicopters will fly from an aircraft carrier, land at Desert One, refuel from C-130s, and pick up combat troops consisting of Delta Force and Army Ranger teams. The helicopters will transport these troops to a mountain location, code-named Desert Two, arriving sometime close to sunrise. The helicopters and ground forces will remain hidden during the day at Desert Two. The actual rescue mission will be launched that night.

CIA agents who are already inside Iran will bring trucks they obtain from reliable sources to Desert Two. Together, the CIA officers and ground forces will then drive from Desert Two into Tehran. This assault team will secure the embassy and Foreign Affairs building, eliminate the guards, and rescue the hostages. The freed hostages and rescue team will then rendezvous with and board helicopters flown in from Desert Two to the nearby Amjadieh Stadium.

While the assault force conducts the rescue operations

in Tehran, an Army Ranger company will capture and hold the abandoned Manzariyeh Air Base about sixty miles southwest of Tehran. Two C-141 Starlifters will fly in from Saudi Arabia and wait on the helicopters transporting everyone from the stadium. Upon arrival of the helicopters, all personnel will board the two C-141s. The eight helicopters will be destroyed before departure, and the freed hostages with the men who rescued them will fly back to an airbase in Egypt.

WHAT COULD GO WRONG?

The aircraft carrier USS Nimitz, on deployment to the Mediterranean Sea since September 1979, is diverted in January 1980 to the Indian Ocean in response to the Iranian crisis. The Nimitz joined a battle group consisting of several other ships to include the USS Coral Sea, another aircraft carrier.

Lieutenant Commander Lee McCormick's Helicopter Antisubmarine Squadron 9 (Sea Griffins) detachment is attached to the USS Nimitz. Since arriving at Gonzo Station, they have been flying diverse missions in support of the battle group. Gonzo Station is the Navy's acronym for Gulf of Oman Naval Zone of Operations. It is used to designate the area of carrier-based naval operations in the Indian Ocean during the Iranian hostage crisis.

It's the evening of April 23, 1980, as Lee rests on his bunk, having just returned from a briefing for the Marine helicopter aircrews assigned to fly in Operation Eagle Claw. Since arriving at Gonzo Station, Lee and his detachment have been flying nonstop missions. He's tired, misses his family, and has serious doubts about the pending operation.

The sheer number of military personnel from all four military branches, the critical element of timing and surprise necessary to be successful, and the types of aircraft involved all contribute to making this a very complex operation. Lee fears for the men involved in the operation, which is scheduled for the following night.

While lying there looking at a picture of Rachel and his son, Josh, who was born in April, 1979 hanging next to his bunk, Marine Captain Barry Phillips enters the room. They are good friends and first met at Pensacola, where Lee was one of Barry's instructor pilots in flight school. Barry is one of the RH-53 helicopter pilots slated for tomorrow night's mission.

Barry says, "Sorry to barge in on you, old man, but I need some fresh sea air. You want to join me on a walkabout?"

"Why not? Let's go. I can use some fresh air myself."

The weather on deck is balmy, and a warm wind blows across.

Barry expresses his concerns about the operation. He questions why there is so much commingling of the four branch services. There are many differences between the communication techniques and equipment used by each branch that could cause issues for the men on the operation.

While walking on the deck, they pass by the Marine RH-53 helicopters secured to the deck of the USS Nimitz. They are camouflaged the color of sand and have no indefinable markings. Looking at one, Lee raises a question to Captain Phillips. "I'm curious as to why they chose these model helicopters. Why not the HH-53 models? The Air Force's HH-53 Jolly Green Giant helicopters are better suited for this rescue mission."

Barry replies in a matter-of-fact tone. "I have the same

lingering question. Both are heavy-lift helicopters with a crew of four, have a six-bladed main rotor, four-bladed tail rotor, and they're both fast. But there are differences."

Momentarily stopping to look at one of the helicopters, Lee comments. "The Jolly Greens have three hydraulic systems providing more backup capability. The RH-53 only has two hydraulic systems. A Jolly Green has more powerful engines, a retractable refueling probe, self-sealing fuel tanks, and Doppler navigation radar which operates well in areas that are off the grid. Lord knows you'll be off the grid on much of this operation."

Barry looks at Lee and says, "Any of those differences may prove fatal to us." He pauses, then continues in a sarcastic and somewhat nervous tone, "In keeping with an all four-branch service effort, I guess they chose the RH-53 so us Marines can be a part of the rescue operation."

"I think you're right. But it's too late to give this part of the mission to the Air Force. Sometimes, this interservice rivalry is overdone. Our purpose is to save hostages, not try to prove which branch is better."

They slowly walk back through the massive aircraft carrier to their officer quarters for some sack time. They'll need it. The next few days will be very busy.

RESCUE MISSION COMMENCES

The next evening, the eight Marine helicopters launch from the deck of the USS Nimitz, and head for their first destination, Desert One. Lee and his detachment of three SH-3 Sea Kings launch shortly thereafter. With Lee in the front position and maintaining a safe distance between themselves, they fly in a V-formation. They're several miles behind the Marine helicopters as they follow them to the coast of Iran. Their assignment is to provide air/sea rescue should any Marine helicopter have to ditch in the Gulf of Oman or be forced to land shortly after crossing into Iran.

As the Marine helicopters approach the Iranian coast, Lee transmits to Barry. The call sign for the Marine helicopter force is designated as Bluebeard, with each helicopter given a number from 1-8. "Bluebeard 5, Sea Griffen 24. We're on station and will remain so as long as possible. Safe flying, good luck. Over."

Barry replies, "Sea Griffen 24, Bluebeard 5, Roger, thanks. Out."

Lee and his detachment fly a large circular holding pattern several miles off the coast of Iran until their fuel situation requires them to return to the USS Nimitz. Once on deck, the three Sea Kings are refueled and secured to the deck. Lee's detachment will remain on standby. Lee heads for the combat direction center (CDC) of the Nimitz, where he will join other officers. This area functions as a tactical center and provides processed information for command and control of an ongoing operation.

From inside the CDC, he'll follow the progress of the rescue operation as it unfolds. After gaining entrance to the CDC, Lee slowly scans the room, looking for a place to sit. It's a large area crammed full of computer consoles, radar and sonar displays, radio transmitters and receivers, large maps, and a transparent plotting board. The atmosphere in the room is tense and serious, with concerned faces of sailors working at their stations. Lee finds a space in one corner of the room, works his way over, and takes a seat. Settling in, he becomes absorbed with the radio communications flowing in from the rescue operation in real time.

The first phase of the operation is going according to plan as Air Force C-130's, with soldiers, equipment and fuel, lands on Desert One. Soon after the first crew landed, they begin securing Desert One. As they do so, an Iranian bus approaches them on the road, which now serves as a runway for the aircraft. Army Rangers force the bus carrying civilian passengers to stop. They, along with the driver, are removed from the bus and detained on one of the empty C-130 aircraft.

Only minutes after the bus is stopped, Rangers on the road-watch team observe a fuel tanker truck bearing down on them. The truck ignores their warnings to stop. The Army Ranger team, using a shoulder-fired rocket, blows up the truck. The truck's passenger is killed, but the driver escapes in an accompanying pickup truck. The driver is not considered a security threat to the mission since it's assumed he's smuggling fuel.

The helicopter mission is proceeding as the Marine pilots fly low to the ground to avoid radar. After almost two hours of flying, one Marine aircrew receives cockpit indications of an impending rotor blade failure. They land, verify the malfunction, and abandon their helicopter. They are recovered by another Marine helicopter crew, which continues with the mission. The remaining seven helicopters proceed on to Desert One and notice out their front what looks like a large fog bank. Flying into the mess, they find themselves in the middle of large layers of desert sand and fine dust. They have flown straight into an unexpected weather phenomenon known as a haboob, an enormous cloud of fine dust.

Strong winds batter their helicopters, and visibility drops. The pilots cannot see the ground from their nap-of-the-earth flying, nor can they see each other. They immediately separate and proceed to fly individually to Desert One. The pilots, having no visual references, fly on instruments at low level in the dark, and through turbulent winds. Many are experiencing vertigo but manage to keep their helicopters in the air. Bluebeard 5 flies into the haboob, but electrical problems disable their flight instruments. They fly without visual references or instruments, which quickly proves impossible. Experiencing navigation and flight instrument problems, they decide to abort and return to the USS Nimitz. This leaves six helicopters proceeding to Desert One.

LEE LAUNCHES

Lee is directed to launch his Sea King and fly out to meet Bluebeard 5 off the coast of Iran. He can guide them back to the Nimitz and provide sea rescue should Bluebeard 5 have to ditch in the Gulf of Oman. Lee rounds up his crew, and they launch into the night. It's early morning on April 25, 1980.

On route to their rendezvous with Bluebeard 5, Lee engages with his crew over the intercom. They are anxious for news about how the mission is proceeding. Lee responds to their inquiries. "Gentlemen, it's not going well. My older brother who, was in Vietnam, told me of a term they used over there to describe a mission such as this; it was 'CF,' which meant cluster fuck."

He pauses and then continues. "My father occasionally mentioned a term they used in World War II to describe a bad mission. It was '*FUBAR*,' which meant fucked up beyond all recognition. They're having a hell of a lot of problems already, including flying through a serious sandstorm, which causes all kinds of pilot disorientation issues. One helicopter had to set down inside Iran because of impending rotor blade failure. They were picked up by another crew. Now we have Bluebeard 5 returning due to issues."

Lee takes a few minutes to scan his instruments and look out his window to the far horizon. He sees some faint lights, which should be the Iranian coastline. "That's the situation when we left the Nimitz. Okay, we're coming up on the Iranian coast now. We'll be going into a holding pattern waiting for Bluebeard 5. Stay sharp and keep your eyes open for them."

After a few minutes of flying a large oval holding pattern just off the coast, Lee hears a radio transmission.

"Any aircraft, this is Bluebeard 5. Do you hear me? Over."

Looking out to his front, Lee sees flashing red and green aircraft lights in the distance, possibly those of Bluebeard 5. He responds, "Bluebeard 5, this is Sea Griffen 24. We see you in the distance off to our front. Do you see us? Over."

"Sea Griffen 24, Bluebeard 5. It's us. Boy, are we glad to see you guys. Can we follow you back to the ship? We're bushed and flying on adrenaline. Our navigation and flight instruments are giving us problems. Over."

"Bluebeard 5, that's why we're here. Follow us back. Over."

Bluebeard 5 falls in at a safe distance behind Lee, and they fly back to the Nimitz. Barry's helicopter is given clearance to land first, and when he's safely down, Lee lands his helicopter. After the aircrews perform their respective postflight inspections, they return to their rooms to rest. Lee and Barry stop by their rooms, drop off their equipment then head to the CDC to follow the plight of their comrade's rescue efforts.

As they work their way through the carrier, Lee asks, "Barry, what was it like out there flying through the dust storm? We could hear some of the radio chatter as you fellows were going through it."

"It's probably the worst flying experience I've ever had. It was like being in a huge blender with sand and dirt swirling around relentlessly pelting the helicopter. We had no visibility, total darkness, and a sense of not being in control of the helicopter. It scared the hell out of me."

"How does one train to fly through something like that?" Lee responds, "Well, we better figure it out and get good at it. I think we're going to be spending a lot more time over here in the Middle East."

They reach the CDC. Once inside, they settle into some chairs in one corner of the room and listen to the incoming radio transmissions of the unfolding drama continuing in one part of the Iranian desert.

RESCUE MISSION CANCELED

The ground forces are becoming impatient as they await the arrival of the helicopters. They need to refuel the helicopters, board them, and fly to the hiding site before daylight. Time has become critical, as the sun will rise soon to the east. Running ninety minutes late, the helicopters finally begin arriving. The fire from the destroyed tanker is still burning and provides an unintended but welcome visual guide to Desert One for the disoriented incoming helicopters.

Bluebeard 2 arrives last at Desert One with a malfunctioning secondary hydraulic system. They cannot repair the malfunctioning system, which leaves only one system to control the aircraft. The senior Marine helicopter pilot refuses to use the unsafe Bluebeard 2 on the mission.

Now, with only five fully operational helicopters remaining to transport the men and equipment to Desert Two, the various commanders reach a stalemate. A minimum of six helicopters was the established threshold to continue the mission. Less than that, and the mission is to be aborted.

Army Colonel Beckwith, the field commander for ground forces, refuses to consider reducing the size of his trained rescue team. USAF Colonel Kyle, the field aviation commander, agrees with the senior Marine pilot about Bluebird 2. He radios and recommends to Army Major General Vaught that the mission be aborted. The recommendation is passed on by satellite radio to President Carter, who reluctantly approves it. After two and a half hours on the ground, the presidential abort confirmation is received.

At Desert One, noise, dust, and confusion prevail. Dust and sand fly everywhere. An eerie glow is cast over the scene from the still-burning tanker truck. The assault force begins loading onto the C-130s for evacuation as the helicopters hover toward the C-130 refueling aircraft. Suddenly, disaster strikes.

As the pilot of Bluebeard 3 repositions his helicopter for refueling, he becomes disoriented. In the darkness and swirling sand, the only point of reference the pilot can see outside his window is an Air Force combat controller standing forward and to the right of his helicopter. To avoid being pelted with blowing sand, the combat controller backs away. The Bluebeard 3 pilot assumes his helicopter is drifting backward, which it is not.

Reacting to his perceived drift backward, the pilot moves his cyclic forward and begins hovering toward the combat controller. His rotor blades strike the parked Air Force C-130 aircraft, which is carrying fuel for the helicopters. The crash causes an explosion, which engulfs both the Marine helicopter and the C-130 in a fireball.

After the crash, the commanders decide to abandon the helicopters and order all surviving ground personnel to load into the C-130s for evacuation. During the frantic evacuation, the helicopter crews leave behind their classified mission documents. The five remaining helicopters are operational but lack sufficient fuel to return to the Nimitz without refueling. They cannot be destroyed. They are loaded with ammunition, and any fire or explosion will endanger the C-130s. The entire force needs to extract as quickly as possible. Their mission and location could already be compromised.

The C-130s carry the remaining forces back to the intermediate airfield at Masirah Island, where two C-141 medical evacuation aircraft from the staging base in Egypt pick up the injured personnel, helicopter crews, Rangers, and Delta Force members. The following day the Tehran CIA team quietly leaves Iran, with the Iranians unaware of their presence.

AFTERMATH

Early on the morning of April 25, 1980, the White House announces that Operation Eagle Claw failed to rescue the fifty-three embassy staff personnel held captive at the US Embassy in Iran. The embassy hostages are subsequently scattered across Iran to preclude any second rescue attempt.

The hostages were eventually released on January 20, 1981, after 444 days of captivity. Their release occurred minutes after Ronald Reagan took the oath of office as president of the United States.

Who paid the price for this failure? Three Marines and five Air Force personnel were killed. Four servicemen were wounded.

8
WHERE DOES TIME GO?
TIME PERIOD 1980-1987. UNITED STATES MILITARY ACADEMY-WEST POINT

After returning to Norfolk, Lee is assigned to the United States Military Academy (USMA) at West Point as a professor of mathematics. Assignments are normally for three years and are considered prestigious and career-enhancing.

Upon reporting in July 1980, Lee is assigned to West Point housing. Lee approaches his new assignment with zeal and a sense of pride. Rachel immerses herself in the life of a military wife whose husband is stationed at West Point. Between those activities and Josh, their first-born and a very active toddler, she stays busy. Lee and Rachel sponsor some of the cadets and frequently invite them over for meals and visits. Lee is one of their many mentors.

Lee and Rachel add to their family with the birth of a daughter, Angela, on December 12, 1981. The day Angela is born, the weather outside is freezing and two feet of snow covers the grounds of West Point. The scene outside is gorgeous as Lee looks out the window. He gazes upon a winter wonderland as he holds his baby daughter up to the window and shows her the view on this, her first day outside the womb. Pulling Angela back close to him, he looks into her eyes. She gazes up at him and smiles. His heart melts. They just formed a lifelong bond.

Approaching the end of his second year at the academy, Lee is becoming anxious and misses being at sea and flying. Outside of his family, these are two additional loves of his life, and he yearns to return to them. West Point is a fantastic assignment and a very rewarding experience, which he has enjoyed. However, with Rachel's support, he feels it's time to move on. The social life and academic atmosphere it provides for the cadets flow through to those who live and work at the academy. They will both miss the lifestyle they'll leave behind.

Lee submits his request to return to naval Air-and-Sea duty at the beginning of July 1982, the completion of his second year at West Point. With considerable reluctance, it is approved by his superiors. He's reassigned back to Norfolk Naval Station, Virginia, and reports in at the end of August 1982.

OPERATION URGENT FURY

When they arrive in Norfolk, Rachel insists on living off-base in a new home near the beach. She wants to feel like a civilian family and enjoy a less structured life outside some of the constraints normally found in military establishments. They purchase a new three-bedroom ranch-style home in the Alanto, Virginia Beach area, which is near the Oceana Naval Air Station. Lee reports to his new unit while Rachel sets about making their new home a warm environment.

Lee is assigned to an ASW Squadron and routinely takes a detachment of two or three SH-3 Sea Kings on short sea patrols out of Norfolk on destroyers and frigates. He's back at what he loves to do, and life is good for him, Rachel, and their two children.

In March 1983, President Reagan reveals his Reagan Doctrine, a policy dedicated to ending the Cold War by eradicating communism. As 1983 progresses, Reagan emphasizes the rising influence of the Soviet-Cuban alliance in Latin America and the Caribbean. When protests against the government in Grenada become violent, he fears another Iran hostage crisis. He cites concerns over the 600 American medical students on the island as justification for invading Grenada and approves a military intervention code-named Operation Urgent Fury.

On October 23, 1983, just two days before the invasion of Grenada is planned to begin, terrorists bomb the US Marine barracks in Beirut, Lebanon. The devasting truck bombing takes the lives of 220 United States Marines, eighteen sailors, and three soldiers but doesn't detour the planned invasion of Grenada.

As the United States grapples with the events in Beirut and mourns the loss of life, the invasion of Grenada begins in the early morning hours of October 25, 1983. The United States and a coalition of six Caribbean nations invade Grenada, 100 miles north of Venezuela. At the time, Lee is assigned to the USS Caron, a Spruance-class destroyer as the officer in charge of a detachment of two SH-3 Sea Kings.

Among sailors and Marines on the Caron, first reports (rumors) making their way around the ship point to a severe lack of security procedures, which led to the disaster in Beirut. Apparently, the suicide driver of the truck, packed with explosives, crashed through a barrier of concertina wire and passed between two sentry posts and through an open vehicle gate. He then crashed through a guard shack in front of the building and smashed into the lobby of the building where the Marines were sleeping.

The truck explodes and men die.

Security measures were slack, and sentries at the gate were operating under strict rules of engagement, making it very difficult to respond quickly to the truck. As Lee and his men prepare to go into action once again, they wonder what awaits them. They'll soon find out.

GRENADA INVASION

Shortly after the invasion begins, the USS Caron recovers a twenty-man Navy SEAL/Air Force reconnaissance team from waters off Grenada's southwest coast. The team's mission is to assess the condition of a 9,000-foot runway under construction by Cuban workers at Point Salines. Heavy swells swamped the engines of the reconnaissance teams' small boats before they could reach shore. The Caron spots them drifting offshore as dawn approaches and rescues them.

Later in the day, the Caron recovers ten more SEALs from the waters northwest of the island's capital. The afternoon of the following day, the Caron makes a third recovery. This time, the destroyer takes aboard eleven Army Rangers on a raft who were left behind on Grand Anse Beach following the successful helicopter rescue of 233 medical students and staff. During all these unplanned rescue recoveries, Lee's detachment provides air cover and support without incident.

The military operation only lasts four days, from October 25 to 29. Some of the opposition military forces encountered are well prepared and well positioned. They present a determined and stubborn resistance resulting in two United States battalions of reinforcements being called in on the evening of October 26. The total naval and air superiority of the American forces prevails and overwhelms the defenders. Nearly 8,000 soldiers, sailors, airmen, and Marines participated in Operation Urgent Fury, along with 353 Caribbean allies from the Caribbean Peace Forces. The United States military suffered nineteen servicemen killed and 116 wounded. The operation is deemed a success, and President Reagan asserts, "...our days of weakness are over. Our military forces are back on their feet and standing tall."

However, his comments mask the fact that several issues were encountered during the operation. A lack of intelligence about Grenada caused problems for the quickly assembled invasion force. They did not know the students were at two different campuses. This caused a thirty-hour delay in reaching students at the second campus. Maps provided to soldiers on the ground were tourist maps that did not show topography and were not marked with crucial positions or coordinates. Navy ships providing naval gunfire and Marine, Air Force, and Navy fighter-bomber support aircraft providing close air support mistakenly killed American ground forces. These "friendly fire" instances were due to differences in charts, location coordinates, data, and methods of calling for fire support.

Operation Urgent Fury once again highlights issues with communication and coordination between military branches when operating together as a joint force. As before in Operation Eagle Claw (the failed attempt to rescue

American hostages in Tehran), post-action investigations are undertaken.

Lee and many of his comrades wonder if the United States military will ever get it together.

PENTAGON

Within two months after returning to Norfolk from the Caribbean and Operation Urgent Fury, Lee is assigned to the staff of the Chief of Naval Operations at the Pentagon for a one-year tour. Not wanting to relocate his family again for a short tour of duty, he and Rachel agree to remain in their home in Virginia Beach. Lee rents a small apartment near Arlington National Cemetery while working at the Pentagon and will commute home on weekends. This arrangement provides him with opportunities to visit his grandparents' gravesites at Arlington National Cemetery.

Lieutenant Commander Lee McCormick reports for duty at the Pentagon on January 3, 1984. He is assigned to work on a team developing antisubmarine tactics and shipboard operating procedures for the Navy's evolving Light Airborne Multi-Purpose System (LAMPS) community. Navy helicopters operate as an integrated weapons system, their purpose being to scout outside the limits of a fleet's radar and sonar range. Their objectives are simple: they are to detect and track enemy submarines or missile-equipped escort ships and feed the real-time data back to their LAMPS mothership. They can also directly engage enemy targets with depth charges or torpedoes.

During the year, Lee works on the LAMPS program and commutes back and forth to spend weekends with his family. It's a grueling schedule, but well worth his family's happiness and well-being. Rachel is comfortable and able to oversee family affairs in Lee's absence. She realized early in Lee's career that his profession involves multiple sea deployments, and over time, she has grown to accept and manage it.

With his Pentagon assignment coming to an end as Christmas 1984 approaches, Lee is promoted to commander and alerted for new orders. Rachel informs him she is pregnant, and their third child is due in July 1985.

CHRISTMAS WITH SEAN AND ANA

Lee and his father, retired General Sean McCormick, are sitting in the den of Lee's house, sipping Irish whiskey by the fireplace. Rachel and Ana are sitting at the kitchen table having their own conversation. Both Josh and Angela are napping in their rooms. Light snow is falling this midafternoon on December 20, 1984. Sean and Ana flew in from Pensacola and are here to take care of their grandchildren, while Lee and Rachel sneak away for three days to Colonial Williamsburg.

Sean, looking fit and trim, retired from the military shortly after Operation Eagle Claw in April 1980. He and Ana relocated to Pensacola, Florida, near Eglin Air Force Base. They purchased a newly renovated large Queen Anne-style Victorian home built in 1900 in the coveted North Hill Preservation District of Pensacola.

After settling into their new community in Pensacola, Sean was offered a position with an A.G. Edwards & Sons' local office in town. He accepted the offer and works as a financial adviser and broker for individuals. He specializes in helping military personnel, both active and retired, living in the Pensacola area. He knew when he was offered the position that it was for his military network.

After taking a few sips of his Irish whiskey, Lee looks at his father and says, "Dad, Rachel and I really appreciate you and Mom joining us for Christmas and watching Josh and Angela. We love the idea of spending a few days alone. It's hard for us to do that now with the children."

Sean smiles at Lee as he takes another sip of his whiskey and replies. "Lee, it's not a problem. Your mother and I were in your position many years ago ourselves. Believe me, we know and can appreciate you wanting some time alone."

Lee, in a very thoughtful and inquisitive tone, asks, "Dad, I've been wanting to ask you a question. If it's none of my business, I'll understand."

"Go ahead, Son. What is it?"

"Why did you retire from the Air Force when you did?" He pauses, looks for a reaction, and, seeing that stoic expression on his father's face, wonders if he should have just taken another sip of Irish whiskey.

The expression on his son's face causes Sean to grin as he slowly responds. "Son, there are two reasons. The first one is simply that I served on active duty for forty years. That's a long time, and I was due to retire. Could I have continued for a few more years? Maybe."

Sean stops, leans forward, and pours some more whiskey in both their glasses. He leans back, glancing over at the fireplace, taking in its warm glow and listening to its crackling sounds. "I was at the Pentagon when the ill-fated Iranian hostage raid was planned and executed. I was one of many senior officers who thought it was ill-advised and poorly planned. A fundamental issue, which turned out to be a real problem was the commingling of all four service branches. Personnel should have been selected purely based on who was best qualified at the time and which military assets would provide the best chance of success. It didn't help that the president basically micromanaged the operation from the White House."

Sean takes a moment and looks at Lee, "Son, I just had enough of interservice rivalry, politics, and what I perceived to be the ever-expanding role of support staff instead of frontline warriors. It was time for me to retire and try something new."

Lee, looking back at his father, says, "As you know, I was there, off the coast of Iran. It was a mess. It cost the lives of eight men, and four were badly wounded. The morale of the men I served with during this operation took a real hit. Many of them, including me, felt as you did before the rescue operation was launched. Then along comes Operation Urgent Fury, and we experience many of the same issues. Will we ever learn?"

The conversation ends as Sean stands and says, "Let's hope so."

They go to the kitchen, where they join their wives. Ana stands up when Lee walks in and gives him another long hug. She's missed him greatly and has looked forward to this visit for a long time.

After celebrating Christmas and ringing in the new year of 1985 with his family, Lee shares with them his new orders. He'll transition to the Sikorsky SH-60B Seahawk helicopter, which will be deployed in Helicopter Anti-Submarine, Light (HSL) squadrons starting in 1985. Upon completion of his flight training, he will report with his family to the College of Naval Warfare at Navy Station Newport, Rhode Island for a year.

9
NAVY STATION NEWPORT, RHODE ISLAND

While Lee is away transitioning to the Seahawk, Rachel lists their house for sale. Their home sells to another Navy family moving into the area in March, the same month that Lee returns from his flight training. The stars are aligned in heaven.

Shortly after Lee's return on March 15, they close the sale, move out of their home, and travel to Newport, Rhode Island for his new assignment. The trip from Virginia Beach to Newport is slow, uneventful, and tiring for Lee, Rachel, who is showing her condition, and the children. Upon arriving, Commander McCormick is assisted by base personnel in finding a place for his family to live. Within a week, Lee and Rachel once again find themselves moving into temporary housing. They both joke about how it feels like déjà vu. Their new neighbors drop in to welcome and assist them and provide meals for several days.

Rachel takes charge once again and busies herself, making the house a warm and cozy place for her family. Josh, at the age of six, is the little man of the house when his dad is not home and takes to helping his mom. He goes about it very seriously. Rachel adores him for it. Angela is just over three years old and very much an active little girl. She's not the little helper her brother is, but she tries. With his family busy settling in, Lee reports to the College of Naval Warfare on April 15 and begins his formal program on May 1, 1985.

Lee considers adding another graduate degree to his resume as a career-enhancing accomplishment. As important to him as that is, allowing him to be home with Rachel and the children for over a year without repeated deployments is reward enough.

Rachel enjoys their life together as a family, no deployments, just college classrooms and Lee being home nights and weekends with her and the children. Rachel senses in Lee a contentment and tranquil peace that he's not experienced in many years. He is relaxed, has grown closer to Josh and Angela, and enjoys working out at the base gym, playing tennis, and swimming. Lee carries a demanding academic program but has no trouble adjusting. He thoroughly enjoys his current assignment at the college.

On July 10, 1985, Rachel gives birth to their third child, a son. They name him Bryan. Ana flies up and spends two weeks with them to help take care of the children and Rachel. Until her arrival two days after Bryan is born, Lee cares for Josh and Angela, who are anxious for their mother to come home. They want to see their new brother. Ana arrives just in time to accompany Lee, Josh, and Angela to the hospital to bring Rachel and Bryan home. With Ana's arrival, all is well. Lee returns to his classroom studies, and Ana looks after his family.

The night before Ana is scheduled to fly back to

NAVY STATION NEWPORT, RHODE ISLAND

Pensacola, Lee, Ana, and Rachel enjoy the evening. The children are asleep in their rooms as the adults indulge in small talk. Lee is privy to recent developments he feels compelled to share with them. With a serious, measured tone, he begins.

"Mother, Rachel, there is another development in the Middle East which will impact us."

They both look over at Lee as their facial expressions slowly change from one of contentment to concern and fear.

"The Iran-Iraq War began back in 1980 when Iran invaded Iraq. Well, it's taking another turn and getting worse. It's spilling out into the Persian Gulf area. Their targets are oil export facilities and oil tankers whose cargoes help replenish both Iran and Iraq's war chest."

Lee stops for a moment, gathers his thoughts, then says. "I heard today that Kuwait is considering asking the United States to help protect its ships. In my opinion, it's not a question of if they will ask, it's when. It could be a year or more before they come to us for help. When they do, I'm sure the Reagan administration will honor their request."

Ana interrupts Lee, "Why should we get involved in that? Don't they have their own military?"

"Unfortunately, we are captive to the oil coming from that region, and so is much of the free world. If the oil supply is cut off or significantly disrupted, our economy and much of the free world's economies could be severely impacted."

Rachel looks to her husband, and as she speaks softly, her voice begins to tremble and crack. "Lee, are you going back to sea again?"

He gazes lovingly at her and his mother. "If the president agrees to their request, it will require several of our warships and could be the largest maritime convoy operation since World War II."

Lee pauses, contemplates what to say next, then continues. "They won't come to us anytime soon, but when they do, and we get involved, it could well last a few years. I'm confident that I'll remain here until I finish my college program. After that, they'll probably send me back to sea."

With Lee's response, both Rachel and Ana bury their heads in their hands and begin to weep silently.

Rachel sobs, "Will it ever end? Ever?"

Ana gazes at her son, tears streaming from her eyes, and in a soft, emotional voice, says, "Lee, my son, you have a father, a grandfather, and an older brother who have all served and seen action. Your younger brother lives on the edge with his CIA exploits. You serve now and have experienced conflict. How much can and should one family give to their country?"

Lee's response, "I don't have an answer for you, Mom… but if not us, then who?"

10
THE TANKER WAR - 1
OPERATION EARNEST WILL

Desperate to bring foreign powers into the Iraq-Iran War, Saddam Hussein expands the fighting in the Persian Gulf area. Iran retaliates by attacking Kuwaiti tankers carrying Iraqi oil. Their war continues to escalate as both countries sharply increase their attacks on oil tankers and merchant ships of neutral nations. Their goals are the same—to deprive each other of trade with their respective allies. The resulting chaos is disrupting the flow of oil from the region and drawing other regional countries into the conflict.

In December 1986, the government of Kuwait asks the Reagan administration to protect their tankers from attack by Iran. They request the United States Navy be sent into patrol and escort all their ships in and out of the Persian Gulf until hostilities cease. The president authorizes the American military to protect Kuwait-owned tankers from Iranian attacks. It's given the name Operation Earnest Will and is scheduled to commence in July 1987. No end date is established.

LEE RETURNS TO SEA AND AIR DUTY

Completing his program at the College of Naval Warfare, Lee is awarded his graduate degree and is reassigned to NAS Norfolk in December 1986. Not knowing what his future holds, Lee and Rachel decide to forgo buying another home. They find suitable rental property near the Navy base. Rachel knows the drill and goes about making their new temporary home comfortable, inviting, and child-friendly. The McCormicks have three small children. Josh is enrolled in the second grade at the local elementary school. Angela now attends kindergarten, and Bryan, who is not of school age, stays home with Rachel.

Lee's first month back at Norfolk is devoted to flying and requalifying on the Seahawk. He then reports for duty with an ASW Seahawk Squadron on NAS Norfolk and trains with squadron aircrews in preparation for deployment as a detachment commander. On Monday morning, March 30, 1987, Lee receives a call from his squadron commander to join him for a meeting with the chief of staff and regional operations officer for the commander of Navy Region Mid-Atlantic. This command structure is headquartered at Naval Station Norfolk. During this meeting, Lee is briefed on Operation Earnest Will and the planned deployment of multiple US Navy ships to provide protection for oil tankers in the Persian Gulf.

He's told by the regional operations officer that he's been assigned a special mission of vital importance. He's to deploy immediately for forty-five days to the Persian Gulf. Commander McCormick will be instrumental in helping plan helicopter support during the upcoming operation. His orders are straightforward and simple: proceed to the

Persian Gulf, familiarize yourself with the region, its weather patterns, and friendly naval facilities in the area that can be trusted to provide shelter, supplies, and maintenance assistance. Lee is also instructed to observe and report on tactics and weaponry deployed to date by the warring factions. Any other observations or planning points to consider are at his discretion. Upon return, he'll work with headquarters staff personnel to develop the operational plans for deploying helicopter assets and their necessary support requirements. He's to join the crew of the USS Stark being deployed to the region this month and will report on board as soon as possible.

On the drive home later that afternoon, Lee dreads and ponders how to tell Rachel of his new orders. That evening, over a glass of wine, he explains to Rachel his new temporary assignment. She handles the news with grace and a calmness that reflects years of being a Navy wife. It doesn't make the news any easier to accept, but there is no alternative. Lee is a naval officer, and he must follow orders from his superiors. She can only pray he'll survive and return home.

USS STARK

Commander McCormick reports on board the USS Stark on April 15 after spending several days meeting with senior staff members of the Navy's Middle East Force located in Manama, Bahrain. The information he is provided while in Bahrain is not encouraging. The Persian Gulf is a hotbed of activity. Placing multiple American ships in the Persian Gulf is like placing them in a small pond. They can become ducks in a shooting gallery, vulnerable to air and sea attack, with little time to react. Lee concludes for himself that ships deployed to the region will need to maintain a high state of combat efficiency and awareness on a 24/7 basis.

After landing on the USS Stark's flight deck, Lee disembarks the helicopter and is met by the ship's executive officer (XO) and a young sailor who takes his travel bags. They clear the flight deck quickly, allowing the helicopter to depart. As it clears the ship, the wind from the rotor wash ceases, and even with a sea breeze, Lee feels the heat from the early afternoon sun. The XO welcomes Lee on board and escorts him through the ship up to the Combat Information Center. Entering the center, Lee is confronted with a room full of sailors performing their assigned duties with minimal conversations. The XO guides Lee over to the ship's captain and introduces him to Lee. The captain welcomes Lee aboard then introduces his tactical action officer (TAO) and weapons control officer (WCO).

Looking at his XO and Commander McCormick, the captain says, "Gentlemen, follow me. Let's go to my quarters and talk." Once inside his quarters, the captain has them take a seat then begins their discussions.

"Commander McCormick, we've been briefed as to your assignment while with us. We'll cooperate fully and help you in any way possible. My XO will be your point person for anything you need."

Lee responds, "Thank you, sir."

The captain continues. "We are on a six-month deployment over here as part of a seven-ship complement. We're charged with safeguarding merchant shipping in the Persian Gulf. Sounds straightforward and simple. It is not. It's fraught with pitfalls and danger."

The captain continues to give Lee an overview of the

situation as he sees it. Lee listens intently, absorbing what he hears. The captain pauses, allowing Lee to respond with any comments.

Lee says, "I'll be no bother and will stay out of your crew's way. I'm on your ship primarily to gauge how Iran and Iraq act and react to our operational escort tactics. My time back in Bahrain was devoted mostly to meeting with staff personnel in other areas I'm tasked with reviewing while here. My early impression is that we have placed ourselves in the middle of a small fishbowl, caught between two warring countries, both of which make up the rules as they go."

Both the captain and XO manage a small grin as the captain responds. "That pretty well sums it up!"

The captain continues in a serious tone. "We see the war around us daily out here. Tankers are being sunk, planes are firing at one another, and we have even been chased by an Iranian ship. They instructed us to shut down our engines, or they would shoot down our helicopter. The Iraqis haven't presented us with a threat yet, but tensions are running very high. Our time window to react to any kind of a threat, perceived or real, may only be a matter of seconds."

Lee simply responds. "On first pass, it appears we are in a no-win situation."

The captain looks down and simply says, "You may be right. I hope not."

Lee spends his time over the next several weeks observing what happens around him as he interacts with the USS Stark's officers and sailors. He witnesses firsthand the daily tedium of escort duty with its hours of sheer boredom, sometimes punctuated with moments of heightened tensions as they are subjected to Iranian harassment and close encounters. Lee is impressed by the crew's overall morale and daily attention to their duties but also senses lingering questions in many.

Why are we here? How long before we are the victim of our circumstances and men on this ship are killed?

It's May 17, 1987, and the USS Stark is sailing through the Persian Gulf's war-free zone during a two-day exercise. The weather is calm and hot with the evening sky clear as usual. The ship is sailing at condition 3, which means that all weapons systems should be fully manned and operational. Lee is doing his usual walk on the ship and decides to stop at the CIC to see what's happening. Upon entering, he becomes concerned at the feverish activity he witnesses.

The ship's crew has identified an Iraqi Mirage F1 French-made jet passing closer to the ship than is normal. The captain is present and orders a radioman to send the standard warning by radio message: "Unknown aircraft, this is US Navy warship on your 078 (degrees) for twelve miles. Request you identify yourself."

The Iraqi pilot does not respond to the message. The aircraft is getting closer to the ship. The captain orders a second message sent, but still, no answer. Lee senses the men in the CIC expect the plane to change course and pull away. Their monitors are not giving any indication that the pilot of the plane has locked his radar on the Stark.

The captain is suddenly informed the Iraqi aircraft has locked his fire-control radar onto the Stark. It's too late; they are targeted. The Iraqi Mirage F1 aircraft fires the first French Exocet missile (air-to-ground missile) twenty-two miles from the ship and the second Exocet from fifteen miles. The pilot breaks off his attack and withdraws from the area.

The USS Stark's forward lookout sees the missile launch

and gives warning. It's too late. The missiles are headed straight for the Stark, with impacts expected in seconds. As the majority of the 222 sailors on board are asleep or relaxing, the worst happens just after 2100 hours.

The first Exocet missile hits just above the waterline on the port side of the ship near the bridge. Although it failed to detonate, it left flaming rocket fuel in its path and severed the firefighting water lines to the forward part of the ship. The second Exocet also strikes the port side thirty seconds later. It follows almost an identical path to the first missile. This missile detonates, leaving a ten by fifteen-foot hole in the Stark's port side, causing a large fire that quickly spreads throughout the ship's post office, storeroom, and combat operations center. Electronics for the Stark's missile defense go out, so the captain cannot order his men to return fire.

General quarters are sounded as the ship bursts into flames. Fires ignite and spread rapidly through parts of the ship. The fire, heat, and smoke add to the confusion, terror, and momentary loss of control over many functions of the Stark. The almost simultaneous missile hits are followed by a horrific explosion. Men in the CIC, both those who are standing and many who are seated at their posts, are violently thrown to the deck floor. Lee attempts to stop his fall with his left arm. He's unsuccessful and, in the process, bruises and strains his arm and wrist. His head hits the side of a sonar console table hard as he falls to the deck, gashing his forehead resulting in an open wound, which begins to bleed.

Lee, dizzy and shaken, slowly picks himself up off the deck, checks himself over to see if he has all his limbs then moves about the room, checking the condition of the other men. He's in a mild state of shock and is not yet aware of his head wound, even though there is blood trickling down his uniform. The CIC sustains damage, and several men are wounded. The captain leaves the CIC for the bridge area to better determine the extent of damage. Lee takes charge in the CIC and assists in the movement of wounded men out of the room. The ship's medical treatment room is unavailable due to structural and fire damage. The Stark's hangar area is designated as the causality receiving area.

Damage reports come in slowly. The crew's berthing areas sustained a direct hit. It is feared there are many sailors dead in those areas. The chart room, pilot house, sonar control room, officers' stateroom, the ship's store, port bridge wing, and the communications center are all damaged. The engine room is still operating, providing propulsion to the ship's engines and electrical power. The Stark's combat systems are severely degraded. The USS Stark's fate rests in the hands of the surviving crew members.

The captain arrives on the bridge and oversees firefighting efforts fore and aft. The XO is on the flight deck directing firefighting efforts. Since the missiles struck, the ship has been taking on water from the hole on the port side and is now listing to port about sixteen degrees. The captain orders the starboard side flooded to keep the hole on the hull's port side above water. This helps prevent the Stark from sinking. The captain dispatches a distress call which is received by the USS Waddell and the USS Conyngham on liberty in Bahrain.

Lee continues his search for wounded men. Those he finds, he helps move through the smoke and heat of crowded passageways to the hangar for medical assistance. Stepping out on the aft deck area for a breath of fresh air, Lee gazes upon blazing fires and billowing smoke. It's a scene from hell. Men are moving around with a sense of purpose as they try to save their ship and help wounded comrades. It's not until one of the corpsmen tells him to take a break and let them check his head wound and arm that he realizes the extent of his wounds. To that point, Lee was oblivious to his situation, driven by rage, adrenaline, and a desire to help save the ship and the sailors on it.

As the corpsman treats him, Lee wonders, *How many men died tonight?*

THE USS STARK SURVIVES

The quick action of the sailors onboard that fateful night saved many lives and kept their ship from sinking. With the assistance of firefighting crews from nearby ships, the crew battles the fire over the next twenty-four hours. With the flames extinguished, the USS Waddell and USS Conyngham escort the USS Stark to Manama port in Bahrain.

A total of thirty-seven crew members were killed in the attack, twenty-nine from the initial explosion and fire, including two lost at sea. Many of them were still in their bunks and burned to death. Eight sailors later died from their injuries. Twenty-one others survived their wounds.

The Stark arrives in Bahrain on May 18, 1987. The ship will remain there to be repaired. Once deemed ready, the ship will depart for Mayport Naval Station, Florida, the ship's home port. The wounded are evacuated as deemed appropriate for further medical attention, and the deceased are sent home in flag-draped caskets. Many of the dead are so badly burned their families may not recognize them.

There are also some body bags containing only body parts for further medical analysis to determine who they are.

Lee is taken to the Bahrain Navy medical facility to recover from the injuries he sustained in the attack. After settling in at the facility, Lee communicates with his family to inform them that he's alive. While recovering, he works on the preliminary draft report relating to his assignment.

LEE'S RECOMMENDATIONS

On June 1, Lee returns to Norfolk, rejoins his family, and prepares his report. He then submits it to the chief of staff and regional operations officer for the commander of Navy Region Mid-Atlantic. He encourages countermeasure squadrons and the use of more helicopters. He outlines why the actions reveal that Iran and Iraq truly hate each other. He ends with, "The danger will only grow—from mines, from warplanes, from warships."

As initially tasked, Lee participates in developing operational guidelines for Navy helicopter assets to be deployed to the Persian Gulf in support of Operation Earnest Will for most of June. He then rejoins his squadron, returns to flight status, and resumes flying routine missions in support of short sea deployments on surface ships stationed at Norfolk.

THE BRIDGETON INCIDENT

Several Kuwaiti tankers are reflagged as American vessels in preparation for convoy operations to begin. On July 22, 1987, American warships and combat aircraft began escorting them on the 500-mile run between the Gulf of Oman and home waters of Kuwait. The dangers became apparent on the very first convoy of Operation Earnest Will.

Two days into the Persian Gulf, on July 24, 1987, the Kuwaiti oil tanker al-Rekkah, reflagged as the US tanker MV Bridgeton, strikes an Iranian underwater mine. On the bridge, the Bridgeton's captain says, "The explosion felt as if a 500-ton hammer had come down on the 400,000-ton ship." No injuries were reported, and the tanker's double hull and compartmentalized structure kept the damage to a minimum. The MV Bridgeton continued on under her own power with three Navy escort ships following in the tanker's wake to avoid mines.

Iran's Prime Minister called it an "irreparable blow to America's political and military prestige" and said that it was the "invisible hands of God" that hit the US-flagged ship and expressed hope that the US Congress would put an immediate end to the administration's plan.

In this unforeseen development, the task force commander admitted that despite intelligence warnings, no one had thought it necessary to check the route for naval mines. They could not have checked for mines anyway. It was quickly determined that there were no minesweepers in the Persian Gulf, nor were any easily accessible. The escort operation was placed on hold until minesweepers could be deployed. The Pentagon ultimately sends in five oceangoing minesweepers, six small coastal minesweepers, and Helicopter Mine Countermeasures Squadron 14 (HM-14) with eight minesweeping helicopters.

Upon learning of this incident and the failure to deploy necessary mine detection assets, Lee wonders, *Did anybody read my report? Is this becoming another Operation Eagle Claw and Urgent Fury?*

11

THE TANKER WAR -2
USS SAMUEL B. ROBERTS

The USS Samuel B. Roberts deploys on her maiden voyage from Newport, Rhode Island, in January 1988, heading for the Persian Gulf to participate in Operation Earnest Will. Commander Lee McCormick is assigned to the Frigate USS Roberts as the ship's air detachment commander of two Sikorsky SH-60B Seahawks. He takes with him five other pilots and sixteen experienced enlisted maintainers. Before leaving his family once again for an extended sea tour, he and Rachel have serious conversations about their future in the Navy. Lee has spent more time at sea away from his family than on land where he can be with them. Rachel is the mother of their children but has become their de facto father as well. She is growing weary of long-term separations as is Lee. They part again, with Lee promising to address the issue when he returns from Operation Earnest Will.

Since arriving in the Persian Gulf, the Roberts has participated in escorting thirteen convoys. Lee soon learns that convoy duty is just the public face of Operation Earnest

Will. The primary role of the Navy contingent in the Persian Gulf is to run off Iranian warships and warn off Iraqi fighters. They also guard secret mobile operating bases in the northern Gulf, which launch Blackhawk Army helicopters on shadowy missions.

Danger is ever present with no room for error. It is a daunting task. Down in the darkened CIC, radar operators sort masses of green specks into tankers, warships, armed speedboats, airliners, and fighter jets. Every dot can represent a way to die.

Early on the morning of April 14, 1988, Lee and his pilots have breakfast together, then proceed to the hangar bay in the aft section of the ship. The morale of his men is good as they look forward to another day of flying. Lee has flown missions the last three days and will stay onboard the ship today. He begins his short briefing.

"Gentlemen, it's just another routine day of flying support for the Roberts. We'll launch both aircraft today with a twenty-minute separation time between liftoffs. The weather is the same: hot and muggy with clear skies. I'll be in the CIC most of the day monitoring activity."

"Fellows, stay safe, keep alert, and we'll see you this evening for dinner." The aircrews then begin their pre-fight checks in preparation for launch.

Later in the afternoon, the USS Roberts is heading east in the main shipping channel. They're ordered to rendezvous with the combat stores ship USS San Jose for a resupply mission. A lookout spots three black spheres in the water and calls out "mines." The officer of the deck swiftly brings the frigate to a halt and calls for the ship's captain. "Sir, we have two mines off the starboard bow, and one just about 300 yards off the starboard beam."

The captain orders his ship to general quarters to secure watertight boundaries throughout the ship, get above the main deck, and report in when all is secured. Once the ship is manned and ready, they will back, out following their own ship's wake trail to exit the minefield. The churn of a ship's screw can leave long wake trails. The sailors on deck can look back and see their ship's trail for miles.

With the sighting of mines, Lee immediately departs the CIC and proceeds to the hangar deck. One of his two helicopter crews recently landed and is preparing to go back out. As he heads for the hangar, the captain reverses engines and attempts to back out of the minefield area through his ship's wake trail. As they start to move back, the unthinkable happens. The USS Roberts hits an underwater mine. Two hundred and fifty tons of TNT explodes, shaking the Roberts from stem to stern.

The explosion lifts the ship into the air, drives her bow down into the water, and blows a twenty-one-foot hole in the port side. Sections of the deck are blown upward. Superhot gases rush through a truck-sized hole in the hull, setting fires at the ship's core, and a wall of seawater soon follows. The fireball created from the explosion is intense. The blast sends burning jet fuel, oil, and pieces of the main engineering spaces rocketing up through the ship's exhaust stacks. The explosion shatters anything that is horizontal on the ship: counters, Plexiglas, tables, etc. The superstructure (parts of a ship that project above the main deck) separates from the main deck and then crashes back down, compressing itself.

The explosion violently thrusts some sailors up into the overhead and throws others across compartments. Smoke is everywhere. Flaming pieces of insulation and debris rain down on sailors caught outside on deck. They scramble for cover. As soon as all the debris falls, they start hauling hoses down to areas with fires. Repair teams send out investigators, hose teams form, and engineers take stock of what equipment they have left.

Lee reaches the hangar area just when the explosion occurs. He is knocked to the deck by the mine detonation's terrific force, his ears ring, and his head hits the flight deck hard. He gradually picks himself up off the deck, checks himself over for any wounds, and looks around at the devastation before him. His world is going in slow motion as he witnesses men moving in all directions, some screaming, as they react to the explosion. Fire and smoke billow from several areas of the ship, adding to the chaotic scene before him.

On the flight deck, the helicopter crew immediately stops their engines as the explosion occurs. The blast sends fluid spewing onto the nonskid flight deck. The first reaction of Lee and his men is that they have a fuel leak, another potential fire hazard. Realizing it is not fuel, they perform a detailed check of the helicopter to determine if it's ready to fly. Lee is certain severe casualties on the ship will need to be airlifted out.

The impact damages the hull and deckhouse as well as foundation structures. Burning fuel shoots a column of fire from the stack. The blast shakes the main engines from their mountings, floods the engine room, opens cracks in the superstructure, and causes a split in the ship's main engine room bulkhead (dividing wall between compartments on a ship).

The bad news keeps coming. Three of the Roberts's four generators are dead, and the power demands of the ship quickly overwhelm the fourth. It's only been a few minutes since the mine blast, and the ship is without electrical power. They cannot operate their pumps to fight the fires raging on board.

An eerie silence fills the ship. Only the occasional shouts of men and the noise of equipment being dragged from repair lockers is heard. An unearthly metallic groan emanates from within the wounded ship.

Through the heroic efforts of one fireman, the big diesel that powers Generator Number One is brought back to life. The lights come on. Another pair of generators soon comes back online, which activates three fire pumps. The USS Roberts now has water for their fire teams to attack the fires.

Deep within the USS Stark's hull, seawater gushes through several cracks in the aft bulkhead of one of the ship's biggest compartments. If it floods, as the engine room has, the ship could sink. Repair teams are sent to shore up the bulkheads and stop the seawater from entering the compartment. During the desperate fight to stop the fire, the crew is spraying so much water that it's adding to the flooding of the ship. The Stark takes on an eighteen-degree list as the dewatering pumps can't keep up with the flooding.

When the captain realizes they are so focused on fighting the fires and not thinking about staying afloat, he races to the bridge. He shouts into the ship's intercom, "Now hear this! Stop fighting the fires. I repeat, stop fighting all fires." Shortly after the order goes out, the ship stops sinking. The repair crews go about plugging holes and leaks in the ship as the dewatering pumps begin removing seawater from the interior.

Several sailors are injured in the explosion, with the

most severe ones taken to the hangar to be medevacked. Lee observes two sailors escorting a naked sailor into the hangar area who is bloody and horribly burned over much of his body. He's in considerable pain but doesn't yell out; he just endures it. As the severely injured sailor moves slowly by other men who are yelling and working desperately to save their ship, they become quiet and stare at him in disbelief. Lee can't believe the man is even walking.

Working now with his men, Lee and the helicopter crew determine their helicopter is airworthy. The aircrew climbs in the helicopter, strap into their seats, start the engines, and checks to ensure their instruments are in the green and all the controls have free movement. Satisfied they are good, the pilot powers up, pulls up on his collective, and lifts off. After flying a few low-level circles around the stricken ship and feeling confident they can fly, he lands his helicopter. Lee and some other sailors help load the most seriously injured. With the wounded placed on board, the pilot lifts off and speeds toward the USS San Jose, where the wounded will receive medical attention.

As darkness surrounds the ship, the crew is making considerable progress in bringing things under control. It's been a few hours since the explosion and the series of repairs and improvisations by the crew results in a steady stream of water to the firehoses. Around 2200 hours, the ship's crew extinguishes the last major fire and smaller reflashes from heat stored up in the ship's steel. The captain announces to his crew that the situation is contained and the ship is saved and tells the men to relax and take a breather.

Lee checks to ensure his men are accounted for, not injured, and both helicopters are secured on the deck of the

USS San Jose. The helicopters and their crews will remain there for the night. He then takes time for a corpsman to check him over. The corpsman informs Commander McCormick that he's alright but needs to take it easy for a few days and check in with a flight surgeon before getting back in the cockpit.

Feeling good about his condition and the fact that he's still alive, Lee decides to stroll around the ship and take in the nightly show of bright stars in the heavens above. As he makes his way around the USS Roberts, he observes a subdued crew that is at peace and proud of how they performed in saving their ship.

Late into the next morning, Commander McCormick's two helicopters depart the USS San Jose and fly back to the USS Roberts. After the helicopters land on the flight deck and are secured, Lee requests that his full detachment join him for an early lunch and briefing.

With his men present, relaxed and enjoying their meal, Lee stands up and, looking around the room at his men, briefs them on the situation.

"Gentlemen, welcome back. It's good to see all of us together as a detachment. You performed very well during our horrific situation. I'm proud of you. As you can see, the USS Roberts has sustained considerable damage."

Lee stops for a moment, then continues. "The crew of the USS Roberts saved their ship with no loss of life. Ten sailors were medevacked to San Jose for injuries sustained in the blast. Your efforts in that regard expedited their medical treatment. Well done. Six of those sailors will be returned to the Roberts within two days. The other four sailors are burn victims who are being sent to a military hospital in Germany for treatment. Initial reports indicate they will all survive."

He pauses, looking around the room to gauge the men's reactions. Sensing they are listening intently, in a calm tone, he says what the men are waiting to hear. "The ship will be towed to Dubai, United Arab Emirates, for initial assessments. They should hook us up tomorrow and begin towing. The USS Roberts will ultimately be taken back to the States for repairs. As for us, the detachment will remain on the Roberts until we arrive in Dubai. Once there, we'll be offloaded and reassigned. There is no indication at this time what the new orders might be or where we'll end up. When I know anything new, you'll be the first to know."

OPERATION PRAYING MANTIS

On April 18, 1988, the United States initiates Operation Praying Mantis which is an attack on Iranian assets. It is retaliation for their acts of aggression and damage to the USS Roberts. The mine that the Roberts struck was one placed there by Iran. The United States retaliates fiercely and attacks with several groups of surface warships plus aircraft from the aircraft carrier USS Enterprise.

By the end of the operation, American Marines, ships, and aircraft destroyed Iranian naval and intelligence facilities on two inoperable oil platforms in the Gulf and sank at least three armed Iranian speedboats, one Iranian frigate, and one fast attack gunboat. Another Iranian frigate was damaged in the battle.

This battle is the largest US naval surface engagement since the end of the Second World War. It also marks the Navy's first exchange of anti-ship missiles with opposing ships and the only occasion since World War II that the US Navy sinks a major surface warship.

THE IRAQ-IRAN WAR SETS THE STAGE FOR FUTURE CONFLICTS

In the aftermath of the fighting, both Iran and Iraq find themselves in precarious positions. Ultimately, both sides damaged more than 500 ships from various nations in the Tanker War.

Iran becomes militarily depleted, economically bankrupt, and politically isolated. The regime did succeed in driving Iraq from its soil, and it would survive. Iraq emerges from the struggle as a virtual pariah on the world stage. Despite earlier support from Western governments, the international community recoiled from the country's use of chemical weapons and its brutal suppression of the Kurds. Although Saddam Hussein's military is the fifth largest on earth, he owes billions to his neighbors, and his war-ravaged economy is susceptible to fluctuations in the global price of oil.

It will only be a short time before another major war breaks out in the Middle East, with Saddam's Iraq in the middle of the conflict.

12
NAVAL AIR STATION NORTH ISLAND
THE SEASNAKES

After returning home from the Persian Gulf and the Tanker War, Lee and Rachel have long discussions about his staying in the Navy and continuing his career. Over many evenings of deliberation, they both agree to give it one more chance, but only if Lee can be assigned long term to one duty station for several years. This may give the children a chance to enjoy a normal life and spend more time with their father.

Lee meets with and presents to his superiors a professional, straightforward case for continuing a Naval career. He is committed, lives to fly, serve his country, and deploy to sea when ordered. He also loves his family dearly and has found the multiple long-term deployments increasingly more difficult for his wife and children. He wants to, and in fact, needs to, have a better balance between the two for him to continue serving. This is a universally shared sentiment with many career military personnel, particularly those with a family.

His superiors are sympathetic to his concerns, hear his

position, and ultimately offer him reassignment on a long-term basis to San Diego. After talking it over with Rachel, they agree to give it a go. Whereupon, Commander Lee McCormick is promoted to captain and transferred to San Diego, California to command Helicopter Antisubmarine Squadron (Light) 33 in August 1988. The squadron is based at Naval Air Station North Island, located at the north end of Coronado in the San Diego Bay.

The squadron is called the Seasnakes and Lee's call sign is Seasnake 1. The men assigned to the squadron affectionately refer to their unit area as Snake Town. Lee is proud of his squadron, the men with whom he serves, their record, and the reputation they have established. The squadron has made several short cruises, one month or less, with several of the surface ships operating out of Naval Station San Diego.

CHULA VISTA

Family life is good for Rachel, the children, and Lee. Shortly after arriving in San Diego, they purchase a new home in Chula Vista, which is one of the larger cities in the San Diego metropolitan area. The military transports their household furniture and belongings and helps where possible as they settle into their Spanish-style ranch home. Their back courtyard overlooks a canyon facing south toward Mexico and out to the west, the Pacific Ocean. The air has a sweet smell blowing in off the desert to their east. With the cool, dry, sweet-smelling air, Lee feels so alive and enjoys waking up in the early morning to begin his day. Both Rachel and he regularly sit outside in the morning, drinking coffee as they watch the sun slowly rise.

Josh will start fifth grade in September, Angela third grade, and Bryan begins his education with kindergarten. Josh is drawn to sports, particularly swimming and baseball. Angela has been taking piano lessons and according to her teacher, has a rare talent and many would consider her gifted. Bryan is a mischievous little boy who loves playing catch with his brother and incessantly talks about playing baseball when he grows up.

Rachel has settled into the community and is enjoying her home, new lifestyle, and having Lee around most evenings. If there is anything she has learned over the years of being a Navy wife, it's how to relocate and settle into a new community. For Lee, it's almost nirvana. He's home with his family, he's watching his children grow, Rachel is happier than he's seen her in years, and he enjoys a sense of satisfaction and pride in being Commander of the Seasnakes.

ALAN AND SHARON VISIT

It's early Tuesday morning on August 8, 1989, and Lee is waiting at the arrival gate for Delta Flight 807, arriving from Atlanta, Georgia. He's here to pick up Alan and Sharon, who are flying in to spend the week with his family. Rachel is at the house with the children, who were still asleep when Lee left to drive to the San Diego County Regional Airport. Alan and Sharon emerge from the exit gate and, sighting Lee, head straight for him. Sharon, looking tired but radiant, reaches Lee first and gives him a big hug. Alan, also looking tired from their early morning flight, walks up to his brother. They shake hands and then hug briefly, as Lee steps back.

"Well, brother, did you have a good flight?"

"We did. It was good. We had smooth weather, and although it was dark, the sky was clear most of the way."

Lee looks over to Sharon. "Sharon, you look terrific." He then looks at both of them and says, "Welcome to Southern California. Rachel's home with the children. When we get there, they'll be full of energy. So enjoy the drive and try to rest—you'll need it."

Lee takes Sharon's travel bag and carries it as he guides them through the terminal to the baggage claim area. After securing their bags, they step outside and walk to Lee's car. The weather is gorgeous. The air is cool, has a fresh smell, and the sun is bright.

Alan takes a few deep breaths of fresh air and smiles at his brother. "Lee, this weather feels great. I'm tired, but something about your climate makes me feel more alive." He inhales a few more times and continues with, "Is it always like this out here?"

"If you like it here, wait until we get home. The air out that way has a sweet smell to it as it blows in off the desert. You're going to love it here."

Sharon comments about the weather in Atlanta at this time of the year being hot, humid, and sticky. It can drain you of your energy. Lee smiles and replies, "Welcome to paradise...almost."

Lee takes the long way home, giving his family a little more time to wake up and start their day. Arriving home, they are met by Rachel and the children, who rush them as they get out of the car. Angela goes straight to her father, and the two boys head for Alan and Sharon. Rachel stands at the doorway and smiles at the scene unfolding before her.

Particularly Angela and Lee, who have a very special bond. She is clearly her father's favorite.

During the week, Lee and Rachel, along with their children, entertain Alan and Sharon. They visit historic sites around the San Diego area including Old Town San Diego State Park and the San Diego Zoo, which is famous for its lush, naturalistic habitats and animal encounters and is home to over 3,700 rare and endangered animals.

Balboa Park is on the list with its many museums and a large carousel for the children to ride. After a long and traffic-filled drive to Hollywood, they spend another day seeing its tourist sites. One afternoon is spent at Hotel del Coronado's beach area, followed by lunch at the sundeck restaurant. Later is a quick trip over to the Cabrillo National Monument and the Whale Overlook. While there, the children insist they saw a whale way out in the ocean while the adults looked in vain for the whale.

Late into the week, they all spend the day at Disneyland. Both Alan and Lee reminisce with their wives about the first trip they made to Disneyland when they met Walt Disney. At first, Rachel and Sharon believe the McCormick brothers are just feeding them a line. Their reaction changes late into the afternoon when they meet Ken Jones, a retired Air Force General and lifelong friend of Sean McCormick. He and his wife live in the area and Lee called him earlier asking that they join the family for dinner in the park.

During dinner, Ken tells the story of how he set up a day for Sean and his family to join his family for a day at Disneyland in Anaheim, California. He arranged for Sean's family to meet Walt Disney to celebrate Alan's birthday back in 1955. At that time, he and Sean were stationed together at March Air Force Base in Riverside, California, near Anaheim.

Ken's family owned the land that Mr. Disney purchased to build Disneyland. Both Rachel and Sharon are impressed.

On the last full day of Alan and Sharon's stay, Lee arranges a short visit to the Navy base and a tour of the USS Okinawa for Alan. The Okinawa is a large amphibious assault ship, which carries twenty-five helicopters and a contingent of US Marines when deployed. Lee shares with Alan that he deployed once on the Okinawa for a short cruise and enjoyed the experience.

When they return home later in the day, the boys are waiting to play catch with them. Josh and Bryan are eager to demonstrate their baseball skills and keep both men active outside, playing catch in the fresh air and bright sun. Alan has no sons, but on this day, he feels like he's on *Field of Dreams,* playing catch with his nephews.

Later that evening, when the children are asleep, the adults sit in the courtyard enjoying a lovely evening while drinking wine and sharing conversation.

They have had one bottle of wine and just started a second when Alan offers a quick toast. That is followed by him saying, "Lee, Rachel, we've had a lovely time this week and can't thank you enough for sharing your home with us and taking us to see so many sights. The scenery out here and the weather are just great. I can see why you enjoy being here. I would love to capture and place in a container some of your air and take it home with me."

Lee laughs at that and responds, "Well, you and Sharon need to plan another trip out this way again. We've loved having both of you here. The kids, well, they just adore you."

Sharon also thanks them and expresses her thoughts about the area and its beauty and climate, which are similar to Alan's. As the evening progresses, Lee and Alan move to another area of the courtyard and continue their conversation.

Looking to his brother, Lee says in a serious, almost ominous tone, "Alan, our military is going to have to go back into the Persian Gulf and get involved in more fighting with Iraq. That idiot Saddam is creating another serious situation in the area. I wouldn't be surprised if he attacks one of his neighbors."

"Why do you say that? The news from that area has been somewhat quiet since the Tanker War ended."

"I'm not privy to any inside information or knowledge of pending actions on our part or theirs. I just have an uncomfortable feeling about it." Lee takes a few minutes, then continues in a melancholy tone. "While I was over there during Operation Earnest Will, I was on two different ships when they sustained massive damage. What are the odds of that? I could have been killed, but here I sit. Another deployment over there could be the one that gets me."

Alan, seeing the concern on his brother's face, leans forward and responds. "Let's hope it doesn't come to another deployment. If it does, you'll do fine. As our dad told me on my first and then second deployment to Vietnam: 'Trust your men, take care of your men, train and plan for the worst, and lead your men when you do engage the enemy. If you've done that, the rest is in God's hands.' His advice helped me deal with being 'in the shit' while in Vietnam."

Meanwhile, at the other end of the courtyard, Rachel and Sharon are engaged in conversation. Rachel has been sharing her concerns about Angela's health.

Rachel says in a soft, concerning voice, "Angela is only eight and has been experiencing occasional periods of mild fatigue, for no apparent reason and some joint pain. Occasionally, she has a red, butterfly-shaped rash over her cheeks and nose. When this occurs, she has usually been playing outside and exposed to bright sunlight which may account for the redness."

Sharon asks, "What do the doctors tell you and Lee?"

"We've taken her to a few over the last year. None have expressed concern or see any reason to suspect something is wrong. But I'm concerned. If anything were to happen to Angela, Lee would be devastated."

This hits Sharon hard; she knows the feeling of having lost their own daughter to cystic fibrosis at a very young age. Sharon moves over to Rachel, who has become emotional and tries to comfort her. As she does, she too becomes emotional. Sharon hugs Rachel and whispers in her ear, "We are here for you and Lee."

13
GULF WAR - 1
DESERT SHIELD-CAPTAIN LEE MCCORMICK DEPLOYS

On a beautiful early afternoon in June 1990, Captain McCormick is standing on the upper bridge of the USS Okinawa carrier's island. The island, as it's called, is the control center for the ship and towers above the flight deck. Lee gazes upon his family standing on the San Diego Naval Station pier. On the pier, along with hundreds of other wives and children, is Rachel and their three children, all waving up at Lee. Struggling to control her emotions as tears slowly slide down her face, Rachel discreetly attempts to hide them. Lee, standing erect as part of a small group of senior officers on the bridge, also struggles to keep himself together. By this time in his career, he's mastered the art of hiding his emotions from the other men around him but knows many of them feel the same way.

As is the custom, the ship's company lines up at regular intervals along the weather deck rails and flight deck wearing their full-dress white uniforms, standing at parade rest as their ship is slowly pushed away from the pier. This is a Navy tradition referred to as "manning the rails" and goes back to the early days of naval history. When a Navy warship entered a foreign port, the crew would man the rails to demonstrate that there was no hostile intent on their part. If they were all on deck, they could not man their guns to fire.

The USS Okinawa is heading out to sea on a routine WESTPAC (Western Pacific) six-month deployment to the Indian Ocean. The Okinawa is the command ship of the 13th Marine Expeditionary Unit. The five-ship squadron has equipment and supplies to sustain a 16,500-person force. The primary purpose of forward-deployed naval forces is to project American power from the sea.

Lee serves as the Air Boss on the helicopter carrier USS Okinawa for this deployment. He was reassigned from the Seasnakes to the Okinawa. The Air Boss is an experienced aviator and is responsible for all aspects of operations involving aircraft, including the hangar deck, the flight deck, and airborne aircraft out to five nautical miles from the carrier. Standing on the bridge as the carrier proceeds under its own power and heads out into the Pacific Ocean, Lee watches as the coastline of California disappears over the eastern horizon. He returns to his duty station in the primary flight control or "pri-fly" area of the bridge. From here, the Air Boss, Mini-Air Boss, and their team use an array of computers and communications equipment to keep tabs on everything. They may also obtain information just by looking out their windows a few stories above the flight deck or by walking out onto "vulture's row." This is a balcony platform with a great view of the entire flight deck. For the next seven months, this will be Lee's office.

IRAQ INVADES KUWAIT

On August 2, 1990, Saddam sent his Iraqi army into Kuwait, his neighbor, and commenced a brutal invasion. Iraq invaded with four elite Republican Guard heavy divisions and the equivalent of a fifth, composed of special operations commandos. President George H. W. Bush quickly announced that the United States considered Iraq's aggression unacceptable. On August 7, the president backed up his words with a military response named Operation Desert Shield and organized a coalition of thirty-five nations to defend Saudi Arabia and liberate Kuwait.

At the time of the invasion, the Navy was already on station in the region with two battle groups led by the USS Independence and USS Eisenhower carrier groups. The initial buildup of Navy forces drew upon these forward-deployed assets of the fleet. By August 8, both battle groups were on station and ready, with the USS Eisenhower carrier group in the Red Sea and the USS Independence carrier group in the Gulf of Oman.

The USS Okinawa and its five-ship squadron have joined the Independence battle group and are now part of a massive buildup of naval forces in the area. The United States Navy has been tasked with providing sea control and maritime superiority, which will pave the way for the introduction of American and allied air and ground forces.

TRAINING FOR WAR

The USS Okinawa is carrying twenty-five Marine helicopters and a large contingent of US Marines. Marine Heavy Lift Squadron 461 (HMH-461), the Ironhorses, consisting of several CH-53K King Stallion transport helicopters, is on the Okinawa and commanded by Lieutenant Colonel Barry Phillips. He and Lee are friends and first met at Pensacola, where Lee was one of Barry's instructor pilots in flight school. They last served together during Operation Eagle Claw and hadn't seen much of each other since. They're now serving on the same ship in significant leadership roles. Although it's been several years, they rekindled their friendship.

Training takes center stage as the men on board the Okinawa train and prepare themselves for what is to come. The helicopter and deck crews practice launching and landing procedures. Helicopter crews practice with their Marine units rappelling from their choppers to the deck of the Okinawa. Other helicopter missions include aerial reconnaissance and patrolling around the operational area of the carrier and its squadron ships, which includes day and night flying.

Marine units on the Okinawa perform daily physical exercises and weapons training. Weapons training includes live-fire exercises. Live-fire rounds penetrate targets and continue their trajectory harmlessly out into the open sea.

Helicopter crews are required to look through photo albums full of crash pictures to give them an idea of what they may face. The Gulf of Aman and the Persian Gulf have an overabundance of sharks, as many as twenty-six species, and Persian Gulf sea snakes. These snakes are completely aquatic, live below the water surface, but must periodically surface for oxygen. Their venom is ten times more poisonous than that of the king cobra. If bitten by a sea snake, the venom damages the nervous system and stops blood from clotting properly. It can also cause nausea, vomiting, thickening of the tongue and numbness. On occasion, death is imminent.

MULTINATIONAL MARITIME INTERCEPTS

After diplomatic efforts failed to resolve the situation with Saddam, the United Nations Security Council passed Resolution 665. This authorized multinational naval vessels to begin enforcement of UN sanctions against Iraq. On station in the Persian Gulf, the USS Okinawa and its squadron of ships begin patrolling to stop the flow of oil out of Iraq and prevent the import of war materials into the country.

Within a few days of the interception mission, coalition warships effectively seal off commercial shipping inside the Persian Gulf. Once-crowded Gulf ports are now empty of oil-shipping traffic, and incoming merchants change course to avert confrontation with coalition forces. Going into November, the number of maritime intercepts number several thousand. Boarding teams of US Marines and Navy SEALs are routinely sent in to perform the intercept boardings. With few exceptions, they are non-confrontational, but tensions can always arise, and American forces remain extremely vigilant and alert.

Lee oversees the launching and recoveries of Marine units sent on boarding missions via helicopters from Okinawa. When missions end, and the helicopter crews return, he sits in on their debriefings. He observes firsthand the gradual increase in the strain, frayed nerves, and frustrations of the aircrews from their daily grind of intercepts. They never know how the target ship's crews will react when they are closing in on them for boarding. If they're armed and fire shoulder-held missiles, the helicopter crews and their boarding teams have no time to react. Their mission could well be their last day on earth.

After the latest mission, Barry and Lee are relaxing in the officers' wardroom and Barry shares what happened.

"The ship we were sent out to inspect was attempting to break through the blockade with prohibited cargo. We had two helicopters with Marine boarding parties and a small boat of men approaching the ship. We flew around the ship several times, threatening them with our weapons. We finally forced them to stop so our teams could board. We closed in and hovered over two separate locations on the ship, allowing the Marines to rapel down to the deck. One Marine was hurt when he hit the deck hard. When the remaining men were lowered to the deck, the injured Marine was secured to our host, and we brought him back up. His fellow Marines then went about their assigned tasks."

Barry pauses, then continues. "On board the ship and waiting were about 250 passengers, later identified as peace activists protesting the allied embargo of Iraq. The activists attempted to interfere with our boarding teams by forming a human chain to obstruct their movements. Team members fired warning shots into the air after several protesters grabbed their weapons. The team also had to use non-lethal smoke and noisemaker grenades for crowd control. The teams were able to subdue the activists without incurring any injuries and then proceeded to inspect the ship."

Lee, in a sarcastic and somewhat forceful tone, comments, "Isn't it enough we have to deal with the Iraqis? Now we have peace activists to contend with."

Barry grins, then says, "During their inspection, they located cargo which violated sanctions. The ship's captain was informed that he could not continue to his planned destination. He was told his ship would be escorted by two Navy frigates to Muscat, Oman. He became belligerent, and the atmosphere, which was already tense, became volatile. The Marine commander on the scene stepped in and handled it well. He lowered the hostility growing on the bridge and convinced the captain to comply. We then withdrew our teams from his ship and waited around as he fell in between the two frigates and headed for Oman."

Barry sits back in his chair, reflecting on what he just shared with Lee, and concludes his story. "Lee, this is becoming really intense. I hope it ends soon. These men are working under extremely difficult conditions."

Lee looks at his friend and, with a serious tone, responds. "We are going to move into another phase of this operation soon. It's only escalating. I think we both know where it's headed...war with Iraq."

WAR LOOMS

As Operation Desert Shield continues into December, the planned coalition invasion is moving rapidly forward for a mid-January start date. The USS Okinawa is the command ship of the 13th Marine Expeditionary Unit. The five-ship squadron has been at sea since departing San Diego in June. They are directed to proceed to Dubai for resupply, make any repairs to their ships they can during their short port call, and provide shore leave to the sailors and Marines. They'll be headed back in early January to take up their station in the Persian Gulf for the start of Operation Desert Storm.

With war looming and Lee's squadron making a short port visit to prepare, he reaches out to his brother Alan for a favor. Rachel is flying into Dubai for a visit while they are in port. He asks his brother and Sharon to take care of his children while he and Rachel spend time together. They readily agree and plan for Lee's children to fly to Atlanta and spend seven days with them.

Before departing for Dubai, Rachel takes her children to the San Diego airport and sees them off to Atlanta. Later that evening, she begins her long trip to the Middle East to spend a few days with Lee before he sails back into harm's way.

14
GULF WAR - 2
DESERT STORM

Soldiers, sailors, airmen, and Marines of the United States Central Command, this morning at 0300, we launched Operation DESERT STORM, an offensive campaign that will enforce the United Nation's resolutions that Iraq must cease its rape and pillage of its weaker neighbor and withdraw its forces from Kuwait. My confidence in you is total. Our cause is just! You must be the thunder and lightning of Desert Storm. May God be with you, your loved ones at home, and our Country.

— GENERAL H. NORMAN SCHWARZKOPF, USA COMMANDER IN CHIEF US CENTRAL COMMAND, IN A MESSAGE TO THE COMMAND—JANUARY 16, 1991

BATTLESHIPS

The Navy dispatched two naval battle groups built around the aircraft carriers Eisenhower and Independence to the Middle East region at the beginning of Operation Desert Shield. They now send in the battleships USS Missouri and USS Wisconsin to the region on the eve of Operation Desert Storm. Once on station, the two battleships will alternate positions on the gun line, using their 16-inch guns to destroy enemy targets and soften defenses along the Kuwait coastline and Iraq.

The evening the two battleships sail toward the Kuwait coastline to take up their positions Lee is standing on the "vulture's row" balcony platform. He's enjoying the clear night sky and the breeze created by the ship's movement through the Persian Gulf. Off the Okinawa's port side, at a distance and silhouetted against the horizon, he sees the USS Missouri gliding majestically through the water. It's a beautiful, awesome, and yet troubling sight to behold as this mammoth warship from World War II sails past. The destructive power of the huge shells this ship will rain down on targeted zones will create mass extinction events for anyone caught in them.

On the decks of the USS Missouri, affectionately called "The Mighty Mo," are three massive gun turrets—two in the front and one in the back. Each turret has three 16-inch guns, which are The Mighty Mo's trademark feature. Each gun barrel is sixty-five feet long, weighs 116 tons, and can fire a 2,700-pound shell twenty-three miles in fifty seconds—with pinpoint accuracy. Following at a safe distance behind The Mighty Mo is the USS Wisconsin, the most recently recommissioned battleship. Lee watches them disappear and wonders what it would be like to serve on battleships of that stature and history. He retires to his quarters for a night of rest and letter writing.

LETTERS HOME

Dear Mom and Dad,

Just a few short updates from the Persian Gulf. As you know, Rachel and I enjoyed a brief visit while our squadron was ported in Dubai. I'm sure you can relate to our situation. Our time together was too short, but it was great to be with her. I miss all of you very much and look forward to coming home soon.

I'm prohibited from communicating about anything we're doing over here militarily. However, with all the news that flows from here, you know we are close to starting a war. The amount of military equipment, ships, and personnel I've seen arriving in the Gulf area is staggering. It's an incredible array of military force, probably not seen since WWII. I believe the coalition forces gathered for this operation, can deal with anything Saddam throws at us when the war starts. I know I'm ready, as are the people I'm serving with over here. They are well trained and motivated to do what is necessary to win. Then we can go home.

I want us to become energy independent, so we don't have to find ourselves constantly over here protecting the free flow of Middle Eastern oil. I know there are other reasons for our continued involvement in the region, but many of us believe that oil is at the center of it.

As I first said when we lost Grandmother Marie on January 10, I wish I had been home for both of you. Grandmother was a terrific person, a loving and caring woman. She was ahead of her time in many ways. The world has lost a wonderful lady. Rachel sent me some pictures of the service and the private burial at Arlington National Cemetery where you interned Grandmother with Grandfather Sam. They convey somber scenes, yet a peaceful and comforting atmosphere and presence comes through in the pictures. When I return, I plan on taking my family to Arlington to pay my respects and visit my grandparents, as early as possible.

I need to go for now and write a letter to Rachel and the children. Take care of yourselves and pray for the men and women over here who will soon be going to war. I love you both very much, miss you greatly, and look forward to coming home soon.

Your loving son,
Lee

My dearest Rachel,

It's only been a short time since we were together, but I'm already missing you greatly. The brief time we spent in Dubai was terrific. As always, you looked fantastic, and I enjoyed every minute with you.

I was happy and relieved to learn that you made it home with little difficulty and reconnected with our children. Flying halfway around the world to spend a few days with your husband is beyond the call of duty, but I'm so thankful you came. I love you very much. I received a letter from Alan and Sharon, who said they had a wonderful time with our children. and look forward to their next visit.

It was heartbreaking to learn of the passing of Grandmother Marie. Mom and Dad told me she passed away peacefully in her sleep. Grandmother was a fine woman and always good to me and my brothers. I love her very much and will miss her greatly. Dad will struggle with her loss for some time. He loved his father and mother greatly and has tremendous respect for what they did with their lives. He's always lived his life to emulate theirs and strived to pass his pride in them on to my brothers and me.

I can't say enough about how you stepped up and joined them in their time of need. Having just returned from over here, you had to have been exhausted, yet you immediately went to them and provided comfort. My God, you're incredible!

We will be going to war over here very soon. Of this, I am sure. When we do, I'm going to have to stay totally focused on every aspect of my job and the well-being of the men and women with whom I serve. I tell you this to say: Know that I love you very much, have total confidence in what you do, and know that you can handle whatever comes your way. We may not be able to communicate for a period of time or for long when we do talk until after this situation is resolved. Just realize that's the way it has to be for now. It will end soon, and all this madness will be behind us.

In closing, be strong for our children, support Mom and Dad as best you can, and take care of yourself.

Know that my parents and both brothers are there for you, so lean on them whenever you need to. Don't be shy about it; they want to help and will support you.

I have to go now. Give the children my love and kisses and rest assured we will be together once again, and soon.

Your loving husband,
Lee

OPERATION DESERT STORM COMMENCES

IN THE EARLY morning hours of January 17, 1991, Operation Desert Shield gives way to Operation Desert Storm as the air campaign begins. The war commences when nine AH-64 Apache helicopters from the US Army's 101st Aviation Regiment, accompanied by four Air Force special operations helicopters, flying low and fast, open fire on their ground targets. Their twenty-seven Hellfire missiles destroy Iraqi radar sites, and their 100 Hydra-70 rockets knock out antiaircraft guns trying to defend them. The attack creates a twenty-mile gap in the enemy's air defense network. Through the wide corridor, coalition aircraft and cruise missiles pour into Iraqi airspace unopposed and rain down death and destruction from the sky.

BATTLE FOR QURAH AND UMM AL MARADIM ISLANDS

United States Navy ships move closer to Kuwait and the islands off its coast in the Persian Gulf. They're tasked with taking the islands back from Iraqi forces and securing them. On January 24, 1991, two Navy attack jets sink an enemy minelayer, a minesweeper, and a patrol boat near Qurah Island. A second minesweeper is sunk when it runs into one of its own mines, trying to evade the attacking jets. Navy helicopters are sent to pick up Iraqi survivors. As they pick up survivors, Iraqi troops on Qurah fire at the helicopters, forcing them to fall back. This starts a short battle to retake the Kuwaiti island. When it is over, three Iraqi soldiers lie dead and fifty-one have surrendered. There are no American losses; however, helicopters sent in to rescue the Iraqis sustain combat damage.

It's early morning on January 29, 1991, and the five-ship squadron, led by the USS Okinawa, sails near Umm al Maradim Island. Lee and Barry are in the Air Boss's primary flight control area of the bridge. They had attended a flight briefing for the impending attack on Umm al Maradim. Barry will lead the Marine helicopter unit into the fray.

Lee looks to his friend. "This sounds trite, but I wish I were going with you. I'm not looking for trouble, but we're here, and I'm watching and hearing the action unfold around me and feel like a coach on the sidelines. I want to get in the game…but it's not in my current job description."

Barry responds with a grin. "I'll trade places with you. Just kidding. Take care, and I'll see you later this evening."

Lee says in a serious, matter-of-fact tone, "Best of luck to you and your crews, Barry."

They shake hands as Barry thanks him and heads down to the flight deck to join his aircrews.

The assault Marines are airlifted in by Barry and his men. They attack the 300-by-400-meter island twelve miles off the Kuwaiti coast and come under heavy ground fire. Lee listens to radio traffic between the Marine helicopter crews and ground forces. Their adrenaline is running high, and they're under considerable stress. Although stressed, their radio communication is professional, with short, direct, and specific transmissions.

Barry is heard directing fire missions on targets as needed and leading his aircrews throughout the engagement. After several hours of intense combat, the Marines succeed in liberating the second Kuwait island. Once secured, the Marines destroy Iraqi antiaircraft weapons and artillery stored on the island. They then raise the Kuwaiti flag over the island, which had been used as an early warning post.

Later that day, Navy helicopters are tasked to check on reports there are Iraqis surrendering on a nearby island. Lee, tired of being on the sidelines and wanting to join the fray, requests that his superiors allow him to lead the mission. Permission is given, and he turns over duties to his Mini-Air Boss. He then leads a small detachment of Navy choppers to the suspect island. As they approach, Lee notices in the distance, several Iraqi small boats. For this mission, Lee uses the call sign Ironhorse 25.

"Ironhorse flight, this is Ironhorse 25. Be advised we have several Iraqi small craft near the island. Go hot. Over."

The Ironhorses "Roger" his transmission. The aircrews prepare their weapons to return fire if they come under attack.

Closing in on the island, they face at least twenty small watercraft, who open fire on them. Lee suspects they have been lured into an ambush. He flies at a rapid speed straight at the Iraqi boats. Flying in a V-formation with Lee in the lead spot, his detachment follows. Lee's gunners, along with the other helicopter gunners, open fire on the Iraqi boats and pour a murderous volume of lead into them.

Radio transmissions are sparse as the aircrews go about their deadly work. Several of the boats are hit and smoke billows from them. The merciless pounding they take from helicopter gunners starts fires onboard their boats. Many of the boats are decimated, and several Iraqi bodies float in the water.

Lee transmits. "Ironhorses, this is Ironhorse 25. Break off and pull back. Let's see what we did. Over."

They pull back and compare notes. The tally is four boats sunk and twelve others damaged. The Iraqis stop firing, head for the coastline, and retreat from the area. After they retreat, Lee flies over the small island, doesn't see any signs of life, and leads his detachment back to the USS Okinawa. Lee concludes his first inclination was correct—it was an Iraqi ambush.

BATTLESHIPS JOIN THE FIGHT

On February 3, the USS Missouri sends 2,700-pound shells crashing into an Iraqi command and control bunker near the Saudi border. It is the first time since the Korean War the battleship fires her main battery in combat. From February 5 to 7, The Mighty Mo fires 112 of her 16-inch shells at infantry battalions, a mechanized unit, an artillery battery, and a command bunker. The USS Wisconsin joins the battle and answers her first combat call for gunfire support since March 1952. The battleship sends eleven shells across nineteen miles to destroy an Iraqi artillery battery in southern Kuwait on February 6.

On February 23, both the USS Missouri and USS Wisconsin are directed to bombard the large island of Failaka off the coast of Kuwait as a diversion. The Mighty

Mo goes first and expends her shells. The Wisconsin, still over the horizon and not visible to the Iraqi forces, launches an Unmanned Aerial Vehicle (UAV) Pioneer drone as a spotter for the battleship's big guns.

As the Wisconsin's drone approaches Failaka Island, the drone pilot is instructed to fly the vehicle low over Iraqi positions. They want the Iraqi soldiers to know that they are once again being targeted by a battleship. Iraqi troops on the ground hear the drone's buzzing, and, having seen what the battleship Missouri strike did to their trench line earlier, decide to surrender.

On February 25, Iraqi ground forces launch a pair of Silkworm antiship missiles at the USS Missouri. One of the missiles splashes harmlessly into the sea, and the other is intercepted by Sea Dart missiles fired from the HMS Gloucester, a British destroyer escorting the battleship. Shortly afterward, the battleship's Pioneer drones locate the missile launchers. The Mighty Mo targets the launchers, fires several 16-inch shells, and destroys them.

During this engagement, the Missouri becomes involved in a friendly-fire incident when it fires off chaff (aluminum-coated glass fibers) as a counter measure against incoming radar-guided enemy missiles. The USS Jarrett, a nearby guided missile frigate, fires its Phalanx (referred to as a Sea Wiz) weapons system at the chaff, believing it was incoming enemy missiles. The Sea Wiz is an automated gun-based system to defend warships against incoming threats such as aircraft, small boats, and missiles.

Stray rounds from the Sea Wiz strike the battleship, and one penetrates a bulkhead in an interior passageway of the ship. A sailor is struck in the neck by flying debris from the stray round and screams out in pain as blood flows from his wound. Some of the sailors near him rush to his aid. They lay him on the deck as another sailor takes his shirt off and uses it as a temporary bandage to stop the bleeding. They rush him to the ship's infirmary. He suffers minor injuries and will survive his ordeal.

Although Lee did not witness any of the battleship engagements firsthand, he hears about them through briefings and conversations between sailors. During some of the nightly bombardments by the battleships, Lee could hear their shells being hurled out into the darkness, headed for specific targets and certain death for anyone on the receiving end.

DESERT STORM ENDS

The war ends on February 28, 1991, with the USS Wisconsin's big guns firing their last naval gunfire support mission of the war. The human cost of the war to the United States is 149 soldiers killed in action and 145 non-hostile deaths. An additional 849 military personnel are wounded in combat.

The USS Okinawa and its supporting squadron depart the Persian Gulf region on March 13, 1991, and sail to Naval Station Subic Bay, the Philippines. From there, the five-ship squadron sails home. They have been deployed since June, 1990 and are one of the longest deployed naval units participating in Operation Desert Shield and Desert Storm. Captain Lee McCormick returns in early April 1991 to San Diego Naval Station and his family.

AFTERMATH

During the fighting to expel Iraqi forces from Kuwait, Saddam ordered his forces to set fire to around 700 oil wells under a scorched-earth policy. The retreating Iraqis placed land mines around the wells to prevent coalition forces from extinguishing the burning oil wells. Widespread pollution began almost immediately and continued unabated. Eventually, private contract crews, paid by Kuwait, were hired at a cost of 1.5 billion American dollars to extinguish the fires. However, by that time, the oil well fires had been burning for approximately ten months. The fires started in January and February 1991, and the last one was extinguished by November, having consumed about six million barrels of oil per day over the ten-month period.

Because of the devasting pollution created from many sources during the forty-seven-day war, another legacy of war, similar to Agent Orange, was in the making. It will manifest in the form of what will be called Gulf War Syndrome.

15
WELCOME HOME
NATIONAL VICTORY CELEBRATION

Returning from the Gulf War in April 1991, Captain Lee McCormick and his fellow sailors receive a warm welcome at the San Diego Naval Station from their families, friends, and senior naval officers. The officers and sailors of the USS Okinawa are given leave to spend time with their families, after which they must report back for future assignments. Lee rejoins his family, and as so many times before, they set out to reestablish their lives. Lee remains assigned to the USS Okinawa as one of the senior officers responsible for its refurbishment. Because of the extensive deployment at sea, the ship requires a robust cleanup.

On June 8, 1991, the National Victory Celebration is held in Washington DC to celebrate the conclusion of the Gulf War. Lee and his family sit around their television and watch the parade and festivities that follow. It's the largest American military parade since the end of World War II. Desert Storm troops march in the parade and are joined by a small group of Vietnam veterans. General Norman

Schwarzkopf, Jr., himself a Vietnam combat veteran and commander of Desert Storm forces, leads the parade.

When it is over, Lee looks to Rachel. "I wonder what my brother thinks. He and his fellow Vietnam veterans certainly weren't honored in this fashion."

"No, they weren't. Why don't you call him and find out?"

Later that evening, Lee calls Alan, and they talk over the day's events. Although both believe it may have been a little over the top, given the brevity of the war, they are impressed. Alan appears at peace with the celebration, and loved the fact that Stormin' Norman, the Vietnam combat veteran, was leading the parade and is a national hero. They conclude their conversation with the same question.

How long will this national pride and outpouring of support for the military last? We are a nation that lives for today, and thinks about tomorrow, but tends to have short memories.

16

NAVAL AIR WARFARE CENTER TRAINING
LIFE SEEMS GOOD

In late January 1993, Lee and his family relocate to Orlando, Florida. He is the new program director for the Naval Air Warfare Center Training Systems Division located on the campus of the University of Central Florida. They have no problem selling their beautiful home in San Diego and moving back to the East Coast. After arriving in Orlando, Lee temporarily rents a house until Rachel finds them a new home in a development near the campus.

As program director, Lee is responsible for overseeing the development, testing, evaluation, and acquisition of all aviation training systems for the United States Navy and United States Marine Corps. In this role, he maintains an active schedule while on duty and travels occasionally to meet with vendors. Lee pursues golf and finds it relaxing and a good way to interact with his many clients, both military and civilian. Since this assignment is a desk job, he's not able to fly, and for the first time in his Navy career, he doesn't miss being in the cockpit. His new position allows him to enjoy a normal family life.

Josh, now fourteen, has decided to apply for admission to the United States Naval Academy as soon as he's eligible. He wants to pursue a career as a naval aviator, hopefully flying jets. He often spends time talking to Navy pilots who are friends of his father. Josh is a young man who's found a sense of purpose, is focused, and is driven to succeed.

Bryan, who is now nine, plays in the community Little League baseball program, is one of their right-handed pitchers and is already considered their best power hitter. He loves the game and looks forward to playing in the Little League World Series when he's older.

Angela is now twelve and has become enamored with the law. She is harboring thoughts of going to law school and becoming an attorney for the indigent and less fortunate. She considers herself a female version of Clarence Darrow, remembered as a fierce trial attorney who, in many cases, championed underdog causes.

Angela is still Lee's favorite. Whenever he looks at her, he sees that small baby girl he first held when she was born. They bonded then and there, and their relationship has been strong ever since. Rachel sees in Angela many attributes of Lee, especially his drive, determination and, yes, his stubborn streak. She often says fondly, "They are like two peas in a pod."

Both Rachel and Lee continue to worry about Angela's health. The loss of their niece, Allie, due to cystic fibrosis, haunts them. Angela's issues are not as severe and only center around occasional bouts of fatigue and some joint pain similar to arthritis. Doctors have run routine medical tests, but no discernible culprit has emerged.

Lee's branch of the McCormick family settles into a middle-class suburban family lifestyle. Lee's current position, although very challenging and stressful, suits him well and allows him to participate in his family's activities. It's a good life for him, and he looks forward to the future.

GULF WAR SYNDROME

Over the next two years, Lee begins suffering from occasional muscle aches, joint pain, headaches, fatigue, and insomnia.

Many returning coalition soldiers have been reporting similar issues following the Gulf War. Although combat lasted only forty-three days and the ground war, only 100 hours, the harmful health effects for many who served in the conflict have begun to surface. The cluster of unexplained symptoms which are becoming more prevalent and debilitating to some veterans of the war are collectively being referred to as Gulf War Syndrome (GWS).

There is widespread speculation and disagreement about the causes of GWS. As was the case with Agent Orange, the Veterans Administration is slow to react and respond. They are failing to even acknowledge an evolving body of evidence that Gulf War veterans are suffering from exposure to any number of harmful chemicals unleashed into the environment they lived and fought in during the war. The Gulf War veterans, like their Vietnam brothers, consider the VA's inaction as incomprehensible, disingenuous, and increasingly frustrating for them. Knowing that Saddam had used sarin gas in the past on his own native Kurds, American and coalition forces sought to eliminate the likelihood of sarin being deployed against them. They bombed Iraqi chemical storage and production facilities, resulting in the release of sarin into the atmosphere, thus exposing troops to toxic substances.

This nerve gas, along with other chemicals released from oil well fires set across Kuwait polluted the ground and air which American forces operated in during and after the war. Even Navy personnel operating in the Persian Gulf were exposed to toxins carried in the atmosphere with wind patterns flowing out across the Gulf. We've once again managed to poison our own fighting men and women with chemicals we made.

The irony of it all!

FAMILY REUNION

Lee and Rachel host the McCormick family at their home for the Thanksgiving holidays in November 1995. Sean and Ana drive down two days before Thanksgiving and settle into their room on one side of the house. Alan and Sharon arrive the following day. The family is together. Scott, as always, is away on another assignment overseas and hasn't been heard from in several weeks. His CIA adventures keep him busy, traveling to always secret distant locations.

On Thanksgiving Day, Rachel, Sharon, and Ana, with the assistance of Angela, busy themselves preparing the traditional Thanksgiving meal. Both Josh and Bryan are in the den watching the Macy's Thanksgiving Day Parade in New York. They're looking forward to an afternoon of football games. The McCormick men sit outside near the pool, sipping Irish whiskey and conversing. Their conversation now centers around Lee's health issues.

In a calm voice, Lee describes his symptoms. "Shortly

after returning from the Gulf War, I started to feel occasional muscle aches, some joint pain, fatigue, and at times I have difficulty sleeping. It's frustrating."

Sean, looking at his son with an understanding expression, reacts. "Lee, I've heard from many clients of mine who are Gulf War veterans that they're experiencing similar health issues. I also know VA personnel are dragging their feet again. They just keep kicking the proverbial can down the road."

Lee responds, "Dad, for those of us who served over there and survived, the war continues in our hearts, minds, and souls. There are several Gulf War veterans dealing with post-traumatic stress disorder, and the rate of suicide among them is growing. Many of these veterans are seeking help from the VA for their issues. So far, the VA has been unresponsive."

Lee pauses, sips some more whiskey, looks at his dad and brother and continues. "There are figures being thrown around that over 250,000 Americans who served in Iraq and Kuwait in 1991 were exposed to deadly chemicals to include sarin."

Both Sean and Alan nod their heads in agreement, for they, too, have heard similar comments. The McCormick men take a moment, reflecting on what's been said as Sean refills their glasses. Then, looking serious and pensive, Sean comments.

"The ground war ended in 100 hours, with a small number of casualties compared to what war planners anticipated. Now, questions swirl around the war. Why did we go to war? Where were the weapons of mass destruction? We'll struggle for some time as a nation about what the war meant, what parts of it we should remember, and what parts we should forget."

Alan, looking at Lee, interjects, "As sure as we're sitting here, the national pride generated by the victory parade following the end of the war, will fade as the Gulf War becomes an insignificant footnote. Just like the Vietnam War. But, for those of us who fought and came home, our wars feel as if they ended only yesterday."

Alan mentions that he hired an Atlanta law firm to represent him and challenge the Veterans Administration in regard to his lingering health issues from Agent Orange.

Asked by Lee, "What happened?" Alan responds, "Nothing. We're still battling them."

Alan pauses and with a look of frustration mingled with resolve raises his whiskey glass in a toast. "Welcome to the club, brother."

Sean, looking at his two sons with pride, feels compassion, understanding, and remorse for what they have both endured. As a World War II veteran, he reflects back to what his generation came home to and how they were treated. To this day, they are held in high regard, as they should be, but Sean wonders.

What happened to change the attitudes and perceptions of so many of our countrymen and women over the years since WWII ended?

Their conversation shifts as Alan and Lee share opinions of Saddam. Both believe the United States will go back into Iraq at some future date and finish what President Bush started. Many in the military, for different reasons, believe that we should have finished the job and gone all the way to Baghdad. Sean doesn't weigh in on this but believes it's much more complicated than many in the higher echelon of the military and defense establishment comprehend.

Their conversation ends on a happier note when Lee shares with his father and brother that he's on the list for promotion to Rear Admiral (One Star.) Sean stands up and Alan follows his lead, as he raises his glass in a toast to Lee. As congratulations are being given, Ana walks outside and tells the men to join the family inside for their Thanksgiving dinner.

17
WHAT IS LUPUS?
NAVAL AIR WARFARE CENTER ORLANDO

In the summer of 1996, Lee is promoted to Rear Admiral, which would normally involve a transfer to another assignment commensurate with his Admiral ranking. However, Lee and Rachel want to remain in Orlando until Angela's health issues are identified and resolved. At the advice of local doctors, they are planning a visit to the Johns Hopkins Hospital in Baltimore, Maryland, for a complete workup and evaluation.

Lee makes a compelling case to his commanders that his tenure at the Warfare Center be extended. They are sympathetic to his situation and give him and Rachel time to work with their doctors to diagnose Angela's health issues.

Rear Admiral Lee McCormick continues as commander of the Warfare Center while his family goes about their daily lives. Josh is a junior in high school and has applied to the United States Naval Academy with the goal of becoming a Naval aviator. He has the backing of many senior naval officers and friends of his grandfather. There have been several letters of recommendation sent to the academy supporting Josh. He is a fine young man, athletic, academically sound, and, like his father and grandfather, has leadership potential.

Bryan has taken to baseball in a big way. He is twelve years old, in the seventh grade, plays in the Little League system, and attends summer baseball camps. He's actively being recruited to join his high school baseball team. Bryan is a natural athlete. He's a tall, right-handed pitcher who can throw a fastball in excess of eighty mph and is consistently ranked high in pitching statistics. He can throw sliders and curve balls with ease and controls the pitcher's mound with authority and confidence. He's also a power hitter who can switch-hit at the plate. His future is bright in the world of baseball if he continues to mature and develop. His great-grandfather would be proud of him, for he loved baseball and the Cleveland Indians.

JOHNS HOPKINS HOSPITAL

Finally, progress is made when Angela is sent to Johns Hopkins Hospital in November 1996 for a complete workup and evaluation. Rachel accompanies her while Lee stays home with their two sons.

Within a week of arriving at Johns Hopkins and undergoing extensive testing, Rachel and Angela sit in the office of the lead doctor for her case. Lee has been dialed in and placed on speakerphone. Dr. Lawrence Moore is discussing the results with them as he converses in a soft and caring tone.

"Mrs. McCormick, Admiral McCormick, Angela, based on our testing and analysis of all data collected, we have arrived at a consensus. We believe Angela is suffering from a mild case of lupus. There are many types of lupus, and they all share some common symptoms and similarities. However, each type has its own unique set of symptoms and complications."

He gives them a moment to absorb what he just conveyed and then continues.

"Angela, young lady, you are suffering from 'systemic lupus erythematosus' most commonly called lupus. Lupus induces fatigue and causes inflammation, which can affect your joints and muscles. These are areas where your symptoms have manifested themselves."

Rachel asks, "Why has it taken so long to diagnose what our daughter has been suffering from?"

He responds sympathetically, "Lupus causes are not well understood. Symptoms of lupus vary depending on how the condition manifests itself in the patient. Also, symptoms may come and go. Many other health issues have some of the same symptoms, making it more difficult to diagnose."

Lee interjects with a question. "Dr. Moore, in Angela's case, what do you think caused her lupus?"

He responds, "That's a tough one to answer. Lupus occurs primarily in women between the ages of fifteen and forty-four and can be triggered by exposure to sunlight, medications causing drug-induced lupus, or certain types of infections causing the autoimmune system to become overactive. Another possibility is a genetic link to an overactive immune system...perhaps inherited from a family member."

Rachel asks, "What about Angela? Is her lupus hereditary?"

Dr. Moore takes a moment to ponder his response and

then continues. "From our interviews with your family members, we detected no other cases of this nature in any of their medical histories. We did note, Admiral McCormick, that your brother Alan had a daughter with cystic fibrosis. These two health issues are not directly linked but have some similarities. It is our opinion that your daughter's lupus is not hereditary. Unfortunately, we could not identify any specific cause. That's just the nature of lupus."

Dr. Moore speaks directly to Angela. "Angela, your lupus is treatable with various medications and lifestyle changes. We'll be discussing those with you and your parents and laying out a treatment plan. Do you have any questions for me right now?"

Angela simply says, "Dr. Moore, thank you for helping me. I finally know what I'm living with. I hope you can make my daily life more productive and active. If we can do that, I'll be happy and very appreciative."

That night the McCormick family enjoys their first peaceful night's sleep in a long time.

ADMIRAL LEE MCCORMICK RETIRES

Although Lee enjoys his role as commander of the Warfare Center, he has been pondering retiring from the Navy. His decision is made easier when the Navy alerts him with new orders to relocate back to San Diego Naval Station for another high-level command with sea deployments back in his future. Lee doesn't regret being in the Navy, but upon reflection, realizes he's paid a heavy price. Not being around his family to watch them grow or witness their lives unfold, enjoy their triumphs, and be there in their times of need have all taken an emotional and physical toll on him. The letters, tapes, and occasional videos he received throughout his Navy career, all intended to help him feel as if he were a part of his family's daily lives, did not capture what a lifetime of living in their presence would have.

Looking back on his career and the time he's spent away from his family, the reality of it all sinks in. *That is time he'll never get back. It's history.* If he wants to wake up every morning and be with his family, he needs to find another line of work.

His decision is a tough one to make, but after conferring with Rachel, he informs his superiors it's time for him to retire and pursue other options as a civilian. His retirement from the Navy is reluctantly approved, and he retires on June 1, 1998.

18
"A MESSAGE TO GARCIA"
NAVAL ACADEMY—JOSH MCCORMICK

The McCormick family is very proud of Josh being accepted to the United States Naval Academy at Annapolis, Maryland. Shortly after graduating from high school, Josh reports to the academy for plebe summer at the end of June 1998. Plebe summer is the summer training program required of all incoming freshmen to the Naval Academy. Its purpose is to turn civilians into midshipmen, which is the lowest officer rank in the Navy. The end of plebe summer is marked by the beginning of plebe year, which is just as rigorous, but with the added challenge of academic classes.

After Josh successfully completes his plebe summer and is set to begin his plebe year, Lee feels he should share some words of wisdom that his father shared with him when he went off to college. Lee sits down at his computer and types out an email titled "A Message to Garcia," which reads:

Dear Son,

Now that you're beginning your Navy training and education, I want to share with you excerpts from a letter written to me by my father. I was about your age and starting my college education at the University of West Florida. This was a big crossroads in my life because not only would this be the place where I started my naval flying career, but your mother and I were married there.

Your grandfather titled his letter to me "A Message to Garcia." He drew from "A Message to Garcia," which is a widely distributed essay written by Elbert Hubbard in 1899, expressing the value of individual initiative and conscientiousness in work. The essay's primary example is a dramatized version of a daring escapade performed by an American soldier just before the Spanish-America War. The essay describes the soldier carrying a message from President McKinley to General Calixto Garcia, a leader of the Cuban insurgents, somewhere in the mountains of Cuba. I hope these words help you as much as they did me.

When war broke out between Spain and the United States at the end of the 19th century (1898), it was necessary to quickly communicate with General Garcia, the leader of the Cuban insurgents. Garcia was somewhere in the mountains of Cuba, but the American leaders were not sure exactly where he was. No mail, telegraph, or telephone could reach Garcia. But President McKinley had to secure his cooperation, and quickly.

Someone said to the president that there is a fellow, by the name of Lieutenant Andrew Rowan, who will find Garcia for you if anyone can. Lieutenant Rowan was summoned and given a letter to deliver to Garcia.

How Lieutenant Rowan took the letter, sealed it up in an oilskin pouch, strapped it over his heart, disappeared into the jungle, and in three weeks came out of the other side of Cuba, having traversed a hostile country on foot and delivered his letter to Garcia will not be discussed here.

The point of the story is President McKinley gave Lieutenant Rowan a letter to be delivered to Garcia. The lieutenant took the letter and did not ask: "Why me? Who is Garcia? How do I find him? Is there any hurry? Can I have the rest of the day off? What's in it for me?" He simply accepted the challenge and immediately proceeded to overcome it.

Military commanders, corporate chieftains, managers, and coaches are continually annoyed, delayed, and distracted by the average person's inability or unwillingness to concentrate on a thing and just do it. Excuses, inattention to detail, indifference, and halfhearted efforts seem to be the norm.

The incapacity for independent action, intellectual laziness, this unwillingness to utilize all of our abilities to their maximum potential are the things that separate the real leaders from the average pilots, workers, players, and managers. In every organization, there is a weeding out process going on by supervisors, managers, coaches, and military commanders. This sorting is a continuous process.

I appreciate the man who does his work or trains when the boss or coach is away, as well as when he's present. A person with a goal and the same determination to achieve it as Lieutenant Rowan exhibited in accomplishing his mission is rare today. The world cries out for such individuals. They are needed—this person who can carry "A Message to Garcia."

Ask yourself, "Will I be one of those people?"

Josh, you have what it takes, you come from good stock and your family is behind you. Go out into the world. Pursue your dreams and ambitions. If you get knocked down, get back up. If you make a mistake, learn from it and do better next time.

I'll end with this partial quote from President Theodore Roosevelt.

"It is not the critic who counts; not the man who points out how the strong man stumbles, or where the doer of deeds could have done them better. The credit belongs to the man who is actually in the arena, whose face is marred by dust and sweat and blood; who strives valiantly;...who, at best, knows in the end the triumph of high achievement, and who at the worst, if he fails, at least fails while daring greatly."

Love,
Dad

PART THREE
THE YOUNGEST DESCENDANT
SCOTT MCCORMICK

1
SCOTT, THE DEFIANT ONE

Scott is a natural athlete, makes friends easily, and is a maverick with an independent streak. He's always looking for excitement and that next adrenaline rush. He admires the characters Steve McQueen and Sean Connery portray in the movies. McQueen in *The Great Escape* and *The Magnificent Seven* and Sean Connery as James Bond, the debonair, super sexy British Spy 007, captivate his imagination.

After graduating from high school in June 1970, Scott enrolled with the Selective Service (draft) and received a college student deferment. The Vietnam War is raging, and many young men are being drafted. Scott will have to maintain his grades and remain in college to continue with his student deferment.

Scott began his freshman year in September 1970 at the University of West Florida (UWF) in Pensacola. He finds studying and college coursework to be more difficult than he imagined. He struggles with his courses and is beginning to believe he's not ready for college.

Completing his first quarter at UWF with poor grades, Scott is placed on academic warning. He flies home to be with his family in Omaha, Nebraska, for Christmas. While home, he informs his parents that he's not comfortable at college and believes he's not ready for the challenges or has the dedication it will take for him to obtain a college degree.

His father, Sean, disagrees and encourages him to return to college for another quarter and give it a chance. Scott values his father's advice, and they have several discussions about his future while he is home. Scott shares with his father that he gave it his best effort, but it didn't go well. He was spending more time enjoying college life and the freedom of being on his own than studying. Against his father's wishes, he decides to drop out and not return for the second quarter. His parents are disappointed but respect his right to make his own choices and now worry about his immediate future.

Neither Scott nor his parents have to wait long. He receives his military induction physical notice in mid-January 1971. Scott reports for his physical, passes the exam, and is immediately inducted into the United States Army. He reports to Fort Benning, Georgia, for his basic training, and upon completion, is sent to Fort Polk, Louisiana. At this time in the Vietnam War, men who go to Fort Polk for infantry training inevitably end up in Vietnam.

Alan is serving a second tour in Vietnam, and Lee is training to be a naval aviator. The worst fears of Sean and Ana may well come true. All three of their sons could end up serving in Vietnam.

2
KOREA
THE SECOND KOREAN WAR

The Military Demarcation Line (MDL), sometimes referred to as the Armistice Line, is the land border or demarcation line between North and South Korea. On either side of the line is the Korean Demilitarized Zone (DMZ). Both the MDL and DMZ were established in 1953 as part of the Armistice Agreement that ended three years of brutal fighting between North and South Korea. Stretching across the 155-mile width of the Korean peninsula, the DMZ's approximately two-mile-wide swath of land is bound on both sides by several lines of barbed wire fence and one of the largest concentrations of soldiers and artillery in the world.

Since the DMZ was established, there have been numerous incidents and incursions by both sides, although the North Korean government typically never accepts direct responsibility for any of these incidents. Tensions between the two Koreas from 1966 to 1969 are so high that the period has been labeled the Second Korean War or the DMZ War.

During this period, North Korean commandos attempt

to assassinate Park Chung Hee, president of South Korea, at his residence at the Blue House in Seoul on January 21, 1968. Unit 124, a thirty-one-man commando team from North Korea, infiltrates the DMZ but are intercepted by police near the residence. In the ensuing battle, all but two commandos are killed; one is captured, and one flees back to North Korea. South Korean casualties total twenty-six killed and sixty-six wounded, including twenty-four civilians. Four Americans are also killed. President Park is unharmed.

On January 23, 1968, North Korean patrol boats operating under cover of fighter planes capture the USS Pueblo in international waters, killing one crewman. Before American forces can react to the hostile takeover of the Pueblo, the ship and her remaining crew are taken into the port of Wonsan. Before the crew is released, they are moved twice to prisoner-of-war camps.

On December 23, 1968, the USS Pueblo crew is taken by buses to the Korean Demilitarized Zone, and released. They cross over the "Bridge of No Return." Crew members report upon release that they were starved and regularly tortured while in North Korean custody.

During March 1969, seven American soldiers patrolling along their sector of the DMZ are killed in a North Korean attack. On April 15, 1969, a US Navy reconnaissance aircraft is shot down ninety miles east of the North Korean coastline in international waters. All thirty-one crew members are killed. On August 17, 1969, three US soldiers are wounded and captured when their helicopter is shot down for straying into North Korean airspace. They are released 108 days later when the United States apologized.

During October 1969, North Koreans murder four American soldiers while on patrol in the DMZ. The four soldiers from the 7th Infantry Division are traveling in a truck marked DMZ Police and have a white flag affixed to their truck. They are ambushed by a North Korean patrol with rifle fire and grenades. The North Koreans then approach the truck and shoot each soldier in the head at close range to ensure they are dead.

As 1969 ends, the intensity level of the conflict reduces substantially. Isolated incidents continue to occur particularly along the South Korean-controlled sectors of the DMZ. During the three-year period of the Second Korean War, South Korean forces suffer 299 soldiers killed and 550 wounded. The United States loses seventy-five soldiers, 111 are wounded, and eighty-five are captured and later released. The North Koreans are relentless in their hatred of South Koreans and American forces.

3
COMBAT PATROL

It's early evening in late October 1971 and Corporal Scott McCormick is sitting in the cabin riding shotgun on the second vehicle in a two-vehicle patrol. They are following about fifty yards behind the lead truck on a routine nightly patrol of his unit's sector of the Korean DMZ. Scott is a squad leader in Company B, Second Battalion, part of the Second Infantry Division stationed at Camp Casey, South Korea. The sky is overcast, with a cold, damp breeze flowing through the open windows of their US Army three-quarter-ton truck. In the truck's open bed are the remaining six soldiers in his squad. All are armed with M-14s. Each man is in full combat gear, including a flak jacket, which is a form of body armor.

The two-vehicle patrol has been driving their assigned route along the fence line for several hours. As the sun sets the usual tedium with its accompanying tension has settled in on most of the men.

Patrolling for twelve hours a day for several days in a row and staring into the barbed wire wilderness is a long time for soldiers to stay focused. They can see all kinds of things moving out there. At night especially, soldiers often fire at something that stirs. Even under the strong spotlights illuminating the American sector, branches rustling in the wind look and sound like potential infiltrators.

Private Bill Johnson, who joined the unit two days earlier, is driving the truck while he and Scott make small talk. Bill asks, "Scott, how did you end up here in Korea? Some of the fellows told me you have an interesting story about that."

Scott responds, "Oh, they did? What did they say?"

Bill, in a low-key manner, says, "Basically, that you came down on orders for Nam, but you were placed on hold at Fort Polk. Sometime later, your orders were changed, and you were sent here."

"Bill, that's the short version. It went down something like this. My brother Alan is an infantry captain on his second combat tour in Vietnam. When I was alerted to go to Nam back in May, my parents, particularly my mother, were devastated. When Alan received the news, he contacted the Pentagon and reminded them that two or more family members didn't have to serve in Vietnam at the same time unless they both agreed. He told them they could send me somewhere else or send him home. One McCormick in Vietnam was enough."

Scott pauses, looks at Bill with a grin, and says, "It was a no-brainer, even for the Pentagon. Do you send an experienced infantry captain home and ship over a green draftee? Or do you leave him there and send me somewhere else? They left him in Vietnam and ultimately sent me here. End of story."

Bill laughs, "I'll bet that makes for some fun family conversations."

"It does."

Scott's reply is stopped cold when the lead truck is hit by a heavy volume of machine-gun fire, and several grenade explosions besiege the truck. Bill slams on the brakes as Scott yells for the men to jump out of the truck and take cover. Before he or Bill can exit, a murderous volume of bullets hits their truck. Bill is thrown back in his seat violently as several rounds penetrate his body. Scott reacts instinctively out of self-preservation knowing that Bill is dead. Kicking the door open, throwing his M-14 to the ground, and leaping out of the truck, he crawls over to a ditch near the truck carrying his weapon.

Four of the six soldiers in the back of the truck manage to join him. The other two are cut down by machine-gun fire before reaching the ditch. Scott organizes the remaining men, and they begin returning fire in the direction of incoming tracers. Scott and his four squad members are on their own.

Scott's radio operator is one of the men killed. Without hesitating, Scott crawls out to him, retrieves the radio, and heads back toward the ditch. Bullets and red tracer rounds stream over his head and around him. As they crack by him, a chill runs down his spine. He wonders, *is one of those meant for me?*

Reaching the ditch, he feels a sharp stinging sensation in his left arm. Back in the ditch and safe for the moment, one of his soldiers checks his arm and tells him he took a bullet, and it's bleeding badly.

Scott, in pain, responds, "Wrap the wound in gauze and

tie it tight to stop the bleeding. I'm going to try and reach our company's command post."

In a controlled but frantic voice, he transmits. "Command Post 3, this is Corporal McCormick. We're under attack by North Korean infiltrators at marker 12. Need help. Several KIA's. The lead truck was hit first. We are about fifty yards behind them and under heavy fire. Over."

The officer on duty responds, "Roger, understand. We heard the explosions and firing. Our reactionary force is en route. They should be there in ten mikes (minutes). Over."

Scott responds, "Roger, hurry. Out."

As fast as it started, the attack and ensuing firefight is over. The area returns to an eerie quiet. All that is heard is the wind blowing across the open expanse of the DMZ dead zone on the other side of the wire.

With his arm throbbing, Scott struggles to his feet and checks on his men. They are unscathed but shaken to the core. They're all draftees who have been in the country less than a month, and this was their first time under fire. Scott has been here three months and experienced two previous encounters. Neither of them was this intense or resulted in casualties.

He organizes his squad and leads them forward with their weapons, ready to check on the first truck. Approaching with caution, they find all eight Americans still in the truck and dead. They have been shot multiple times and are almost unrecognizable.

There is nothing they can do for them as Scott and his remaining squad take cover in another ditch and wait for their relief force to arrive. Scott's been functioning on an overdose of adrenaline. As his breathing and heart rate slow, almost reaching normal, he collapses from exhaustion.

The next day he awakens from a long sleep and finds himself in the hospital unit at Camp Casey. His left arm is wrapped in heavy bandages from his shoulder to below the elbow. His arm rests in a sling suspended from a pole next to his bed. As he slowly regains consciousness and an awareness of his surroundings, his arm begins to throb, and he calls for a nurse. A nurse walks over and welcomes him back to the land of the living. She calls for his doctor while administering morphine to the drip bag hanging from the pole. Almost immediately, his pain disappears as a doctor approaches.

"Corporal McCormick, I'm Captain Jones, your attending physician. Good to see you back with us."

Scott responds, "Thank you, sir. What can you tell me about my wound? Will I fully recover?"

Captain Jones pulls up a chair next to Scott and tells him that he sustained a bullet wound to his upper arm, and there is some muscle and bone damage. They've stabilized him, and he'll be medevacked to the US Army hospital in Seoul for further treatment and rehabilitation the next day. His wound is serious, and it will take some time for him to recover. However, he'll make a full recovery and should be able to rejoin his unit later.

That evening, with the aid of his nurse, Scott dictates a short letter to his parents to let them know he's fine. The nurse tells him the military had already reached out to his father, informing him of the incident.

After lights out in Scott's hospital ward, he lies there staring up at the ceiling, reflecting on his time in Korea and the firefight that nearly killed him. He recalls being told that he was lucky to be reassigned to Korea.

American soldiers in South Korea serve thirteen months,

which is one month longer than those assigned to Vietnam. Men on duty facing the North Koreans draw the same additional monthly combat pay given to those in the Vietnam war zone. Scott now realizes why.

It may not be Vietnam, but you can still get killed in Korea.

4
ASSIGNED TO CAMP KITTY HAWK

As the most forward-deployed unit in Korea, Camp Kitty Hawk has suffered several American casualties in action against North Korean soldiers in and around Panmunjom since the signing of the Armistice Agreement. More recently, on August 29, 1967, a North Korean commando force attacked Camp Kitty Hawk, killing two soldiers and wounding twenty-four others. On April 14, 1968, they struck again and ambushed a resupply truck en route from Camp Kitty Hawk, killing four soldiers and wounding two more. Sporadic incidents continue, and American soldiers must remain ever vigilant.

After Scott recovers from his wound, he is promoted to sergeant, awarded a Bronze Star and Purple Heart for his actions the night of the ambush, and is assigned to Camp Kitty Hawk in late December 1971. Since arriving in camp, he's pulled his share of guard duty within the Joint Security Area (JSA), where a number of buildings for joint meetings referred to as conference rooms are located. The MDL goes through conference rooms and down the middle of conference tables where North Koreans and the United Nations Command (primarily South Koreans and Americans) meet face-to-face. The MDL is painted on the floors and tables to depict the boundary between North and South Korea.

Pulling guard duty is not one of Scott's favorite assignments. American troops sometimes find themselves nose-to-nose with their North Korean counterparts while on patrol in the conference rooms area. These encounters can become very tense and require level heads to prevail. Recently, Scott had a North Korean soldier unholster his pistol, bring it up a few inches, and look at him straight in the face. He was about a foot away. Scott stood his ground, and the North Korean eventually walked away. If Scott had put his hand on his gun holster, North Korea would use the image for propaganda, saying that America is threatening North Korea. No American soldier stationed at Camp Kitty Hawk wants to be responsible for starting another Korean War or possibly World War III.

Scott has been so busy with his duties the first month at Camp Kitty Hawk, he's not had a chance to write his parents. He's received several letters from them and knows they worry. Compelled to correspond with them, he takes some time, and composes his first letter since arriving.

January 30, 1972

Dear Mom and Dad,

First, I need to apologize for not writing sooner. Since reporting to Camp Kitty Hawk late last month, I've been pulling twelve-hour-duty shifts and training constantly. The pace can be very hectic, and the constant fear of infiltrators and physical confrontation with our North Korean counterparts keeps me on edge. They tell me I will grow used to it and be able to deal with the stress and uncertainty, but I have my doubts.

Since my last letter to you after being released from the Army hospital in Seoul, I'm happy to report that my wound has healed, and I'm doing fine.

I'll give you an idea of my current duty station and our routines. Camp Kitty Hawk is a small collection of buildings surrounded by triple coils of razor wire just 440 yards south of the DMZ. It is often described as looking like a Boy Scout camp with minefields and soldiers.

There is a base exchange with limited merchandise. We have a barber shop, laundry, mess hall, and living quarters. Our existence at this camp is spartan by any standards. We do have a small par three one-hole golf course. The hole is made of green AstroTurf and is surrounded on three sides by minefields. Sports Illustrated calls it "the most dangerous hole in golf," and supposedly, at least one shot detonated a land mine.

When we are on standby, our time is spent training. The camp has its own shoot-house, which is a live ammunition small arms shooting range where we can train for close contact engagements in tight spaces such as the conference rooms we guard. We also train at ranges outside the camp, including one that has a mock-up of the Joint Security Area we're tasked with patrolling.

Our training time is mostly spent on infantry

tactics and personal security techniques, such as hand-to-hand combat. We want to handle any situations that occur between us and our North Korean counterparts. Unfortunately, these guys always seem to be trying to create an incident. We, the Americans, are constantly reminded to temper our reactions and control the situation. Easier said than done. Over the years, there have been many confrontations around here, resulting in American soldiers being harmed.

Working here is like being on a school playground where all the bullies are trying to start something, and you're ordered to just take it. If the North Koreans do start something, we always seem to be on the short end of the stick, so to speak. The North Koreans train to create situations, which can quickly escalate into an incident.

There are constant ongoing propaganda campaigns between the North and South Koreans. Both sides broadcast audio propaganda across the DMZ. Massive loudspeakers mounted on several of the buildings here broadcast North Korean propaganda directed toward the South Koreans.

Both sides launch balloons targeted at the DMZ and beyond. Many North Korean leaflets provide instructions and maps to help targeted South Korean soldiers in defecting. In addition to using balloons as a means of delivery, North Korea is suspected of using rockets to send leaflets into the DMZ.

Dad, you flew in the Korean War, which ended in an Armistice. Now it seems that all the North Koreans want to do is start another war. I wonder if the Korean people, both north and south, will ever be able to come together and form a peaceful and united country. I hope someday they can, but seriously doubt they will.

Well, I've rambled on long enough. Rest assured, I'm doing well and look forward to coming home at the end of August when my thirteen-month tour over here ends. I love you both very much. Please give my best to Alan and Lee when you see them again.

Love,
Scott

ANOTHER INCIDENT

With only three weeks to go on his tour before he rotates home at the end of August 1972, Scott is assigned to patrol the conference room area within the JSA. The day starts out as any other, with breakfast, followed by drawing weapons and a briefing before going on patrol. Tensions within the camp have increased over the last few weeks as North Korean guards have become more aggressive and unpredictable. As a result, more American soldiers are added to the guard patrols and armed platoons are maintained on close standby.

Sergeant McCormick is assigned a squad of ten men to patrol one small area near the conference rooms. He has his men patrol in teams of two, but close enough to each other to assist their fellow soldiers if attacked. His squad has been on duty several hours, the environment is tense, and he and his men feel that something is about to go down. The number of North Korean guards roaming around the area has slowly increased to the point where the Americans are heavily outnumbered. Seeing this, Scott alerts his commanding officer and recommends they send in a reserve platoon ASAP.

As he does, four North Korean guards attack two of his men with clubs. Scott leads his other squad members to their defense, and a brawl breaks out. The four guards retreat back to their side, the north side, of the MDL and out of sight. Just as Scott and his men regroup and check each other over for wounds, more than thirty North Korean guards return. They are armed with clubs, rocks, and shovels and attack Scott and his squad.

Outnumbered three to one, they fight desperately, hoping the reserve platoon arrives quickly. Scott is wielding his club with ferocious force, knocking two North Koreans to the ground, where they lie motionless. He then hears one of his men screaming.

"Sergeant McCormick! Help! They're trying to kill me."

Scott looks over and sees Danny being dragged by three North Koreans across the DML and behind one of the conference rooms. Scott yells, "I'm coming, Danny! Hold on."

Scott grabs two of his men and runs over to help Danny. As they do, the reserve platoon of Americans rushes in and joins the fray. They rapidly isolate and disable the North Korean guards on their side of the DML and gather them up.

Rounding the corner to the building, Scott and his two men come upon a horrific scene. Danny is being beaten over the head repeatedly by the North Koreans using their shovels as a weapon. Scott doesn't hesitate. He charges into them, swinging his club with malice, knocking two to the ground where they lie, moaning. The third North Korean attempts to hit Scott with his shovel. Scott's two men step between them, club the North Korean to the ground, and continue to beat him. Scott has to pull them off. They then pick up Danny's motionless body and quickly head back to their side of the DML.

Almost as fast as the melee started, it ends when two North Korean guards armed with AK-47s emerge from their guard posts on the north side of the DML. Simultaneously, several Americans armed with M-14s, emerge from their guard posts on the south side of the DML. Senior officers from both sides quickly arrive to defuse the situation. With the incident over, Scott sees to his men. Five have suffered minor injuries, and Danny is in serious condition. He is immediately medevacked to Camp Casey for medical attention. It does not look good.

Scott and his men are praised for the way they conducted themselves during the North Korean incident. With the exception of Danny, all the men quickly recover from their ordeal. Danny is moved to the Army hospital in Seoul and will eventually be sent home, where he's expected to make a slow recovery. United Nations personnel file formal complaints against the North Korean guards and their officers surrounding the incident. However, like every preceding incident, they just ignore them and insist they were the aggrieved party.

Scott is scheduled to return home on September 1, 1972. Unfortunately, he is not able to accelerate his departure date for early August and will miss Lee's Naval Wing ceremony in Pensacola, Florida. His middle brother will become a naval aviator and part of their helicopter community. Scott is proud of him and would very much like to be there with his family to witness the ceremony. But it is not to be. He must complete his full thirteen-month tour in Korea before he rotates back to the States.

5
COLLEGE, ALLIE, AND THE CIA
UNIVERSITY OF FLORIDA

After returning home and taking a few months to unwind and chart his future course, Scott enrolls in the University of Florida in January 1974. Having tasted foreign travel on a small scale, he's leaning toward pursuing a career that affords him opportunities to travel the world and live life on the edge.

During the fall quarter of his junior year, Scott commits to pursuing a degree in accounting with a concentration in international business. He's proven himself ready for college, does very well in his studies, and is a quick learner with the ability to retain whatever he reads. He plans on graduating in December 1977.

Having settled on his degree programs, Scott begins interviewing with various companies and United States governmental agencies, including the CIA. They present him with a career path with opportunities to travel internationally and engage in challenging endeavors. They gloss over the stress, danger, and potential life-threatening assignments that are part of the job. Scott knows they come with the job, but in his youth, finds them appealing.

While attending an off-campus keg party, Scott meets Stephanie Young, a senior who will graduate in June 1977. The chemistry between them is spontaneous, and they're immediately drawn to each other. She is an attractive, athletic brunette who's planning a career with the CIA. They become passionately involved in a sexually driven relationship, which neither surmises will lead to any long-term commitments. They're both too adventuresome and seek youthful lives full of action tinged with danger. A loving and close relationship is not in their DNA.

VISITING ALAN AND HIS FAMILY

Finishing his junior year, Scott travels to visit his brother Alan as a show of support for him and Sharon. They're struggling with the serious deterioration of their daughter's health. Stephanie accompanies him as they arrive on Saturday, December 11, 1976, for a three-day visit. It's midafternoon when they pull into the driveway of Alan's home in Decatur, Georgia. The weather is cold, damp, and overcast.

Alan greets his brother and Stephanie as they exit Scott's 1966 Ford Mustang GT Fastback. Looking at the car, Alan comments to Scott, "Great car. What have you done to it?"

Scott replies in a quizzical tone. "What do you mean, Brother?"

"Looks like it could use a little TLC, don't you think?"

Laughing, Scott says, "You know me; I'm just not good at taking care of stuff. I just use it." They both laugh, shake hands, then hug.

"It's really great to see you, Scott. Both Sharon and I appreciate you visiting."

With that said, Alan walks over to Stephanie, gives her a light hug, and says, "Thanks for coming. It's great to finally meet you."

She responds, "Thank you, and you too. I wish it were under different circumstances." Alan nods his understanding, offers to help with their bags, then guides them inside and out of the weather. Entering the house, Allie runs to her uncle. Scott picks her up, gives her a big hug, and says, "How is my favorite girl?"

Allie is frail, weak, and has a raspy voice as she responds. "I'm okay. I can't wait for Christmas and Santa to come."

Scott smiles, "I'll bet you can't. I can't either."

He places her feet back on the floor and has Stephanie give Allie the wrapped gifts they brought for her. Allie smiles, takes them, and walks over to the Christmas tree, placing them underneath. Scott, remembering what it was like at that age waiting for Christmas morning to open presents, looks over at his brother and whispers to him.

"Is it okay for her to open them now?"

Alan nods his approval, and Scott, looking down on Allie, says to her, "Go ahead, young lady, and open them. I'm sure there'll be many more presents under the tree come Christmas morning."

With a look of pure delight, she sits down and tears into the gifts.

Sharon approaches Scott and Stephanie and gives them both a big hug. She thanks them for the gifts and the joy they gave her daughter. Scott senses her appreciation but feels her pain. He wishes there was more he could do to help but knows Allie's future is in God's hands, not mortal man's.

Over the next few days, they all enjoy each other's company. Sharon, Stephanie, and Allie make cookies, go shopping, and enjoy coffee and hot chocolate at Sharon's favorite coffee shop. Scott shares with Alan some of his experiences in Korea and gives him an update on college life. Alan shares his frustrations with the VA, Agent Orange, and the slow start to his banking career.

LAST DAY OF VISIT-CIA DISCUSSIONS

Alan is able to take Monday off so he can enjoy his brother's company. He's curious about Scott's CIA ambitions and the relationship with Stephanie. On Monday, he and Scott visit a local pub, have a few beers, and engage in conversation.

"You know me, Alan. I like adventure, sometimes living on the edge, and traveling. I'm rather a free spirit, born to travel and seek adrenaline rushes. The CIA will offer me opportunities to do that."

Alan responds, "Just what are they looking for and what are the qualifications you need to be considered? I'm not familiar with that aspect of the organization. I can tell you I was around some CIA operatives while in Vietnam. They're definitely a rare breed. Some of the men I came across who professed to be CIA impressed me with their abilities and absolute fearlessness. Their Black Ops guys were men I would not like to have as an enemy."

With that said Scott tells Alan that the CIA is a massive US government agency whose basic objectives are to collect foreign intelligence, provide objective analysis, and conduct covert action as directed by the president. If tasked to perform covert acts, the CIA attempts to carry them out.

Some previous covert operations were considered

successful, such as the Phoenix Program in Vietnam. This program has been heavily criticized on various grounds, including the number of neutral civilians killed, the nature of targeted assassinations of suspected Viet Cong, and the use of torture to extract information. Nevertheless, the program was considered successful at suppressing the Viet Cong's political and revolutionary activities. Other covert acts were not successful, such as The Bay of Pigs. Both brothers are familiar with this failed attempt to overthrow Fidel Castro, as they lived at Homestead Air Force Base during that tumultuous time.

Scott sits back in his chair, finishes the draft beer he's been nursing, and concludes his summary. "Alan, it's the CIA's Clandestine Service that I'm interested in. They're the unit responsible for covert operations."

Alan leans forward, looks closely at his brother, and says, "You're serious, aren't you?"

Scott simply replies, "Yes! Yes, I am. I've already begun the application process. Which, I might add, is very comprehensive and lengthy."

"When are you planning on telling our parents?"

"I'm waiting to see if I get accepted then I'll make another trip home and tell them."

Both brothers sit back and share a quiet moment together. Alan breaks the silence with, "So tell me about Stephanie. Where did you meet her? Is it serious? What is she planning to do after graduation?"

In a more upbeat and lighter tone, Scott responds. "We met in October at a keg party before the Florida Gators homecoming football game. We were drawn to each other and have enjoyed our time together ever since. We have much in common, to include the CIA."

Alan interjects, "The CIA! In what way?"

"She has been accepted to the CIA and will begin her training in August of next year. She'll be trained as an analyst."

Alan, with some concern, says, "Sounds interesting. How dangerous is it? Does she have to go out into the field as a covert operative?"

Scott says in a straightforward tone, "It can be dangerous depending on the situation…and yes, she may have to go into the field on covert operations. Again, it depends on the issues at hand."

Closing out their conversation before returning to Alan's house, Alan jokingly asks, "What do you call yourselves in the CIA? Secret agents, agents, special agents, spies, CIA spooks, or secret agent men?"

Somewhat laughing, Scott replies. "That's just in the movies. The CIA uses the terms operations officers or case officers, or officer, for short."

ALLIE-MARCH 30, 1977

Scott and Alan maintain regular communication with each other as Allie's health rapidly deteriorates and she slips into a coma. On Friday, March 25, 1977, Allie succumbs to the deadly disease of cystic fibrosis,, which she's lived with since birth. At the news of her death, Scott rushes to his brother's side. Stephanie is out of town dealing with an emergency in her own family and cannot join him.

6

CENTRAL INTELLIGENCE AGENCY TRAINING

REPORTING TO CIA

After graduating in December 1977, Scott reports to CIA headquarters in Arlington, Virginia during the second week of January 1978 to begin his training. His first course of action after reporting is to spend time with Stephanie, then find a place to stay. Stephanie graduated in June 1977 and began her training in August. She has an apartment near Arlington. When Scott contacts Stephanie, she insists he share her apartment while he's in this phase of training. The majority of CIA basic training is held at office buildings in the urban areas of Arlington. Scott agrees and moves in with his limited possessions. They rekindle their relationship, keeping it secret and quiet.

Scott's training will prepare him to become a paramilitary operations officer for the CIA. In this capacity, he'll use his CIA training and military experience to conduct air, ground, and maritime paramilitary operations. When fully trained, Scott will spend most of his career on numerous short-term deployments or multi-year assignments in a variety of overseas locations. This scenario is right down his alley.

Stephanie's training schedule keeps her in the Arlington area where she will be initially stationed as an analyst after completing her training. The CIA runs at least two operations training facilities. One is known as The Farm at Camp Peary, Virginia. The other is known as The Point at Harvey Point, North Carolina. After completing basic training in Arlington, Scott is going to The Farm, where he'll undergo extensive training for at least six months. Nestled in a secluded area of Virginia, The Farm encompasses a sprawling campus of numerous buildings and training facilities. The exact location remains undisclosed for security reasons, further adding to the mystique surrounding the institution.

STEPHANIE'S REQUEST

While living with Stephanie, they both enjoyed romantic evenings and outings together when time permitted. Their relationship, from the first encounter, was and still remains, one of convenience and sexual gratification. They both realize, as they move forward with their CIA careers, that remaining single and uncommitted is in both their best interests.

On Scott's last day in Arlington, he and Stephanie go out to dinner and later to a local disco club for some dancing. Returning to her apartment, they share a bottle of wine while enjoying the view from the balcony overlooking the Potomac River in the distance.

Stephanie shares with Scott that she had a wonderful evening and will miss him. She tells Scott she cares for him deeply and hopes they work together on future assignments. She wants to stay in touch as they progress in their careers. Scott conveys similar feelings about her and is reluctant to share that he's falling in love with her. This feeling has slowly evolved since living and socializing with her over the last few months. She is beautiful, talented, confident, and career-driven. He senses she'll go far in whatever field or organization she chooses. However, he is more of an adrenaline junkie who lives for adventure. This is not a good recipe for long-term commitments, or for that matter, a long lifespan. For these reasons, he chooses to maintain the status quo with Stephanie.

Retiring to her bedroom, they enjoy a long night of satisfying their sexual desires. The next morning as Scott prepares to leave for The Farm, Stephanie pulls him close and asks him to write her, saying she'll do the same. She hopes they'll reconnect sometime in the future. He feels the same and shares his feelings with her. They tightly embrace and kiss passionately as Stephanie slowly pulls back from him. They separate, and Scott slides into the front seat of his Mustang GT, starts the engine, and drives out of the parking area as Stephanie waves goodbye to him. Scott watches in his rearview mirror as she slowly disappears from view. Tears form at the corner of his eyes.

CIA'S CLANDESTINE SERVICE TRAINING

On Scott's first day at The Farm, he and his fellow recruits are presented with what they can expect while there. The last session of his first day ends with an experienced CIA Clandestine Service Officer leaving the recruits with the following to consider.

"CIA Clandestine Service Officers are responsible for covert paramilitary operations. As such, you'll find yourselves serving anywhere in the world. Your services are required when the United States government does not want to be associated with the collection of intelligence in hostile or denied areas. You will not carry any objects or clothing that could associate you with the United States when assigned covert missions. If compromised during a mission, the government of the United States may well deny your status and all knowledge of your mission. In essence, you are on your own! If anyone wishes to drop out, now is the time! Sleep on it."

Scott retires that evening to his room, and while lying awake in bed, he asks himself. "What have I gotten myself into?" He awakens the next morning and, after a restless night of pondering the question, commits to a life of danger.

He begins his CIA training to become a clandestine service officer. Over the ensuing months, he learns about explosives, booby traps, escape and evasion techniques, survival training, and interrogation techniques. He's subjected to mock interrogations designed to familiarize him with what to expect if taken prisoner. Waterboarding, sleep deprivation, constant harassment, and threats of torture are all thrown at him during these sessions. He's taught there is no room for error, no detail too small, or precaution too minimal when dealing with life-and-death situations.

As Scott and his fellow recruits close in on the completion of their training, the experienced CIA Clandestine Service Officer they met at the beginning of their training shares some words of wisdom.

"It will probably take each of you several years into your

careers with the CIA to fully understand and appreciate all the tools, training, and knowledge you learned while here at The Farm."

He pauses, looks out over the room at each recruit, then, in a serious tone, continues. "Having spent many years in the field and living in the psychology gray zone, walking a tightrope between loyalty and betrayal, I can assure you, every person here will face situations on their missions requiring choices. What is the right thing to do? What is right? I leave you with the following."

He pauses again, looks pensive, and continues in a slow and deliberate tone. "Being able to wade through that grayness is probably one of the key things to take away with you when you leave here and begin your careers. There's never a right answer. The answer is, and it is used every day here at The Farm, every operations officer knows this phrase."

He stops, takes his time, and says, "The phrase is—it depends!"

Scott's not sure what to make of this phrase and commits to himself that he'll do what he believes to be right, learn from his mistakes, and press on. Scott begins his CIA career with the phrase "it depends" lingering in the back of his mind.

What happens to me if what I believe to be right at the time and what others not present or involved in the action deem to be right after the fact do not agree?

7
OPERATION CYCLONE
SOVIET-AFGHANISTAN WAR

The Afghan War was launched with the overthrow of the centrist government of Afghanistan in April of 1978, by Nur Muhammad Taraki, a revolutionary communist politician. The Democratic Republic of Afghanistan was formed, and power was shared between the various factions within the country at that time. They forged ties with the Soviet Union, purged domestic opposition, and began a series of social and land reforms. Mass executions and political oppression unprecedented in Afghan history soon followed. These actions ignited a revolt by Afghanistan's anti-communist population.

Widespread opposition to the government spread quickly and caused insurgencies to form among various tribal and urban groups. They would come to be known as the Mujahideen. This resistance, coupled with internal fighting among the communist government factions, contributed to the Soviet Union's decision to invade Afghanistan in December of 1979. The Russians sent in massive numbers of troops and installed a client state with a new leader, Babrak Karmal. This invasion inflamed the Mujahideen, and their rebellion accelerated across the country.

Earlier in 1979, Pakistan intelligence officials privately lobbied the United States and its allies to send resources to Afghanistan's anti-communist insurgents. The United States viewed the conflict in Afghanistan as another Cold War struggle and responded to their request. They established Operation Cyclone. This was the code name for the CIA covert program to arm and finance the Mujahideen in Afghanistan.

PAKISTAN

Scott was assigned to his Pakistan CIA post in early April 1979 and works under the guidance of two more experienced covert officers. This is his first post after completing training. All three men are single and live in temporary quarters near the American Embassy in Islamabad. Scott finds both men, who go by their first names, Jim and George, to be amiable and more than willing to share their knowledge and experiences with him. They have been with the CIA for several years.

Jim, George, and Scott are operating under what is known as "official cover," which means they are posing as employees of another government agency. In this assignment, they are diplomats with the State Department on temporary assignment to Islamabad. The State Department allows hundreds of its positions in embassies around the world to be occupied by CIA officers representing themselves as diplomats.

Upon his arrival, Scott was assigned to work with Jim and George on Operation Cyclone. Up to now, all they know is they've been given an important assignment to meet with Afghan rebel leaders through Pakistani government contacts. President Jimmy Carter authorized a collaboration between the CIA and Pakistan's Inter-Services Intelligence (ISI), Pakistan's powerful intelligence agency, and through the ISI, the CIA will begin providing non-lethal assistance to the Mujahideen.

Scott arrives at his office in the American embassy early and begins his normal routine of checking security alerts. It's April 30, and he's anxious to get started on their assignment. His routine is interrupted when George walks over to his cubicle and, in a low voice, says, "Scott, come with me."

Scott follows him without conversation as they walk down two flights of stairs and through a maze of hallways. They eventually arrive at an unmarked door. Entering, Scott finds Jim and two other men whom he has not met sitting at a small conference table. Jim motions for George and Scott to take a seat. Jim doesn't introduce the two men by name but says, "These men just came in from DC and will brief us on our mission assignment for the coming months."

Both men are slender in build, look unimpressive in nature, and could pass for a couple of tourists visiting the embassy. If it weren't for their dark suits, ties, and close-cut hair, you would not guess they were CIA officers. The older man looks over at them and begins. He speaks in a low, professional tone.

"Gentlemen, your mission has a simple goal: meet with Afghan rebel leaders favored by Pakistan's leaders, then set up and coordinate the delivery of non-military assistance to the Mujahideen. Over time, they will become our allies in an effort to combat the spread of communism in Afghanistan."

He stops, reaches into his briefcase on the table, pulls out three file folders, and slides one over to Jim, George, and then Scott.

He continues. "Everything you need to know at this point to make it happen is summarized for each of you in the documents contained in these folders."

He waits until all three men pick up their respective folders and begin thumbing through them. He gives them a few minutes to look over the contents and then directs their attention back to him.

"Take the rest of the morning to review this information, discuss it between yourselves, and begin planning a course of action. Later today, you're scheduled to meet with representatives from Pakistan's ISI."

He leans forward in his chair and gazes intently at all three men. He closes their meeting in a calm, authoritative tone.

"Gentlemen, that was easy to say. Now for the hard part...make it happen!"

With that said, the two men stand up, bid them farewell and good luck, and exit the room. There's dead silence in the room as Jim, George, and Scott, still sitting, look at each other, wondering what is next.

After spending the morning reviewing and studying the contents of their folders, they have lunch together and, later in the afternoon, meet with two ISI men in the same room. They're provided with detailed plans for meeting Afghan rebel leaders of various small groups over the next several months at safe houses in and around the city of Torkham, a Pakistani town in Khyber District. This is the location of the

Torkham Border Crossing with Afghanistan just to the west of the Khyber Pass. The Khyber Pass is a historic mountain pass that links Pakistan and Afghanistan.

They'll be accompanied by members of the ISI on each trip and flown from Islamabad to Bacha Khan International Airport in Peshawar. From there, they'll be driven in unmarked escort vehicles to Torkham for their meetings. Each meeting will be set up by ISI on short notice for safety purposes and will require only one to two days for travel and discussions with the leaders they'll meet.

Their first meeting takes place in late May 1979 and is followed by others in June and July. Each meeting is meticulously planned and results in establishing the necessary coordination for the deliverance of CIA assistance.

Much to the delight of Jim, George, and Scott, their encounters with the Afghan rebels are cordial and non-threatening. They are not without stress, however. Each man must remain vigilant, alert, and constantly aware of their surroundings. After every mission, Scott is physically and emotionally drained. Following their return to the embassy, Scott looks forward to a few days of rest without worrying about whether or not he'll be taken prisoner or murdered.

As the Soviet Union becomes more involved in Afghanistan, the CIA begins considering other options for assistance beginning in October 1979. These options include direct provisions of combat arms from the United States to the Mujahideen through the ISI.

Jim and George, working with the ISI, are setting up a meeting with Gulbuddin Hekmatyar, an Afghan Mujahideen with a growing following. He had spent time in Pakistan and returned to Afghanistan as war with the Soviets grew closer.

They're meeting with him in mid-November. The CIA plans to fund his rapidly growing Hezb-e Islami organization through the Pakistani ISI. It is believed that Gulbuddin Hekmatyar's Afghan rebels will eventually become one of the largest of the Afghan Mujahideen.

Among Hekmatyar's friends and contacts is Osama bin Laden, who was born in Riyadh, Saudi Arabia, to an aristocratic family with close ties to the Saudi royal family. He had been studying at local universities until late 1979, when he traveled to Pakistan. Using money from his own construction company, bin Laden helps establish an operation to recruit and assist Afghan Arab volunteers to fight in Afghanistan. These are Arabs and other Muslims who are drawn to Afghanistan to help their fellow Muslims fight the Soviets and pro-Soviet Afghans. Despite being called Afghan, they are not from Afghanistan nor legally citizens of Afghanistan.

SCOTT RETURNS HOME FOR THE PATRIARCH'S FUNERAL

On the morning of November 11, 1979, as the hour approached 11:00 a.m., Scott's grandfather, Sam McCormick, passed away peacefully in his sleep. Within twenty-four hours after being told about his grandfather, Scott finds himself back in Louisville on the morning of November 13th. Taking a few hours to rest and make himself presentable, Scott joins his parents, brothers, and their families at the funeral home in Canton as they interact with a multitude of visitors who steadily pass through. Although exhausted by his travels and events leading up to him being here, he stands tall with his family.

Looking down on his grandfather, he marvels at how peaceful and relaxed he looks. The last time Scott was with him, he struggled to breathe, needed assistance for the simple things, and lacked an appetite. Scott reflects on the many fond memories of the times he and his grandfather spent together over the years. He was a good man and took great pride in his family and country. Scott never knew but wonders what the patriarch thought of his career choice.

Following his grandfather's funeral at Arlington National Cemetery on November 18, Scott must return to Istanbul. The Islamic region is aflame with dissent and chaos, much of it directed at the United States and fostered by Iran. After saying farewell to his family members over breakfast the next morning, he's accompanied to the Washington National Airport by his father.

While waiting for the announcement to board, Sean and Scott enjoy a cup of coffee. Neither man talks; they're both lost in their thoughts as the moments tick down before Scott must once again depart. The announcement comes, and Sean walks his son to the gate entrance. They hug and shake hands, and Sean says, "Son, take care of yourself when you get back over there. It's a damn mess."

Scott replies, "I'll do my best, Dad. I love you and hope to see you again soon." He starts for the gate entrance, stops, turns, and says to his father, "Dad, I'm really sorry about Granddad. He was a fine man. We'll all miss him. I hope someday to be considered a man of similar stature."

Scott's comments catch him off guard, and Sean chokes up. He simply responds. "I'm sure you will, Son."

8
AMERICAN EMBASSY IN PAKISTAN ATTACKED

Before the death of Scott's grandfather, student followers of the Ayatollah Khomeini stormed the US Embassy in Tehran, Iran on November 4, 1979. The radical Islamic fundamentalists took ninety hostages. Two weeks after the embassy was stormed, the Ayatollah released all female and minority Americans and retained fifty-two hostages. Tensions are high in the region.

Landing at Islamabad Airport early in the afternoon of November 20, Scott is met by George and two armed plainclothes ISI men for protection. Clearing Customs, Scott walks up to the waiting men and extends his hand to George.

"Thanks for meeting me. This place looks like an armed camp. Things must really be bad since the Tehran Embassy attack."

George is serious and scans the area around them, as do the two ISI men who keep their hands close to their concealed 9mm Beretta pistols. George shakes Scott's hand as he replies, "Welcome back. Your timing is impeccable.

This place is a powder keg right now. We're hearing all kinds of rumors. Let's get out of here and back to the embassy grounds."

Scott replies in a somewhat shaky voice. "Is it that bad? Hell, why don't we just get back on the plane and go home?"

George leads Scott and the ISI men toward their waiting vehicle and responds to Scott, "Not a bad idea!"

They return to the American embassy without incident. George gives Scott twelve hours to rest before returning to his office the following day.

The next morning, Scott is scanning the morning reports on his computer, and the news does not look encouraging. The Islamic region is aflame with unrest. At the insistence of the American embassy staff, Pakistan increased its police presence to twenty-four armed police officers on the grounds of the compound. The chancery or principal office of the embassy has both front and rear entrances. In response to attacks on other US missions elsewhere in the world, the front entrance had been made impregnable. Neither the back entrance nor cafeteria windows have been made impregnable, even though plans call for that by the end of 1979.

From his workstation, Scott hears protesters shouting anti-American slogans. At first it seems to be a small protest outside the embassy walls, but the rhetorical intensity and level of noise increases. Scott goes to a window near his work area on the third floor, staring out in disbelief as hundreds of people climb over the walls while others try pulling the walls down using ropes. The Marine guard unit responds with non-lethal gas canisters, trying to disperse the growing crowd. It doesn't work. Pakistani police begin to panic as they try to disperse the protesters, firing into them, killing two and wounding several. This only enrages the surging crowd of rioters. The police are overwhelmed and seek shelter for fear of losing their lives.

Scott is watching this unfold in front of him when Jim and George rush over. They all look down in disbelief at the courtyard. Not succeeding in climbing over or pulling the walls down with ropes, the rioters are now driving trucks through the embassy compound's outer walls.

Looking at Scott and George, Jim says in a calm manner, "We need shelter now. Everyone is being moved to the communications vault. This is totally out of control and only getting worse. Let's go!"

Scott interjects, "Let's spread out on the floor and help ensure everyone makes it to the vault. The Marines are outnumbered and have their hands full. We can help."

Jim and George agree, as all three men pick an area to check. They separate and make hasty searches. Much of the building's interior, excluding the communications vault, is filled with tear gas fired by the Marines who attempted to hold back the rioters. Scott rushes over to their break area, grabs a washcloth, soaks it in water, and places it over his mouth and nose to help filter out the tear gas. He then works his way around his area and helps guide stragglers to the communications vault.

After completing his sweep, Scott makes his way to the vault door being guarded by some Marines. He doesn't see Jim or George and inquires if they've made it inside. One of the Marines replies they just returned and are inside. Before Scott enters, two other Marines carrying a wounded soldier go into the vault ahead of him. He then steps inside as the vault door closes.

Scott asks one of the Marines what happened to their

comrade. The man replies that Corporal Crowley was stationed on the roof guarding the area when he was shot by one of the rioters.

The embassy is at full strength during the attack and numbers about 137, including fifty Americans and eighty-seven Pakistanis. They're now inside the vault when the door is bolted. Scanning the area around him, Scott sees people sitting on the floor, consoling each other as an eerie calm has settled among those present. He makes his way around the area looking for his two associates, and finding them, asks about their situation.

Jim tells Scott that Herbert Hagerty, political counselor for the embassy, is in the vault, as is one of the senior men in charge. Confidence is high that help will arrive soon. The American ambassador, who was home having lunch when the attack took place, is secure in his quarters outside the embassy grounds and is working the phones. They've abdicated the chancery building to the rioters, believing they can hold them off by staying in the communications vault.

The wounded Marine is moved to a small enclave in the vault, where he is attended by a nurse. His gunny (Marine Gunnery Sergeant) checked the blood types of various people in the vault and had two volunteers ready to go with him if they could get him air evacuated from the roof.

Another Marine, who was posted near the back entrance to the chancery and still outside, was instructed by phone to try to make it to the vault. It was risky, but he agreed. Wearing a gas mask and carrying a shotgun to protect himself, he made it to the vault door and was allowed in.

Jim, George, and Scott check in with the gunny to see what they can do to help. He's stationed four of his Marines

AMERICAN EMBASSY IN PAKISTAN ATTACKED

to guard the small room directly underneath the hatch to the roof. This is their only escape route to the roof and could be used by the rioters to enter the vault area. The Marines have taken up positions at the four corners of the room with their shotguns ready should anyone attempt to breach the hatch door. Scott asks the gunny if they can help relieve his Marines periodically. The gunny welcomes their help and Scott volunteers to go first, followed by George then Jim. Each man will do half-hour shifts.

About midafternoon, Scott is one of the guards on duty in the room when they hear a helicopter overhead. It's apparently there for observation, as it doesn't attempt to land on the roof. After it flies away, Scott and the Marines hear rioters on the roof beating on the hatch above their heads, trying to open it. One Marine rushes to alert the gunny as the others raise their weapons and aim at the hatch. The rioters are working feverishly to open the hatch. Gunshots are also heard being fired into the air vents as bullets whizz through the ventilation system.

What goes through a man's mind as he sits there waiting for an unknown outcome to befall him? Scott is no novice when it comes to danger, having served on the DMZ in Korea and skirmished with the North Koreans. Although his visits to the Afghanistan border to meet with members of the Afghan Mujahideen were stressful, he encountered no hostilities. Now he stands here looking up at an exit hatch with an undetermined number of rioters beating on it, wondering what happens if they succeed in opening it and storming the vault. What weapons are they carrying? Do they have explosives? He feels like an animal trapped in a cage with no way out.

The noise above begins to abate as the gunny enters the

room. Looking around at the men, a smile crosses his face as he sees anger in their eyes and an expression that conveys a sentiment of, "Come on in and get it, you lousy bastards."

Scott speaks up first, and in an agitated voice, says, "Gunny, what's going on out there?"

He shares with them the latest. The nearby British embassy informed them by phone that they could see the chancery had been set on fire. There's a lot of smoke and tear gas making its way through the building.

An air conditioner is working in one room of the vault, so they are taking turns rotating people in by that air conditioner to get some fresh air. When not near the air conditioner, everyone needs to breathe through wet paper towels or washcloths and a gas mask if they have one. Those with masks are instructed to share them.

One of the Marines asks the gunny how Corporal Crowley is doing. He takes a moment, then responds slowly, struggling to keep his emotions in check.

"Corporal Crowley died of his wounds. They did all they could to keep him alive. We are keeping this news quiet for now from the others. Our situation is dire. We do not want to cause a panic among the staff."

Later in the afternoon, Scott, who has been resting in one of the larger areas of the vault, notices, along with others near him, that the floor is beginning to get hot. The temperature inside is rising because the fire beneath them is growing in intensity. The carpet begins to smolder in one corner. This doesn't go unnoticed by some of the staff members who look very concerned. Scott, feeling a similar concern, moves over to them, offers some reassurance, and moves them to another area of the vault.

Meanwhile, it's been reported to the political counselor

that huge columns of black smoke are rising above the embassy. There were about eighty cars in the parking lot. Several of the rioters, in a planned action, drained their gas tanks, took gas in buckets, poured it all over the embassy, and set it on fire. An embassy is not particularly easy to burn. It is made of masonry and brick without a lot of flammable stuff, but if you use enough gasoline, you can make anything burn. So, it wasn't long before the whole embassy was on fire.

The fire is bad enough, but reports are coming in that truck after truck of yelling, chanting rioters are pouring into the compound. At this point, the police are useless. Scott and the people in the chancery need regular Pakistan Army troops in large numbers to have any hope of surviving.

By 5:30 p.m., the building is engulfed in flames, and it's so bad in the vault from the heat that the floor tiles start popping off. Scott, Jim, and George, along with some Marines, move among several of the staff employees, doing what they can to maintain calm. They know they cannot last much longer.

Eventually, word is received from the Canadian residence compound nearby that the crowd is thinning and those on the roof are gone. After a brief discussion between the senior people present, it is agreed to send an armed group up to the roof by a route the rioters don't know exists.

A group of volunteers is formed and led by the gunny. It consists of Marines and Army personnel, a Pakistan interpreter, and Scott. They're armed and slowly work their way through the smoke-filled route toward the roof with their weapons ready. The Marines gain access to the roof where the hatch is located just as the last of the rioters climb down. The crowd is growing smaller, the building is burning, and smoke is everywhere. They quickly clear the entire roof of any stragglers and establish a secure perimeter.

It's apparent that the rioters, after realizing they could not open the hatch, tried to jam it so no one inside the vault would be able to exit. Scott and one of the Marines work to free the hatch from the outside while two Marines struggle to open it from inside. After some effort, they open the hatch, and embassy personnel begin to climb up the ladder through the hatch and onto the roof. Emerging from the vault area, they get their first breath of cool, fresh air in several hours.

Their exit is orderly and involves small groups of five at a time. While waiting for the roof to be secured and the hatch opened, senior officials set in motion a plan for evacuating everyone quickly and with minimal confusion. First, the Pakistani women, then American women, then Pakistani men, and finally the American men. They are followed by senior staff members who are the last to climb out.

Trapped embassy personnel, after exiting the vault, step onto the roof area and gaze up at a clear sky with stars. But, looking around at the roof's edges, all they can see are flames. Scott, not one to believe in miracles, witnesses one as fire trucks and large numbers of Pakistani Army troops pour into the compound. For the first time since the ordeal started, Scott and other embassy personnel feel safe enough to descend from the roof.

With everyone evacuated from the building to the courtyard outside, the gunny is overheard saying, "I'm not going to leave my dead Marine in there." So he goes back into the building, places the Marine over his shoulder in a fireman's carry, and carries him out. He is still dripping blood.

Those who witness this, including Scott, become emotional as Corporal Steve Crowley is carried out, placed on a blanket by his fellow Marines, and covered by another blanket. He was the youngest Marine at the embassy and very popular.

AFTERMATH

When the Pakistani Army finally arrives, and the attack ends, security around the embassy and for American personnel increases substantially. The morning following the attack, remaining embassy personnel are moved into the US Agency for International Development building a short distance away. By this time, a significant number of Pakistani Army units are in complete control of Islamabad.

The attack on the American Embassy in Islamabad was incited by false Iranian radio claims of an American attack on Islamic sites in Saudi Arabia. When it was over, two Americans and two Pakistani foreign service employees working at the embassy lost their lives. Two student attackers were killed, and seventy were injured by the Pakistani Army and police forces in their efforts to end hostilities. The entire embassy was burned, determined to be unusable, and ultimately will be rebuilt. All nonessential embassy personnel were evacuated back to the United States within a few days.

9
CIA OPERATIVE IN IRAN- EAGLE CLAW
COVERT ASSIGNMENT

On November 4, 1979, a group of Iranian students stormed the United States Embassy in Tehran, Iran, taking more than sixty American hostages. Images of blindfolded American Embassy staff spurred outrage and calls for decisive action across the United States. Four days after the hostage crisis began, Ted Koppel's *Nightline* debuted on ABC to provide in-depth coverage of the events. Walter Cronkite began ending every CBS News broadcast by announcing the number of days the embassy workers had been held hostage. Under tremendous political pressure, on November 12, President Jimmy Carter ordered the Pentagon to begin drawing up plans for a daring rescue.

The CIA's Iran station chief was one of the hostages taken in the capture of the American Embassy in Tehran. He needed a replacement since planning for any rescue of American hostages would require the CIA to assist in critical intelligence gathering and securing transportation assets.

Following his Pakistan assignment, Scott is reassigned in early January 1980 to a highly classified covert operation.

He'll join a CIA in-country team of several Iranian and American Persian speakers in Tehran, Iran. While training with the CIA, Scott learned to speak French, Persian, and Arabic and studied Islamic history and culture. Jim and George remain in Pakistan to continue working on Operation Cyclone, which is growing in size and importance.

Scott arrives in Tehran using the alias Johnathan Sullivan, an Irish businessman pursuing opportunities for his trucking company to expand. His CIA job category of nonofficial cover, simply referred to as "NOC" (pronounced knock), is rare and dangerous. Covers such as this provide believable reasons to work long periods overseas and interact with foreign nationals.

The CIA's Tehran in-country paramilitary team, led by a retired US Army Special Forces officer, has been tasked with obtaining information about the hostages, security measures established by the Iranian guards to confine them and securing reliable truck transportation for a rescue attempt. After arriving in Tehran, Scott settles into his cover role and contacts the CIA team leader, who assigns two local Iranian assets to work with him. Scott is apprised of their requirements and learns the rules of working with his Iranian assets, then goes about the business of locating and securing several trucks for use in a rescue attempt.

From the beginning of the crisis, ongoing diplomatic negotiations were pursued but failed to release the hostages. Facing reelection and with little to show from negotiations, the Carter administration ordered the State Department to sever diplomatic relations with Iran on April 7, 1980. On April 11, President Carter approves a plan, code-named Eagle Claw, to rescue the American hostages.

OPERATION OVERVIEW

Scott and the other paramilitary team members are briefed by the team leader on the operation the day after the president's official approval. They gather in a safe house near the American Embassy in Tehran, which serves as their meeting and planning center. The location is considered safe and convenient, and has escape routes if needed. While they meet, two team members remain vigilant to ensure they're not approached by any suspicious groups or individuals. Feeling secure, the team leader speaks in a professional, matter-of-fact tone as he conveys the basics for the plan.

"Eagle Claw, the operation to free the hostages, will involve all four branches of the military. Marine helicopters and Air Force C-130 aircraft are the designated air assets for this operation. It entails the Air Force flying Delta Force troops into a location 200 miles southeast of Tehran, code-named Desert One. This location is a large salt flat, which can be ideal for landing aircraft. After Delta Force troops secure Desert One, eight Marine helicopters launching from an aircraft carrier will fly in, land, and refuel from the C-130s, then pick up their Delta Force teams. They will transport them to a mountain location, Desert Two, closer to Tehran."

He pauses, looks around at each man, and continues. "This is where we come into play. We'll be there waiting on them with our trucks and equipment. Upon their arrival, the troops will disembark and join us. We'll hide out during the day and rest. The helicopters will fly on to another secure location nearby and remain concealed. The actual raid into the city will be initiated later that night."

Allowing the men to digest his comments, he continues with their part of the operation.

"Scott, working with local assets, has obtained several vehicles and has them stored in a secure warehouse on the southeast outskirts of Tehran. When the operation commences, we'll drive to Desert Two, where we'll meet the incoming Delta Force troops."

Looking over at Scott, he asks, "How are we looking, Scott? Everything set at your end?"

Scott calmly replies, "Yes, sir. We have several Mercedes trucks and a Volkswagen bus ready to go—more than we should need. I wanted to account for any last-minute changes in Delta Force numbers or issues with truck engines. Some of their vehicles are not well maintained or very reliable. Each truck will be carrying some construction material, and false walls have been installed inside the covered truck beds to hide the occupants."

"Anything else, Scott?"

He replies, "No, I think we're good."

The team leader continues.

"When we get the order to go, Delta Force teams will board our trucks, and our team will drive them to the American Embassy in Tehran. Their teams will storm the US Embassy, free the hostages, and we'll transport everyone to Amiadieh Stadium, a nearby soccer field. Marine helicopters will be waiting. They'll fly the freed hostages and Delta Forces to Manzariyeh Airfield, about sixty miles southwest of Tehran. The airfield will be secured by Army Rangers arriving aboard Air Force C-141s. Everyone will then board the C-141s for final extraction to Egypt."

Almost jokingly and as an afterthought, he adds, "What could go wrong? Nothing to it; just a simple plan."

From the facial expressions of many men present, they appear to agree with his sarcasm and wonder what their fate will be in this audacious undertaking. Scott speaks up.

"What about us? What do we do?"

The response is terse and brief. "If we make it that far, and we're in a fight for survival, we'll extract with the others. If all goes well, we'll return to our NOC covers and quietly leave Iran as quickly as possible."

Later that evening, back in his hotel room, Scott relaxes while drinking a Doogh and sitting on his fifth-floor room balcony overlooking the Tehran street scenes below. Doogh, a Persian yogurt drink, is found almost everywhere in Iran and is one of their popular soft drinks.

Scott is aware that his brother Lee deployed to the Mediterranean Sea in the fall of 1979. He was then dispatched to the Indian Ocean as part of a large naval buildup in response to the embassy attacks. He does not know if Lee is participating in the operation but hopes his brother is safe.

Enjoying the night air and serenity of his room's balcony, Scott's thoughts drift back to their planning meeting earlier in the day and the coming mission, *The operation is very high risk. The men and equipment are being called upon to perform at the upper limits of human capacity and equipment capability. There is no margin for mistakes or plain bad luck.*

There are too many moving parts and using all four branches of the military is risky. Scott is the product of a military family and knows political posturing often occurs behind the scenes. Posturing may not result in the best planning or utilization of equipment or talent available.

FINAL INTELLIGENCE

On March 31, anticipating the need for military action, an Air Force combat controller is flown into Desert One by covert CIA operatives. His mission is to perform a reconnaissance of the proposed landing areas for the helicopters and C-130s. He successfully surveys the airstrip and installs remotely operated infrared lights and an IR strobe to outline a landing pattern for the pilots. He also determines the ground is hard-packed and can support aircraft landings.

Scott and the other clandestine agents have spent months setting up the infrastructure and resources necessary for Eagle Claw's success. They have scouted the road connecting Tehran and *Desert Two* several times. They conclude that Delta Force teams could easily navigate the few obstacles that exist. Also, the CIA team leader has staked out the Desert Two location and considers it remote enough to ensure absolute secrecy.

Information, referred to as intel, concerning the location of the hostages, has proven elusive until just before the operation is to commence. Through a stroke of luck, the most important information comes from a Pakistani cook for the embassy hostages. He confirms that the hostages are centrally located in the embassy compound on the two lower levels of the chancery. He also provides intel concerning the number of guards inside the chancery at night and where they are positioned.

OPERATION EAGLE CLAW

Late in the evening on April 24, Operation Eagle Claw commences. Scott is riding shotgun in the second truck as the CIA team heads for Eagle Two. The stars are visible in abundance above them, and a calm, cool breeze flows through the truck's open windows. The landscape they drive through is arid desert with open terrain, contributing to a sense of loneliness. There is no sign of human presence, such as lights, building structures, cars, or trucks—just the sounds of their own trucks.

Each operator carries thousands of dollars in Iranian currency, fake passports stamped with fake visas, documents containing key words and phrases in Farsi, and tourist maps marked with escape routes should the mission go south. Staring out his window, Scott wonders how the operation is unfolding. They've prepared for any eventuality, including escape and evasion out of Iran. The items he carries provide testament to the possibility they may need to use them.

Arriving at Desert Two without incident or detection, the covert team sets up a defensive perimeter, conceals their vehicles, and awaits communication updates from the leaders at Desert One. Unfortunately, it doesn't take long for the mission to break down. Radio communications are brief, highly tense, and laced with stress as they are alerted to the debacle unfolding. Only delivery of the Delta Force equipment and fuel by the C-130 aircraft has gone according to plan at Desert One.

The CIA team leader, Scott and the radio operator listen to incoming radio transmissions. It is apparent that they're facing a no-go situation. Only six of the eight helicopters make it to Desert One, and one of those is deemed unsafe to continue flying. For them to proceed with the hostage rescue requires at least six operational helicopters. The Delta Force commander in charge of the ground element calls for the abort. The White House concurs, and Operation Eagle Claw comes to an end. The American hostages will not be going home this day.

The CIA team leader gathers his team around him and briefs them. Their mission is canceled. Given the severity of the debacle at Desert One, there is no assurance the Iranian military is not already aware of the incursion into their country. The CIA team is facing a serious, potentially volatile situation. The men on the team are stunned by the terrible news.

What happens now? Does the Iranian military know about the failed rescue attempt at Eagle One? If so, what are they doing about it? So many unknowns, so many questions.

Scott retreats unto himself briefly, *Oh my God, the worst scenario just unfolded. Will he survive the day? Will he see home again or join the fate of the other American hostages? His brother's face flashes before him. What about Lee?*

The team leader shakes Scott's shoulder, bringing him back to reality. In a command voice and a rough tone, he says, "Scott. Scott. Are you with us?"

Scott looks around at the men and then at the leader, "Yeah, I'm here. I was just thinking about my brother."

Until now, Scott has not shared with the group that his brother is part of the Navy contingent supporting the operation. The team leader looks at Scott again and, in a compassionate voice, asks, "What's this about your brother?"

Scott takes a moment and shares with him and the men his brother's situation. The team leader looks at Scott, nods his concern and understanding for his brother, and says, "Scott, he'll be fine. He's a Navy pilot."

Scott thanks him for his genuine concern and then asks, "What's next? Time is critical."

The team leader gazes at his whole team. "Gentlemen, we're going back to Tehran. Gather your gear, store it in your trucks, and when ready, we'll depart as single trucks staggering our departures. I'll be the last truck to leave. Good luck, gentlemen, and God be with you."

Scott can't help but feel apprehensive about Lee and hopes he was not in one of the helicopters or worse, wounded or killed. His drive back is long, lonely, and fraught with apprehension.

The White House announces the failed rescue operation at 1:00 a.m. the following day, April 25, 1980. Over the ensuing days, the Tehran CIA team quietly leaves Iran with the Iranians unaware of their presence. Scott returns home sporting a beard and mustache, learns that Lee is fine, then settles in for a week of rest and decompression from his ordeal. He spends much of his time with Stephanie, who is working at CIA headquarters in Langley, VA. Ten days after his harrowing ordeal in the desert of Iran, he reports to Langley for a new assignment.

10
BEIRUT LEBANON
UNITED STATES EMBASSY BEIRUT

Scott is working in the United States Embassy in Beirut with several other CIA case officers. He arrived in the country shortly after the Marines were deployed to Beirut in August 1982. Stephanie was temporarily assigned to the Beirut Embassy in February 1983 for a special fact-finding and data analysis assignment related to the various militias engaged in fighting. Her assignment will last well into 1983.

Both Scott and Stephanie had worked at separate locations in the Washington, DC, area before being assigned to Beirut. During that time, they rekindled their relationship and enjoyed many nights of heated passion. While neither Stephanie nor Scott consider their relationship to be a romantic one, they do maintain a heartfelt connection with each other.

Scott lives in a small apartment with a balcony that provides a view of the Mediterranean Sea in the distance. He was able to secure Stephanie an apartment in the same complex shortly after she arrived. Although they have separate accommodations, much of their time is spent together, rotating between apartments.

April 18, 1983, dawns with a cool, comfortable breeze and a partially overcast sky. Scott has been sitting on his balcony enjoying the early morning serenity. Stephanie walks out to join him, wearing a robe over her work dress and holding a cup of coffee. They spent the night in his apartment. As she walks out, looking radiant as always, Scott looks up at her. If she was still in her nightgown, he would coax her back to the bedroom.

"Good morning. Did you enjoy the night?"

She looks into his eyes and, in a low, sexy, teasing voice, replies, "Did you?"

He gives her a James Bond look and says, in his best British accent. "I did! I'm looking forward to a sequel later tonight."

She smiles slightly, runs her hand through his hair, and replies, "You might just get lucky 007."

Scott grasps her hand and lightly squeezes it a few times, acknowledging her teasing, then continues. "Stephanie, it's going to be a comfortable day but a little chilly later this evening."

Stephanie looks out at the view of the Mediterranean Sea, sits next to him, and responds.

"Then we should probably take a sweater or light jacket with us to the embassy. After work, we're meeting our Lebanese friends for dinner."

"Sounds like a good idea."

Stephanie is already dressed to go to the embassy. She's ready, but Scott is not. He hurries to dress. When ready, they ride together in an embassy vehicle to work. By design, their vehicle has no official designations and blends in well with other local vehicles.

Arriving at the American Embassy, they park the car, proceed through security, then head to their respective offices on separate floors. Scott's office is on the fifth floor near the back of the embassy building, and Stephanie's is on the third floor in the front of the building, just over the front entrance. Around noon, they join some other associates for a light lunch at the embassy canteen, then return to their respective offices.

Scott's looking forward to dinner and then another passion-filled night with Stephanie. He's developing stronger feelings for her and has started thinking about a long-term commitment. Stephanie would make any man proud to be her husband and go through life together. He wonders how she really feels about him.

Not far from the American Embassy, a suicide bomber driving a van packed with 2,000 pounds of explosives is headed straight for the embassy.

Upon returning from lunch, Scott is informed he's to attend an unscheduled emergency meeting at 5:00 p.m. which could last an hour or more. He calls Stephanie on the office phone system.

She answers, "This is Stephanie Young."

"Hi, lady, I enjoyed lunch. I'm looking forward to later this evening. I need to give you a heads-up. I was just told I have an emergency meeting to attend at..."

It's 1:00 p.m., and the suicide bomber just gained access to the embassy compound, drives his van through an outbuilding, and crashes it into the lobby door. There is a horrific explosion as the van disintegrates. The force of the blast collapses the entire center of the horseshoe-shaped building. Balconies and offices in this frontal section collapse, creating tiers of rubble and spewing masonry, metal, and glass fragments in all directions. The explosion is heard throughout West Beirut and breaks windows over a mile away.

Stephanie's office is two floors above the blast. She is killed instantly as the blast collapses her lungs and tears into her body. The floors above crash down on her floor, sending it to the ground. She's buried in debris along with several other embassy workers. It will be some time before rescue workers retrieve her body. Scott is two floors above Stephanine, and in the back of the building. The blast does not collapse the floors in his section but does extensive damage.

Scott is talking to Stephanie when the explosion occurs. He's knocked to the floor by the force as the windows behind him shatter, sending glass flying everywhere. He's cut by small pieces of flying glass in the face and hands which he was able to place over his eyes just as the blast occurred. Looking at his blood-soaked hands, Scott surmises he has several facial wounds. His ears are ringing from the incredibly loud blast. Lying there on the floor wondering if he'll ever hear again, he checks for additional wounds and finds none.

Looking around his office, he finds it in shambles. His body is dealing with a traumatic event, and yet his first inclination is to run to Stephanie. Regaining his senses, Scott slowly lifts himself up from the floor as his world unfolds around him in slow motion. His office is full of smoke, dust, and tear gas. There were tear gas canisters stored on the first floor near the air shaft, which the explosion set off. With the windows blown out through much of the building, a wind tunnel effect is created as air rushes through the shaft, circulating tear gas throughout the embassy.

Scott slowly works his way out into the hallway and goes into the nearest restroom. He checks his facial wounds and determines they're not severe. He cleanses them and uses paper towels to wipe the blood off and as gauze to stop the bleeding, which is beginning to coagulate. Satisfied he's not incapacitated, Scott rushes out and sets a course for the third floor and Stephanie's office.

Arriving at the location where the central stairway near the front of the embassy should be located, he finds it gone. It's been destroyed in the blast. There are other stairwells near the back of the embassy, so he sets out for the nearest one, picking his way carefully through the rubble. Approaching a back stairwell, he runs into survivors who are covered in white dust. They appear as ghosts to him and just stagger around in a state of shock. These folks must have been in the back of the building away from the main blast area.

Scott does what he can for the wounded, organizes them, and begins leading them down the stairwell to the first floor. As the group works its way to the first floor, Scott notices more wounded and helps them join in behind the others making their way to safety. The level of destruction is overwhelming. Sobs, gasps, and moaning are heard from many of the survivors as they work their way down and out the back exits.

Reaching the first floor, Scott comes upon two women who worked in the same area as Stephanie. Their faces are bloody from glass cuts. They're in shock as he asks, "Have you seen Stephanie? Do you know where she is? Did she make it?"

They don't answer him. They just stare at him with empty eyes. He helps them out of the building, then returns to the back stairwell and makes his way up to the third floor. Arriving there, he steps out of the stairwell and into what was a hallway. It's now an open space looking out over the total devastation of the central part of the third floor. What had been offices now lies in ruin.

Parts of all six floors in the front section of the building disintegrated and lie at the foot of the embassy in a big pile of rubble. The other part of those six floors separated and pancaked onto the lower floors as they fell to the ground. If anyone survived this blast area, they're extremely fortunate. Scott works his way forward to the edge and, peering down into the abyss, sees no one. Rescue workers will work around the clock, unearthing the dead and helping the wounded they locate during their search of this area.

The full realization of what happened crashes down on Scott. It's clear they are victims of a massive car bombing, and many people were killed, including Stephanie. He lowers his head, begins to sob, then openly cries out loud as he falls to his knees. Looking up at the sky he yells out.

"God! Why? Why? Can't these people just live in peace? If they can't live with each other, why do they have to take it out on us?"

Rescue workers hear his cries. Two come to him, help him up, and lead him out of the destruction to waiting medical aid.

Later that evening, after being helped by medical personnel, he's driven to his apartment where he'll spend time recuperating. Stepping into his empty apartment, which still radiates with the scent of Stephanie, he goes to his liquor cabinet and pours Scotch into a large glass. The sun has long since set as he steps out on his balcony. Slumping down into his chair, he gazes out over the Mediterranean Sea and retreats into himself. For the next several days, Scott alternates between drinking his whiskey, fits of melancholy, and periods of loneliness for Stephanie. He cries himself to sleep when exhausted.

He vows revenge for the atrocity committed and his loss of Stephanie.

RETALIATION

American responses to the various terrorist attacks were minimal and considered ineffective. Many believe that terrorist organizations were emboldened to conduct further attacks against United States targets because of the perceived inaction.

On March 8, 1985, a truck bomb blew up in Beirut, killing over eighty people and injuring more than 200. The bomb detonated near the apartment block of Sheikh Mohammad Hussein Fadlallah, believed by many to be the spiritual leader of Hezbollah. This is a major terrorist group that was deemed responsible for bombing the American Embassy in Beirut on April 18, 1983. Although the Americans did not engage in any direct military retaliation for the attack on the Beirut barracks and the American Embassy, this bombing is widely believed by Fadlallah and his supporters to be the work of the United States CIA. Although Fadlallah was not killed in the bombing, he supposedly got the message.

Lebanese intelligence personnel and other foreigners

were undergoing CIA training in Lebanon at the time of the bombing, but the CIA maintained it was not their operation and they knew nothing about it. Shortly after the attack, American officials canceled their covert training operation in Lebanon.

Somewhere in the Middle East, Scott sits drinking an Irish whiskey, smoking a Cuban cigar, and enjoying the evening sunset while lamenting that Fadlallah did not die in the bombing.

11
IRAN-IRAQ WAR
TIME PERIOD 1984-1989-IRAQ INVADES IRAN

The Iraqi military campaign against their neighbor began in 1980 when their armed forces crossed the international border and invaded Iran, igniting the Iran-Iraq War. The war was preceded by a long period of tension between the two countries throughout 1979 and 1980, which included frequent border skirmishes.

Their war continued, and by the middle of 1982, Iran gained the upper hand and invaded Iraq to depose Saddam's government. These developments caused the Reagan administration to fear that Iran's army might slice through Iraq to the oilfields of Kuwait and Saudi Arabia.

The United States proceeds to actively support the Iraqi war effort by supplying them with billions of dollars of credit and military intelligence, and assists in the sale of non-US origin military weapons, ammunition, and vehicles. The Reagan and Bush administrations approve of US companies selling chemical agents, including anthrax, to Iraq.

The CIA becomes involved in secretly directing

armaments and high-tech components to Iraq through false fronts and friendly third parties such as Israel, Jordan, Saudi Arabia, Egypt, and Kuwait while also quietly encouraging rogue arms dealers and other private military companies to provide arms to Iraq.

Enter Sarkis Garabet Soghanalian, nicknamed the Merchant of Death.

SARKIS GARABET SOGHANALIAN

Sarkis Garabet Soghanalian is a Syrian Lebanese Armenian international private arms dealer. American intelligence officials describe him as a cooperative and reliable source in Lebanon, making him an ideal candidate to conduct arms deals with Iraq. He's also close to Iraqi leadership, intelligence officers, and others in the Reagan administration. In many respects, he is the living embodiment of plausible deniability, serving as a key conduit for CIA and other US government operations.

Soghanalian is contracted with the CIA to sell arms to help Iraq during the Iran-Iraq War. With the backing of American intelligence agencies, he brokers vast military weapons sales to Iraq from Eastern Bloc countries, the French, and other countries. He is the largest arms dealer and the lead seller of weaponry to the government of Iraq.

SCOTT ASSIGNED TO JORDAN

Scott is assigned to the United States Information Agency (USIA) in Jordan during the summer of 1985. He's using the alias Jarrett Andre, an American of French descent who works in the broadcasting information division. The USIA is responsible for promoting America's image throughout the world while trashing the Soviet Union. They do so by broadcasting thousands of hours a week, affectionately referred to as "the tower of babble," to over 150 different countries in more than seventy languages.

Scott's mission is devoted to working with Soghanalian and other rogue dealers and private foreign military companies. Their efforts concentrate on providing Iraq with computers, communications equipment, radar equipment, vehicles, and weapons. Although not officially assigned to the CIA team at the American Embassy in Amman, Jordan, he does interact with the CIA station chief as needed.

Jordan is a moderate Arab country and a major recipient of American assistance. It's not considered an especially risky posting for Americans, and the embassy is part of the city's pulse. The embassy is housed in an older building with a non-discreet facade. The front of the embassy is heavily sandbagged as a precaution following the bombing of the American Embassy in Pakistan.

Compared to where he had been, Scott feels safe working here in his day job. It's different when he goes out at night or during off-hours to pursue his actual CIA job. That's when he fears for his life.

A major source of stress for case officers working a cover job is they must become accustomed to leading a double life. It can be exhausting with twelve-hour days and six-to-seven-day workweeks. Case officers are there to do their mission. Their cover job is there to protect them and their operations. All this can take a toll on one's personal life. Up to this point in his career, Scott has handled it well and thrives on the action and adrenaline rushes.

He does have his limits, though.

WORKING FOR IRAQ

Shortly after arriving in Amman with the help of the USIA, Scott finds suitable accommodations in the Jabal Amman neighborhood. His cover job as an international broadcaster entails authoring news-related stories and feature stories on a variety of subjects for radio, television, speaker engagements, and lectures hosted at the USIA. He also initiates and conducts interviews on a wide variety of subjects with many individuals and organizations. It is this aspect of his cover job that affords Scott the most flexibility to perform his CIA job—secretly directing armaments and high-tech components to Iraq through false fronts and friendly third parties.

Working through his intermediary contacts and Sarkis Garabet Soghanalian, Scott has been active in a military aid program known as Bear Spares. Through this program, the United States makes sure that spare parts and ammunition for Soviet and Soviet-style weapons are made available to countries seeking to reduce their dependence on Russia. At the start of the Iran-Iraq war, the Soviet Union stopped its arms shipments to Iraq. The United States added Iraq to its Bear Spares aid program and worked to provide them with parts and ammunition for Russian or Russian-style weaponry.

Scott's efforts have taken him on clandestine meetings with Egyptian General Intelligence Service (GIS) agents and Mossad agents at all hours of the night to facilitate deliveries of Bear Spares. These meetings are not without risks to him. Everyday things he takes for granted back home can be problematic in Jordan. He must always remain vigilant in not setting patterns. Patterns can be used against him. Terrorists find their assignment to kill a target much easier when they leave their apartment or house at the same time every day, using the same route. Scott must continuously be aware of not eating at the same time or place. He's always alert to his surroundings and routinely gives his car a quick inspection before starting it to ensure no one has planted a bomb.

Over time, a vast network based in the United States and elsewhere is established and feeds Iraq's warring capabilities. Scott has immersed himself in this world of deceit, lies, and contradictions, which challenge his own sense of values. He consoles himself with the belief that what he's doing is in the best interest of the United States. He's finding that belief harder to accept the longer he's immersed in the shadowy world of the CIA. Scott also still struggles with the loss of Stephanie and misses her companionship, understanding, and counsel.

CIA operatives interact with and deceive scores of people throughout their careers, a process some believe can leave a person feeling jaded. This can lead agents to engage in sexual trysts and sometimes infidelity if they're married. Scott is no exception. To relieve anxiety and stress, he pursues lust-filled encounters with secretaries, coworkers, and women he meets while out on assignment. These trysts take place outside of his apartment at hotels and safe houses, which are not supposed to be used for trysts. His escapades, although discreet, have not gone unnoticed by the opposition—his enemy.

Scott is living a life of danger and must always remain vigilant in his actions, communications, and relationships. All his activities, minor or major, must be done right each and every time. Sometimes, he might come up short, get lucky, and get away with it. However, his enemy only has to get lucky once to catch and kill him.

AN IRAQI WOMAN

Working at his office on a midmorning in September 1986, Scott's phone rings. He picks up the receiver and, speaking in English, answers, "Good morning, this is Jarrett Andre of the USIA. How can I help you?"

The voice on the other end of the phone is that of a young lady with an Iraqi accent, speaking English with an enticing female inflection to her voice.

"Mr. Jarrett Andre, my name is Amina Mansour. We have a mutual acquaintance who suggested we get together."

Scott replies quizzically, "Oh, and who is this person?"

"Sarkis Garabet Soghanalian. Would you care to meet with me? It concerns dual-use exports."

Scott, starting his second year in Jordan, is assigned to work on facilitating the flow of what they refer to as dual-use exports to include chemicals from the United States to Iraq. Shipments of pathogenic (disease-producing), toxigenic (poisonous), and other biological research materials are to be shipped from the United States to Iraqi government agencies. They'll occur in accordance with legal application and licensing by the US Department of Commerce. These biological materials won't be weakened and are capable of reproduction. Iraq will use them to further their chemical weapons development.

Digesting what he heard and realizing he's just beginning his efforts to establish contacts for this assignment, he responds calmly and in an authoritative tone with a little flirtation to his voice.

"Yes, Miss Mansour, I would."

"How did you know I was Miss?"

"Just guessed. Should we meet for an early dinner and some conversation? Say around six o'clock this evening?"

Amina responds, "That's fine. What if we meet at the Romero Restaurant? It's close to you and very nice."

"I'm familiar with the place. Good choice. How will I recognize you?"

She describes herself and what she'll wear. Although Scott goes through the effort of briefly describing himself, he's certain she's seen pictures of him. After their conversation, the rest of his day is devoted to preparing for the evening. The first order of business is to confirm with his contact the authenticity of her call and relationship with the Merchant of Death.

After confirming Amina's story, he moves forward with preparation. Up to this point, he's run into a wall trying to establish a contact inside Iraq to coordinate shipments of dual-use materials—chemicals. That situation appears to have changed with one phone call.

Arriving at the Romero Restaurant at the designated time, Scott walks into the reception area and immediately notices Amina sitting at the bar nursing a glass of wine. She recognizes him, sets her wine glass down, stands up, and walks toward him.

Amina is a very attractive, vivacious young lady with medium-length dark hair resting on her shoulders, brown eyes, and a welcoming smile. The woman captivates him as she approaches. Closing the distance, she extends her right hand and says in a low, inviting tone.

"Mr. Andre, I'm Amina Mansour. I'm very pleased to meet you."

Scott extends his right hand and lightly clasps hers. It is soft, elegant, and inviting. His inner thoughts start to go on hyperdrive, thinking about how this relationship might develop.

"Miss Mansour, I'm Jarrett Andre. I'm pleased to meet you. Please, call me Jarrett. It's a beautiful evening, so I called ahead and reserved a table on the veranda. We can enjoy the city view while we dine and talk."

She smiles and replies, "Excellent. Jarrett, it is. Please call me Amina."

He nods and says, "I shall." Scott then motions for the maître d' who leads them to their table. While enjoying some wine and a light dinner, they share a little about themselves then move on to the business at hand. Amina shares with Scott that she is of Iraqi descent on her father's side, while her mother is Lebanese. Amina works at The University of Jordan School of Science, where she specializes in Biotechnology and Genetic Engineering research. She knows Sarkis Garabet Soghanalian and acts as a conduit between him, contacts inside Iraq, and chemical companies in America and Europe.

What isn't shared with Scott is that she is an agent of the Iranian Ministry of Intelligence and Security (MOIS), which is responsible for both intelligence and counterintelligence. They also conduct covert actions outside of Iran in support of Islamic regimes. Amina is a member of the notorious Department 15, a group within MOIS tasked with assassinations. Like the CIA, their operatives travel the globe under various disguises, often using the cover of an embassy, a front company setup, or, in her case, a well-established college researcher. She was recruited years earlier and is paid handsomely for her services.

Hearing her story, Scott asks, "Exactly what have you been told about this dual-use assignment, and why do you want to be involved?"

"Fair questions. First, you're looking for contacts inside Iraq to facilitate the flow of dual-use chemicals. I have some. Second, my father is Iraqi, which makes me Iraqi, and third, I get paid for my assistance. Does that cover it for you?"

A slight grin crosses Scott's face as he quips, "Good answers."

During their time together, he senses a strong vibe coming from Amina. His training cautions him to go slow as this is all an act. She, in turn, senses his initial reluctance and holds back. She suggests they meet again in a few days for dinner. Scott agrees.

Over the next two weeks, they meet after work several times for dinner and conversation. Scott finally succumbs to her charm, and they have a passionate evening of unbridled sexual pleasure, which carries into the next morning. This leads to many more trysts as they indulge their sexual desires freely, rotating between her apartment and various local hotels preferred by Scott.

After several weeks, Amina finally sets up a meeting for Scott (Jarrett) with two Iraqi contacts. After the meeting, Scott takes stock of the assignment. His suspicions have become more acute as he believes Amina is just stringing him along while trying to entice him to divulge information about his operations and other associates. The two Iraqi contacts are already known to the CIA as low-level and questionable bureaucrats. Although the sex is great, the unfolding scenario is not good. His senses are on high alert, and his actions become very measured. He believes she may be on to him, as he is to her.

It's a clear, cool, and refreshing evening on October 12, 1986, as Scott steps out of a taxi a few blocks from Amina's apartment. She called earlier in the day, inviting him over for dinner to meet another Iraqi contact. He is leery of the late call setting up this meeting as, heretofore, they've always established their next meeting before departing from their existing one. No big deal, but in his business, everything must be considered, no matter how insignificant or innocent it may seem.

Arriving at her third-floor apartment, he knocks on the door, careful to be standing to one side and not in front. After a brief moment, Amina opens the door and invites him in. As always, she looks stunning, seductive, and inviting. But he immediately senses something is amiss as she welcomes him, turns, and slowly walks over to her countertop bar.

Scott instinctively scans the room to his front and sides. His peripheral vision detects two male figures, one on each side of him, stepping forward out of the darkness, wielding knives.

Without hesitating, his close combat training and a surge of adrenaline take over. Instinctively, he reacts, deflecting the closer man's knife thrust with his left arm as he drives the palm of his right hand into the man's nose with a powerful thrust. This has the intended effect of pushing the nose bone and cartilage well into his attacker's forehead, impacting his brain. Without making a sound, his body goes limp as he collapses to the floor.

The other man closes in on him, quickly wielding his knife as he yells in Arabic, "God is great."

Scott steps back as his second assailant almost makes contact. Using the assassin's own forward momentum, Scott knocks him to the floor. Before the assassin can recover, Scott grabs a heavy lamp from a nearby table and, using it as a weapon, strikes the man in the head repeatedly. The first blow probably cracked his skull. But Scott, who is enraged and in full attack mode, continues until his assailant's head is crushed. Blood flows from his skull onto the floor.

Gasping for air as he straightens up, he looks over at Amina. He stares intensely at her with glazing hatred in his eyes. Scott doubts she's seen this level of intensity in the eyes of any previous adversary. Amina's confidence in her own skills as a killer is shaken to the core. She moves behind the counter as if looking for someplace to hide. Her face betrays a look of disbelief over what just happened to her two assassins. Is she next?

She grabs her Beretta pistol, which is lying on the counter under a newspaper, and raises it. She's too late. Scott, wearing a shoulder holster under his coat, withdraws his own pistol with a silencer attached and shoots her in the head. The back of her skull explodes, sending gray matter splattering over the kitchen wall as she falls straight back onto the floor. Her last facial expression of fear is frozen in her eyes.

Standing there looking down at the three people he just killed, no remorse sets in, no regret for what he had to do—just relief that he's standing and they're not. He calmly shoots each of his assailants with a double tap to the center of their chest. He then leaves the apartment, exiting the building by a back stairwell. Having no concern, he walks several blocks while blending into the evening crowd before catching a taxi. With his night's work done, Scott relaxes at one of his favorite lounges near his apartment.

Earlier in the day, before going to Amina's apartment, Scott had received feedback from a request he sent to CIA headquarters the week before, listing his concerns and suspicions about Amina Mansour. They were confirmed, and none too early. She was an Iranian Department 15 special operator and assassin. Her orders were to befriend him, milk all the information about the CIA's Iranian network she could, and then kill him, thereby disrupting his ongoing operation to send weapons to Iraq. The CIA maintains a network of spies in Iran, and she was responsible for identifying some who were subsequently deported or murdered. With his termination of Amina, the outing of CIA operators in Iran slows to a trickle for the time being.

Scott is given a week off and travels to Rome for a brief R&R. While there, he refrains from female companionship, opting instead to just enjoy Italian culture and food and explore some of Rome's historical sites. Returning to Amman, he resumes his assignment of aiding the flow of weapons and materials into Iraq for their war with Iran.

Scott questions if they are doing what is right. Saddam is a butcher. He deploys chemical weapons and is not to be trusted. Iran is no better and certainly no friend of the United States. He recalls the last day of his CIA training and the closing words from his instructor, "The phrase is—it depends!"

12

MIDDLE EAST TERROR ARRIVES IN AMERICA
FIRST GULF WAR

The Iran-Iraq War comes to an end when both countries agree to a United Nations-brokered ceasefire on August 20, 1988. In October 1989, President George H. W. Bush signs National Security Directive 26, which begins, "Access to Persian Gulf oil and the security of key friendly states in the area are vital to US national security." This becomes the baseline for future United States involvement in the Middle East region. With respect to Iraq, the directive further states, "Normal relations between the United States and Iraq would serve our longer-term interests and promote stability in both the Persian Gulf and the Middle East." In theory, maybe. Time will tell.

On August 2, 1990, Saddam launches an invasion of his neighbor, Kuwait, and fully occupies the country within two days.

The invasion of Kuwait was immediately met with international condemnation. The United Nations Council unanimously imposes economic sanctions against Iraq in

Resolution 661. British Prime Minister Margaret Thatcher and President George H. W. Bush deploy troops and equipment into Saudi Arabia and openly urge other countries to send their own forces. Several countries join the American-led coalition, forming the largest military alliance since World War II. The United States provides the bulk of the military power projected and deployed. Operations to force Saddam out of Kuwait are code-named Desert Shield, preparation for war, and Desert Storm, the actual war.

Scott finds himself back in Jordan again, working to obtain and provide intelligence support for US military operations. The CIA also attempts to mobilize Iraqi officers against Saddam's regime. At the center is Mohammed Abdullah al-Shahwani, a charismatic Iraqi commander who made his reputation in 1984 with a helicopter assault on Iranian troops atop a mountain in Iraqi Kurdistan. His popularity made him dangerous to Saddam Hussein who arrested and interrogated him in 1989. Al-Shahwani fled Iraq in May 1990, just before Saddam invaded Kuwait. He returns to Jordan and works with Scott and other CIA case officers to collect intelligence on Iraq and begin organizing a military coup utilizing former members of the special forces that Saddam had disbanded.

The First Gulf War only lasts forty-three days and ends on February 28, 1991, when Saddam is forced out of Kuwait and his military significantly degraded. There's not enough time to organize a coup and Scott is ordered back to the United States. He reports for his new assignment in New York City, close to the Twin Towers.

The CIA's New York station is behind a false front of another federal organization located in the Seventh World Trade Center building, which is part of the World Trade

Center complex. This station is a base of operations to spy on and recruit foreign diplomats stationed at the United Nations. Scott absorbs himself in his new responsibilities and finds time to enjoy the nightlife of New York City.

AFTERMATH

Following the war, United Nations inspectors identify many United States-manufactured items that were exported from America to Iraq under hundreds of different export licenses approved and issued by the Department of Commerce. Included were biological materials obtained under the dual-use program, which the CIA and their operatives played a role in securing and ensuring delivery to Iraq. These materials and items were used in Iraq's chemical weapons development programs.

New fears, suspicions, and rumors gain traction concerning Saddam's efforts to build weapons of mass destruction (WMD). The United Nations puts in place severe economic sanctions against Iraq and establishes enforcement inspection requirements on Saddam. The UN Special Commission is charged with investigating Iraq's WMD program and begins conducting inspection missions at targeted locations throughout Iraq.

Scott questions his own role in helping Saddam gain access to materials necessary for building WMDs. Why did we provide Saddam with these materials? What did we think he would do with them? Could we have been that naive? Are we now laying the groundwork for another confrontation with Saddam and his military forces?

WORLD TRADE CENTER BOMBING

On Friday, February 26, 1993, Kuwait-born Ramzi Yousef and a Jordanian friend, Eyad Ismoil, and two other terrorists, drive a yellow Ford Econoline Ryder van into lower Manhattan. They pull into the public parking garage beneath the World Trade Center complex around noon and park on the underground B-2 level. The van is loaded with around 1,500 pounds of urea nitrate (an explosive material made from fertilizer), hydrogen gas cylinders to magnify the explosion, and cyanide. Yousef ignites a 20-foot fuse, and then the four terrorists flee. Twelve minutes later, at 12:18 p.m., the bomb explodes, opening a blast crater six stories deep and 200 feet wide. Initial news reports are that a main transformer might have blown before it became clear that a bomb exploded in the basement.

The bomb cuts off the World Trade Center's main electrical power line, knocking out the emergency lighting system. It causes smoke to rise to the 93rd floor of both towers through the stairwells and up the damaged elevators. With thick smoke filling the stairwells, evacuation becomes difficult for people working and visiting the buildings and many suffer injuries from smoke inhalation. Hundreds are trapped in elevators in the towers when the power is cut, including a group of seventeen kindergartners.

Scott and his coworkers immediately realize that a massive explosion has just occurred at the World Trade Center. The blast knocks out their power and their building goes dark. There is calm as the case officers wait for their emergency power system to activate. When it does, Scott, along with other CIA officers, grab their coats, gloves, and hats and spill out onto the street. As Scott steps out into the cold air and snow on the ground, he gazes upon a scene of mass confusion. First responders are arriving with their sirens wailing as people scurry from the Twin Tower's various exits. Smoke billows out from the exits. Scott rushes across the street and over to the nearest exit to help those struggling to leave the building. Their faces are partially black, particularly around their noses, from the smoke. Some are hysterical, others are crying and in shock, and most are coughing as some fall to the ground.

Triage areas are set up, as oxygen masks and bottles of water are provided. The noon rush hour is a scene of confusion and hysteria. In the middle of it all are citizens doing what they can to help fellow Americans in their moment of need. The evacuation and rescue efforts continue all afternoon, with Scott and many of his associates assisting any way they can.

On this cold wintery day in February 1993, Middle East terrorism arrives on American soil.

Ramzi Yousef's plan called for the North Tower to fall onto the South Tower, collapsing them both. He wanted the smoke to remain in the towers, smothering people inside, killing them slowly. The North Tower did not collapse, but the garage was severely damaged in the explosion. Six people are killed and over 1,000 injured, most during the evacuation that followed the blast. Scores of first responders, firefighters, police officers and EMS workers are also injured in dealing with the fires and other aftermath.

The small band of terrorists scurry away from the scene unnoticed. Eyad Ismoil flees to Jordan, and Yousef, the mastermind of the operation, is on a flight to Karachi, Pakistan, that evening.

BACK TO JORDAN

Within weeks of the bombing, the terrorism task force identified seven terrorists involved in the attack. Four were apprehended within months, tried in New York, convicted on March 4, 1994, and each sentenced to 240 years in prison.

Ramzi Yousef is captured in Pakistan in February 1995. After his arrest, Ramzi said to investigators, "This is only the beginning." He and Ismoil, who is arrested in Jordan in August 1995, stand trial and are subsequently convicted. Both terrorists are sentenced to multiple life sentences amounting to over 240 years each. Scott worked on the task force and, with the capture of six of the seven terrorists, he is reassigned to Jordan.

Arriving in Amman in January 1995, he joins the CIA's efforts to indirectly support bombing and sabotage campaigns in Iraq conducted by insurgents in their efforts to topple Saddam's rule. It is believed that Saddam might have played a role in the World Trade Center bombing and that he's moving forward with efforts to build WMDs. These assumptions elevate him to the status of Public Enemy Number 1 in the Middle East.

The United States has no significant intelligence sources in Iraq. There are various rebel groups attempting to oust Saddam with hit-and-miss bombing campaigns. Scott reconnects with Mohammed Abdullah al-Shahwani, who is planning another attempt at a coup against Saddam. Al-Shahwani has enlisted the support of his three sons, who serve in the Republican Guard.

The Clinton administration has come under political pressure to do something about Iraq. The CIA informs the White House they have a plan called the Silver Bullet Coup, to rid Iraq of Saddam. Central to this plan is Mohammed Abdullah al-Shahwani. The White House approves the plan but orders that it be accomplished by early summer in advance of the presidential election in November 1996.

The only problem is the coup is well-known to the Iraqi government. Many of the defectors being used by the CIA are actually Mukhabarat (Iraqi Intelligence Service) double agents. The Mukhabarat learns every detail of the plan, including that the CIA is planning for the coup to correspond with the next United Nations Special Commission WMD inspections. These inspections will include Iraqi Special Republican Guard facilities scheduled for early June 1996. One of the facilities houses the 3rd Battalion (Special Forces), 1st Brigade of the Special Republican Guard. This is the unit that is central to the CIA's planned coup and includes al-Shahwani's three sons.

When the United Nations team arrives in Baghdad on June 10, 1996, under the watchful stares of Iraqi handlers, the team is completely unaware of the CIA's plan to initiate a coup. On the very first day of scheduled inspections, one team is prevented from entering a Special Republican Guard barracks in Abu Ghraib. The following day, another group set out for the headquarters of the 1st Brigade, Special Republican Guard, and was denied entry.

Two days later, the inspectors were still parked in the sun while the CIA station in Amman is desperately trying to contact the ringleaders of the coup in Baghdad. But their entire network is silent. It's as if they had disappeared. In reality, Saddam's intelligence service so thoroughly infiltrated the plot that there isn't a single CIA-controlled asset left in Iraq who has not been arrested by the Mukhabarat.

The coup against Saddam Hussein fails. The CIA's Amman station receives a transmission on one of their secure satellite phones. On the line is the Mukhabarat, which informs CIA agents that the game is up. Within days, Scott, al-Shahwani, and the CIA team in Amman vanish. Saddam's security services round up more than 800 suspected plotters, most of whom are tortured and executed, including al-Shahwani's three sons. All traces of the CIA's involvement in a coup plot against Saddam are eliminated.

Scott returns home for some much-needed rest. After visiting with his family, he sets out on a two-week Caribbean cruise, including a few days in San Juan, Puerto Rico. He enjoys the pleasures of female companionship various Caribbean rums, and the warmth and beauty of the many islands he visits.

Upon his return, he's relaxed, well-tanned, and looking forward to his next assignment in Cairo, Egypt. He'll work out of the American Embassy under his official cover as a diplomat. His CIA job centers around collecting information related to terrorist activities in the Middle East. He and his fellow case officers are also directed to recruit human assets —spies—from Iraq, Iran, and Saudi Arabia. The CIA must expand its network. The expectation is extremely high that Islamic terrorists are planning major attacks on the United States and its Western allies.

13
SEPTEMBER 11, 2001

Scott returns from Cairo and is assigned again to the CIA's New York station across from the World Trade Center. It feels like déjà vu to Scott. Little does he know. With the arrival of Islamic terrorism in the United States, the station is heavily involved in counter-terrorism efforts in the New York area, working jointly with the FBI and other agencies.

BEAUTIFUL SEPTEMBER MORNING

In the early morning hours of September 11, 2001, nineteen terrorists smuggle boxcutters and knives through security at three East Coast airports and board four flights bound for California. This destination is chosen because the aircraft are loaded with fuel for their long transcontinental flights. Soon after takeoff, the terrorists hijack the four planes, take over the controls, and transform the commuter jets into guided missiles.

Scott arrives to work early in the morning and is

attending the daily station briefing with other agents. His commute to work was pleasant as he enjoyed the early fall-like weather outside with its cool, crisp, clean air that made him feel alive.

Their daily briefing is in the early stages when outside, high above them, American Airlines Flight 11, a Boeing 767 that departed from Boston's Logan International Airport earlier, flies south over Manhattan in its final moments. Heading for the Twin Towers, the jet smashes into the northern facade of the North Tower, hitting between the 93rd and 99th floors. It's 8:46 a.m., and the tremendous explosion from the jet's impact reverberates within the confines of the CIA station. Scott and the other men in the room look at each other in shock. Without saying a word, they know what happened. They're under attack by Islamic terrorists.

As televisions are turned on, the word spreads throughout the station that a jet just crashed into one of the Twin Towers. Scott and some other agents rush out of the building to see what's going on. They step outside to a scene playing out high above where several floors of the North Tower are ablaze, with smoke pouring out the windows. In disbelief, they watch as United Airlines Flight 175, another Boeing 767, heads straight for the South Tower. It's 9:03 a.m., just seventeen minutes after the North Tower is struck. The jet flies into the southern facade of the South Tower, striking it between the 77th and 85th floors.

The collision of speeding jets flying directly into the sides of the Twin Towers creates enormous explosions. Glass, metal, asbestos, and other debris rain down, crashing onto parked vehicles as people run for cover. Scott and the people standing near him are sheltered from the falling debris at this moment, but caution prevails, and Scott moves back into the station. Rejoining many of his associates who are gathered around televisions watching the unfolding tragedy, he pulls out his cell phone.

He calls Lee in Orlando. Both Lee and Alan are already on their phones talking to each other as they watch the events unfold. Lee connects Scott to their conversation and as the brothers converse, Scott tells them his firsthand account of what he's seen.

As millions watch the horrible events on television, American Airlines Flight 77, a Boeing 757 headed to Los Angeles, circles over the nation's capital. Flight 77 had taken off earlier from Dulles International Airport. The jet drops down and heads for the Pentagon, slamming into the west side of America's military headquarters at 9:37 a.m., creating a devastating inferno. Within moments, news channels begin reporting this attack.

Alan speaks first and says, "Brothers, we are witnessing our own Pearl Harbor. War with somebody is eminent."

Scott says in a calm, matter-of-fact voice but with an angry tone, "I'm going to the top floor of our building to see if I can get a better view."

His brothers respond simultaneously. "Be careful!"

Scott catches an elevator to the top floor and goes to a conference room with windows facing the towers. Scott witnesses people falling and some intentionally jumping out of windows from floors above those that are burning in both buildings. What a scene of desperation. People are trapped and deciding to leap to certain death. How does one do this? Never before has he witnessed such carnage. He vows revenge.

TWIN TOWERS

Scott's brothers are still on the phone, as he provides them with commentary on what he's witnessing. Standing there looking out at the Twin Towers, he notices the South Tower starting to buckle on the floors where the jet struck. At 9:59 a.m. the South Tower suddenly collapses after burning for fifty-six minutes. It pancakes as each floor falls on the one below. The South Tower's collapse shatters windows and damages other exterior elements along the North Tower's southern and eastern facades. It's a scene from hell as Scott witnesses the tragedy and is helpless to prevent it or save lives. He's furious and conveys his emotions to Alan and Lee who feel the same way as they watch the South Tower collapsing on television.

As the tower falls, Scott tells his brothers he has to hang up and return to his station. He'll call them later. They both tell him to be careful and that they'll call their parents to let them know he's alright.

Entering his station office, Scott finds it almost abandoned as the remaining CIA employees gather up critical files and head for the exits. Scott is told by the station chief to do the same, as they've been ordered to evacuate the building.

With his briefcase stuffed full of folders, Scott rushes out of the Seven World Trade Center building. He's joined by the last two case officers. They step out into a world of sirens, people running in all directions, most with looks of disbelief and many in shock. First responders are everywhere trying to bring some order and help those they can. Moving away from their building, Scott stops for a moment and gazes out over the scene. As he does, another horrific noise rocks his world as the North Tower collapses. The time is 10:28 a.m. and the tower has been burning for one hour and forty-two minutes. The collapsing tower generates enormous clouds of dust and debris, which envelop lower Manhattan. The windstorm it creates knocks over people who cannot get behind a wall or inside a building before it overtakes them.

Scott and his associates manage to duck into an alley near their building as the windstorm overtakes them. They, along with everyone caught outside, are covered with light white dust. Scott struggles to see and chokes on the smoke as he looks for a building entrance to duck into. His eyes are itching, scratchy, and it's hard to focus as tears stream down onto his cheeks. He doesn't know if it's from crying, effects of the dust, or both. He hears other people yelling that they found a building entrance and to follow them.

Scott and the two case officers make their way to the entrance and enter the building's lobby. It's crowded with people covered in white dust, several in a state of shock, some crying, others cursing, and many looking for water to wash their faces and cleanse their throats. A snack vendor in the lobby opens his refrigerator doors and passes out water bottles to everyone. On this day, Scott witnesses many acts of courage, compassion, self-sacrifice, and resolve. If the terrorists thought they would destroy this country's will to fight, they've made a terrible miscalculation.

SEVEN WORLD TRADE CENTER

As the North Tower collapses, heavy debris hits Seven World Trade Center, Scott's office location, causing damage to the south face of the building and starting fires on various floors. Firefighters enter the building searching for people to evacuate. They attempt to extinguish small pockets of fire, but low water pressure hinders their efforts. Fires burn into the afternoon on several floors, and many are out of control.

Around 2:00 p.m., firefighters notice a bulge in the southwest corner of the building between the tenth and thirteenth floors and hear cracking sounds. These are indications the building is unstable and might cave to one side or collapse. Around 3:30 p.m., the FDNY chief halts all EMS operations near Seven World Trade Center and evacuates the area. At 5:21 p.m., the forty-seven-story building collapses after burning for hours. It is the last of the Twin Towers complex to fall.

UNITED FLIGHT 93

United Airlines Flight 93, a Boeing 757 with forty-four people aboard, takes off at 8:41 a.m. from Newark International Airport for San Francisco. It had been scheduled to depart at 8:00 a.m., around the same time as the other hijacked flights. Shortly after takeoff, three terrorists overpower the cockpit crew and hijack the aircraft. Passengers and crew members learn about the attacks in New York and Washington, devise a plan to fight the hijackers, and attempt to retake the plane.

The following are actual communications that were recorded in the fateful minutes before the jet smashed into an open field. Forty-one Americas are killed trying to stop the hijackers from reaching their intended target. The heroic efforts of these men and women save the lives of many more Americans who were potential victims in the Washington, DC, area.

9:35 A.M. FLIGHT 93 FLIGHT ATTENDANT REPORTS HIJACKING

Flight attendant Sandy Bradshaw dials the United Airlines Maintenance Facility in San Francisco from the Airfone in Row 33 (the next to the last row on the plane) to report the hijacking. The manager who takes the call later describes the flight attendant as "shockingly calm." Bradshaw says that the hijackers are in the first-class cabin and cockpit and have announced they have a bomb. She says they have pulled a knife and killed a flight attendant. This begins a series of thirty-seven phone calls made from the plane, most of them made on Airfones in the last nine rows.

9:55 A.M. OPERATOR HEARS PASSENGER DECLARATION

The Airfone operator, who has been on the line with passenger Todd Beamer since 9:44, reports that someone says, "Are you guys ready? Okay! Let's roll!"

10:02 A.M. THE STRUGGLE CONTINUES

Passengers and crew members keep up their assault. An English-speaking male shouts loudly, "Turn it up!" A hijacker says, "Pull it down! Pull it down!" The plane noses down begins a rapid descent, and the control wheel is turned hard to the right. The airplane rolls onto its back.

10:03 A.M. FLIGHT 93 CRASHES IN STONYCREEK TOWNSHIP, SOMERSET COUNTY, PENNSYLVANIA

With sounds of passengers and crew fighting the terrorists, Flight 93 crashes into a field near Shanksville, Pennsylvania, about twenty minutes from Washington, DC, and all on board are killed.

9/11 AFTERMATH

Numerous people fall or jump to their deaths from the burning Twin Towers. Almost all the deaths occur in the zones above the points of impact by the jets flown into the Twin Towers. Toxic powder from the destroyed high-rises is dispersed throughout the city.

Close to 3,000 people died on this fateful day in the World Trade Center and its vicinity, at the Pentagon, and on United Airlines Flight 93. A staggering 343 firefighters and paramedics, twenty-three New York City police officers, and thirty-seven Port Authority police officers who were struggling to complete an evacuation of the buildings and save office workers trapped on higher floors all perished doing their jobs.

There is no greater sacrifice than forfeiting your life to save the lives of others.

14
CIA GOES INTO HYPERDRIVE

Scott survives 9/11 but carries the memories of that day with him. He believes the feeling of utter hopelessness with no ability to fight back will haunt him for the rest of his life. The mass killing of thousands of innocent Americans going about their daily lives is repugnant to him. He's spent considerable years traveling, working, and interacting with people in the Middle East. He's befriended several of them and grown to respect along with many of their cultural beliefs and norms. However, this radical Islamic al-Qaeda organization, no matter where they're hiding, must be hunted down and destroyed before they carry out any more devasting terrorist attacks on America. Of this, Scott is sure and vows to do his part.

Back in early 1996, United States authorities determined Ramzi Yousef, the master planner for the first World Trade Center bombing, in February 26, 1993, and nephew of Khalid Sheikh Mohammed (KSM) was wired money from his uncle before the bombing. KSM has evaded capture, and rises in the ranks of Islamic al-Qaeda to become one of Osama bin

Laden's top lieutenants. KSM is identified as the principal architect of the terrorist attacks of 9/11. He succeeded where his nephew failed. He, along with Osama bin Laden, orchestrated the destruction of the Twin Towers and mass murder of thousands of civilians on American soil.

Now, Osama bin Laden and KSM join the ranks of Public Enemy Number One along with Saddam. Scott recalls the comic duel of Abbott and Costello and their "Who's on First" routine. These terrorists are no joking matter—they're for real and must be stopped. But do we prioritize them or go after them all simultaneously? No matter in what order they're pursued, the US will need more personnel, reliable intelligence operatives, and effective coordination between its many security agencies and those of friendly foreign government agencies—a daunting task.

The Taliban is an extreme Islamic group that has ruled Afghanistan from 1996 to the present, 2001. The Taliban government in Afghanistan has been harboring al-Qaeda's leaders, including Osama bin Laden, for some time. Less than a month after the 9/11 attacks, the United States and allied forces invade Afghanistan. The Operation is called Enduring Freedom. The United States leads an international effort to remove the Taliban from Afghanistan and destroy Osama bin Laden's terrorist network.

The CIA undertakes a large-scale kill-or-capture campaign against operatives of al-Qaeda. In 1976, President Gerald Ford prohibited the CIA from carrying out assassinations. However, President George W. Bush believes that the assassination ban does not apply in wartime, particularly the current war on terror. The CIA is given the green light to hunt down and kill al-Qaeda terrorists who are threatening the United States.

CIA GOES INTO HYPERDRIVE

The CIA's campaign against al-Qaeda also involves the interrogation and indefinite detention of terrorist suspects. The CIA establishes a network of secret detention sites outside United States territory, called black sites, where suspected terrorists are sent and subjected to enhanced interrogation techniques.

The Global War on Terror (GWOT) commences, and the CIA tasks their paramilitary officers in Afghanistan with aiding the United States' attack on that country by collecting information and identifying military targets. Scott is sent to CIA headquarters at Langley, VA, where he's assigned to the newly formed KSM Targeting Team. Their job is to gather, compile, and analyze all information available to help in the hunt for and capture of Khalid Sheikh Mohammed.

15
CAPTURE OF KHALID SHEIKH MOHAMMED
BACK TO PAKISTAN

The KSM Targeting Team in Langley assembles a massive file with considerable information previously collected by security agencies but not analyzed for connectivity. For instance, almost every al-Qaeda suspect captured during much of 2002 had some connection to KSM. Although many had no ties to one another, they all seemed to know him.

Based on the information gathered and analyzed by the CIA targeting team, they believe KSM is hiding in Rawalpindi. This is a large city near Islamabad, the capital of Pakistan. It has a chaotic and lively atmosphere, with crowded markets, colorful rickshaws, and historic buildings. Rawalpindi is the headquarters of Pakistan's army. It's believed that KSM is there because of the huge military presence which affords him the opportunity to essentially hide in plain sight. Scott, who has become one of the experts on KSM, is sent to Islamabad to join the CIA's paramilitary unit assigned to capture KSM.

REPORTS TO CIA STATION CHIEF IN ISLAMABAD, PAKISTAN

Scott arrives in Islamabad, Pakistan on November 15, 2002. After settling into his quarters at the American Embassy compound, he reports to the station chief at his office in the rebuilt embassy. Twenty-two years earlier, on November 21, 1979, Scott was assigned to the American Embassy in Pakistan when it was attacked and burned down. Since then, relations with the Pakistanis have been more cordial but strained. Many believe that Islamic terrorist attacks and activities emanate from terrorist leaders hiding in Pakistan.

Walking into the station chief's office, Scott is greeted by him and another CIA operative with their paramilitary unit.

Scott walks up to his new boss and introduces himself. The chief, in turn, welcomes him. "Scott, welcome to Islamabad. I trust you'll find your accommodations and relations with the locals much more to your liking than the last time you were here."

Scott grins as he replies, "I certainly hope so."

The chief introduces him to the other man present. "Scott, this is Andy Nada he's in charge of our paramilitary unit working to capture Khalid."

The two men shake hands and engage in momentary small talk. The chief invites them to take a seat around his conference table and calls for some coffee.

He starts their conversation by saying, "Andy will brief you on what has happened recently. But before he does, I want to say a few words about our working relationships with the FBI and ISI (Inter-Services Intelligence) Agency, Pakistan's top-secret spy organization."

"All three agencies want to catch this guy...but we each have some underlying motives, priorities, and to some extent, are seeking different results. For example, after 9/11, the FBI hoped to capture all the masterminds and punish them. The CIA hoped to prevent future deaths of Americans. The FBI wanted evidence; the CIA needed intelligence. ISI just wants to capture and kill these guys. They believe many in the free world think they're sheltering these terrorists. Their national reputation and pride are being tarnished in their minds, and they want to change that."

He stops and looks at Scott. "Any questions?"

Scott replies, "No, I've run into that myself. That was one of many obstacles we faced back at Langley trying to compile all the data about KSM. It was challenging on many occasions to obtain cooperation. American security agencies and other friendly agencies around the globe are protective of their information and sources. I learned to work around that to the extent possible and will do my best here."

The chief nods his head in approval and looks over to Andy. "It's your show."

Andy lays out where they are to date.

"We've concentrated our searches on Karachi, which is an easy place to hide and a very dangerous place in which to operate. Terrorists can slip in and out of empty places every day if they so choose and rent them for almost nothing. A series of raids conducted this spring and summer resulted in nothing but empty flats. In early September, we got lucky when the Pakistani police were told there was an awful lot of traffic through a house in the Gulshan-e-Iqbal neighborhood of Karachi."

Andy stops for a moment, finishes his coffee, and refills his cup.

"A four-story building identified to the Pakistani police in that neighborhood resulted in a massive two-hour gun battle when they attempted entry. The building was ultimately secured and then searched room by room. In a storage space under a stairwell, they found Ramzi bin al-Shibh. He's the man who declared himself the coordinator of the 9/11 attacks."

Pausing, then looking directly at Scott, he says with some glee in his voice.

"Here's the kicker. One of the prizes in the bin al-Shibh raid was a large suitcase that contained a virtual road map of KSM's life, including bank records and his framed diploma from North Carolina A&T. More importantly, this stuff is evidence that KSM is in touch with bin Laden and his family and on the move. He isn't fixed, but mobile. He's built an elaborate network of safe houses to move and shelter al-Qaeda operatives through Karachi, perhaps as many as fifty houses."

Scott asks, "So what now? Where do you plan on searching for him? Do we have any concrete leads?"

"Based on your KSM Targeting Team assessments and having no luck finding KSM in Karachi, we'll concentrate on Rawalpindi. Let's hope we get lucky soon."

The general conversation continues between the three men and concludes with the chief coming back to relations between the CIA and FBI.

"Scott, just another little piece of information in case it comes up. Remember that diploma from North Carolina A&T that was just mentioned? Well, that piece of paper has become another battle in the turf war between FBI and CIA agents. The FBI wants it as evidence and is accusing a senior CIA officer of hanging it on his Karachi office wall as some sort of trophy. Just be mindful of your dealings with the FBI. We're on the same team."

Scott replies, "Yes, sir. Not a problem."

THE NOOSE TIGHTENS AROUND KSM

Asset X, as he's called, first came to the CIA's attention in the spring of 2001. He had access to KSM through a third party who trusted him. On September 27, 2001, a CIA case officer sent an email to his colleagues about Asset X titled "Access to Khalid Shaykh Muhammad." In it he emphasized that, for a price, Asset X is willing to help.

Something goes wrong when the case agent requests approval to pay the informer for his information. The request is denied, and Asset X disappears. Through June 2002, the CIA continues to believe that Asset X can provide information about KSM, but they've been unable to reestablish contact with him. Nine months later, in February 2003, he reemerges and says he's still willing to help. Something goes wrong again. Asset X's original CIA handler is transferred, and his replacement, Scott, is not made aware of his real value. Scott sends several cables to CIA headquarters seeking guidance. His cables disappear into a black hole with no response.

With nothing to go on, Scott prepares to terminate the relationship with Asset X. While explaining his dilemma to a colleague and another visiting CIA officer in their field office, the visitor informs him that Asset X is extremely valuable. Scott reaches back out to Asset X, trying to reestablish contact. With no advance warning, Asset X travels to Pakistan and meets with KSM. While visiting with him, Asset X goes into a bathroom and sends a text message to Scott: "I M W KSM."

KSM CAPTURED

It's the last day of February 2003, and Scott has been working with the paramilitary team in Rawalpindi when he receives the electrifying text message from Asset X. Within hours of receiving the text, a raid is conducted by members of a joint Pakistani American team consisting of ISI officers and some CIA paramilitary operatives in the early morning hours of March 1, 2003. They go in like a SWAT team, heavily armed, expecting everything and anything. Twenty-five men dressed in blue, their faces covered with masks and carrying automatic weapons, break down the door and enter the house.

ISI officers enter first and systematically move through the house, securing each room. As they enter the room where KSM is sleeping, he snatches an AK-47 assault rifle next to his bed and starts firing. The assault team returns accurate fire near him, being careful not to hit him. They're under orders to take him alive. He surrenders and lays down his weapon as they rush him. He's violently thrown to the floor, and his hands are tied tightly behind him. CIA operatives, including Scott, enter the room. Looking around, ensuring there are no other threats, Scott sees an ISI colonel sitting up against a wall being attended to by one of his men. He was shot in the foot by KSM as he entered the room.

The other occupants of the house are moved to a separate room, told to be silent, and are guarded by some ISI men. They'll be taken to ISI headquarters for further interrogation. With the house secure and KSM captured, several members of the raiding party search the house for computer hard drives, discs, cassettes, documents, and cell phones. Everything and anything that could possibly contain the names, locations, and other clues to al-Qaeda cells in the United States and around the world is confiscated.

KSM is turned over to members of the CIA and immediately removed from the house under strict security, then relocated to a CIA safe house in Rawalpindi. Scott is assigned to this detail as part of the team's security while trained CIA interrogators work on him. KSM is held the next two days in Rawalpindi, where he is questioned by CIA agents who use force to try and extract information from him.

Scott witnesses some of KSM's interrogation while providing security. He's totally indifferent to the treatment being rendered. He has not forgotten 9/11 and all the death and destruction he witnessed. As he stands there looking at KSM, the mastermind of 9/11, he feels no sympathy or compassion for him. If he weren't a potential source of valuable information, Scott, with no remorse, would prefer to put a bullet in his head and send him straight to hell.

As he watches the interrogators work on KSM, Scott wonders if it will bear any meaningful intel. He believes people in pain will say anything to get the pain to stop. Most of the time, they will lie—make up anything to get their tormentor to stop hurting them. That means the information provided could be useless or just made up to give the interrogator what he wants to hear.

Looking at KSM, a mass killer, Scott sees a pathetic man. But his eyes reflect defiance, arrogance, and pure hate. Scott simply doesn't care what they do to him if it will prevent the deaths of more Americans.

A twenty-five-million-dollar reward was promised to anybody who helped find KSM. It will ultimately be given to the mysterious man called Asset X.

16
ANOTHER WAR

On March 19, 2003, the United States, along with coalition forces primarily from the United Kingdom, initiates a war with Iraq. The president and his advisers built much of their case for war with Iraq on the claim that, under dictator Saddam Hussein, the country was in possession of or about to build weapons of mass destruction. After explosions began rocking Baghdad, Iraq's capital, President George W. Bush announces in a nationally televised address the beginning of hostilities with Iraq.

"At this hour, American and coalition forces are in the early stages of military operations to disarm Iraq, to free its people, and to defend the world from grave danger."

Coalition forces are able to topple Saddam's regime and capture Iraq's major cities in just three weeks, sustaining few casualties. President Bush declares an end to major combat operations on May 1, 2003, from the flight deck of the aircraft carrier USS Abraham Lincoln. Despite the defeat of Iraq's conventional military forces, an insurgency springs up and spans an intense guerrilla war in Iraq.

After the capture of KSM, Scott returns to Islamabad, where he works with the task force trying to locate and capture Osama bin Laden. His efforts while stationed in Islamabad keep him in the field chasing leads and interviewing assets, trying to zero in on his hiding place. It's a frustrating exercise. Bin Laden is like a ghost—he's everywhere but nowhere. Scott grows weary of the hunt and aches for another assignment placing him in the unfolding action in Iraq.

The situation in Iraq is deteriorating further as the most serious fighting of the war begins on March 31, 2004. Iraqi insurgents in Fallujah ambush a Blackwater convoy led by four American private military contractors providing security for food caterers delivering their supplies. The four men are murdered by insurgents, their bodies dragged from their vehicles, beaten, set on fire, then hung from a bridge crossing. Photos taken of their death and the following degrading treatment are sent out to news agencies worldwide, creating outrage in America.

The United States military responds with Operation Vigilant Resolve. The operation begins on April 4, 2004, and ends on May 1. It's the First Battle of Fallujah, resulting in thirty-nine American servicemen killed and ninety wounded. The operation is unsuccessful in pacifying the town. With only a third of the town taken, the Iraqi government requests the United States military pull back.

They oblige and turn over remaining operations to the newly formed Iraqi Fallujah Brigade on the first of May. This security force is formed by the CIA, which arms them with American weapons and equipment. The Brigade soldiers shortly thereafter dissolve, declare themselves loyal to the insurgents, and turn over their supplied weapons to the insurgency.

Following these embarrassing developments and increased chaos unfolding in Iraq, more CIA assets are being sent into the country. Scott is notified he's one of them and will be deployed to Baghdad, Iraq. He'll be embedded with American units operating around Fallujah. Before reporting to Iraq, he's given a thirty-day leave to return home, spend some time with his family, and relax. His new assignment will be dangerous and demanding.

17
IRAQ WAR
CONVOY

It's late in the afternoon of August 24, and Scott is riding shotgun with the convoy commander in his Humvee. Scott's been in Iraq for three weeks and is traveling back from Camp Anaconda to Baghdad Airport. He was at the camp working with a reconnaissance team for several days, assisting them with linguistics as they follow up on some rumors of WMD locations. Hunting for WMDs continues to this point in the war but has turned dry. This was one of the main reasons for launching a war with Iraq and is proving elusive. Any and all rumors, even at this late date in the war, are chased down.

The weather is stifling outside the vehicle, and the only relief for Scott and the crew inside is airflow through the open gun turret. Scott grasps a Red Bull from the cooler behind him, opens it, and chugs the drink down. He then works a large piece of ice around his neck and drops it down his body armor to cool his chest. He feels a momentary boost of energy from the drink and a little cooling sensation from the ice. His efforts only result in a few minutes of relief.

The convoy consists of five United States Army vehicles armed with crew-served weapons escorting a convoy of twenty-five fuel trucks and four semi-tractors pulling flatbeds loaded with building supplies. These trucks are driven by civilians working for Halliburton subsidiary KBR. Every day, hundreds of civilian American truck drivers working for KBR make their way across Iraq. For many drivers, the main attraction is the chance to earn a decent paycheck. Yet, like any job in a war zone, this one involves considerable risk—roadside bombs, gunfire, and even rocks are a daily danger.

Scott wanted to ride in the lead vehicle, but the convoy commander insisted he ride with him further back in the convoy line. In the lead vehicle is Staff Sergeant Reeves, the Humvee truck commander who is just starting his fifth year in the Army. His wife, two-year old daughter and six-month old son are living with her parents back home in Augusta, Georgia while he's deployed. His driver, Specialist Tucker, is barely able to shave, hails from Southern California, and was a surfer before joining the Army. He will not reenlist. Private Rameriez is the gunner on top manning the turret's fifty-caliber machine gun. He hasn't contemplated his future beyond his current position.

As the lead Humvee commander for a large convoy, Sergent Reeves has a daunting challenge for a twenty-two-year-old. He's not only responsible for his crew's safety but also that of the convoy's civilian drivers and soldiers providing security for the convoy. Scott met these soldiers earlier in the day and was looking forward to riding with them at the front of the convoy. He's not sure why he wanted to do so but just thought it would be interesting to see how these young men carried out their duties.

Riding with the convoy commander, Captain Smith, Scott engages in small talk, asking several questions about their convoy tactics and risks. Scott's heard they are becoming more dangerous. They're traveling on one of the main convoy routes, which is a paved two-way road with considerable traffic. Combat checkpoints (CP) are dispersed along the route and manned by Iraqis charged with monitoring activity in their sector. As they pass through each CP, Captain Smith calls ahead to Combat Outposts (COP) to get a situation report (SITREP) on the next CP. A COP is a small base established in combat zones and manned by American troops.

After passing safely through their third CP, the captain calls ahead.

"COP 3, this is Grizzly 5...radio check."

The Humvee's radio crackles as they respond. "Grizzly 5, Roger. We have you. What is your status and location? Confirm!"

"COP 3, we are inbound for BIAP (Baghdad International Airport) with thirty-four vehicles and 120 paxs (passengers)—requesting a SITREP. We just passed CP 11. Over."

They respond, "Roger Grizzly 5. No IEDs reported in the last twenty-four hours. Small arms fire at CP 12. Rock throwing incident at CP 14."

The captain acknowledges their last transmission. "Roger, understand. Thanks. We'll check back with you again when we pass through CP 12. Out!"

Captain Smith, who's driving, looks over to Scott. "Can you get me a Red Bull and open it? I need an energy hit."

Scott responds, "Sure," as he pulls one out, opens the can, and hands it to the captain.

"Thanks, Scott." Scott nods.

Although they're in the middle of the convoy, the captain continuously scans the road from the left to the right shoulder as he drives. He's searching for anything that's out of place, appears unusual, or just doesn't look right. As Scott watches him, he wonders what would trigger a warning to the captain. As they drive through the terrain, it all looks similar to Scott and, at their speed, it would be hard to focus on any one area, let alone a spot. He concludes it must be experience, intuition, and luck.

Captain Smith insists that all his men driving convoy security remain vigilant. Staff Sergeant Reeves in the lead vehicle is charged with the important task of trying to identify any threats in front of them first and hopefully spot any IEDs.

The sun is setting as the convoy speeds down the road with Reeves leading the way, traveling over fifty miles per hour. On the left side of the road, just ahead of him, is a large, camouflaged IED. It's a mixture of grey, brown, and tan paint that's dusted with sand and dead plant material indigenous to the surrounding terrain.

Reeves doesn't see it and enters the kill zone. A massive explosion lights up the night sky, temporarily blinding the men immediately behind the lead vehicle. The Humvee disappears in a massive fireball. The driver of the fuel truck following behind Reeves hits his brakes and comes to a stop before crashing through the burning mass to his front. This causes a cascade of convoy vehicles following him to apply their brakes and stop. The military vehicles in the convoy immediately take up defensive positions on both sides of the road.

Staff Sergeant Reeves and his crew perish in a nanosecond. They've been hit by an IED on the left side of their

Humvee. They are consumed in a plasma fireball, which compromises the vehicle's armor and subjects the occupants to a firestorm that engulfs the interior of their vehicle. Staff Sergeant Reeves leaves a wife, two small children, and many other family members. Private Ramirez leaves his family and a girlfriend who never told him she was pregnant. Specialist Tucker leaves behind his parents and grandparents. His dream of traveling the world's beaches in search of the perfect wave comes to a sudden end.

In Scott's Humvee, chaos is heard over the radios as men are shouting out potential targets on either side of the extended convoy's length. Captain Smith orders his men to give him a SITREP, return fire, and calm down. Within a few minutes of his communication, insurgents launch rocket-propelled grenades at several vehicles. Three fuel trucks scattered through the convoy take direct hits and explode in massive fireballs. Their drivers and the men riding shotgun with them perish instantly.

Scott yells to the captain, "We've just driven into a shitstorm. They have us trapped."

By hitting the fuel trucks scattered through the convoy, they've made it very difficult for the trucks to drive out of the large extended kill zone. Scott, no novice to combat, grabs the radio transmitter and calls COP 3.

"COP 3, COP 3…this is Grizzly 5. We're under attack. I repeat, we are under attack. We're between CP 11 and 12. Send help. We'll need Medevacs. Over!"

The Humvee's radio crackles again as they acknowledge his transmission and respond help will arrive ASAP.

With the salvo of RPG fire over, the insurgents lay down heavy rifle- and automatic-weapons fire up and down the convoy. They're trapped in a kill zone, and men are dying as they struggle to return accurate fire at an elusive enemy. Scott doesn't hear their gunner returning fire with his .50-caliber machine gun. He looks back and into the turret area. Their gunner was hit in the head and slumped down through the turret. His lifeless body, bleeding profusely over his body armor, lies on the floor of the vehicle.

Captain Smith is working the radios, trying to rally his men to stay in the fight. Scott instinctively climbs up and into the turret. He wraps his hands on the trigger of the .50-caliber heavy machine gun and relentlessly fires in a wide arc, creating a 180-degree field of fire. The other gunners up and down the convoy see his burning hot red tracers know what he's doing, and follow his lead.

Forget looking for targets. Just blow the hell out of everything to your front using a wide arc as your field of fire. Traversing his .50-caliber back and forth, he fires low to the ground, keeping his bursts short as he sweeps the area to his front. With Scott's actions and those of the other gunners, the insurgents' attack subsides as their incoming tracers taper off until there are none. The insurgents fade back into the night as quickly as they rose from their hiding places to rain death on the infidels. They leave behind them a partially destroyed convoy with several wounded and dead Americans.

COMMUNICATIONS HOME

After surviving his harrowing convoy trip, Scott is assigned to FOB, Camp Baharia, in late September 2004. He's now attached to the 3rd Battalion 5th Marines who took over the camp in September. They're responsible for operating in areas outside the FOB. Camp Baharia, also known as Dreamland, is the smaller of two major United States military bases maintained just outside the city limits of Fallujah.

It's been another long, hot day as Scott sits at his computer reviewing the latest emails. After a late dinner at a Camp Baharia dining facility and a cold shower, he feels a little more human. Sitting at his computer, he opens his father's latest email. The news from home is the same, everyone is doing well, staying active, and enjoying their lives.

They are not, however, at all pleased with what is going on in Iraq. His father has been against the war in Iraq since the initial invasion. He believes it's misguided, the strategy is not well articulated, and he's skeptical about the validity of claims made to start the war. Scott shares his father's opinions.

After reading his current emails, Scott responds to his father.

Good evening, Dad.

It's rather late over here in Iraq, but all is well with me. However, the situation here is not getting any better, and I'm afraid it continues to deteriorate. I'm not at liberty to talk freely, as you can appreciate. But there is more action on the horizon coming our way soon.

As you know, I'm now with the Marines at Camp Baharia. Before this assignment, I had spent a little time out on a small combat outpost, a COP, as we refer to them over here. That was an experience. The outpost sprouted up from an unbroken moonscape and looks like a medieval castle, complete with towers and several vehicle-fighting ramps. The rectangular perimeter covers about two acres and is protected by twelve-foot-high T-walls (portable, steel-reinforced concrete blast walls). There are four towers on the perimeter walls, which are manned by soldiers, armed with .50-caliber machine guns. The inner redoubt is protected by walls and two thirty-foot towers, which are vacant unless the outer perimeter walls are breached in an attack.

The COP is home to fifty-five soldiers who lead a spartan life. There is no PX, Pizza Hut, or Burger King. No USO shows. No morale, welfare, or recreation facility—only old magazines and worn-out playing cards. The men have no privacy, no place to escape for a moment of peace, and no time off unless you consider their few hours of sleep. Water supplies are limited, and the constant noise of diesel generators and suffocating sandstorms exist almost daily. Scorpions and camel spiders thrive everywhere out there. Care packages occasionally arrive and have almost always been picked through by troops back in the main bases.

The COP is tethered to a larger combat base and is dependent on convoys to truck everything soldiers need to survive in their harsh and deadly environment. These men are some of the best I've met over here, and I certainly respect them.

I got a little carried away, but have been meaning to share with you what life is like for our men and women who are placed out on these smaller combat outposts.

I'll sign off for now give my love to Mom and the others when you see or talk to them. I miss all of you and look forward to being assigned back in the States. I'm getting rather old for this macho lifestyle.

Love,
Scott"

18
2ND BATTLE OF FALLUJAH- OPERATION PHANTOM FURY
OVERVIEW

Insurgent strength and control over Fallujah increases dramatically by late September 2004. The United States military is once again going back into the area. The most wanted man in Iraq is Abu Musab al-Zarqawi, the leader of an extreme and violent element in the insurgency. He's been implicated in over 2,000 deaths since the invasion of Iraq, mostly from bombings. He's notorious for capturing and killing hostages by decapitating them, videotaping it, and placing it on the internet for the world to view. Zarqawi is the highest priority in Iraq, with the number of insurgents following him estimated at over 5,000 men, mostly non-Iraqis. They are jihadists who just want to kill Americans and are believed to be in Fallujah.

The second battle for control of Fallujah is expected by military planners to be brutal and could well be the costliest battle of the war. The joint military effort will be led by the United States, supported by the United Kingdom and the Iraqi Interim Government. The actual battle for the city will be led by units of the United States Marines and Army.

2ND BATTLE OF FALLUJAH-OPERATION PHANTOM FURY

They call it Operation Phantom Fury.

Scott travels into hell embedded with the 3rd Battalion, 5th Marine Regiment.

IS THIS HELL?

Day 1

Scott is attached to K Company (Kilo), of the 3rd Battalion and will go into battle with them. His knowledge, experience, and ability to speak Arabic are valuable assets they can use as they fight their way through Fallujah. As night settles, the Marines spend their time waiting for orders to move out by checking and rechecking their gear and battle plan. Kilo Company has several Humvees and some troop carriers to take them into battle. Scott is with the second platoon of Kilo and has spent some time among the men.

They are young, some are quiet, while others are boisterous, and some can't wait to get into a fight. They're good men, and like many men before them, they anxiously wait for the order to go into battle.

With Navy SEAL and Marine Recon snipers providing reconnaissance and target marking on Fallujah, ground operations commence late into the evening of November 7, 2004. The initial attacks come from the west and south of the city and are intended to distract and confuse insurgents holding the city. The main offensive will follow.

Day 2

It's early morning on November 8, and the sun has yet to make an appearance. Scott's unit is poised to attack from their line of departure and await the order to advance. Sitting in the back seat of the platoon leader's Humvee, Scott rechecks his weapon, armored vest, helmet, sidearm, and other gear while waiting for the go signal. The platoon leader, Lieutenant Harper, Scott, and the other Marines in the vehicle listen intently to communications traffic coming in over their radio. A massive artillery barrage and air strikes have just commenced within the city. From their location, they can see flashes from explosions, hear the noise, and, in some cases, feel the shockwaves and ground tremors from close hits.

The intense bombardments taper off, and the order to move out is given. Under cover of darkness, they begin the assault. Mortar shells and rocket-propelled grenades hit Kilo Company as the Marines pile out of their troop carriers. They fan out and take defensive positions as the Humvee gunners return fire. Emerging from their bunkers, insurgents shoot at them from rooftops, houses, sewers, or wherever they can take shots at the Americans.

Scott disembarks the Humvee and runs to join a squad of Marines who've taken cover behind a wall on one side of the street. Dirt kicks up from a mortar shell hitting nearby and partially covers him. He shakes it off and joins the Marines at the wall.

They have no tanks with them, and their troop carriers move back. Throughout this battle, American Marines and soldiers will systematically go from house to house, room to room, as they fight their way through the city. They'll move through almost entirely on foot, into the heart of the resistance, rarely protected by tanks or troop carriers, working their way through Fallujah's narrow streets with seventy-five-pound packs on their backs.

Lieutenant Harper calls for immediate, indirect fire support on buildings to his front. Within moments, 120mm mortar shells are heard by the Marines as they arch up and fly over them. They reach the apex of their arcs and fall to earth, destroying whatever they hit. Some of the Marines yell out cheers as they explode on impact. Scott would join them but knows this just started and chooses to wait until the battle is over before displaying any joy. They have a long way to go.

The insurgents retreat from the area to regroup as the Marines seize the initiative and press forward. Scott sticks with the squad as they advance and slowly work their way down a side street. Five three-man fire teams maintain their separation from one another and scan rooftops and windows as they cautiously move forward. Making their way into a courtyard of a three-story building, the first fire team comes under heavy attack. A brutal gun battle begins, killing one of the Marines instantly and wounding a second Marine. He falls to the ground and is trapped in the open courtyard. The third team member holds back and ducks inside a door just before they fire on him. The other fire teams hold their positions outside the courtyard until they know what they're up against.

As the gunfire subsides, they hear the screams of their injured man. The third Marine in the fire team and another from the second fire team rush into the courtyard to save him. They come under intense fire as one dives for cover behind a dead insurgent and the other Marine behind a large tree in the middle of the courtyard. Both men are pinned down.

Seeing this, Scott takes off his pack, lays his M-4 against the wall, and pulls out his M9 Beretta. He yells to the men in the courtyard, "Hold on. I'm coming." Looking at the Marines near him, he watches as they instinctively move into position to provide suppressive fire on the insurgents.

Firing his weapon, Scott rushes over to the wounded Marine, who has gone silent. Marines provide cover fire as Scott reaches the man. His adrenaline is running on overdrive and his heart races as he leans down and picks him up. He throws him over his shoulder and rushes back to safety. Insurgent gunfire rains down on all the men in the courtyard. As Scott approaches the corner, two Marines step into the open and let loose with their SAWs. They traverse their weapons, firing into the buildings' windows and doors around the courtyard's interior. These lightweight machine guns rip up the exteriors, killing anyone they hit. Within moments, the courtyard is quiet.

A Navy corpsman joins the Marines and feverishly works to save the injured man. He's been hit by several insurgent bullets. One hit him in the thigh, severing his femoral artery, causing excessive loss of blood. The corpsman cannot save him as he fades away and succumbs to his wounds. Scott leans against the wall, still catching his breath as he sips water and pours some over his head. Looking down on the man he just tried to save, he feels remorse for him and his family. He's Bill Shaffer, a twenty-year-old Marine who had spent some time with Scott earlier, trading stories about their shared experiences living on military bases. Bill's father is a career Marine whose son now joins the unwavering line of Marines who predeceased Bill on this day.

Bill's body is carried back to one of the Humvees, placed in a body bag, and carefully laid on the vehicle's floor. The platoon resumes their forward movement. As they do, several of the Marines approach Scott and thank him for what he did. Others give him nods or handshakes. Scott returns their gestures as a genuine show of respect and appreciation.

He's become one of them now—a part of their brotherhood.

By late afternoon, under the protection of intense air cover, the Marines move through districts on their way to the center of the city. As they move forward, they're followed by Navy Seabees who bulldoze the streets, clearing off debris from the bombardment that morning. Shortly after nightfall, the Marines reach Phase Line Fran at the center of the city. Kilo Company takes a break to rest, have some food, resupply with ammo and water, and wait for further orders to advance once again.

On this particularly grim night on the first day of the battle and after a short rest, Kilo Company is ordered to continue their advance. The third platoon moves out to lead the company. As their first squad turns a corner in the darkness and heads up an alley, the squad leader, Sergeant Jim Reece, sees movement to his front at twenty meters. He halts the squad as he peers through the darkness. As his night vision adjusts, he observes men dressed in uniforms worn by the Iraqi National Guard. The uniforms have pieces of red and white tape affixed to them—the signal agreed upon to assure American soldiers that any Iraqis dressed that way are friendly. All others can be killed.

The Marines, spotting the red and white tape, wave, thinking they're friendly. The men in Iraqi uniforms open fire on them. One Marine is killed instantly with a headshot. Another lies on the ground screaming from his left leg being severed above the knee. The remaining squad members take cover and open fire on the insurgents to their front.

Several SAWs are employed against the enemy who melts back into the darkness, leaving their dead scattered around the alley. The commanding officer (CO) of Kilo Company orders his men to fan out and set up defensive positions. As they do, the wounded Marine is stabilized, the deceased Marine is placed in a body bag, and they are both transported to the rear. The CO orders their company's fire support and tactical air controller personnel to join him. He uses these men to call in artillery and fixed-wing assets to engage the enemy.

Scott joins the CO at his command post and observes the interactions between the CO and the men directing the fire support. They use a language consisting of multiple acronyms, target grids, slang, and many other word phases that, even if you had a glossary of terms available, would be overwhelming to the untrained observer. Scott doesn't try to follow their dialogue; he just listens and admires their professionalism. He hopes they're raining hell down on the insurgents.

With a break in the action, the CO turns to Scott.

"It's been a hell of a day out here, Scott. What do you think?"

Scott replies in a tired but calm voice.

"These bastards are learning quickly that fighting us on the open streets is a death sentence. They're changing tactics and fighting from inside buildings and in smaller groups."

The CO agrees and adds, "Their fighters largely fall into two categories—terrorists who try to kill as many of us as they can before withdrawing—and martyrs who stay hidden in place until they can kill themselves and as many Americans as possible."

Scott nods agreement. Both men fade into silence as they try to rest while reflecting on the horrors they've witnessed since the battle began.

Day 3

It's late morning on November 9, and Kilo Company cautiously moves forward toward its next objective. They receive orders to stop, secure the area, and set up their sniper teams. They'll move out later in the day after some rest and food. Sergeant Johnson and his spotter are directed to set up on the roof of the building they just secured. He's joined on the roof by Scott and some other Marines who post on all four sides to provide security.

As a sniper, Sergeant Johnson sits on roofs for hours at a time, looking through the scope pm his bolt-action M-40 rifle, waiting for insurgents to step into his sights. The scope is big and wide, and to improve his view, he often removes his helmet. In the first battle for Falluja in April, American snipers were especially lethal and feared by the insurgents who didn't wish to become martyrs.

Scott watches as the sniper team sets up and begins their search for targets. As they work, Sergeant Johnson looks over to Scott. "Do you know we've been warned we're major targets of insurgents? They're trying to take us out."

Scott responds, "Yeah, I've heard that. I also heard they've placed bounties on your heads."

Sergeant Johnson removes his helmet and finishes adjusting his M-40 rifle. "Yeah, I heard that too."

The impact of a bullet fired from a high velocity sniper

rifle hits Sergeant Johnson in the head, knocking him backward and onto the floor of the roof. The back of his head explodes as an insurgent sniper finds his target. The Marines seek cover behind the low wall around the building's rooftop. They restrain their immediate impulses to rise up and start shooting back. Experience has taught them that the sniper is well back from their location and would be extremely difficult to locate. They stay low to the floor, not wanting to become the sniper's next victim.

Scott crawls over to Sergeant Johnson to see if he's alive. He's not. His spotter is in shock as he looks upon his friend and starts weeping. Scott tries to console the man while keeping him from raising his head and becoming another sniper target.

The senior Marine on the roof reports to the platoon leader what happened. They're ordered off the roof and back down to the first floor. Carrying another dead Marine and his M-40 rifle, they join the rest of the platoon. Gathered around another fallen brother-in-arms, the men once again grieve, but this time more in silence. They're becoming more hardened to the fact that in war, people die.

One of the young Marines standing near Scott, who is the oldest person he's seen in the battalion, looks to him.

"Sir, I've heard you've been around and seen some shit. Is this hell?"

The other Marines look over at Scott for his response. He gazes at each one as he responds in a low, mature, and melancholy tone.

"Son, I don't know. But it sure as hell isn't Kansas."

Sometimes casualties come in volleys, like bursts of machine-gun fire. Late into the afternoon, Kilo Company's first and second platoons become involved in a ferocious struggle for a mosque. Fallujah, referred to as the City of Mosques, has over 200 mosques. Many of the mosques are being used as arms caches and weapon strongpoints while their towers, which have commanding views, are being used by insurgent snipers to target Marines.

The Marines of the second platoon, along with Scott, dash across an open field in a mass movement toward the mosque. They are supporting the first platoon, which is attacking from the other side of the mosque. Closing in on the mosque, they maneuver right into interlocking streams of fire. By the time they make it through the killing zone and to the other side of the open field, six men lie wounded and bleeding in the field. Scott is one of them. Lying there, bleeding into the Iraqi soil, he looks up to the heavens with life fading from him. He questions in a faint voice, "Why are we here? What are we accomplishing? Why me?" He slowly slips into darkness.

While some of the Marines risk their lives to drag the men to safety, 120mm mortar rounds begin raining down on the mosque, destroying it and killing everyone inside. The area goes quiet. Medevac Black Hawk helicopters are en route to the battlespace.

Scott is severely wounded. He's not responsive to the Navy corpsman attending him and barely clings to life. To the corpsman and the Marines looking down on him, his wounds look mortal. They are devastated and fear the worst. Scott has earned the respect of every Marine he's served with since being assigned to their battalion. They have come to depend on his knowledge, experience, and wisdom.

MEDEVAC HELICOPTER

Scott and two Marines are placed in the first Black Hawk to land. They're secured inside the helicopter as it lifts off, creating a dust storm. The second one arrives, lands, and takes the other wounded Marines. It lifts off quickly and trails behind the first helicopter. The two helicopters gain altitude, settle into their fastest cruising speed, and head for Camp Baharia and medical attention.

Before clearing the battlespace they're flying through, both helicopters come under RPG attack. The trail helicopter has two rockets approaching, but they miss, passing harmlessly beneath them. A volley of three are headed directly for the Black Hawk carrying Scott. Two of the rocket-propelled grenades impact the tail, blowing off a section of the tail boom and all four of the five-foot-long tail rotors. Chunks of the stabilizer, missing tail, and tail rotor blades strike the main rotor system.

Without tail rotors or its stabilizer, the fate of the Black Hawk is sealed. Having also lost his main hydraulic system, the pilot fights valiantly to control his helicopter. With the earth looming closer through his cockpit window, the pilot tries a series of desperate control movements to place his dying helicopter on the ground. It looks like he might make it, allowing some of them to survive. Then the backup hydraulics fail, and it's game over. Impact with the earth is horrific. The helicopter rolls over several times as the main rotor blades hit the ground, destroy themselves, and send pieces of blades flying in all directions.

Men, equipment, and weapons in the helicopter break loose and are thrown about inside as the Black Hawk tumbles and flips over several times. Finally, it stops, settles itself, and all that is heard are sounds emanating from a dying helicopter heavily loaded with aviation fuel that is gushing out. Then a spark sets off the volatile fuel, and the resulting explosion engulfs the helicopter.

It's 18:00 hours on November 9, 2004, and, as the sun is beginning to set in the west, Scott and the men inside the Black Hawk perish in a bright fireball.

Scott's medevac helicopter is captured on film by insurgents as it's shot down. They immediately post footage of the tragedy on YouTube, which finds its way onto televised network programs. Images of the action are shown before Scott's family is notified by the military. The military must first ensure the accurate identification of their dead, the location, and to the extent possible, some information about what happened. Then, military notification teams are sent out to visit their families.

Scott's father and brothers watch the evening news regularly and see the incident broadcast on TV. They immediately recognize the area where the helicopter went down. They know Scott is operating there but have no idea if he is involved. Every news report that includes combat action and causalities where Scott serves, impacts the entire McCormick family, causing them anxiety until they hear from Scott that he's fine. That will not be the case this time.

AFTERMATH

The Second Battle of Fallujah became the bloodiest battle up to that point in the Iraq War. American casualties were ninety-five service members killed and 560 wounded. The battle was not the decisive engagement the US military wanted. Some of the nonlocal insurgents, along with

Zarqawi, fled before the battle started, leaving mostly local militants behind.

In late January 2005, American combat units pull out of the area and turn the heavily damaged city back to the local population. Local insurgents, who remain, slowly regain control of the city's population as the number of insurgents increases once again.

What was it all for?

19
UNWELCOME NEWS
NOTIFICATION

It's a gorgeous midmorning in Pensacola, Florida, on November 11, 2004. Sean and Ana McCormick are sitting on their back porch, enjoying the comfortable weather while they sip coffee and trade small talk. Both had a rough night trying to sleep. They worried about their son.

The phone rings as Sean reaches over to the small coffee table next to his chair and picks up the receiver.

"Good morning, this is Sean. How can I help you?"

The voice on the other end is that of Air Force two-star General Sydney (Sid) Williams, stationed at the Pentagon. Although Sean has been retired for many years, he still has a network of senior officers, whom he relies on to keep him informed of his son's military deployments.

In a low-key, sympathetic tone, the general says, "Sean, this is Sid. Are you alone? Can we talk?"

Sean sits up, knows what's coming, and gazes over at Ana. She sees the dread in his eyes and senses immediately what is to follow. She fights back the emotions swelling within her. Sean also struggles but keeps them in check for the moment.

"Sid, go ahead. What news do you have about Scott?"

There is a long pause on the other end as Sid is slow to respond. "He was killed in Fallujah yesterday when his Black Hawk helicopter was brought down by RPGs. He was being medevacked due to serious injuries sustained while attacking a mosque controlled by insurgents. You'll receive a visit later this afternoon from the military's notification team and a senior CIA officer. I wanted you to know before they arrive. I'm so sorry, Sean."

Sid's comments hit Sean hard. He's always been the one notifying family members of their loss. Now, he's the recipient. Pausing long enough to momentarily control his grief, he responds. "Thank you, Sid."

Sean hangs up the phone, stands up, and walks over to Ana, who's become emotionally distraught and cries uncontrollably. Sean helps her up, wraps his arms around her, and pulls her close to him. She buries her head in Sean's chest and wraps her arms tightly around him. They are as one and grieve openly for the loss of their youngest son.

The military notification team arrives that afternoon. The team consists of an Army captain, an Air Force chaplain, and a CIA senior officer. Thanks to Sid, both Ana and Sean had time to begin grieving over the loss of Scott before the team arrived. Controlling his emotions, Sean greets the team at the door and leads them into the living room. He introduces them to Ana, offers them seats, and asks if they would like anything to drink. They respectfully decline. The team is relieved that General Williams reached out to Sean earlier in the day and laid the groundwork for their visit.

The Army captain, without going into details, gives

them an overview of what happened to Scott. The senior CIA officer briefly comments on Scott's exemplary service as a paramilitary operations officer. He also mentions that Scott has been recommended for the Intelligence Star. The CIA presents this award to its officers for voluntary acts of courage performed under hazardous conditions and grave risk. If awarded, he will be memorialized on the Wall of Honor at CIA headquarters.

Sean and Ana sit quietly and listen intently. At the conclusion of the team's comments, the Army captain asks if they have any questions. Sean stands up and asks once again if anyone would like a drink as he walks over to his bar. They all respond in the negative. He tells them to please remain seated as he pours himself a glass of Irish whiskey, walks over to Ana, and places his free hand on her shoulder. Looking at the CIA senior officer, he speaks directly to him with an inquisitive tone.

"Would you please tell us why he was in Fallujah? What was he tasked with doing?"

The CIA officer responds in a calm but matter-of-fact manner. "That is classified. I'm afraid I can't say."

Sean straightens up his frame, sets his glass down, and gazes menacingly at the CIA officer. "Let me rephrase that. I'm demanding to know what Scott was doing there. You can give me a high-level explanation now, or I'll get the CIA director on the line, and we'll see what he says."

This changes the whole dynamic in the room as the CIA officer is shaken and struggles with how to respond.

Sean steps over to the table where his phone is located and says, "I'm waiting."

Standing before the CIA officer is a retired three-star general of the United States Air Force with a highly distinguished forty-year career and several military decorations. He's also very well-connected but doesn't throw his weight around unless he's extremely agitated. Sean has no patience for bureaucratic nonsense.

After clearing his throat, the CIA officer responds.

"Sir. Your son was on a highly classified mission to assist in locating, capturing, or killing Abu Musab al-Zarqawi. He is the leader of an extreme and violent element in the Iraq insurgency. He's one of the CIA's top targets, along with Osama bin Laden. Your son was involved in several efforts to locate him and other high-value terrorists. On the day your son was killed, he was participating in an attack on a mosque where Zarqawi was rumored to be."

Sean sits back down and reflects a moment on the response. Looking at the CIA officer with appreciation and respect for his candid response, Sean simply says, "Thank you, sir."

He looks at the men in his living room and feels empathy for them. Notifications to families about the loss of a loved one in the service of our country are stressful, emotional, and physically demanding. He knows. He's had to participate in many over his forty-year career.

Sean is aware that current practice allows for fallen troops to be returned home in ordinary commercial jets, their caskets being met by baggage handlers with forklifts and then unloaded like luggage. He will not permit his son to be treated in this fashion. America's fallen soldiers deserve to be returned home to their families with honor and dignity. In closing, Sean makes a request of the team.

"Gentlemen, I want my son to be transported back to the States in a military aircraft only and to be given a dignified transfer at Dover Air Force Base. When his body arrives there, I want him to remain there until his burial date at Arlington National Cemetery. I've already initiated planning for his internment."

All three men acknowledge his request. With their duty complete, they stand as Sean and Ana escort them to the front door. Each member of the team respectfully offers Ana their condolences as they step out onto the front porch. Then, each team member shakes Sean's hand and offers their heartfelt condolences. Without a word, they show their respect for Sean when they all come to attention and render him a military hand salute. They hold it until Sean reciprocates. It's a very powerful moment, not lost on any of them.

The notification team returns to their vehicle. Sean and Ana stand on their porch and watch them drive off until they're no longer visible. Stepping back inside their home, Sean and Ana grasp each other tightly and weep uncontrollably.

ARLINGTON NATIONAL CEMETERY

It's midmorning on Monday, November 22, 2004. The weather is clear and cold with a slight breeze as the sun shines brightly. Sean brought his entire family to the grave site of his father, Sam, and his mother, Marie. They are buried together at Arlington National Cemetery. The McCormick family stands around the headstone of Sean's parents as he looks down on their grave site and speaks softly to them.

"Father, Mother, the entire McCormick family is here with me today. Ana, your daughter-in-law, Alan and Lee, your grandsons and their wives, Sharon and Rachel. Your two great-grandsons, Josh, a naval aviator and Bryan, a college baseball player, and your great-granddaughter, Angela, a law student, are also here."

He's becoming emotional as he speaks and stops for a moment, regains his composure, then continues. "I'm sorry to say that your youngest grandson, Scott, was killed fighting in our latest war. He'll be buried here today on this hallowed ground. He'll be joining you and the other men and women who rest here in eternal peace. Scott was not married, nor did he have any children. As you'll recall, Scott was born to travel, take risks, and see the world. That didn't leave him much time to settle down, marry, or start a family."

Once again, Sean pauses then closes with, "Father, Mother, your descendants are all here today. Scott will remain; the others will follow someday."

Sean steps back from their headstone, bows his head, and asks his family to join him in a moment of silent prayer. When completed, Sean leads them on a short walk over to where Captain Henry Miller, Jr., United States Air Force, is buried. He was a fighter pilot killed in the early stages of the air war over North Vietnam. He was like a son to Sean's parents and a little brother to Sean.

After paying their respects, Sean and his family are driven to the Old Post Chapel on Fort Myer in an Army van provided to the family for the day. The driver is a young Army sergeant who reminds Ana of her son at that age. She silently weeps for Scott.

Arriving at the Old Post Chapel, they are greeted by a large gathering of friends, a small number of CIA officers who served with Scott, and military associates and comrades who span many years. The chapel is full for the service, which is short in duration. They hold many services daily and limit the time for each. Exiting the chapel, they join the military procession and are led through Arlington National Cemetery to Scott's burial site. Sergeant Scott McCormick is laid to rest with full military honors at 1:00 p.m. on November 22, 2004.

The Army chaplain concludes his prepared remarks. He pauses, looks out over the people present, then focuses his gaze on the McCormick family sitting in front of him and offers one final comment.

>To the McCormick family,
>>I close with this passage from Isaiah:
>>"I heard the Lord say, *'Who shall I send and who will go for us?' I answered, 'Here I am, send me.'"*

EPILOGUE

This, the third novel in my historical fiction trilogy of one family's three generations of men serving America during times of conflict, has come to an end. Although it's written as historical fiction, I drew from stories of my family's legacy. In fiction, the characters' personalities and life experiences do not always coincide with the real person. Liberties were taken to make the writing more engaging and dramatic. *The Descendants* is written in three parts and follows the adventures of Sean McCormick's three sons, **Alan, Lee,** and **Scott**, and are loosely based on the lives of my brothers and me.

My brothers and I are the sons of Samuel F. Freeland, a career senior Air Force officer who now rests in eternal peace with his beloved Ann, our mother, at the Georgia National Cemetery in Canton, Georgia.

I'm the oldest, Larry Alan Freeland. My middle brother is Thomas Lee Freeland, and my youngest brother is Robert Scott Freeland. All three of us were born in Canton, Ohio, over a six-year time span. I was born within a year of our parents' marriage, right after our father returned from World War II. Thomas followed about eighteen months later. While our father was in Korea and Japan during the Korean War, Robert was born.

We each grew up to serve in the military, experienced combat and were very fortunate to have survived. However, I live with issues related to my exposure to Agent Orange while serving in Vietnam. Thomas dealt with issues related to Gulf War Syndrome, although never officially classified as such before he died. Robert dealt with PTSD.

What follows are excerpts from both my two brothers' obituaries:

Captain Thomas Lee Freeland, USN (Retired), passed away on October 11, 2016.

His distinguished twenty-six-year naval aviator career included tours as officer in charge of an unprecedented nine detachments, earning the first individual Navy "E" for ASW (AntiSubmarine Warfare) Excellence, and being selected as Naval Helicopter Association 1980 Atlantic Region Pilot of the Year. He capped his flying career as CO of Helicopter Squadron (Light) Thirty-Three in San Diego, California. Following this command tour, he served as Air Boss on the helicopter carrier, USS Okinawa, during Operation Desert Shield and Desert Storm.

Captain Freeland served with distinction in numerous challenging positions, including tours as professor of Mathematics at the United States Military Academy in West Point, New York, chief instructor, and community standardization pilot on the staff of the chief of naval air training for the naval helicopter training community, and on the staff of the Chief of Naval Operations at the

Pentagon. He is the recipient of multiple military awards for his service.

Captain Freeland rests peacefully among many of his peers at Arlington National Cemetery, Washington DC, where he is interned with his younger daughter, Gwen Alicia Freeland, who died of lupus at the age of nineteen in September 1994.

Robert Scott Freeland, who was married with two children, passed away suddenly on September 16, 2014 at Georgetown Memorial Hospital in Georgetown, South Carolina. His career includes two years in the United States Army where he served as an infantryman on the DMZ in South Korea in 1971 and 1972. He went on to serve twenty-four years in federal law enforcement, which included drug-related assignments, tax evasion, anti-government activities, and money laundering activities.

During this time, he also served three years with the United States State Department Foreign Service and traveled extensively in North Africa. He worked within the embassy network. Immediately following the attacks on September 11, 2001, he was temporarily assigned as an Air Marshal and served in this capacity for eleven months until the TSA could rebuild its Air Marshal force.

After retiring from the federal government, he contracted with private firms to serve in Iraq. He then served with the 82nd Airborne Division for two separate tours of eighteen months each. In this capacity, he served with the combat troops stationed on FOB's. After six months home, he once again departed for Afghanistan, where he served thirteen months in the same capacity.

EPILOGUE

Shortly after returning home, he suffered a heart attack from which he did not recover.

LARRY ALAN FREELAND, the author of the *Legacy of Honor* trilogy, comprising *The Patriarch*, *The Air Warrior*, and this book *The Descendants*, joined the United States Army in 1968 and served one tour in Vietnam with the 101st Airborne Division as an infantry officer and a CH-47 helicopter pilot.

While serving with the 101st in 1971, he participated in the last major American helicopter combat operation of the war-Lam Son 719. This was a large-scale combat incursion into Laos by the South Vietnamese military, with American military providing their helicopter support. The operation lasted sixty days and was the costliest period of the war for helicopter pilots and crew members.

Freeland is the recipient of the Distinguished Flying Cross with one Oak Leaf Cluster, the Air Medal with 10 Oak leave Clusters, the Vietnam Service Medal with 3 Bronze Stars, the Bronze Star medal, and various other military service medals.

ACKNOWLEDGMENTS

Telling this story has been another exceptional and rewarding writing experience for me. During my life, I have crossed paths with many men and women who served in the military during our nation's wars and conflicts. Although most have long since passed, I wish to thank them for their shared stories and the inspiration they gave me to write this trilogy.

A special thank you to my wife, Linda, for all her support, encouragement, and understanding as I endeavored to author this novel. It was another journey we traveled together.

We are just one family in our great country, where millions of families have similar stories of men and women who served and sacrificed. To them, we are eternally grateful for their selfless service to this country and the free world.

A special thank you to Frank Eastland and his team at Publish Authority. His professionalism, guidance, and support are very much appreciated. And especially to Raeghan Rebstock, my book cover designer, thank you for everything. It was a real pleasure to work with her once again.

Also, a sincere thank you to Janie G. Mills of Alliance

Book Editing, LLC for all her efforts. She was a pure joy to work with and greatly improved my novel.

To all those who read my novel, I say a special thank you. I hope and trust you found this story insightful, educational, and enlightening.

ABOUT THE AUTHOR

Larry Freeland, born in Canton, Ohio, comes from a family with a strong military tradition. His father was an Army Air Corps/US Air Force officer whose career spanned from World War II to the early Vietnam War. His grandfather served in World War I, and his brothers are veterans of post-Vietnam conflicts.

After graduating high school at Ramey Air Force Base in Puerto Rico, Larry earned a degree from the University of South Florida in 1968. He then joined the U.S. Army, serving in Vietnam with the 101st Airborne Division as an infantry officer and CH-47 helicopter pilot.

After leaving active duty in 1973, Larry pursued a career in banking, retiring in 2001 before working as a financial consultant and later as an instructor in management and leadership at Lanier Technical College.

Now retired, Larry writes full-time and lives in North Georgia with his wife, Linda, a retired educator. Together, he and his wife enjoy traveling, cruising, and visiting historic sites. They are passionate about Le Mans racing, veterans' causes, and the Cystic Fibrosis Foundation.

Learn more about Larry at LarryFreeland.com and follow him on LinkedIn, Facebook, and Instagram.

www.ingramcontent.com/pod-product-compliance
Lightning Source LLC
Chambersburg PA
CBHW051740210425
25478CB00014B/814